EARL INTERRUPTED

AMANDA FORESTER

sourcebooks
casablanca

Published by Sourcebooks Casablanca, an imprint of Sourcebooks, Inc.
P.O. Box 4410, Naperville, Illinois 60567-4410
(630) 961-3900
Fax: (630) 961-2168
sourcebooks.com

Printed and bound in the United States of America.
OPM 10 9 8 7 6 5 4 3 2 1

Praise for *If the Earl Only Knew*

"Once again, Forester earns top marks… [Her] gift for humor and creating memorable characters who have survived wrenching tragedy sparkles like gems in this newest romp."

—*RT Book Reviews*, 4 stars

"Forester, a champ at crafting feisty and independent Regency-era women, has outdone herself."

—*Publishers Weekly*

"Fascinating… Amanda Forester has created another delightful romance, with great adventures, mysteries, and secrets."

—*Fresh Fiction*

"The scandalously independent heroine is a delight… the humor lively and ironic. Highly recommended to those who enjoy a witty Regency romance."

—*Historical Novel Society*

"Enchanting and delightfully refreshing… Forester knows what she's doing and she does it incredibly well."

—*Herding Cats & Burning Soup*

"The rapid pace, lively dialogue, and engaging characters all add up to a highly enjoyable read."

—*Color Me Read*

"Forester combines romantic tension with over-the-top adventures in this witty read for historical-romance fans who like a touch of mystery."

—*Booklist*

Also by Amanda Forester

For the courage to try something new and the wisdom to appreciate what you have, and to Ed, who does both.

Foreword

The Earl of Darington and his sister, Lady Kate, are twins, yet, like any brother and sister, they have their own perspectives on the world. The twin books in the Daring Marriages duo tell the story of a most-impromptu house party at Greystone Hall from the viewpoint of each twin. *If the Earl Only Knew* followed Lady Kate as she fell in love (most unwillingly) with the Earl of Wynbrook. Now, in *Earl Interrupted*, we get an opportunity to see the same house party through the eyes of Lord Darington as he is thrown into the company of the irrepressible Miss Emma St. James. Read the books in any order and enjoy!

One

High Seas, 1810

THE EARL OF DARINGTON WAS HUNTING. HE SHIFTED his stance on the quarterdeck as the ship pitched in the treacherous storm. He squinted into the driving rain at the black outline of his quarry. Captain Esqueleto was rumored to be in these waters. Given the recent discovery of a wrecked ship and murdered crew, Dare believed the tale.

Esqueleto had been terrorizing the high seas for more than a decade. He was known to make a series of calculated strikes on valuable treasure ships and then disappear for years at a time, presumably enjoying his riches.

"Is it Esqueleto?" asked Mr. Everett, his first mate.

"No," responded Dare, the ship finally near enough to determine her identity. "It's the *Jade*, a French privateer."

"Even better," muttered Everett with some relief. No one had ever gone against Esqueleto and lived.

A French privateer would make a handsome prize, though no doubt it would prove a worthy adversary.

Darington's ship, the *Lady Kate*, was as fast as she was tough and was gaining on the French frigate. Dare surveyed his domain, ensuring his experienced crew was at quarters and ready.

"Run out your gun. Prime!" Men scurried to obey Darington's command with skill and precision.

"Aim high, aim for the masts. Fire!" Darington shouted the command as the French frigate came into range. Explosions blasted through the raging storm. The *Lady Kate* shuddered with excitement at the simultaneous blast and recoil of the cannon. Acrid smoke rolled down the decks, a stench not even the torrential downpour could wash away.

"Over again. Lively now." Darington had trained his crew to fire as well as any ship of the line, and a moment later, *Lady Kate*'s guns were singing again in an orderly and deadly chain.

The ships passed out of range and Darington gave the command to come about for a second pass at their enemy. He held up a hand to block the rain from his face, evaluating the damage to the enemy ship. The main-topmast of the *Jade* had shattered and was hanging limply, dragging in the ocean over the port side. The crew on the enemy frigate scrambled to cut themselves free of the broken mast, which was slowing their craft considerably.

"Looks like they're making a run for it, but we got 'em, sir," said Everett with a grin.

Darington squinted into the storm. He had not earned the reputation for being a feared privateer by being foolhardy. While other captains were all flash and bluster, he was somber, steady, and had never failed to take a prize after he set his sights on one.

"No, Mr. Everett," replied Darington calmly. "They are waiting for us."

Everett squinted into the storm. "Well, I'll be damned. You're right."

The French ship had allowed her sails to continue to drag in the waves and slow them down so they could line up their cannon for a direct shot down *Lady Kate*'s bow. That French captain was a tricky one.

"Hard larboard," commanded Darington.

"Cap'n?" Everett gasped. "Heeling so fast, she'll broach."

"She'll hold." His ship, a quick frigate named for his sister, was tough as steel and resilient as the lady for whom she was named. Kate would never go down without a fight, and neither would his ship. "Hard larboard."

Whatever the misgivings of his crew, his command was carried out immediately. Dare had led these men for years. He trusted them as they trusted him.

"Hold tight and ready the port side," commanded Darington, grasping the railing of the quarterdeck as the ship pitched. Frigid ocean waves crashed over him, but he remained firm. The ship groaned and strained, but they were coming around the enemy ship. Instead of sailing into a trap, they were the ones coming up from behind.

They were so close now he could hear the shouts of the men on the enemy ship. By the time the *Jade*'s crew realized what he was doing, it was too late to correct their mistake.

"Fire!" shouted Darington. Canons roared and the main mast on the enemy ship shattered and fell. The ship was crippled but still dangerous. Grappling hooks flew from the deck of the *Lady Kate*, bringing the wounded *Jade* close enough to board.

"Boarders, follow me!" thundered Darington. He jumped through the twisted rigging onto the deck of the *Jade*, pistol in hand, his sword at his side.

Dare quickly dispatched an attacker and scanned the deck for the *Jade*'s captain. He saw the man in a gilded coat fighting on the quarterdeck and made his way through the seething mass of violence toward his object. Darington leapt onto the quarterdeck, just as the *Jade*'s captain knocked down one of his men. The *Jade*'s captain was skilled, but Dare had years of experience and drew his sword, striking fast, using his speed and long reach to his advantage.

The French captain was pressed back and retreated out of range for a moment, glancing down at the fight on the deck, which had turned in favor of the *Lady Kate*'s crew. Darington stepped back to allow the man to accept his defeat as a gentleman.

"I, Captain Lord Darington, demand your immediate surrender."

The French captain's jaw dropped for a moment, but he collected himself and ground his mouth shut, his jaw rigid. "I, Capitaine Desos of the *Jade*, do tender my surrender." At the word from the captain, the crew of the *Jade* surrendered.

Darington gave the glowering French captain and his officers to some of his men to take on board the *Lady Kate* as others in his crew searched the ship.

"Cap'n! Cap'n, you are going to want to see this!"

Dare followed the sound of Everett's voice into the hold. His first mate stood before an open chest, his eyes sparkling. Though Dare had been sailing as a privateer for five years and served with the Royal Navy before that, the sight before him gave him pause.

Gold. *Gold!* And lots of it.

Everett began smashing the locks off of more chests and found them similarly laden. This was not just a French privateer, but a treasure ship.

"Well, Mr. Everett, I do believe we have become rich men. Let's get this cargo aboard the *Lady Kate* before this storm takes us all."

The news spread fast among the crew, and no amount of wind and rain could dampen their spirits at the sudden windfall. In contrast, Captain Desos stood in sodden misery alongside his officers under the pouring rain and the trained rifles of Darington's crew.

The *Lady Kate* was in better condition than the *Jade*, but she also had taken damage in the punishing battle, and debris was scattered across the decks. The ship pitched and everyone shifted to gain footing, while bits of splintered wood and mangled metal slid across the decks. A piece of wood that Dare had found days ago from a submerged gig in shallow waters hit Desos in the foot. The French captain picked up the board and Dare put a hand on his sword, ready for any sign of danger. Desos met his eye, pausing for a moment, then dropped the potential weapon with a shrug.

"I give you the choice of being taken back to Gibraltar in irons or being set in a gig to make it back to shore as you are able." Dare offered the French captain the choice as he was a fair man.

"I take the gig," replied Captain Desos grimly, for it was rough sailing, yet he fared a better chance with the weather than with British justice in Gibraltar.

"So be it."

Dare watched as chest after chest of silver, gold, and other valuables were loaded onto the *Lady Kate*. He had been sailing as a successful privateer for the past five years, but this was the largest prize yet. Even after the admiralty courts had had their say, his portion would be generous. Five years ago he had set out to restore his fortune, and he had more than accomplished his goal. With his latest prize, he had enough to repay the investors in his "shipping" business and still be a wealthy man. Of course, that meant London.

Dare's satisfaction over his conquest of the *Jade* dissipated. Given the choice between the danger of life as a privateer or high society, he vastly preferred the mayhem of the high seas. But he was no coward. Now that his fortune had been restored, it was time to take his place in society. It was time to find a wife.

A...wife?

Suddenly feeling unbalanced, Dare put a hand on the mizzenmast for stability. As the Earl of Darington, he had certain duties and responsibilities. He had no more excuses to avoid them. It was time to take a wife.

The awful reality of his predicament crushed down on him with bruising force. Heaven help him, he might be forced to speak to some young thing just out of the schoolroom to find said wife. And if she declined his proposal, he would have to speak to—oh, the horror of it all—more ladies.

Life as a privateer was dangerous, but stepping into London society to find a wife? That was far more treacherous.

❀

Captain Desos barked orders at his men as they strained against the oars of the gig in the writhing sea. Another wave crashed over the bow, soaking him in the freezing salt water. If he survived, he would see that Darington regretted ever taking his ship.

For a moment, Desos had been afraid Darington would recognize him, but of course, the young captain did not know him. If he had, Darington would never have let him go.

Desos somehow needed to retrieve the treasure Darington had stolen before his father discovered its loss. Cold fear seeped through his skin to his very soul. If his father learned he had lost all their treasure—to Darington no less—his father would kill him.

He expected nothing less from Esqueleto.

Two

Waverley Hall, January 1811

"YOU WANT ME TO MARRY MY BROTHER?"

"Honestly, Emma, must you be so gauche?"

"Forgive me. I must have misheard you." Emma St. James took a breath of relief. "I thought you said you wished me to marry Eustace."

"I only made a suggestion. Something must be done." Regina Ludlow St. James, Emma's stepmother, fanned herself furiously. Regina was of a ruddy complexion, and her coloring always reddened when irritated, angered, or embarrassed. Despite Emma's best efforts, her stepmother always seemed to flush a florid palette whenever they spoke. Emma tried to avoid her as best she could, but her tactics were becoming less and less successful.

"I am sorry if I have distressed you, Stepmother," apologized Emma, eyeing the door. Despite the cold winter day, the brisk walk outside would be a relief from the uncomfortable conversation. "Would you like me to inquire after tea?" Emma began to rise, hoping to make her escape.

"No, no, do not run off again. This needs to be settled once and for all. You will be turning twenty-one in a fortnight!" Regina pronounced Emma's crime with narrowed eyes, as if it were entirely Emma's fault for reaching her majority.

"Please do not distress yourself, Stepmother," said Emma. "I understand I will come into my inheritance, but I have no intention of—"

"Forcing me out of my home? Leaving me destitute?" cried Regina, pulling a handkerchief from her bosom and blotting her puffy eyes. She had once been a beauty but resisted the passing of time with the liberal application of cosmetics, the powder highlighting every line and wrinkle, giving her skin a crepey appearance.

"Of course not," responded Emma, though if she was honest, the thought of no longer living with her stepmother was not an unappealing one. "I understand my father left the estate to me, but—"

"He left everything to you!" cried Regina, her eyes flashing.

"He did leave you a jointure." Emma tried once more to convince Regina that she was not the injured party. Her father's will had left the majority of the estate to Emma, though held in trust until she turned twenty-one. The two trustees, her stepmother and stepbrother, saw Emma's coming into her majority as a threat.

"A mere pittance," said Regina with a sob as she buried her face in her handkerchief.

"I have no intention of casting you out." Emma

intended to be comforting but it came out as more of a sigh. As she drew nearer to her majority, she was having to endure her stepmother's dramatics with increasing regularity.

"No, of course not, dear." Regina looked up with dry eyes. "For you are the sweetest girl, my dear, lovely daughter. I could not love you any more than if you were my own flesh and blood."

Emma smiled tentatively in return, never quite sure about her stepmother's sincerity.

"I…I do have another notion, which would be a great service to an illustrious person, a peer of the realm. You like to be useful, do you not?" Regina gave her a cajoling smile.

"I do like to help as I am able," Emma replied in tentative agreement, doubting she would approve of Regina's new scheme any more than she had appreciated any of the other plans her stepmother had devised.

Regina held up a letter with an air of importance. "I have learned that the Earl of Langley is concerned that his grandsons make appropriate matches. His daughter ran off with an American sea captain, and they live like savages in Boston or some such—oh!" Regina blinked at Emma, clearly forgetting her audience. "But that can be nothing to you, can it, dear? The point is, Lord Langley has eligible grandsons, sea captains I believe, and he has made polite inquiries about sending appropriate brides. He is determined to have his grandsons marry respectable English girls, not one of those brash Americans."

Emma stared at her stepmother. Was she really so desperate to secure her own comforts that she would banish Emma to the New World to get it? Emma paused, waiting for her to say it was all in jest, but Regina returned her gaze with a distressed, pleading one of her own.

"You will forgive me if I will decline to be sent to America to marry a stranger," said Emma stiffly.

"Not a stranger, the grandson of the Earl of Langley. Here, read for yourself. Is it not an excellent plan? Just think—you could be wed to the grandson of an *earl*!"

Emma reluctantly took the offered letter. "Who is still a stranger to me."

"What difference could that possibly make?"

Emma was saved the indignity of reply by a sudden, small intruder. A little girl from the village burst into the room, running directly to Emma. "Please, come quick. It's Tommy. He fell from a tree!"

"What is that to us? Call a doctor or some such," said Regina with a dismissive wave of her hand. "Where is that butler? Can he not keep out such persons?"

"Tommy fell?" asked Emma, jumping up. "Where is he, Kitty?"

"You know this urchin's name?" Regina was aghast, the powder in the lines of her mouth cracking as her jaw dropped. "I suppose you plan to help this child?"

"Yes, of course. They are dear children."

"But that is the same excuse you used last week with the case of measles, and the week before with some old man's gout, and the week before that when some farmer got consumption. Every poor tenant cannot be special to you. Besides, we must come to some resolution. Eustace will be here soon, and he expects things to be settled."

"Forgive me, but I cannot tarry." Emma tucked the letter into her pocket and made for the door, relieved to have an excuse to exit the unpleasant encounter.

Emma followed Kitty to where Tommy was lying inside a modest farmer's cottage, his anxious mother pacing back and forth. The child's arm was propped up on a pillow, twisted at an odd angle.

Emma had followed her father on his rounds ever since she could remember. Some thought it was strange for a gentleman to study medicine, but Dr. St. James was a man who held a particular fascination for medicine. He had become a doctor and a surgeon, and promoted the general welfare of his considerable estate by acting as a gentleman physician to any of his neighbors, tenants, and laborers who should find themselves ill or injured.

Dr. St. James was considered by most to be eccentric, but to Emma he was a wonderful companion. Since Emma's mother had died when she was a baby, Emma and her father were especially close. He trained her to assist him as well as to handle things when he was out of town. They had done everything together, and he claimed her to be an excellent physician—at least, that was what he always said. Emma was completely content in this, ignoring the talk that it was unseemly for a young lady.

Eventually, however, as Emma neared her sixteenth birthday, the talk of the ladies of the neighborhood grew so loud not even her father could ignore it. Emma was not prepared, they said, to be brought out into society. Emma needed someone to guide her. Someone to teach her to be a proper lady. Emma needed a mother.

So her father found one for her. And then he died.

Emma shivered a little at the remembrance. She forced herself to focus on the patient at hand. She would need to set the bone, for it was badly broken. She prayed for guidance to help her heal the little boy and got to work.

The sky was growing dark by the time she walked back to Waverley Hall. She was tired and hoped to sneak back into her room without another encounter with Regina.

"They are waiting for you in the drawing room," the butler said ominously when she returned to Waverley.

"They?"

"Mr. Ludlow has arrived from London."

Emma's heart sank. The last person she wished to see was her stepbrother. Eustace was six years her senior and had rarely lived with the family, as he was at university when Emma's father married Mrs. Regina Ludlow. Eustace came for holidays, glowered at everyone, complained about everything, and left long after everyone tired of his presence.

Emma took a breath and entered the drawing room. Regina and Eustace were sitting near the fire on the cold January night.

"Emma! Wherever have you been?" demanded Regina, though she knew exactly where Emma had gone. "We had to eat dinner without you and I daresay there's none left."

"Emma," acknowledged Eustace Ludlow, his face permanently in something of a sulk. His heavy brow and sullen mouth did nothing to brighten his gloomy expression. After graduating without fanfare from

Cambridge, Eustace had spent several years in London as a man about Town. The experience had only hardened his resolve to find fault with everything and everyone he met. Eustace made a slight movement as if he was begrudgingly obliged to stand since Emma had entered the room, but his mother waved him off.

"Oh, you needn't bother with ceremony. It is only Emma," Regina said with a dismissive flick of her wrist. "Do sit down, Emma, next to Eustace on the settee. Why, you two look like a happy couple."

"Good evening, Eustace," said Emma, perching herself on the edge of the settee as far from Eustace as possible.

"Emma, my mother has informed me that you refuse to sign the property transfer papers," began Eustace, not bothering with pleasantries.

"Yes, I do not feel there is any need—"

"That is because you are a stupid, ignorant girl who does not have the slightest notion what it takes to run this estate," interrupted Eustace. "You cannot manage on your own and are determined to destroy this household and ruin the tenants. I find it selfish in the extreme that you are refusing to sign a very simple document."

Emma clenched her hands together as heat flared up the back of her neck. "My father felt I could manage."

Eustace stood with a snort. "Your father was a dreamer, a friend to the impoverished. Why, he never even raised his rents and kept virtually no records of transactions."

"My father believed a handshake was sufficient. He had known his tenants his whole life. He grew up with them."

"Yes. He did," replied Eustace in an incriminating manner. Since Eustace had taken over the management of the estate as Emma's trustee, Emma had received many complaints of raised rents, reduced charity, and more stringent oversight, all of which Emma suspected went to finance Eustace's preferred lifestyle in London. "This matter needs to be resolved. You will sign the contract."

Emma took a deep breath. "You will forgive me for being disobliging, but I will not sign something that is so clearly against my father's will for my life."

"Mother, make this chit of a girl see sense!" cried Eustace in frustration, turning on his mother.

"I have tried," whined Regina. "You know what she wants. You must be willing to accommodate."

"So it has come to that."

"I fear it has."

They both seemed to know the issue at hand, but Emma was mystified.

Eustace turned to her with a malevolent glare. "So you think to hold out for an offer, is that your game?"

"I...I am not playing any game." Emma leaned farther away from him.

"It all becomes clear. You will not sign over the management of this estate, as is only right and proper. No, you want to hand it over in marriage instead. Our little Emma here has the stone-cold heart of a viper. You refuse to sign and wait instead for me to make you an offer. You wish for the security of my name, is that it?"

"No! No, I assure you it is not!" Emma could not be more adamant. She had hoped she had made her position clear earlier when Regina had suggested it.

"Do not play coy. If marriage is your price, so be it, but let me be clear that I can never respect the manner in which you have trapped me into this union!"

"No!" Emma shouted. She took a breath and tried again at a more moderate, if forced, tone. "Eustace, this is nonsense. We are brother and sister. We cannot be married."

"You are not blood relations," interjected Regina. "So the alliance is legal. I had it checked." Regina gave them a stealthy grin.

Emma gulped for air. If she were forced to wed Eustace, her entire inheritance would be turned over to him. Not to mention the fact that she would be forever bound to one of the most unpleasant men in all of Britain.

In a flash, everything became clear to her. Why she had never been allowed to have a season. Why Regina had carefully kept her apart from others beyond their immediate tenants, ensuring that Emma never visited friends or allowing anyone to visit her. At first, after her father's death, Emma had no interest in seeing anyone, but long after the traditional period of mourning was over, Regina kept her isolated. They had wanted to ensure that Emma could not meet anyone whom she could possibly marry. No, they were determined to have her inheritance, her father's estate.

"Allow me to ease your mind, Brother," said Emma in a measured tone. "In no way do I wish to entrap you to marry me. In truth, I think we both know we would be quite ill suited."

"Emma!" gasped Regina with wide eyes. "Do reconsider. My son makes a great concession for you."

Emma's back straightened at the suggestion that a marriage to her would be a condescension. "I am aware of the…honor he does me, but I cannot accept."

Eustace's jaw tightened. "You are refusing my offer of marriage?" He seemed genuinely surprised she would refuse him.

"I am. Despite everything, I do wish you happiness and I doubt you would ever be pleased with a marriage to me."

Eustace snorted once again. "You are correct at least in that regard. But that does not remedy the situation. You need to sign over control of the estate to me, or I shall be forced to take matters in hand."

"You will regret refusing my son, Emma," muttered Regina.

Emma was certain that was not true. No matter what they would do next, she would never regret refusing to wed Eustace.

Eustace's glower deepened. "I fear we have kept you long after you have been wishing to return to your room. Good night, Emma."

Summarily dismissed, Emma rose, wished them both a good night, and proceeded to her chamber for a much-needed rest. When she reached the darkened staircase, she paused, a sinking feeling overcoming her. Despite her proper upbringing, she removed her slippers and crept back to the drawing room on stockinged feet, pausing just outside the door to listen to the conversation inside.

"…cannot understand why you have not resolved this!" Eustace's raised voice could be clearly heard in the hall.

"I've done everything I could. You know I would do anything for you, my dear boy," said Regina, attempting to placate him.

"Clearly, it is time that I take matters in hand. Emma is an unreasonable chit and demonstrates the inability to make sound decisions. Thus, we shall be forced to have her committed for the utter madness she is currently displaying."

Emma stifled a gasp. She had thought nothing could surprise her. She was wrong. The pressure put on her by her stepbrother had been unpleasant, but she had never felt her very freedom or personal safety to be at risk.

"Oh, Eustace, do you think it has come to that?" asked Regina.

"Yes. I do not see any other option."

Defend me. Emma held her breath, waiting for her stepmother to speak for her.

"But, my dear, only think of the unpleasant gossip this would create for you, to be known as having an insane sister."

It was not precisely the type of defense for which Emma had hoped, but it was something. Eustace paused as if considering how his plan could affect his reputation. He finally muttered, "Not blood anyhow. Can't see as it matters."

"Well, I suppose you must do what you think best." Regina acquiesced without further complaint.

Emma put a hand on the wall to steady herself, suddenly feeling off balance. Regina had abandoned her. Emma wanted to believe that she could not be falsely accused and locked away for madness, but she knew a woman's word was nothing compared to a man's. If Eustace decided to claim she was mad, she had very little recourse.

Her mind spun, trying to think of someone she could turn to for assistance. Regina and Eustace had broken off acquaintances with the families in the neighborhood, and Eustace had fired her father's steward and replaced him with a man loyal to Eustace alone. Most of her friends were the villagers who, though kind, could not help her stand against Eustace. If he claimed her insane, she would be committed to an asylum. She liked to think that some of her father's former friends would help her, but an appeal could take years, and all the while she would be…

Emma crept stealthily back to where she had left her shoes and silently climbed the stairs to her room. She could not allow herself to be sent to an asylum. And yet, her only other options were to sign away her inheritance or marry Eustace.

Emma took a deep breath. There was one last escape. She unfolded the letter Regina had given her about the Earl of Langley's desire to find English brides for his grandsons. Though Regina had suggested it, she knew Eustace would never have approved. He would never let her marry another, not even an American. If she was going to escape, she would have to take matters into her own hands.

She pulled out a sheet of paper and dipped her quill in her ink. She had always wanted to travel. Considering the alternative of being locked away in an asylum, the New World was an excellent place to start.

Three

DARINGTON SWAYED IN SILENCE AS THE COACH SLOGGED through the slush of the cold January day, wondering how long he was obligated to remain in England before he could return to his ship and a warmer climate.

"We are engaged at Mrs. Howell's tonight." Lord Wynbrook smiled at the occupants of his town coach. Darington had met Wynbrook years ago at university and he was one of the few people Darington considered a friend.

"So soon after your sister's wedding?" asked Kate, Dare's twin sister. "It was only just yesterday." Dare agreed that two social engagements in the span of two days was entirely too many.

"Shocking as it may be, there is not a mourning period after a wedding that must be observed before one can show oneself again in public," replied Wynbrook with a muted expression and laughing eyes. With his chestnut hair, green eyes, and impeccable tailoring, he was a stark contrast to the somber color palette preferred by Dare and his sister.

"Ought to be," muttered Kate, staring out the

window as the coach continued to push toward London. She was decidedly unadorned in a plain wool coat and serviceable bonnet. Her straight, brown hair was pulled back into a plain bun, but there was nothing she could do to hide her striking silver eyes.

"Should be a fresh crop of ladies for you to meet." Wynbrook gave Darington a wink. Nothing could fill Dare with greater dread.

Darington had been in the London area for two months. During this time, he had repaid all the original investors in his "shipping" enterprise, become acquainted with London society, and asked two ladies to marry him.

Neither one had accepted.

"Perhaps you can pass along my regrets," replied Darington. He would have much rather spent the evening with a book. Or the paper. Or staring at the blank walls.

"Ah, but you would leave the ladies devastated not to catch a glimpse of the Pirate Earl," laughed Wynbrook.

The Pirate Earl.

When Darington had returned to London with a small fortune, it did not take long for the rumor to spread that he had acquired his newfound wealth through pirating. He had attempted to explain the difference between a pirate and a privateer, but the name Pirate Earl stuck, only increasing his discomfort in society.

London society ran on mysterious, obscure guidelines, for which there was no written rule book. While he was sure in his interactions with his fellow man, attempting conversation with a lady left him

completely at sea. Invariably, he found himself staring, confused, at petite, sweet-smelling, muslin-clad
creatures who giggled and batted their eyelashes and
made him break out in a cold sweat.

If it wasn't for the fact that he was required to
marry and produce a legitimate heir, he would have
returned to Gibraltar months ago. Unfortunately, since
permanent bachelorhood would bring an end to the
line of the earls of Darington, he was obliged to look
for a bride. Though he was beginning to feel he had
done what he could in the matter and a tactical retreat
would be permissible.

After a morning of swaying back and forth in a
carriage, they stopped at a nondescript posting house
for food and a change of horses. Following a reviving
meal with far too many other travelers for comfort,
Dare wandered out into the cold, crisp air. A light
dusting of snow covered the ground and thick, gray
clouds threatened more of the same. He breathed
deep of the refreshing cold air, his breath showing in
the frosty air. He noted boot prints in the snow and
guessed his sister had also gone outside to avoid the
crowded common room.

Kate was generally of a reserved disposition, but she
had become almost hostile toward Lord Wynbrook.
Despite her outward irritation, she put herself often
in his company. They verbally sparred in public and
kissed in the library when they thought no one was
looking. Apparently, Dare was supposed to pretend
not to notice.

A muffled shout caught his attention and instantly
his senses sharpened. Noises of a struggle came from

the other side of the posting house. He strode quickly on long legs and broke out into a sprint when he heard a scream. He knew the voice.

It was his sister.

He rounded the posting house in time to see four men shove Kate into a coach and take off down the frozen road.

"Kate!"

Dare ran to the stables, grabbed the reins of a horse from a surprised stable lad, and took off after the coach. He raced down the road, bits of ice and frozen earth flying as his mount's hooves struck the road.

Who were those men? Why had they abducted Kate? Were they hurting her? He kicked his mount to run faster. Kate was his only family. Nothing could happen to her. Nothing.

∽

"Put on your best frock for dinner. Eustace will be joining us." Regina did not look at Emma as she pronounced the words that filled Emma with dread.

"So soon?" Cold dread ran down Emma's spine.

"Yes. Tomorrow is your birthday. He wanted to be here for it."

"I see," murmured Emma, keeping her voice low to prevent Regina from hearing her panic. Emma had been busy over the past fortnight arranging her escape but had not expected Eustace to return for a few more days. He must also have been busy arranging her demise. She should have realized he would wish for her to be committed before she could assume control of her estate.

Regina had grown quiet over the past few weeks. Emma had hoped when Eustace left, her stepmother would warn her or do something to help her, but Regina had remained silent.

"I had best get ready." Emma turned to leave, her mind spinning. She was not yet ready, but she would have to leave before Eustace arrived.

"You should have married Eustace when you had the chance," Regina called out to her.

"No, I should not," said Emma firmly, turning slowly to face her stepmother. She had second-guessed most of her decisions lately, especially her scheme to leave home and travel halfway across the world to marry a man she had never met. But she had never, not even once, considered marrying Eustace.

"No, I suppose you are not well suited," Regina admitted softly with something akin to true sorrow in her eyes. "Emma…"

"Yes?" Emma waited for her stepmother, hoping to hear a word of warning or at least kindness from the only mother she had ever known.

Regina's face hardened again and she looked back at the window. "Do not run off to the village today. You know Eustace does not like to wait for his dinner."

With any luck, Eustace would be waiting a very long time. "Goodbye, Regina," whispered Emma as she left the room. She had much to do.

⚜

Darington swallowed down emotion and forced himself to return to the cold detachment that was essential in a crisis. He kicked his mount again, speeding down the road in the direction of the coach. He moved the reins to his left hand and pulled out the pistol he always kept in his greatcoat pocket. He knew he was outnumbered and his chances were slim, but this was his only chance to save his sister.

The road curved through the forest, snow and ice glistening off of the stark branches. Dare leaned forward and urged his mount faster. Rounding the bend, the coach suddenly came into view. He veered off the road and through the trees, branches slicing past him. He emerged back on the road next to the coach, the chaos within visible through the frosted window. Inside, his sister, bound and gagged, was fighting four men. One of them grabbed her by the hair and raised a massive fist to strike her in the face.

Reacting by instinct, Dare kicked in the window and jumped into the coach, knocking the large man away from Kate. The three other men in the coach reached for their pistols. Dare shot one, gunpowder and smoke filling the carriage.

One of the men returned fire. The shot missed, but his ears rang. Dare dropped his own weapon, grabbing at the loaded pistol of the third man, holding it away and punching the man in the nose with his right.

Kate yanked down her gag. "Robert, watch out—"

The large man who had attacked Kate crawled up from where he fell, grabbing the pistol from the shot man. The shot sliced into Dare's side, exploding his senses with white-hot pain. His legs buckled and he collapsed to the floor.

"No!" screamed Kate.

"Lie still or I'll kill you!" threatened one of the

abductors, throwing her to the floor of the coach beside him.

He had failed. His vision narrowed, and Dare knew he did not have long before he lost consciousness. He lay on the floor of the coach, his hands at his side where the bullet had torn through. It burned like hell. He let his body move and sway with the jerky motion of the coach, feigning unconsciousness, all the while fighting off the seductive pull to just slip away. Somehow, he had to get Kate out of there. He couldn't die until the job was finished.

He glanced at the door of the coach and then his sister. Kate was lying with her back to it. He had a plan. He moved slightly to get into position. Every movement, every breath, was misery. White pinpricks danced before his eyes. He didn't have long.

He caught Kate's attention, glancing up at the door latch, then back at her, willing her to understand. Her scowl deepened and her lips tightened, but she gave a nod. Slowly, he positioned his feet so they were lying flat against her stomach. He held her gaze, trying to impart his apologies. He was going to hurt her in the process of trying to save her life.

It was Kate's turn now. With a sudden movement, she reached up with her bound hands for the side door latch, opening it. At the same time, Darington kicked her hard against the now-unlatched door. She flew out the opening and disappeared from view. Robert's heart broke, seeing her fall from the coach. He had succeeded in getting her out of the coach; he only hoped she had found a soft place to land.

"What the devil?" yelled one of the abductors.

"Stop the carriage!"

"Get her!"

Several men attempted to run after her, but Darington jumped up, ignoring the screaming pain, and slammed a fist into the soft midsection of one of the abductors. He grabbed at another one, wrapping his arms around the man's head, wrestling him to the floor and blocking the path to the door with a tangled mass of bodies. Every breath was agony and gray haze narrowed his vision.

One man, managed to escape the coach.

Kate, run!

His sight faded to black and he knew nothing.

Four

EMMA RESTED THE BRIM OF HER BONNET AGAINST THE coach window, watching her home grow smaller as they rolled away. She wondered if she would ever see Waverley again. A lump formed in her throat at the thought, yet the place had become almost strange to her.

A house, after all, was nothing more than wood and stone. It was the people inside who made it a home. Once her papa had died, her home had died with him. Waverly might have been hers by right, but it was no longer her home.

Emma took a breath and exhaled it in a short burst. She was ready for a new adventure. She was ready for a new home. She was more than ready to escape the danger of being locked away in an asylum.

The coach bumped over the frozen road and they settled into a rocking pace. It had been a desperate rush to leave without attracting the attention of Regina. Though Emma did not ask for help from the staff, as she did not want to put them at odds with Eustace, they had helped her without words, preparing a basket of food and leaving it in the kitchen, whisking her packed bag to the coach, so she would not have to carry it through the house, and most of all, not saying a word.

Her need to leave immediately meant she had to take her own coach, sneaking out while Regina was taking her afternoon rest. Emma would not take her own coachman, knowing he would be dismissed if he helped her, so she made a last-minute hire of a man who was visiting one of the villagers to act as her coachman—at least until she could reach Portsmouth.

"Well, here we are, on the start of an exciting journey." Emma gave a bracing smile to Sally, her young maid.

Sally stared back at her in wide-eyed dismay, clutching her ragged bandbox on her lap. One of the difficult aspects of running away was the inescapable need to have a chaperone. To arrive in Portsmouth unchaperoned would be unthinkable. The Earl of Langley had arranged for a suitable chaperone to escort her across the Atlantic. If Emma arrived without a maid by her side, it would certainly prevent her from being deemed acceptable to marry the grandson of an earl.

The young maid some four years her junior was a questionable chaperone at best, but she was better than no one. Sally was a relatively new addition to the house and had not impressed anyone with her industriousness. Regina had recently informed Sally that she would need to look for a new position, giving her two weeks to leave Waverley. Given the circumstances, it seemed a perfect match for Emma to offer Sally the option to accompany her.

"I hate traveling by coach," whined Sally. "Makes me sick. And I hate the cold. My feet are like ice."

"Part of an adventure is leaving our comforts behind and experiencing something new," Emma said, trying to soothe her.

"You never said nothing about leaving comforts behind," cried Sally, and instantly burst into tears.

After an hour, Emma gave up trying to console her maid. She found Sally's demonstrative wailing not at all helpful in Emma's attempt to cling to the brighter side of their adventure. The brighter side was admittedly rather hard to discern.

And the Lord, he it is that doth go before thee; he will be with thee, he will not fail thee, neither forsake thee: fear not, neither be dismayed.
—Deuteronomy 31:8

Emma repeated the verse in her head, reassuring herself. Her faith had sustained her since her father had passed. The verse from Deuteronomy seemed particularly appropriate, for, like the Israelites, she was going to a distant land to find a new home.

They traveled on for hours, stopping only briefly for a change of horses. Emma watched the sun dip farther and farther down on the horizon. She wished to put as much distance as possible between herself and her stepbrother, hoping to reach Portsmouth that night.

The coach swayed and bumped along and Emma noted the coachman had picked up the pace after getting fresh horses. She had impressed upon him the importance of getting to Portsmouth, and he was trying his best to accommodate, though perhaps with a little too much haste.

They took a turn so violently that Emma was thrown from one side of the coach to the other, crashing against the wall. She struggled to right herself, fumbling at the window to yell at the coachman to slow down. Before she got the chance, the coach swung the other way and she slid with a yelp to the other side. The coach lurched suddenly, and she experienced the sickening feeling of falling. With a crash of grinding rock and splintering wood, she landed in a heap on the side of the carriage.

The window shattered as the coach was drug on its side until, with a sudden jerk, everything came to a stop. Emma found herself sitting on the door of the overturned coach, gasping for breath. She was bruised and her left shoulder smarted.

"What happened?" asked Sally, wide-eyed from waking from her nap in a much different position than when she started it.

"We have experienced an accident," said Emma, her voice calmer than she felt. "Nothing to fear," she added, more to herself than to Sally.

Sally gasped. "I knew we were going to die in this coach!"

"I grant you that we have experienced a mishap. However, we do appear to be very much alive." Emma attempted to disentangle herself from her own skirts so she could stand up, carefully avoiding the broken glass.

"Miss St. James! Miss St. James. You all right miss?" The man she had hired to be her coachman cried at them from outside.

"Yes, thank you, Mr. Peters. We are quite well. Have you suffered any injuries?"

"I'm wells, miss," he said with a concerning slur. "Lets me help you out." The door above them opened and the head of the coachman burst through, along with a heavy dose of freezing rain.

Emma was able to climb out mostly on her own. This was fortunate, since the coachman's attempts to assist her were clumsy and awkward, doing more to hinder than to help. As Emma drew closer to the man, she could readily smell on his breath the reason for the accident.

The coach jerked, causing Emma nearly to slide off of it. She grasped onto the edge of the door to keep from falling off. "Mr. Peters! Go hold the heads of the horses before they drag us farther into the ditch. And for goodness' sake, man, cut them loose from the coach!"

The intoxicated man stumbled down and swayed his way to the horses. Emma shivered against the driving rain and biting wind. Concealed by dark storm clouds, the sun had set, casting them in almost complete darkness.

"Sally, give me your hand." Emma helped to pull up her simpering maid. Once they were on top, there was no way down but an undignified drop to the ground. She was glad the coachman was otherwise occupied, so no one could witness her embarrassing egress.

"Mr. Peters." Emma marched toward him, her impractical slippers quickly becoming water logged in freezing slush. The coachman was glibly cutting through the harness of their two horses with a knife. "We need to take these horses into the next town.

We cannot stay here in this weather." There were two horses, three people, and no saddles. It would not be her first choice to ride bareback tandem with her maid to whatever the next hamlet might be, but it was preferable to freezing to death.

"Yes, miss. Right away, miss," said Peters in a singsong voice. He must have been seriously foxed not to feel the effects of the cold weather. He dropped the leads to the mounts and gave her a bow.

"Be careful—the horses!" cried Emma, but it was too late. The coachman made a dive for the leads, but the horses were spooked enough to bolt. The man managed to grab hold of one, but the other ran off into the night.

"Mr. Peters," said Emma darkly. "I believe you are experiencing the ill effects of drink."

Peters shrugged. "It's too cold to work wi'out drink. You wouldn't know about cold, since you're all warm in the coach. You lofty ones is all the same."

"Mr. Peters. Mr. Peters, what are you doing?" Emma grew alarmed as Peters grabbed the reins and jumped up onto the one remaining horse.

"You ain't paying me enough to stand out here and freeze."

"Mr. Peters!"

"I needs me a drink," he slurred and galloped into the gloom without looking back.

"Mr. Peters, come back!" shouted Emma into the driving rain. He had left her. He had left her in the freezing cold.

God has a plan. He will not forsake me. Emma's teeth chattered as she slogged back to the coach, where her

maid was huddled. They were cold, wet, and alone
on a lonely road at night. So far, God's plan wasn't
looking too bright.

"Peters has ridden off," said Emma with a determined smile, as if this wasn't a very bad thing.

"To get help?" asked Sally with a shiver.

"We can hope so," muttered Emma, though there
was little chance of that. The pale light of a lantern
on an oncoming coach filled her with relief. "Look,
someone is coming. I knew the good Lord would not
leave us stranded here to freeze. We are saved!"

The coach came to a grinding halt before them and
two men emerged. They were rough-dressed men,
with mufflers wrapped around their faces, but at least
they had come to render assistance.

"You here alone?" asked a man in a red muffler.

"I fear so. We are very glad for your assistance."

The man in the red muffler glanced at his companion, a large, squarely built man in a black muffler.

"Sad thing for a pretty bit of muslin to be out here
all alone."

Emma took a step back, a new fear growing. "What
do you want?"

"Give me your money, lady," growled the man in
red, drawing a pistol and pointing it at her. "And then
you're coming with us."

Her heart sank to her frozen, wet feet. Eustace must
have hired these men to come after her. "Whatever
Mr. Ludlow promised you, I can double it. The estate
belongs to me, not him." Her only chance was to try
to reason with the men, though they did not look the
reasonable type.

"Quit your rambling and hand over your purse!"

Behind the men, she noted another figure exiting the coach. He was a tall man, hunched over at the waist, in a black greatcoat. He slowly snuck up behind the highwaymen, knife in hand.

She froze, mutely watching the drama unfold. If the enemy of her enemy was a friend, was the man with the long knife her hero?

Five

DARINGTON AWOKE COLD, UNABLE TO MOVE. HIS HEAD swam as he tried to remember where he was and why he was in so much pain. He was aware of motion, a swaying and a jerky bounce. Maybe he was at sea? No, the motion was wrong; he was in a coach. A coach that needed new springs.

And he had been shot.

His mind emerging from the haze, he remembered rescuing his sister and getting shot in the process. He was not sure how long he had been lying unconscious on the cold floorboards. He wondered why the men didn't shoot him again and finish the job. Perhaps they were content just to let him bleed to death. At least he had been spared the disagreeable prospect of having to attend a social engagement at Mrs. Howell's, though a different form of avoidance would have been preferred.

As his faculties slowly returned, he continued to feign unconsciousness with the hopes that his abductors would talk, and he could discover who they were and why they had taken his sister and then him. He noted there were only three left in the coach; the one who had left to go after his sister had not returned. He was not sure if that was a good or bad sign.

The three remaining men wore mufflers, concealing their faces. He found it strange that not one of his abductors had removed his watch or wallet. If they were not thieves, what did they want?

"Why couldn't we stay at the inn?" one of them finally complained.

"'Cause Cap'n said to move on," growled another.

"Couldn't we stop? I'm mighty cold with that broken window," complained the man who had wrapped a blue muffler around his face and head.

Try being shot and lying on the freezing floor of the coach.

"Shut yer trap. Cap'n is already mad as blazes we got the wrong one," said the gravelly voice of the man in black.

Darington tried to place the voices but could not. These men were not known to him. Who was this captain? A sea captain he assumed, though for all he knew, they could have been referring to an army captain. They said nothing more until they rolled to a stop.

"What's wrong?" hollered one of the men out the window to the driver.

"Overturned coach blocking the road," the driver called back.

"Push it out of the way," growled one of the men from inside the coach.

"There's two gentry coves out here."

"Heavy pockets, eh? Let's have us a look, shall we?" said the man in a red muffler. He and the large man in black stepped out of the coach, leaving the complaining man to watch over Darington.

Darington took a breath. Now was his time to act. The remaining man leaned his head out the broken window, interested in what was happening outside. Dare noted the handle of a knife concealed in the man's boot and slowly reached for it, ignoring the pain.

Dare gritted his teeth and sprung forward, grabbing the knife. Pain seared through him, but Dare continued his attack, lunging at the man. The man jerked back in surprise, but Dare was already in midswing, and instead of stabbing him in the chest, the blade struck deep into the man's thigh.

The man opened his mouth to scream in pain, but Dare elbowed him quick and hard in the head, causing the man to slump over without making a sound. Dare collapsed back on the floor, panting.

With a grunt of effort, Dare removed the knife from the man's thigh. He briefly considered dispatching the man, but killing an unconscious man did not sit well with his sense of honor. He could only hope he had nicked an artery and the man would bleed to death.

As quietly as possible, Dare opened the coach door and snuck out into the cold night. A coach had overturned ahead of them and the thieves were busy pushing it farther into the ditch while demanding money from two cloaked figures standing in the road. Dare wanted to help, but he knew he could do precious little in his condition. He hoped the men in the overturned coach could fend for themselves, for Dare could not be of service. If he wanted to live, he needed to flee.

He was about to turn away when a gust of freezing wind blew the hood away from the face of one of the occupants. It was a lady. A young lady, with wide eyes and blond curls. She stood her ground, raising her chin in defiance.

"You a pretty, little thing, ain't you?" The man in red pushed a curl of golden hair away from her face with the muzzle of his pistol.

Dare ground out a curse. He could not flee and leave a lady unprotected. Better to be dead than to live as a coward. He kept his head low, sneaking up from behind in the darkness. He crept closer, gritting his teeth against the pain. He was directly behind the man when the lady turned toward him. Their eyes met for an instant and he froze. If she gave him away, consciously or not, he was as good as dead.

Her focus flickered back to the highwaymen, not drawing their attention to him. At least he was attempting to save a lady with the presence of mind not to get him killed. Well, not yet anyway.

"You, sir, are a cad," said the young lady to the man pointing a pistol at her. She had admirable pluck, he had to give her that much.

"You need to come wi' me, sweet thing," drawled the man in red. "I'd like to get me hands on those—"

Whatever the vile molester was going to say was cut short by the pressure of a knife blade at his throat. Dare grabbed him from behind, holding the man in a headlock with the blade to the man's throat. Pain sliced through him at the effort it took to stand upright, and he wasn't sure if the whimper was from the man he threatened or from himself.

"Drop it!" Dare demanded, and the man in red dropped his pistol to the ground. "You too," Dare commanded the larger man in black.

The surprised man in black lowered the pistol but did not drop it. "Damnation, how did you get out o' the coach?" He followed the statement with a string of curses. The lady backed herself and her companion out of the way, toward their overturned coach. Dare was glad she had the sense to stay out of the line of fire.

"Drop your pistol or this man's dead," Dare commanded again.

"If I let ye go, I'm dead." The man in black raised his pistol and shot.

A flash in the night temporarily blinded him, and the explosive shot rang in his ears. Dare had always suspected the ringing sound of gunfire would be the last sound he would ever hear, and here it was. He had failed.

Dare was in so much pain it was impossible to tell where he had been shot, but to his surprise, both he and the brigand slumped to the ground. The man in black had shot his own comrade. So much the better. Dare grabbed the pistol the dead man had dropped and shot the man in black without hesitation.

The man turned to flee, staggered a few steps, and dropped to the ground. Dare's hands were shaking so much he was surprised he had been able to hit him. Shouts pierced the night and Dare turned to the driver of the coach, who jumped down from the box and rushed toward him with a knife.

Dare stood, trying to devise a plan to counter the attack, but the pain wracked his body and he collapsed right as the man was upon him. The man tripped over him and landed hard. Dare flicked the pistol around in his hand and hit the man hard on the temple with the butt of the gun. The man moaned and lay still.

Dare's breaths came in panting bursts as he struggled to regain his feet. Every inhalation was agony.

"My good sir," said an angelic voice. "You have saved us!"

Dare turned in the direction of the voice and a vision of loveliness met him. The lady was a young one, with large eyes, golden curls, and lips that even in the dim light of the carriage lantern appeared rosy and plump. She smiled at him and her cheeks flushed in the cold. Even standing in the mud of the road, she was the most beautiful lady he had ever seen.

A gray haze impaired the outside of his vision, but his gaze remained on her. It was a nicer view than anything he thought he would see as he died. He was content in that.

"Forgive me," he said in a rasp. "I fear I can no longer be of service." His knees buckled and he fell. He didn't even feel hitting the ground.

Six

Despite the freezing rain and the bodies strewn across the road, Emma was flooded with relief. She had not been abandoned—no, she had been sent a rescuer! He was a handsome one too. Tall and strong. While Emma did not condone violence, in this case, she was willing to think only of the heroism of the swaying man before her.

Emma watched in horror as her protector fell to the ground. She raced to him, kneeling in the mud beside him. She lifted his head out of the icy sludge and rested it in her lap. She drew back his greatcoat, searching for injuries. She did not have to go far before she found a large stain of dark-red blood on his waistcoat.

She put a hand to his chest and was relieved to find him still breathing. He appeared to have lost a good deal of blood, and Emma surmised the wound was not fresh. The man was a gentleman by the quality of his clothes. She surmised he must have fallen prey to her vile attackers earlier that day, though how he had come to be entangled with such company and what connection, if any, he had to her stepbrother was a question for later. The most pressing need was to save his life.

"Sally, bring the luggage. My medicine kit is inside." Emma glanced up at Sally, who appeared frozen in place—her eyes wide, her mouth open in horror. "Sally!" Emma repeated, allowing a rare sharpness into her tone. "Bring the luggage immediately."

Sally blinked. "Yes, miss." She ran around to the far side of the coach, where the luggage had been tied to the top.

Emma shuddered in the cold of the night. Their attackers' coach remained on the road, the horses' breath visible in the pale light of the coach lantern. She needed to get her injured protector inside and somehow drive them all to the next hamlet to get help. To do any of this, she first needed to revive the gentleman.

"Here, miss." Sally returned with all the luggage, dragging Emma's large trunk and carrying her own small bandbox.

"Thank you. That is very helpful." Emma wasted no time in opening her father's medical bag and finding a vial of smelling salts, waving it under the man's nose. The man started and opened his eyes with a gasp.

"W-what? Who—?"

"I am Miss Emma St. James. A pleasure to meet you."

"I am Dare…" murmured the man, his voice trailing off into something inaudible.

Emma smiled at the man. She was not sure what sort of name 'Dare' was, but it did seem an apt description. "I am sorry for the rude manner of your awakening, but you have been injured and we cannot tarry."

Emma spoke plainly and pleasantly, as she had found injured people needed hope and a calm presence.

"Go," the man croaked. "You need to find safety."

"I will not leave you."

"You need to go!" said the man in a stronger voice, his dark eyes blazing with intensity. He had angular features with dark-brown hair tied back in a queue. She might have been afraid had she not been cradling his head in her lap.

"I will not leave you here to die in the road," said Emma firmly. "What a poor way to repay your kindness. I could never live with myself. So we will either leave together or stay here together." As she spoke, she grabbed some bandages from her bag and pressed them to his wound, wrapping a bandage around his blood-soaked clothes.

The man inhaled sharply through his teeth as she pressed hard against the wound. "Sorry," she murmured. "This will stop some of the bleeding, but you need a doctor."

"Your life is in danger," the man croaked, rousing himself to a seated position beside her.

"My life? Did my brother send these men to *kill* me?" Emma gasped.

"Your brother? No, those men are after me."

"After you? But why would my brother be after you?"

They stared at each other, his eyes mirroring the confusion she felt.

"Can we l-leave n-now?" asked a shivering Sally through chattering teeth.

"Yes, let us get Mr. Dare to his feet. If we can get him to the carriage, I can attempt to drive us to safety."

Between the two of them and the man's own efforts, they were able to raise him to his feet. He was a tall man, muscular but thin, which was fortunate in getting him back upright.

"Let us get you to the coach and—"

The man lying near them let out a long, low groan. At the same time, a man cried out from the coach with a string of curses. "That bastard stuck me. Help! I'm bleeding like a stuck pig. Where are you lubbers?"

Emma's heart pounded in her throat. There was another man in the coach. The man in black, the one she thought her rescuer had shot dead, also groaned and moved on the ground. Sally let out a short shriek that was silenced by Dare, who clamped a hand over her mouth. He looked back at the hedgerows. Emma nodded in understanding. Crouching to avoid being seen, they crept off the road and into the bushes. The night was dark and the wind and rain relentless, which made for miserable conditions, yet easier to conceal their movements.

Dare made a concerted effort to move off the road, but once they were behind a large hedge, he collapsed once more. Emma sunk down beside him, out of sight. She peeked over the scrubby bushes at their attackers. One man, the one in the red, remained still, and she was certain he was dead. The man in black and the coachman, though, struggled to their feet.

"Where'd that bastard go?" growled the man in black.

"He took that pretty little ladybird, damn his eyes!" moaned the coachman, rubbing his head.

"He's shot. He can't have got far."

"I've been stabbed," complained the man from the coach.

"And I been shot an' hit my head when I fell. Now, shut yer trap. No one cares for you."

Emma's luggage was still sitting by the road near the bushes, a sure sign of their current location. The men staggered to the coach and while their backs were turned, she darted back onto the road, grabbed all the bags, and sprinted back to their hiding place.

"Someone help! I need a bandage—aaarrrgh!" cried the man in the coach.

"Get moving! We need to find that bastard," snarled the man in black.

Go! Dare mouthed to her as they crouched behind the hedgerow, out of sight.

She pressed her lips together and shook her head.

"Where are they?" called one of the men.

"We'll find them," said another, close enough to make her shudder.

Emma silently motioned to her terrified maid to take their luggage. Sally trembled in fear and cold but nodded in understanding. They had no chance of getting to the coach now, not with one of the highwaymen still inside. Their only hope was to sneak away into the fields and hope to find a farmhouse or some sort of help soon. Emma put a hand to Sally's shoulder and gave her an encouraging nod. They could do this. They had to. She needed her maid and her injured protector to believe it too.

Emma turned to Dare and put his arm around her shoulder with the intent to hoist him up but froze at the sound of voices directly on the other side of their hedge.

"Where are they? Where'd that wench go?"

"Black as sin out here," said a man with a groan.

"Bring the light. They can't have got far," demanded the gravely voice.

"Go!" hissed her protector in her ear. The warmth of his breath sent a strange shiver down her spine. He was glaring at her, and she realized he expected her to comply with his demand. She shook her head. He glared at her or possibly grimaced. It was difficult to tell in the gloom. He reached around for a rock and threw it down the road, wincing in pain with the effort it took to do so.

"What was that?" called one of the men.

"This way!" called another as they moved farther down the road.

Emma braced herself and stood up, attempting to help Dare to stand, but he shook his head.

"Don't wait for me," he whispered. "Go now and save yourself."

"We leave together or we die together," said Emma with conviction. She sincerely hoped her determination could make the man stand, for she would rather not die tonight.

The man's eyebrows lowered into a fierce glare. "Just like my sister," he muttered.

"I am honored if I remind you of your family."

"If you knew her, you wouldn't be." He struggled to stand, and together they were able to get to their feet, hunching over to avoid being seen. She doubted Dare could stand upright even if he had wanted to. She glanced back at her shivering maid, who was following them with the luggage, her face frozen in fear.

Emma gave her a smile of encouragement. Despite Emma's determination to cling to hope, her heart hammered against her rib cage in fear.

Sleet pounded down on them, stinging her face and eyes. Dare leaned heavy on her, making it difficult to walk in the thick mud. The only consolation was she had long lost feeling in her feet. She shivered in the icy wind as they struggled through the hedgerows, making their way overland in the dark. She prayed they could somehow sneak away from their attackers.

A crack of gunfire blasted through the night, and everyone crouched down. A highwayman shouted in the distance. They had not given up the search.

With a flash of fear, she considered leaving her companions and running ahead to find help. She quickly rejected the notion as cowardice, repellent, though enticing. Emma gritted her teeth and spurred their party onward at a faster pace. With every twist and turn, she feared coming upon one of them.

Another shot rang out, this time closer. She could do quite nicely if people would stop trying to kill her. Still, assuming she survived the night, it would make quite a story. She lowered her head and trudged faster, hoping they had not been seen.

Seven

ANOTHER SHOT RANG OUT, ECHOING ACROSS THE FIELDS. It was hard to say if it was nearer or farther away. They needed to find shelter. And fast.

Like a blessed answer to prayer, a light came into view. Emma closed her eyes and prayed her thanks. Lights meant people, and people meant help. She changed course slightly and moved toward the light, though it was still a ways in the distance.

Slowly, they picked their way across the fields and through the hedgerows. Progress was slow, but it seemed they were slowly drawing nearer when the light, their beacon of hope, was extinguished. Emma stopped short in the frigid darkness, a finger of dread running down her spine. She could no longer see where to go. The rain had let up for the moment, but it only brought a harsher wind. She shuddered in fear and cold.

"This way," said Dare in a low voice, pointing in a direction.

"You are good with directions in the dark?" Emma certainly hoped so.

Dare gave the curtest of nods. "Learned to navigate at sea."

She allowed Dare to direct her toward where the light had been. They would get through this, just as she had survived her father's death and the difficulties with her stepfamily. She took a determined breath and continued to tramp through the icy mud at night with a critically injured man and murderers at their heels.

It was going to make for an exciting tale...just as soon as they got there.

If they got there.

"I-I fear I can go no farther," gasped Dare. He had been leaning on her with more and more of his weight until she was almost dragging him along. Sally was also exhausted, dragging her trunk behind her in the mud. In truth, Emma feared she could not go much farther either. But to stop was to die.

"Let us rest a minute. We shall see a house soon. In this dark, we could be right upon it and not see it." She refused to give voice to her own pain or fears.

After a brief rest, they rounded another large hedgerow. Before them, the black shapes of buildings could be seen. Emma took a deep breath of relief. They had found some sort of hamlet, where hopefully they would find help. As they staggered nearer, they could make out more buildings in the darkness. They had approached from the back side, so they went around to the center of the little hamlet, walking back onto a road. It was a cold night and no one was out, but a few lanterns shone in the windows, one illuminating a sign for the Green Man Inn.

The sound of a coach rolling toward them made

them hustle behind a building to hide, fearing they had been discovered by the highwaymen. The coach rolled past them and came to a stop, the markings on the side clearly indicating it was the mail. Relief surged through Emma and she noted Dare dropped his pistol once more into the pocket of his greatcoat.

A man jumped out, mail was exchanged, and the coach rolled on into the night. They struggled back to their feet toward the inn, the orange windows glowing from the lights inside. Emma's hopes soared. They had made it.

Dare winced but managed to stand on his own, though for how long he could manage, she was not sure. His face was pale, and she feared he may soon lose consciousness. She opened the door and they walked into the inn. In the light, Emma realized what a curious sight they must make, dirty and soaked through.

They stood in the entryway, blinking in the light. An open doorway to the right revealed a stairway, which most likely led to the upper sleeping chambers. Doors on the left of the main entryway led into the taproom and pub, though all was quiet in the sleepy hamlet. Despite the relative warmth of the inn, Emma could not stop shivering. Sally's teeth were chattering.

A man appeared, ruddy in cheek and wide in belly, with tufts of white hair circling his bald head. He wore an amiable smile, which sagged when he saw their pathetic, little party. "Oh my, oh my, did you come in on the mail? Looks like you've had a time of it. Come in! Will you be wanting a room for the night?"

"Yes, that would be lovely," sighed Emma.

"Right away, right away. Are you hungry too? We always leave a pot of stew in the hearth for our late-night visitors that arrive on the mail."

"Yes, that would be appreciated, but first a room. Could you send for—" She was about to ask for a doctor and the magistrate when a voice from outside the door made her heart stop.

"Look around. If they're here, we'll find them," rumbled the familiar gravelly voice from the other side of the door.

His comrades responded in muttering growls.

"Well, more passengers from the mail?" asked the innkeeper, looking past them to the door.

"We are completely done in. A room as quick as may be, please," begged Emma, desperate to get out of sight.

"Of course! Martha, show these three to their room," said the innkeeper and bustled past them to the door.

A woman in a white cap and a dressing gown appeared with a yawn and led them to the stairs. Emma wrapped an arm around Dare and practically shoved him out of the entryway just as the innkeeper welcomed the highwaymen into the inn. They struggled up the stairs, out of sight of the man in black, but his voice thundered through the hall.

"We're looking for our friend," said the highwayman in false politeness. "He would have arrived on foot and may be in the company of two women. He is not well, been injured, important for us to find him soon."

"Well now," answered the innkeeper. "We got some

folks that came in from the mail, but no one arrived on foot."

Emma climbed the stairs quickly, pulling Dare along with her. All she wanted was to put a locked door between her and the highwaymen below. She had endured enough excitement for one day, possibly the entire year.

"Here you are," said the landlady, opening one of the doors. "Is he well?" she asked, looking askance at Dare, who looked almost green with a sickly hue.

"Traveling does not agree with him," said Emma quickly, helping him into the room. She wanted to ask for a doctor but feared that would alert the men below that Dare was here. "I'm sure a little rest should right him."

"I hope it will. Beg pardon, but what did you say your names were?" She looked up at them over her spectacles.

"Mr. and Mrs. Anders, and my maid, Sally," improvised Emma, knowing that if those men were after her, giving her real name would be fatal. She also needed to remain with Dare to tend his wounds. If they could not get a proper physician, she would have to do what she could. She realized only after the words had left her mouth that she could have told the innkeeper's wife that she and Dare were siblings, but it hadn't crossed her mind as a possibility.

"Send down your maid when you're finished with her for the night. We can make her comfortable in the servants' quarters," said the landlady.

"Oh…oh, yes. Right." Emma smiled even brighter to hide her sudden panic. She refused to look at the single bed in the room. Where they would be expected to sleep. Together. Without her maid.

Of course, she should not under any circumstances spend the night alone with a stranger. Dare held himself rigid, his teeth clenched from the effort of standing. One glance at the pale, strained face of her protector, and she knew she could not leave him to his fate.

"Magistrate available?" asked Dare in a raspy voice.

"The magistrate?" asked the landlady. "Well, no, sir. Sir Gerald is visiting his mother, but he should be returning tomorrow morning. Have you need of a magistrate?" She wrung her apron in her hands.

"Only a property matter my husband has been talking about," said Emma quickly, not wanting to alert the landlady that anything was amiss if she could not do anything about it. She feared that any sign from them that they needed a doctor or the magistrate would bring them to the attention of the very men they were trying to evade.

"Well then, do have a pleasant stay. I warrant you could use some warming," said the innkeeper's wife, looking relieved. A maid entered and lit a fire in the grate, for which Emma was quite grateful.

"Thank you. We are half-frozen, I fear," said Emma.

"Would you like me to take your cloaks and brush them out and hang them by the fire downstairs? And if you put out your boots, I'll have those attended to as well," said the innkeeper's wife.

"Yes, thank you," said Emma, trying to figure a way to ask for help without raising suspicion. She tugged off her wet, leather gloves and struggled to unbutton her coat with numb fingers, giving it to the landlady. Dare shifted and a glimpse of something red could be seen. The bloodstains, which were dark and muted in the night, were a garish, bright red on the bandage she had hastily wrapped. Emma feared the landlady had seen the blood, but the elderly woman was focused on Emma's cloak in her arms.

"We'll keep his greatcoat. Thank you so much. We are indebted to you." Emma attempted to hustle the landlady out of the room. "Since my husband is feeling poorly, something warm to eat and drink in the room would be ever so delightful, and some hot water and clean towels if you can manage. I fear we are chilled down to the marrow of our bones!"

"Yes, of course, poor dears. I'll send it right up to you."

The innkeeper's wife and the maid left just as Dare collapsed onto the bed.

"Dare!" Emma ran up to him, but he had finally lost consciousness. She wondered how he had managed to stand up for as long as he had. She rolled him onto his back and tried to inspect the wound on his side, but her hands were too cold and numb to do much more than bat at him ineffectually. She pulled a blanket over him to try to keep him warm. It was all she could do for him in her present condition.

"Oh, this is no good. I need to get warm. And so do you," she said, looking at her shivering maid. "Come. Help me into something warm and dry."

Emma shook her head at the state of her trunk. It was of sturdy construction, but was considerably the worse for wear after being dragged through the mud.

She was relieved to find her clothes were cold but not wet.

"You can't undress in front of a strange man," protested Sally.

"He is unconscious and I am freezing." Emma understood Sally's objection, but it was time to be practical. Though Emma dismissed the concern, she was quite conscious of taking off her gown before him, even though she knew he could not see her...but still she was undressing before a strange man and the very thought sent warm tingles up her spine.

"Shouldn't be doing this," muttered Sally as she assisted Emma out of her wet, dirty frock. "That man was with them bad men. He killed one of them. I saw it!" accused Sally.

"Actually, one bad man killed another bad man, which is lamentable, because I suppose somewhere he has a poor mother, but perhaps a predictable end for the manner in which he chose to live." Emma took command of her dressing, changing as fast as she could into a clean, dry gown and rubbing her hands together to bring them back to life. It was a relief to be out of her wet stockings and shoes. Her feet ached as feeling slowly returned, but at least they were now dry.

"Let me help you change, Sally, or you'll catch your death," said Emma.

"I'm not taking off my gown in front of 'im. No, not ever. And you shouldn't have done it either."

"Well, it is done. If you will not change here, you will need to go down to the servants' quarters," said Emma to her shivering maid.

"But you can't stay here with him. Alone. With a man," Sally elucidated the arguments unnecessarily.

"He is unconscious and in need of my help."

"But—"

"I doubt I will get any sleep, what with tending him through the night. You will most likely be safer in the servants' quarters."

"Oh, then I'll go there," said Sally, focused on her own safety. "You don't think those bad men will come back?"

"Not if we do not attract attention to ourselves. Remember we are Mr. and Mrs. Anders and we arrived on the mail."

A short rap at the door brought a girl with a tray. Emma was relieved to see food, towels, and hot water.

"Thank you kindly," said Emma. "Could you show my maid where she can get some refreshment and sleep for the night?"

"Yes, miss," said the maid and nodded for Sally to follow her.

Sally grabbed her bandbox and trailed after the maid out the door. Emma only hoped Sally would not give them away.

Bolting the door after her maid left, Emma took a deep breath. It was all highly unusual, but she would do what she needed to do. She could not allow the man who had saved her to die.

Emma walked to the edge of the bed, watching the slight rise and fall of his chest as the man breathed. She was alone with a strange man. A man who needed her help.

And the first step was to remove his clothes.

Eight

EMMA WALKED BOLDLY TO THE SIDE OF THE BED
where the strange man was lying. She was acting as a
medical practitioner, nothing else. "I need to undress
you to examine your injuries. Would that be acceptable to you?"

Dare gave no response.

"I will accept your silence as tacit approval." Emma
pulled back the blanket and took another deep breath.
She needed to undress him. His skin was like ice, and
she feared that without immediate help, he would not
last the night.

She began by removing his Hessian boots and wet
stockings. She could discern no injuries on his lower
extremities. His trousers were cold and wet, clinging
to muscular thighs, but inspecting his legs did not
reveal further injury, so she ignored them while she
inspected his wound. She glanced quickly over his
midsection and then up to his right side, which was
caked in blood, some fresh, some dried. She removed
the hasty bandage and tugged off his wool greatcoat
and jacket, managing to remove them by gently

rolling him from side to side to get them off. Next
came the cravat, followed by the waistcoat.

His clothes marked him a gentleman. Emma was
no expert in fashion but she had read her fair share of
society papers and fashion plates, and could easily tell
this man was well heeled. What had happened to him?
What kind of a name was "Dare"? Were the men who
accosted her on the road sent by Eustace, or were they
random brigands?

Emma was puzzled to find the man's watch fob
and money pouch still on him. If the motive of the
highwaymen was robbery, they had done a poor
job of it. She hoped he would have answers to these
questions, but the only way to hear them would be to
save his life.

She stared at him in his current state of undress. No
respectable man would ever be seen wearing nothing
but shirtsleeves, and it was only going to get worse,
for his linens must be removed. She pulled his bloody
shirt up and over his head, focusing on her duty to
keep her mind off the fact that she was undressing a
perfect stranger.

A perfect, muscular stranger.

A perfect, muscular, handsome stranger, with rippling abdominal muscles that appeared to be cut from
stone.

Which was completely irrelevant.

Except that it was entirely important.

Emma blinked at the man, now half-naked before
her. He had dark-brown hair tied at the nape of his
neck, though several strands had come loose and rested
on the pillow. His face was tanned from the sun,

showing the effects of working outdoors, unlike the pasty skin of her stepbrother. No, the man before her was one accustomed to action.

She stared at his trousers, knowing she had one last responsibility. He could not remain in cold, wet clothes. To do so was to risk his life. The trousers needed to go. And she needed to do it.

Her hands hovered over the button fall of his trousers. Was she really going to do this? Though she had tended many sick and injured people, this was something she had never done. She forced herself to undo the two buttons on one side of the fall, and then the two buttons on the other side. She glanced at the unconscious man. The wound was still oozing blood. She needed to work fast.

She took a deep breath, her hands hovering over his now-undone trousers. With any luck, he was wearing short pants underneath—or maybe with any luck, he wasn't. She pushed the lecherous thought aside. She was caring for a man in need. That was all. With a quick flick of the wrist, she flipped down the fall of his trousers to reveal he was wearing linen short pants.

"Good. Very good," she said to no one particular. She began the work of pulling off his wet trousers, which required some effort and repositioning of him, not to mention that the short pants wanted to come off with the trousers, since they were all wet. She was forced to come very close to certain parts of his anatomy to effectively remove the trousers, her cheeks burning at the positions in which she found herself. She finally succeeded in her efforts, but not before she had become intimately aware that the man she was assisting was, indeed, quite all man.

Emma cleared her throat and covered the lower half of the man to keep him warm and protect his modesty, not to mention prevent her from becoming overly distracted by the undeniable, chiseled perfection of his physique.

Emma dipped one of the towels into the water and began to cleanse the wound. She needed to stop the bleeding. A close inspection showed he was suffering from a gunshot wound to his right side, several inches above his hipbone. The warm water brought the injury into focus, but also encouraged it to bleed more. She needed to work fast, as he had lost a good deal of blood.

She felt around the wound, trying to ascertain if any major organs had been struck. She was most concerned about his kidney or intestines, but the bullet had angled up and away from anything vital. An exit wound showed the bullet had pierced through, so hopefully it had done so cleanly.

Emma went back to the shirt and laid it out, searching carefully for the place where the bullet passed. A hole in the garment filled her with dread. Any material left within him could cause the wound to fester. She went to her medical bag and selected some long tweezers. She needed to retrieve that bit of material.

"Forgive me," she muttered. She drew a lantern closer and began to probe the wound.

"Arrrgh." Dare's eyes flew open with a start. His hand shot out and grasped her arm.

"Trying to help," she gasped, pulling at his viselike fingers.

His eyes roved around the room in short anxious darts, then fixed back on her and immediately released her.

"Sorry," he rasped.

Emma rubbed her arm where she was sure he had left a bruise. "No, perfectly understandable. It appears you have been shot."

He nodded.

"Did those men do it?"

He nodded again.

She wanted to ask who they were and why they shot him, but she needed to save his life first. "There is a bit of your shirt missing," she began.

He frowned. "Need to get it out. Call a surgeon. No…they may track me. Don't want to put you at risk."

She was pleased at least he understood what needed to be done. "With your permission, I can try to do it myself."

Dare's frown deepened.

"My father was a physician. He trained me to assist."

Dare stared at her, his black eyes piercing through to her very soul. Even lying on his back, bleeding to death, the man was intimidating. As she returned his gaze, she realized his dark eyes were not black, but actually a very dark brown with tiny flecks of amber. It gave him a searing look.

"Are you able to do it?" he asked.

Emma swallowed down doubt. "Yes, I believe I can."

"Then do it."

Emma reached for a bottle of laudanum. "Here, this will help. A little at least."

Dare seemed reluctant to take it.

"I fear you will want it." She prepared a tincture and handed it to him. He swallowed it down with a grimace, for the medicine was extremely bitter.

Emma took a calming breath. She would need a steady hand and a bit of luck. She prayed that luck would be providentially provided. She rinsed the wound and took the long tweezers and a metal probe and began carefully to do her work. Dare gritted his teeth and went rigid.

"I cannot thank you enough for protecting me," said Emma, trying to distract Dare from the pain. "I cannot think what might have happened if you had not come along."

"Did...what anyone would." His words came out in short breaths.

"My dear sir, I fear I do not know anyone who would have done as you did. Forgive me, for I know that I am hurting you but...I think I... There!" Emma pulled out a small piece of fabric. Had it been left inside, it could have cost him his life. "I think we have it." Emma took the piece and compared it to the shirt. It looked complete.

"Now all we need to do is close."

"Thank...you." His low voice was strained with pain.

"Most of my patients are very unhappy with me at this point in the operation. You are very kind. And now I fear you will hate me." Emma cleansed the wound with hot water and then drenched it with alcohol.

Dare gritted his teeth so tight she feared he would

crack a tooth, but he did not cry out. His face was tight, sweat pouring down his brow, as she stitched the wound closed.

"I am sorry. It is for the best, but I know it is unwelcome." Emma took another stitch. The entry wound in the front was not as bad as the larger one in the back. "You are fortunate it did not hit a kidney, or you would be dead by now." She tried to make cheery small talk. From his pallor, she doubted it was working.

She finished stitching and bandaged the wound. She was running short of bandages, so with a nod from him, she cut up the clean parts of his shirt and used his cravat to tie it around him. She removed the towels she had placed under him to soak up the water and blood and helped him to move under the sheets, into the bed. He paused, noting that he was naked but for his short pants. He stared up at her, his eyes questioning.

"You were wet and cold. I...I had to remove the damp clothing or you might take a fever." Heat crawled up the back of her neck as though she were the one with a fever.

He nodded slowly in understanding and carefully slid under the covers. "Most improper."

"Yes, please forgive me."

"No, I am in your debt. Sorry to trouble you so. Few ladies would have the presence of mind you have. Blasted lucky to have met you."

"I suppose now we are even, for you saved me first. I was only returning the favor." She pulled up a chair beside him. "Now you need to rest." She had done what she could for the man. Whether he lived or died was no longer in her hands.

His eyes closed, but his hand emerged from the bedclothes and landed on her knee. "You need to rest too."

She stared at the hand on her knee, warmth spreading from where he touched through her whole body.

She placed her hand over his and held it.

Nine

EMMA WATCHED THE SLOW RISE AND FALL OF DARE'S chest as he slept. Breathing was good. Breathing meant he was not dead. Though whether or not he might still succumb to his injuries was unknown. She was not sure the full extent of his injuries. He could have been bleeding internally. He could become septic. The wound could fester. He was a strong man, and she hoped resilient too. Much could happen in the next few days that could turn the course of recovery. She could only hope and pray he would not die.

She still held his hand. Somehow she could not let go. She leaned her head against the back of the wooden chair and closed her eyes. Her body was sore, but she was so tired she did not even care she was sitting on a chair and not lying on a soft bed. Well, she didn't care much.

She must have dozed, for she felt herself jerk awake. She was still holding his hand in her lap, so she reached over with her free hand and pressed it to his forehead. He was warm, but not hot or clammy. That was good.

She was about to lean back when his hand she was

gently holding suddenly grasped her wrist and pulled her toward him so that she fell over him on the bed. She gasped in surprise to suddenly find herself practically on top of him.

"Who are you? What do you want?" Dare demanded as he struggled to get up. His eyes were barely open and he appeared to linger somewhere between wake and sleep. She had given him a hearty dose of the laudanum, and she feared he was much under the influence of the potent medication.

"It is me, Emma. Do not move about so." Finding herself already half on top of him, she pressed herself onto him farther to try to prevent him from moving. She feared he would rip out the stitches or do himself serious harm.

"Let me go," he growled, thrashing about, his eyes glazed and unfocused. He tried to roll her over but cried out in pain.

Though it was terribly unladylike, she straddled him to gain better leverage and pressed down on his shoulders with all her strength, trying to keep him still.

"Do not move or you will rip the stitches!" She tried to hold him down, her heart pounding in her chest. Though weak, he was still stronger than she was and Emma feared he would try to stand. "Please stay still!" Her face was very close to his. The top sheet had pulled down in the struggle and she was lying on top of his bare chest. He was breathing hard. So was she.

"Dare, please listen to me. You are safe now. I am trying to help you." Her breath was hitched from the exertion of trying to keep him still and the strange sensations that coursed through her from lying so intimately on a man.

He blinked, focusing on her for the first time. He stopped struggling and stared at her. His gaze traveled down to her natural assets, a sizable portion of which had spilled out of her bodice and was pressed against his bare chest. The moments stretched on, and had he not been injured, she might have feared he was gawking at her, but she knew he was only injured and thinking slowly.

"You are not one of the men who attacked me," he finally said, addressing her breasts.

"No, indeed," she replied, grateful he had been returned to sanity. "I am here to help."

"Help," he said slowly. "Help is good."

Something in the way he spoke flushed heat through her. She was suddenly aware that she was sprawled in a most suggestive fashion over a man who was staring down her bodice. She should have been horrified. Instead...she was intrigued.

"If you promise not to rip out your stitches, I will move away now."

"And if I don't promise?" He turned his dark eyes to hers.

Her cheeks went warm. "I should move." She sat up and peeled herself off him. There simply was no way to do so with any dignity. She finally managed to return to a standing position and turned away for a moment to straighten herself. She wished to withdraw, but given that they were in the same room, she was forced to make adjustments to her person in his presence.

She turned back to him with a bright smile born of

embarrassment and something warmer she could not readily name. "I had best check your stitches to see what damage you have done to yourself."

"Apologize. Not myself today." His eyelids grew heavy.

"Of course not. You have been shot."

"No excuse," he murmured.

"I do not mean to be disagreeable, but I think it is a better excuse than most I have heard." Emma pulled down the blankets a bit farther and checked her handiwork. "There now. I do not see any torn stitches. Could you roll over just a tad so I can check the back?"

Dare locked his eyes on hers before slowly rolling to his side. She was acutely aware of his body.

"Thank you," she said briskly before helping him roll back and covering him with the blankets. "Everything is looking well, despite your best efforts to make me do this stitching twice. I hope you can return to your family soon." Emma spoke quickly, but the thought lingered in her mind. Surely this man must have some family.

She busied herself in straightening the sheets. "Have you a wife we should notify?" She had not considered the possibility that he was a married man. Suddenly, she was deeply interested in his reply.

"No wife."

Not married. Somehow this made her quite happy. "Is there anyone I should contact for you?"

"Should let my sister know I am well," he said, his eyes half-open.

"I can do so. How should I direct the letter?"

"Not sure. Been traveling." Dare shook his head and as his eyes closed. "The rogues may return. I should stay awake. Keep watch."

"Sleep now," said Emma as the man drifted unwillingly back to sleep. She took a deep breath and tried to calm her own scampering heart. Even injured and unconscious, the man before her had a commanding presence. Emma settled herself on the hard, wooden chair. It was going to be a long night.

◈

Dare opened his eyes, confused about where he was. His thoughts seemed to crawl slowly though his mind. He squeezed his eyes shut, then opened them again, trying to clear his head. He was in a plain room, dimly lit by a small tin lantern.

Vaguely, the events of the past day dragged themselves across his mind. The lady who had helped him to the inn and then tended his wound was asleep on a wooden chair, her head fallen to one side. Golden ringlets, messy and all the more beautiful for it, fell across her face as she slept. He had thought her a pretty thing before, but in the flickering candlelight, she was nothing short of perfection. She had a smooth complexion and a small rosebud mouth, and in repose, she had the face of an angel.

Perhaps he had died and gone to heaven. His thoughts came slowly, as if trying to pull threads of coherence from a great tangle of wool. He tried to speak, but the words only came out in a low rumble. He cleared his throat to try again and the lady woke up with a start.

"Oh!" she exclaimed, looking at him in surprise as if she also needed to get her bearings. It had been that kind of day. Her wide-eyed response only enhanced her beauty. She had large, blue eyes and plump, rosy cheeks. She blinked at him and smiled. Something within him melted.

Now it all made sense. He was dead and being tended by an angel. She had no wings, but truly, with radiance like that, she needed none. He was a little disappointed to be dead, but at least it was not without its benefits. She leaned forward and he could not help but notice her natural endowments. He had not expected angels to have so many curves, but he wasn't complaining.

He tried to sit up, but the pain shot through him and he lay back down. He thought he would not be in so much pain in heaven. Perhaps this was hell, and she was there to tempt him into madness. Oh well. At least she was there.

"How are you feeling?" she asked, blinking impossibly long lashes at him.

"Am I dead?" he croaked.

One side of her mouth twitched up. "Not yet. But you have certainly tried to put an end to your existence today. Would you like to tell me what happened?"

"I got shot."

"That much I know."

"Thank you for helping me." Dare tried again to sit up. He should not be lying on his back in the presence of a lady.

"Please do not move. I want to give the stitches time to set a bit."

He lay still, though his movement brought the reminder that he was practically naked. The only clothes he had left were his short pants, which barely covered his manhood. He had always been nervous around women, and now he was lying next to one who had seen, well, probably everything. He wondered if he had passed inspection.

He wished to ask if she was pleased with what she had seen, but of course that was entirely out of the question. Instead, he realized he knew nothing about her, which bore remedying immediately. "Forgive me, I believe you told me your name, but in all the confusion…"

"Yes, it has been a trying night. I am Miss Emma St. James. It is a pleasure to make your acquaintance."

Miss. She was a *miss*. This was suddenly extremely important to him. "Where were you going, Miss St. James? And why were you traveling with none but a maid?"

"I was on my way to Portsmouth. Unfortunately, our coach took a curve in the road too fast and we overturned. The driver had indulged in too much liquor, I fear, and ran off with our horses after the accident."

"What?" Dare tried to sit up again and was settled back by her hand on his chest. Her bare hand on his bare chest. She was saying something about stitches or some other meaningless thing, with her hand still on his chest. He lay back down and she smiled at him. For that reward, he would do much. "I will kill the man for you." It would be a gift from him to her.

Her smile vanished and she snatched her hand away. "Oh, no, please do not. I am sure he is a perfectly nice man but was rendered short of reason by an excess of drink."

Dare was torn. He felt certain killing the man was the right answer, but her smile had gone away, which was not good. "As you wish," he conceded, thinking of many things short of death that would be instructive to the lad.

The smile returned and he was happy again. Her hand, however, remained demurely in her lap. A hand that was cold. A closer inspection of his current situation brought an injustice to light.

"You are sitting in a chair on a cold night while I am in the bed," he accused.

"You were cold from your ordeal. You needed—"

"I am sufficiently warm, but you are not. You must take a turn in the bed. I will sit up."

Emma shook her head firmly. "You have been shot and need to recover. I am fine. Truly."

He frowned at her. He was not accustomed to having people disregard his commands. On board ship, one word, one gesture of his hand, and all the men jumped to comply. His sister, of course, had her own mind and would do what she thought right, but even she would see the logic of warming herself. "You will at least take the blanket, or I will sit up and put it around you myself."

"No, you'll pain yourself and rip your stitches."

"True, but I cannot call myself a gentleman if I do not."

Her eyes met his. She seemed to be sizing him up, judging if he meant what he said. Sighing, he began to raise himself to his elbows only to be rewarded with her hand on his chest again, gently pushing him back down. Truly, if she wished to discourage the behavior, she should not touch him, for it only enticed him to do it more. Pain be damned.

"If I remove the blanket, you will grow cold," said Emma logically. "I cannot allow that to happen. I worked very carefully on you and I'd hate to have all my efforts go to naught."

Dare took a breath and blew it out again. She was arguing with him. Nicely. Intelligently. But she definitely had a mind of her own and she was not afraid to speak it. The thought was comforting, for the ladies he met in London had a circuitous manner of speaking, which Dare found baffling. If Emma was one who spoke her mind, he should be all right.

"Join me." It was the only logical answer.

"Oh, no, I couldn't."

"You need to warm yourself and rest, or you will catch cold, and then who will I have to tend me?"

A smile slowly graced her face. "I see you are using logic against me."

"As you did against me."

"I am tired, I confess, but I simply could not."

"Miss St. James—"

"Do call me Emma. We have gone through much, and besides, we are pretending to be married, so it won't do to let anyone hear you call me that."

"Well, as your pretend husband, I demand you take your rightful place beside me. I assure you I can barely roll over, let alone molest you."

"Well…"

"We have already broken almost every social

convention. Remaining in that chair cannot improve your situation. Will only harm your health."

"Oh, have it your way." She threw up her hands in a gesture of surrender. "You do seem to be determined in your opinions." She walked around the bed with a yawn. She put her hands to her hair and paused. "The pins."

"Remove them. Hate to be stabbed after I've already been shot."

She giggled. "Yes, I suppose that would be terribly unkind." She pulled out one after another of the pins.

Had he been a true gentleman, he would not have looked, but he could not turn away as her thick, blond hair fell down like a cascade of gold. How he longed to touch her hair. Of course, he had not the right and, at the moment, not even the ability.

She pulled back the covers and lay beside him. Her mere presence made his heart pound. She gave a little, contented sigh as she sank into the mattress.

He expected to feel wildly uncomfortable with some strange female sharing his bed. Instead, he felt oddly content, as if he had been missing her presence for years and she was finally where she should be.

"Good night, Emma." His eyelids grew heavy once more.

"Good night, Dare."

Ten

DARE WOKE IN THE EARLY MORNING TO A FAMILIAR ache. This time he was clearer headed regarding the dramatic events of the night before. What he was not prepared for was the image of the sleeping Miss Emma St. James, her hair splayed out around her like rays of sunlight.

Even in the pale light of morning, her beauty was undeniable. Her skin was flawless, her cheeks plump and rosy. Her full, pink lips parted as she slept, drawing him to her in a manner he found disconcerting and yet appealing. He watched as her ample chest gently rose and fell as she breathed.

Her thick hair was too enticing to ignore and he reached over and wound a golden curl around his finger. The simple act caused his heart to pound. Spending the night with her, no matter the circumstances, would require him to make an offer of marriage. Strange, but for once, the thought of matrimony did not fill him with a clawing sense of dread.

Emma was not only sensible, but also beautiful. He had never before considered the physical attributes of the woman he would marry. He had focused on rational thought as the primary criterion and assumed such a person would be plain. Emma did not fit that description at all. How could such a beauty still be unwed? The face of an angel and a backbone of steel. A dangerous combination.

He was so accustomed to pushing his emotions far beyond conscious awareness that he had not been troubled by them for as long as he could recall. Yet with Miss Emma St. James, he was definitely feeling…something.

The thought that he was obliged to offer marriage made him perfectly content. He just needed to keep her safe, track down the men who had attacked them, and then marry her. He slowly wound and unwound the lock of her hair around his finger. Yes, that would be quite acceptable.

Beside him, Emma stirred. She turned toward him with a sleepy noise, opened her eyes, and sat bolt upright. He released the lock of hair immediately, hoping she had not noticed his indiscretion.

"Oh!" She stared at him with wide eyes. "Oh dear, I fear I must have been overcome with fatigue."

"You are a sensible lady and made a sensible choice," he reassured.

She smiled. "Thank you for that. Well, I should remove myself." She sprung from the bed like it was on fire.

He was actually pleased at her reaction, for it showed that she was not accustomed to waking up in bed with a strange man. Something important in a future wife. She looked quite wild with a blush on her cheeks and her curly, blond hair shimmering around her.

"You must be in need of some relief from the pain." She rummaged through one of the traveling bags.

"Do not wish to lose my wits." In truth, Dare was in a great deal of pain but could not risk being put under again.

"This dose is lower than what I gave you last night."

"That was a heavy dose."

"It was intended to be," she replied, "for I was performing surgery."

He silently conceded she had a point. She offered him the small cup and he drank down the wretched concoction.

A small rap at the door brought a chambermaid to tend the fire in the grate. Emma's cheeks flushed pink at the presence of the sleepy maid. "Is there anywhere I can tend my morning ablutions in private?" Emma asked the maid.

"Room next to you ain't taken, ma'am."

"Thank you, that would be appreciated," responded Emma with a certain tone of relief.

The chambermaid nodded and left as quietly as she had entered, leaving a modest fire.

"I fear your shirt and cravat are a loss," said Emma, still in heightened color. "But I laid your trousers by the fire last night so hopefully they will be dry."

Dare nodded in appreciation. He would like to get dressed, though unlike Emma, he had no change of clothes. Emma laid his trousers within reach and, gathering up a few things, hustled herself out the door.

He stared after her, indulging in a small sigh before preparing for the day. The pain required him to move cautiously, and he kept his focus on Emma to distract himself. She would make him a fine wife. He could not wait to make things official between them. He frowned, recognizing that though he should request her hand in marriage immediately, it would be more seemly if he was not half-naked when he proposed.

Emma glided back into the room in a white frock, looking fresher than he would have thought possible considering the events of the prior day. Her hair was pulled back, with natural ringlets framing her face. She stopped in the middle of the modest room, rocking back and forth on her heels, as if not sure what to do next.

"Please sit, or I will be forced to attempt to stand," he directed.

"You would not dare," said Emma with twinkling eyes, and she returned to her station on the chair beside him.

Normally he could not think of anything to say to a female, but in this case, he had a true interest in her—one really should get to know one's future wife.

"Why were you traveling to Portsmouth at such a time of night with only your maid as a companion?" Someone had failed her and he meant to discover who it was.

Her smile faded a bit, and he could see stormy seas in her blue eyes. "I thought I could get to Portsmouth in one day. Unfortunately, with the weather, it proved too difficult." She gave an excuse he found rather flimsy. He would never send his sister out in such weather with only a young maid for protection.

"Have you relatives in Portsmouth?"

"No, I am meeting a traveling companion. I am sailing to America. There, I will meet my intended. I am to be married."

Engaged. She was engaged to be married.

He tried to wrap his mind around this new revelation. He wanted to resist the unwanted news, but of course she was spoken for. How could such a beautiful creature not be?

"I wish you much joy," he said mechanically. He suddenly realized what the emotion he had been experiencing was called. It was happiness, strange and rare. And now it was gone.

He closed his eyes as every drop of joy drained from his soul.

⌒

Silas Bones glared at the broad-shouldered man in the black muffler, a bloodstained bandage on his shoulder. Silas had not wanted to come back to England; it was dangerous for him to do so, but more dangerous if he did not retrieve his lost cargo. *Capitaine Desos* was only one of the many aliases Silas had used through the years, but not one he would use in Britain.

"What do you mean you lost them?" Silas grabbed the man by his black scarf and twisted until the man's breath came in ragged gasps. "I told you to bring me Lady Katherine." He twisted again. "We were going to use her to get Darington to pay me a ransom." He twisted once more and the man's lips turned blue. "I need to take back what he stole from me!"

Silas released the large man, who slumped to the floor of the tavern's back room. The man coughed and gasped for air. Bones cared not for the misery of this man. It was only a taste of what was to come.

"Do you have any concept of what Esqueleto will do

to you, to all of us, if he finds his treasure has been taken by Lord Darington? Bloody Darington of all people!"

"Y-yes."

"No, you do not. The only ones who truly know the depths of his depravity do not live to tell the tale."

"He can't have gone far. He's been shot," the man said, still gasping, trying to stand once more.

"Good. But we need to find him before he dies."

"He might be with a lady we met on the road. He defended her." The man managed to get back on his feet.

"Bring her too, then, and hope he cares enough for her to pay a ransom." Silas slammed a fist against the table, causing the bottle of whiskey to jump. "I cannot believe you let them both get away."

"We found this on the floor of the coach. Must have fallen from his pocket or something." The man handed over a silver ring.

Silas snatched it and held it up to the light. "His signet ring. Do you think I am going to be mollified by a damn ring? Now go! Find Darington and whatever chit he has with him and bring them both here. I don't care what it takes. I don't care who you have to kill to do it. Just get it done, or I will turn you over to my father myself!"

"Aye, sir."

The man stumbled as he ran out of the room. Silas could hardly blame him, for Esqueleto was a name that struck fear in all, and he was no exception. Slumping down at the table, Silas tried to pour himself another shot but the glass had hit the floor. Without pause, he drank deep from the bottle. Silas had to get the treasure back or his own life was forfeit.

Eleven

EMMA COULD NOT BELIEVE SHE HAD WOKEN UP IN BED next to a stranger. A practically naked stranger. The blush heating her cheeks showed signs of permanence. She would not be surprised if it lingered for days. She had shared a bed with a man whose full name she did not even know!

When Dare had become agitated in his sleep, demanding that she lie down, she had planned to pretend to give in until he fell back asleep and then return to the uncomfortable chair. She feared he would rip out his stitches and cause himself more harm, so it seemed best to humor him.

She had underestimated how exhausted she was. Wrapped in the thick covers, she had sunk into the mattress, soothing her aching muscles. She had closed her eyes just for a moment, and the next thing she knew, it was morning.

And she was still in the bed.

Next to a half-naked man.

A gorgeous, muscular man.

A man about whom she knew practically nothing, not to mention she still had no idea who had attacked her on the road or why.

"I believe you said your name was Dare?" she asked, sitting primly in the chair, her hands folded on her lap…as if a demure posture could erase the fact that they had slept in the same bed.

"Robert Ashton, Earl of Darington," he responded without fanfare.

Emma caught her breath and stared at the strange man. Did he say…*earl*?

Her heart pounded and emotions fluttered through her at this startling revelation. She had read the name in the society papers. He was the one they called the Pirate Earl. She thought for a moment of doubting his declaration but could not do it. His clothes, his manner, his actions all betrayed the truth. He must be the Earl of Darington.

"I beg your pardon, my lord." She could not believe she had behaved in such a familiar manner with a member of the nobility. A dangerous member of the nobility.

"Call me Dare. What friends I have call me by that name. You have earned the doubtful privilege more than most."

"Dare, then." She gave him a hesitant smile. Given how he had defended her, she should not have been surprised to learn he was a man of action.

"Miss St. James." He did not smile in return, but his eyes grew softer.

"If I am to call you Dare, then you must call me Emma."

Dare gave a slight bow of his head. "I would say 'at your service,' but it seems you are at mine."

"No, indeed, I cannot imagine what would have happened to us if you had not helped," exclaimed Emma. "If you had not bravely stood to defend me, goodness only knows what would have been my fate. And you being shot too! What an adventure we are having!"

Real-life adventures were much more uncomfortable and messy than reading about them in books, but Emma was no less enthralled. Now that they had survived to morning, the events of the previous night were taking on epic proportions.

The crease between his eyebrows deepened. He did not appear to have the same enthusiastic view of adventures. Of course, he had been shot, so his perspective was not quite as bright. "Only did what had to be done. Any gentleman worth his salt would have done the same."

"I have not a wide knowledge of gentlemen with which to judge," replied Emma, thinking of her step-brother. "But I can say for a certainty that many men would not have acted as you did. It is pointless to try to convince me otherwise. You are a hero to me, and you always will be, my lord."

"Dare."

"Dare." She smiled. Her hope for one in return was in vain. Perhaps he was not the smiling type.

She paused, hoping he would say more, but they lapsed into silence. "I confess, that I have been greatly interested in the circumstances that led to you being shot. I hate to press, but if you are up to it, I should like to hear the story." One could only be polite so long.

Dare paused and seemed to consider his options. "I hate to involve you."

"I believe I am already involved."

"Not sure where to start," he began. "My sister and I had attended a wedding for the Earl of Wynbrook's sister. We were all riding back to London and stopped at a posting house. Kate, my sister, went outside. I followed just in time to hear her scream and see her being pulled into a coach."

"Your sister was abducted on a public road?" gasped Emma. "What did you do?"

"Grabbed a horse from the stable. Chased the coach. I managed to get her free but got shot in the process."

"I cannot believe such a brazen attack! Who attacked you?"

"Not sure. But I expect we were targeted."

"You were targeted?" she asked, hoping he would explain, but he frowned as if remembering something.

"Did you say you thought the men were after you?" Dare asked.

Emma sat back in the chair, not sure how to respond. "I…I thought perhaps."

His eyes narrowed. "Why?" His voice was so low it came out as a growl.

Emma took a breath, trying to determine how much to reveal. "Well, you might as well know. I have run away from home."

The eyebrows rose in surprise. "Why?" He caught himself and shook his head. "Not used to female company. Don't mean to make you uncomfortable."

"No, I understand. I have been curious about you too. My problems come from inheriting my father's estate. I come into my majority…well, actually, today!" She realized it was her birthday.

"Many returns of the day."

"Thank you. My stepbrother, Mr. Eustace Ludlow, was not pleased with me inheriting. He made things… uncomfortable, so I decided to accept an offer of marriage and have an adventure."

Dare's frown returned. "I see."

She was not exactly sure what he saw, but he clearly wasn't pleased with the view.

Dare cleared his throat. "Miss St. James, I am greatly indebted to you. Without your help, I would be dead in the hedgerows. But you need to leave. Now. Get somewhere safe."

Emma shook her head. "I cannot abandon you while you are still injured."

"It would be different if we…" He paused and pressed his lips together, giving his angular face a severe expression. "You are engaged to another man. I have no right to trespass on your time and your good name. You need to leave."

Emma swallowed hard. She acknowledged the sense of his words, but still, it was difficult not to feel rejected. "I would not feel right leaving you in such a condition. Besides, we have taken this room as husband and wife. It would look rather strange should I abandon you now."

"But in truth, we are not married, and your reputation will be irrevocably damaged by remaining here."

"Fortunately, my betrothed is an ocean away," she said lightly.

"In addition, we do not know who those men are,

why they attacked, or if they are still looking for us. You need to run as far and as fast from here as you can." His voice was firm, and it was clear he was a man accustomed to giving orders. She, however, was not easily cowed.

Once she had grown into womanhood, and her body had developed a decidedly rounded and unabashedly plump figure, most men addressed themselves to her bosom and never gave her another thought. Apparently, according to conventional wisdom, a lady with a generous bosom must not have a logical thought in her head. People seemed to believe one could only grow brains or breasts. Not both.

"I will do as my conscience dictates," she said calmly, folding her hands in her lap.

He glared at her. She continued to regard him with placid determination. If Eustace, with all his threats and unpleasantness could not force her to obey his demands, surely an injured man could have no hope in securing her compliance.

"You need to leave." He also was a man of determination.

"Even if I were inclined to leave, I have no way to do so at this point. My coach is quite damaged and... Oh, the coach."

"What about it?"

"Well, I had to leave a little earlier than I planned and so I took my own coach. It is still lying there in the road. Even if those men were not sent by my brother-in-law, he will certainly come looking for me." The overturned coach would be a beacon telling him she was in the area.

"The mail coach comes by in the evening. You will be on it," said Dare firmly.

They shared equal looks of resolve, in a silent battle of wills. Finally, she acknowledged his plan with a slight incline of her head. "As long as you are recovering and can manage without me."

"I hope your future husband is of an understanding sort," he muttered.

"I hope so too." She sighed when she said it, and a spark of suspicion ignited on Dare's face.

"May I ask the name of the fortunate man who has won your heart?"

Emma smiled to cover her discomfort. Her intended may have a marriage contract on his side, but certainly not her heart. "He is the son of Captain Redgrave, an American."

"I am familiar with the name. Fearsome opponent. Good privateer. I have not met him in battle. Which son are you to wed?"

Emma looked away and busied herself with smoothing her skirts. "I am not rightly sure." She coughed a little in a futile attempt to hide her discomfort.

"You are not sure?" He raised an eyebrow.

"Oh, it is a long and boring story. I think you need some rest."

"I think you need to tell me the story."

Emma again struggled with how much to reveal. In truth, she longed to share her situation with someone. Someone who might be sympathetic. Someone like Dare. And yet as she turned her predicament around in her mind, the story sounded rather sordid. She wanted to reveal herself but maybe soften the edges a bit, for she could not bear to be pitied.

"It is an arranged match," she began hesitantly. "The Earl of Langley's daughter married the American, Captain Redgrave, apparently against her father's will. The earl is now concerned that his grown grandsons find English brides. I am being sent as a bride for one of them."

Dare's frown etched deeper onto his forehead. "You are being sent to wed some man you have never even met? And you don't even know which brother you are to wed?"

"I have always wanted to travel." Her smile was beginning to hurt her face. "I am very excited to see the New World. I feel I am a great explorer."

Dare's face told her he did not like her arrangement. He opened his mouth to speak, but closed it again, deciding instead to glare at her in an accusing manner.

"And your guardian has agreed to this?"

Her smile vanished. "My stepmother and stepbrother have served as my trustees. My father passed away when I was sixteen."

"I am sorry for your loss." He was silent for a moment. "Both my parents have passed also."

"I am sorry for your loss as well," said Emma.

"It is hard to lose a parent."

"Yes." Emma's first instinct was to brighten the maudlin conversation. She never wished to burden anyone with how much her heart grieved the loss of her father, so she typically kept the conversation light. In the immediate aftermath of her father's death, Eustace had taken great offense at her grief, calling her tears childish and manipulative. Emma had learned to smother her feelings behind a calm facade. Yet one look at Dare's somber eyes told her that he would prefer honesty over superficial pleasantries.

"When my father died, it was quite a blow to me." Emma glanced away from the intense, black eyes of the Earl of Darington.

"Where were you when he passed?"

Emma looked up. It was a question she had never been asked before. It took her back to that moment in time.

"I was beside him. He had been injured, shot by accident by one of the village lads hired to help with the annual hunt. A shotgun had accidentally discharged, and he had been struck. I tended his wounds, following his instructions. It seemed as though he would recover, but then the wound turned hot and festered. I did everything I could to save him, but he grew weaker and weaker every day, until finally…"

She could not stop the memories from flooding back. The night before he passed, he told her he was dying and not to blame herself. She had begged him not to leave her. She stayed by his side, trying anything to help. By the morning, his breathing was ragged and labored. She knew it was close to the end. She held his hand and told him she was sorry. When he breathed his last, she had cried until her breath came in silent gasps.

Regina had blamed her for his death, saying Emma should have let them bleed her father, and that if they had called a proper doctor, his death could have been prevented. Her stepmother's words still haunted her. "I miss him greatly," Emma whispered.

"Forgive me the lack of a handkerchief."

Emma started and looked up at Dare, confused by

the comment. Why would she need a handkerchief? She blinked and tears fell down her cheeks. She quickly found her own and attempted to remedy the situation. "Please do forgive me." She feared his recrimination.

"It is a natural thing to mourn one's parent." The only thing she saw in his eyes was compassion.

"Yes, yes it is." She was enormously relieved by his acceptance. Dare did not attempt to fix her tears and make her stop, nor did he seem inclined to run away. Of course, he had little option to flee. "How old were you when your parents passed?"

"My mother died bringing my sister and me into the world. My father died when we were twelve. I was at school and not able to be present at his passing."

"I am sorry for your loss. My mother also died in childbirth when I was young, attempting to bring a son into the world. Unfortunately, neither survived."

They were quiet for a moment.

"I think, perhaps, losing a mother early, it is not good for a child. I felt I missed something," confessed Emma.

"Yes. If my mother had lived, life would have been very different."

"Yes. Very different," agreed Emma. No stepmother. No stepbrother. Mothers were the protectors of children; they stood in the gap to shield their offspring from pain. Without them, children were vulnerable.

It was odd that in the sparse room with a complete stranger, Emma felt she could talk about things she could never share with her family. The Earl of Darington was different. Though she was supposed to be taking care of him, it was he who was providing comfort to her.

Twelve

DARE HAD NEVER BEEN MORE CONFUSED. HE HAD SPENT a good deal of time and energy trying to avoid young women, especially the possibility of awkward conversations, and yet here he was, talking about the death of his parents, something he had never done in the entirety of his life, with a beautiful young lady without feeling a qualm of discomfort. He should have been running for the door, injury or not, yet instead, he hoped she would speak more about her life.

Their honest conversation was interrupted by a knock on the door and a maid brought in a repast, basic in nature yet delicious in scent. Emma jumped up to accept the offerings and placed them on a small wooden table. "I asked for some broth for you," she explained, bustling about to prepare to break their fast. "Have you any appetite?"

At the scent of food, his stomach rumbled audibly. "Yes, indeed." It had been a day since his last meal and he felt the deprivation. "Is that bacon I smell?" Dare was taking a distinct interest in the breakfast tray.

"Yes, but let's start with the broth."

His enthusiasm waned. He thought nothing could reduce his regard for Miss Emma St. James, but coming between him and bacon came close.

"We can work up to bacon," she conceded.

He tried to sit up a bit more so he could eat, but his wound throbbed with pain. He had been hurt before, but never this bad. It was going to take time to heal—time he did not have.

"Now let me raise your head a bit with another pillow so you can try this broth," said Emma in a mothering fashion.

"I can feed myself," he complained and took the spoon from her hand. She held the bowl and he ate. Slowly at first, then faster, trying to fill his empty belly.

"Easy now," she gently chided. Dare did not care to be treated like an infant, but he did appreciate her leaning over him with warmth in her eyes and a smile on her face. He could see where the role of invalid could have its advantages.

"So I understand you took to the sea as a young man." She smiled at him, her bright-blue eyes crinkling at the edges.

"Yes. I have only recently returned."

"I know."

He frowned, wondering how she would know of his movements.

"It's been in the paper," she admitted with a guilty shrug of a dainty shoulder.

So she had read of the Pirate Earl. He wondered what she thought of such an unfortunate title.

She appeared to have something on her mind as she gazed at him intently, but then she turned away when he looked at her. She hummed a song as she cleared the dishes, nibbling on her bottom lip in an unconscious manner.

"Was there… Do you have any concerns?" He was not sure how to ask what she was thinking and, for the first time in his life, wished he had been blessed with more social graces.

Emma glanced up with bright eyes and returned to her post on the chair by his side. She did not seem to mind his awkward attempts at conversation. "I do not mean to pry, but you said you thought those men had targeted you. I was wondering why. Please do forgive me my awful curiosity."

Dare never spoke of his past, but if there was ever a time to break this rule, it was for Emma. If those men were still looking for them, the truth might help her stay alive. He owed her that much at least.

"It's a long story," he hedged.

"I adore long stories." Her eyes sparkled with an adoring enthusiasm, and he found he was not so opposed to talking of his past after all.

"My father died when I was twelve," he began, trying to stick only to the basic facts. Facts were easier. "We were called back to our family house and found that it had been gutted. The silver, the china, and anything of any value were gone—the furnishings, pictures, rugs, all gone. Everything."

"You were robbed?"

"We were told my father had not managed his finances well and everything was being sold off to pay the creditors. Hours after the funeral, we were packed in a carriage and taken to London, to what we thought was the home of our guardian. Instead, we were handed off to some rough men who took us to Fleet."

"Debtors' prison?" she gasped. "But I thought a peer of the realm could not be imprisoned there!"

"That is true, but they lied about our identities. They said we were children of a merchant who had gone deeply into debt and we liked to pretend to put on airs. I explained who I was, but nobody would listen."

"That is horrible!" Emma rose to her feet in indignation. "How did you escape?"

Dare searched her face for disapproval or rejection. Yet in Emma's eyes, he saw only sincere concern. "We were in Fleet for a few weeks before my tutor found us and helped secure our release."

"Well, I am certainly glad you were able to escape, but who did this to you?" Emma began to pace in the small, sparse room.

"After we escaped, I was able to win my majority in court and take control of my finances. Our steward had robbed us of all monies and property beyond the land entailed to the title. He stole everything and left us in prison."

"The thief! What happened when you confronted him? Was he arrested? Did he hang?"

"No. He was found murdered in an alley behind his lodgings, his throat slit, no trace of the fortune he stole. He must have been working for another and was killed to ensure his silence."

Emma's jaw dropped at his frank words, and he belatedly remembered this was not the type of conversation one was supposed to have with a lady.

"How horrible! Who would do such a thing?"

Emma sat back down in the chair beside him and leaned close.

"To this day I do not know." Dare felt the weight of the unknown enemy that he had carried his entire adult life. Someone had gone to great lengths to cause him pain. "I joined the Royal Navy and served for years until I returned to England for university. Afterward…as you have read in the papers, I sailed as a privateer. Despite what the papers infer, I was not a pirate."

"No, of course not. You are an honorable man," she reassured, her eyes gleaming. "What stories you must have to tell."

"I was able to restore my fortune…more than restore." He could not help but voice a small boast. "Unfortunately, the wealth may have made us a target."

"Do you think someone tried to abduct your sister to hold her for ransom?"

"Perhaps. We have recently been the target of several attempted robberies."

She paused, a wrinkle forming between her eyebrows. "Do you think what happened to you as a child, the attempted robberies, and the abduction yesterday are connected?"

"I do not know." He did harbor suspicions. "But I will find the truth."

"Yes, but you must heal first. I do hope you can find the answers you seek. I will pray for a solution to present itself. I have had to rely quite a bit on the good Lord these past few days, and I have not been disappointed."

"You are sincere in your faith?"

"Why yes, of course." Emma's expression brightened into a natural smile. "I would not know how to survive without it. After my father's death, my faith was the only solid ground on which to stand. Is not your faith of importance to you?"

Dare shifted a bit in the bed. "I have not the fortune of experiencing any understanding of the deity."

"Well, it's rather difficult to understand the creator of the universe, so I would hardly hold that against you."

"Perhaps I have never seen the hand of God in my life." Dare took a breath and blew it out again. He was sure that she would not approve of what he was going to say but was unwilling to deceive her since he had been frank about so much. "In truth, I have doubted the existence of God. Either he has no control over the circumstances of my life, or he does not hold me in high regard."

"So you think that the Lord should protect you from any adventures?" She tilted her head to one side.

"Only the bad ones."

"How do you know the good from the bad?"

"When you end up shot and bleeding on the floor of a coach, you're in a bad one."

Emma inclined her head in acknowledgment. "That does sound rather awful. But then, if you had not been in that carriage, I shudder to think of what would have happened to me. I fear your misfortune was the answer to my prayer."

Dare grunted. "To follow your logic then, God does exist, does act in the lives of men to protect those he chooses." He gestured toward Emma. "He just doesn't like me."

"Now do not say such. I am certain God loves all his children."

"If he loved me, he would have found a way to protect you without getting me shot."

"I can see you are rather firm on this position."

"I was *shot*."

"I concede the point. I would likely feel the same if I was shot. It cannot be comfortable."

"No, it is not."

"Would you like another dose of—"

"No, no, I am well enough. I do not wish to be medicated into unconsciousness. I am simply saying that faith is easier when one has very little to complain of."

"Well, I suppose you are going to find me argumentative, for I cannot agree. I tend to ignore my faith when things are going well and cling to it desperately when they are not. I suppose that says a little about my capricious nature. There now, you have induced me to reveal myself in a very unflattering manner, and I was so determined to present myself in an admirable light."

"Nothing you can say will reduce my admiration for you." Darington spoke in earnest. He appreciated her candor and even her willingness to disagree. She was a lovely, capable creature, with a mind of her own.

She would make the perfect bride...just not for him.

Thirteen

THE EMERGENCE OF SALLY, THE PETULANT AND RATHER tardy maid, ended the interesting conversation Emma was having with the Earl of Darington. Sally returned in a silent sulk and took up residence on a stool in the corner of the room.

Though Emma could no longer press him for more details of his life, she marveled at the new information she had learned about the Earl of Darington, the Pirate Earl himself. She had always secretly enjoyed reading the London society papers, thinking the aristocracy far beyond any true problems. Dare had certainly experienced more than his fair share of difficulties, and it only made her hold him in higher esteem.

She only wished he could experience the comfort she had in her faith. Without that, she did not know what she would do. A slight rustling got her attention, and she realized Dare was attempting to sit up.

"What do you think you are doing?" she accused.

"'Tis morn. Must inform the magistrate of all that has occurred." He glanced at Emma. "Well, not all that occurred, but we need to inform him about the men so he can try to apprehend them."

"Yes, of course we must, but you cannot walk downstairs."

"I must."

"But you cannot. I will go."

"No!"

She paused, startled by his emphatic response.

Emma tilted her head slightly to one side. "Whyever not? Surely, we must report such evil deeds to the proper authority."

"A magistrate will ask questions. Some of which may be difficult to answer."

Emma blinked. "What questions?" Though she feared she knew.

"Like your name and what you are doing here and why you were spending the night with a man not married to you," Dare said ruthlessly.

Emma smoothed her skirts. "You make it sound very sordid."

"They will think it very sordid. You have been of great service to me. I would not repay you by ruining your reputation."

Emma shrugged. "I do not think it matters if my reputation is ruined in this hamlet. Besides, I had no intention of giving my true name." She had no desire to be found by Eustace.

"Still it would be a shabby repayment. Besides, we do not know where those men are. I must go." Dare attempted to sit up in bed.

Emma immediately rushed to his side. "No, please do not move. You know how I feel about the stitches. I will be ever so angry at you if you force me to do them again. That, indeed, would be a poor repayment."

Dare winced and lay back down, the pain clear on his face. "I will not let you leave this room without me to protect you." He looked at her with such intensity she did not doubt him. If she were to leave, he would drag himself after her.

"May I suggest that I ask the innkeeper to request the magistrate to come here so you can make the report?"

Dare glowered at her, but she could tell she was winning the argument.

"I will go no farther than the common room of the inn, and I will even take Sally with me. Now what could possibly go wrong with that plan?"

Sally shook her head in protest, but Emma was firm. This would be simple. She knew it must have been safe, for Dare reluctantly agreed to it.

Emma walked down the stairs to the common room, having to stop several times to encourage the recalcitrant Sally to come along. The maid did not want to become involved with anything to do with the men who had attacked them and complained about having to spend the night in the servants' quarters of the inn with a maid who snored. Emma attempted to be sympathetic, though she had no real empathy.

"My husband would like to speak with the local magistrate," Emma told the innkeeper when she found him in the entryway. "Could you tell me how I might direct a letter to him?"

"Why, you are the second person to ask for the magistrate today," commented the innkeeper, scratching the white tufts of hair on the side of this head. "Must have been some excitement, for Sir Gerald is being kept busy." He paused and gave Emma the expectant look of one hoping to be given more information.

Since that was one thing Emma could not do, she merely gave him one of her brightest smiles. "My goodness. How unusual. How might I contact Sir Gerald?"

"Why that's no trouble at all. He's here to talk to them other fellas. He's talking to them right now, in the private room off the common room. You can talk to him yourself when he finishes with his business."

"Thank you. I will wait for him in the common room with my maid," replied Emma. Only a few people were in the main room—a pair of older gentlemen playing chess in a corner and two women knitting near the window. It all looked rather mundane, a relief from the excitement of the past day. She sat at the table nearest to a closed door on the far side of the room, which she assumed led to the private room. Sally stood beside her, looking miserable.

"Why don't you ask the staff here to prepare a tray for Mr. Anders," Emma suggested.

"Mr. Anders?" Sally clearly forgot the assumed name they had used when they checked in.

"Yes, my husband who is sleeping upstairs," said Emma in an undertone with a knowing look.

Sally continued to stare at her for a moment before realization dawned on her face. "Oh yes, of course, miss."

"'Missus' or 'madam,' if you please," hissed Emma.

Sally frowned and slunk off without another word. Emma sincerely hoped Sally would not blurt out the wrong information at the wrong time. A waiter left the private room, accidentally leaving the door open a few inches. Emma did not intend to eavesdrop, but she could not help hearing the raised voices coming from the private sitting room.

"That is unconscionable," exclaimed a voice she did not recognize. "You say this happened along the main road?"

"A horrible circumstance. Robbed us of all our worldly goods. Shot me in the arm and murdered our poor friend in cold blood," said the gravelly voice.

Emma froze. She knew that voice. It was the man in black who had attacked them while they were stranded. She remembered his voice, his face, the stench of his body when he came close.

The brazen highwaymen were at the inn. And had gotten to the magistrate first.

Fourteen

EMMA FROZE, NOT KNOWING WHAT TO DO. SHOULD SHE rush in and defend herself? No, that would only reveal herself to the men who had threatened her and shot Dare.

"There were two of them you say. A man and a woman?" asked an unknown man whom she assumed was Sir Gerald, the magistrate.

"Yes, indeed. A sad day when a woman goes bad like that," replied one of the robbers.

"I say, I am shocked, *shocked* by what you have related. These are troubled times, troubled times indeed. What did they look like?"

The man with the gravelly voice gave apt descriptions of her and Dare and mentioned there may have been a maid with her. They even reported that Dare had been shot in the attack. Emma wanted to run but could not resist trying to learn more about the men.

"I shall inquire for a man and a woman with her maid who may have arrived yesterday. This is a small hamlet. We should be able to find strangers if they are here. We shall hold them for trial," said Sir Gerald ominously.

The man in black growled. "If you can locate them, we will assist to bring in these dangerous criminals."

"A generous offer, sir," said the magistrate. "Do not fear. We shall catch these villains."

Emma had no doubt that if the blackguards found him, Dare would not have long to live. The sound of wooden chairs scraping on the stone floor got her legs in motion. If they walked out the door, they would trip over her. There was no hope of going to the magistrate now, poisoned against them as he was.

She rose and walked calmly but quickly toward the stairs. She had almost made her escape when she remembered she had sent Sally to prepare a tray. If they saw her, Sally would be in danger, and the killers would know Dare was here. Emma hustled toward the kitchen.

"Can I help you?" A red-faced cook, two kitchen staff, and Sally, all stopped what they were doing and stared at her. Emma knew for a patron of the inn to suddenly run into the kitchens was most unusual, but she could still hear the voices of the highwaymen in the common room behind her.

"I do apologize. I need to speak with my maid. Most urgently." She hoped they would go back to their business, but instead, the kitchen staff all continued to stare, foregoing their work for unabashed curiosity. This was not good. "Mr. Anders would like some tea, but he is particular. I feel I must prepare it myself."

Emma knew this was a very poor explanation for her behavior, but she could think of none other.

"I got the hot water, miss. You can prepare the tea how you like," said Sally, completely unable to play along. And she called her "miss." A slip Emma hoped would not be noticed by the staff.

"Did you get the biscuits? You know how he likes biscuits."

"Yes, miss. I got biscuits." Once might pass, but calling her "miss" twice? Sally was clearly no help in a crisis.

"Miss? Why, Sally, have you forgotten the wedding? We are such newlyweds my maid is hardly accustomed to it." She smiled at the kitchen staff, hoping they would accept her explanation. The staff regarded her coolly.

"Hey there, wench! We're thirsty!" The man with the gravelly voice shouted from the common room. Emma had hoped the brigands would move along, but instead, they seemed to be staying for a meal.

"New customers?" she asked one of the kitchen maids as she moved to go out to serve the men.

The girl shrugged. "They came last night, shortly after you did."

"Ah, a busy night for you, I see." Emma tried to make the circumstance not seem as desperate as she feared it was. The men who were hunting her were staying at the same inn! They had convinced the magistrate she and Darington were the wrongdoers, and now she was trapped in the kitchen with a curious staff. *Lord, help me to know what to do!*

Emma spied a small door leading outside from the kitchen. "I know what we need—some nice flowers to brighten up this tray." Everyone in the kitchen stared at her as if she were mad, and she remembered it was January. "Or perhaps some evergreens. Have you anything green outside?" she asked the cook.

The cook shrugged. "Suppose so."

"That will do nicely, I'm sure. Sally, please come with me and we will decorate this lovely tray." She smiled so hard her face hurt, as if the fake grin could make up for the nonsense she was spouting.

"But…why…" stammered Sally.

"Come along now." Emma grabbed the arm of the recalcitrant maid, who was still holding the tea tray, and firmly guided her out the door. It was freezing outside, and she shivered in the cold.

"What are you doing?" complained Sally as they were enveloped by the damp chill.

"Hush now. The men who attacked us last night are in the common room. We must get back to our room and quick."

Emma's pronouncement did not have quite the impact she intended, for instead of moving faster, Sally stopped dead in her tracks and began to shake. "They are going to find us and kill us." Sally's teeth chattered along with the clattering of the china, which vibrated as she trembled.

"That is why we need to move a little more quickly," said Emma, taking the tray from the girl's hands. "Come along now."

Emma led them around the building, stepping in more than one freezing puddle along the way as her foot broke through the thin layer of ice to the frigid water below. They finally got to the edge of the building facing the road. Emma handed the tray back to Sally and flattened herself along the stone side of the building, then peeked out to make sure the men were not out on the road.

She could not see very far without revealing herself, and she knew she would have to take a chance that one of the highwaymen would not step outside the inn or look out of the common room and see her walk back inside.

Emma had a sudden desire to run away. She could hide until the mail coach returned, then flee to Portsmouth and sail away to America. She could leave Darington and all this behind her.

For God hath not given us the spirit of fear, but of power and of love and of a sound mind.
                                        —2 Timothy 1:7

The verse came powerfully to mind, and she knew she could never live with herself if she abandoned Darington in his hour of need. She would not be bound by a spirit of fear. With a silent prayer for help, Emma squared her shoulders, took the tea tray back from Sally, and boldly walked onto the road.

Emma walked as confidently as she could holding a tea tray and strode to the door of the inn. Emma held her breath as Sally opened the door. The entryway was empty and she breathed a sigh of relief. She wasted no time in hurrying up the stairs and down the corridor to her room, Sally following closely behind.

Emma launched the tray onto the table, spilling some tea, and locked the door behind her, collapsing into a chair. Sally returned to her stool in the corner to sulk silently, where she sat with arms folded and an accusing glare on her face.

"What happened?" asked Dare with a frown, struggling to sit up.

Emma wanted to pretend it was all nothing so as not to worry him, but this was not something she could keep from him. She wasted no time in conveying to Dare what had happened.

Dare did sit up this time and grimaced in pain. "We must leave."

"And go where? Where can we hide? And how could we leave without drawing the attention of those brigands? We have no carriage, so we would have to leave either on foot or hire a coach. Either one would be sure to attract notice."

As she spoke, she plumped the pillows behind him so he could lean back. She tried not to notice his bare chest, but it was unavoidable. His form was chiseled perfection. She pulled up the blankets to preserve his modesty…and her ability for rational thought.

The Earl of Darington glowered at her in return, and she feared he recognized her errant thoughts regarding his pleasing appearance.

"Besides, someone might notice that you are less than fully clothed," said Emma in a breezy manner, as if looking at perfection of the male form was a perfectly natural part of her day. "Surely it would lead to an awkward conversation at the very least. Already the staff here think I am quite mad. I fear that our presence and the descriptions the men gave the magistrate cannot go unnoticed for long. I suspect they will soon come to ask questions and I am not sure what we are going to say."

Even as she spoke, a knock came on the door. Emma felt her stomach sink to her cold, wet toes.

"Yes?" she called, stepping near the door.

"This is Sir Gerald. May I have a word with you and your husband?" said the voice from the other side of the door.

She glanced back at Dare. What were they going to do now?

Fifteen

"I AM SORRY, BUT MY HUSBAND IS ILL. MAY WE SPEAK to you at a different time?" called Emma, in a desperate attempt to put off the magistrate.

"I won't keep you long. Just a few questions will do."

"Yes, all right," said Emma, for what else could she say? "One moment while I make ourselves presentable."

She ran back to Dare's side. "Do we dare trust him?" she whispered.

Dare frowned and shook his head. "Too great a risk he would tell those men. If they should learn we are here, they could kill us at their leisure. I fear I am in no condition to protect you."

"We need to convince him you are sick," whispered Emma. "Not shot. The pox would do. That would keep everyone away. What can we use to make red spots?"

"Miss St. James," Sally interjected, head down.

"Yes, Sally?"

"I…I…" She turned quickly to her small bandbox and rustling through it pulled out a small case. "Here."

Emma took the case from her and stared at the lid.

"Pear's Liquid Blooms of Roses? Why Regina was furious looking for her rouge."

"It fell behind the cabinet and I found it cleaning. She threatened anyone she caught stealing it, so I was afraid to give it back."

"This carmine color will work nicely for the illusion. You probably should have returned it as soon as you found it, but I am glad you did not, for it will render us a service. Thank you, Sally."

A knock came again on the door, causing Emma's heart rate to climb. She was a country girl. She could not lie to a magistrate and pretend to be someone else. What was she doing?

"It will be fine. You can do this." Darington's low voice broke through her worries.

She realized she was trying to open the rouge with trembling hands. "Yes, of course."

The knock sounded again, louder this time.

"One moment please," called Emma. She opened the carmine rouge and dabbed her pinkie finger into the dark-red paste to apply spots to Darington's face and hands. It would not serve under close inspection, but she counted on a fear of smallpox to prevent anyone from coming close. She tossed the case to Sally as she walked to open the door.

She opened the door halfway, blocking entry into the room, though the large man before her would have no difficulty barging in if he so chose. His mouth and eyes were grim, and he looked her up and down as if weighing her worth. He was wearing a wool hunting jacket and riding boots, clearly called away from an intended day of sport.

"Yes, may I help you?"

"I am Sir Gerald, the magistrate here. Do I have the honor of addressing Mrs. Anders?" The man spoke in a deep voice and had a salt-and-pepper mustache that almost completely hid his mouth. His tone was reserved and she was certain he was irritated at having been kept waiting at the door.

"Yes. How can I help you, Sir Gerald?"

"There has been a report of a serious nature. I need to speak with your husband."

"I fear my husband is not well."

"Forgive this intrusion, but my business cannot wait."

"I do not wish to raise alarm, but my husband is quite unwell."

"I hate to be blunt, Mrs. Anders, but a man is dead. Three men report the culprits are individuals fitting your description, who would have come to this hamlet around the same time as you. Now I will speak to your husband." He stepped forward, and there was nothing she could do but step back.

"As you wish, but I fear my husband's illness has taken a turn for the worse. We were traveling by post, and he took ill. I am not familiar with this but…" She lowered her voice to a whisper and leaned closer to the magistrate in a conspiratorial manner. "You do not think it could be smallpox, do you?"

Emma's heart was beating so fast she hardly had to act to give her tone a tremble of anxiety. She stepped aside to reveal the patient. Dare was doing an excellent job at looking ill. Of course, he was already pale from his ordeal and the smattering of small red dots across his face was convincing. He lay still, eyes closed, mouth slightly ajar.

"The fever burns him so," added Emma, hoping to keep the man away.

Sir Gerald took a step back and put a handkerchief over his mouth. "Yes, well, I see, very ill indeed." He backed up as he walked until he had removed himself from the room and was standing in the hallway, still staring at Dare. "He is clearly not the man we seek. Thank you for your time. I wish your husband well. I will notify a doctor for you."

Emma had been relieved to see the man go, but a new danger gave alarm. She was about to protest the sending for a doctor when the magistrate continued.

"Though I know he is visiting his sister. Probably won't be able to get him until tomorrow morning."

"Please, do not trouble yourself. I am sure he will be well." She gave him a nervous smile. She certainly did not have to fake her concern.

Sir Gerald looked over her shoulder at Dare in the bed. "I'll send for the doctor," he said in a low voice. He shook his head and walked back down the corridor.

Emma closed and bolted the door and breathed a sigh of relief. "Well, at least that has bought us a little time." She smiled at Dare and Sally.

Dare revived himself and passed a hand over his eyes, smearing his spots. "Won't be long before those men hear of us and come to look for themselves. Wish I knew who they were or why my sister and I were targeted."

"Come now. Do not fret. You are smearing your spots." Emma took a handkerchief, dipped it in water, and proceeded to scrub the red off of his face. He might have been able to do it himself but put up no resistance to her ministrations. "I am sure help will come or we will think of something." He had encouraged her and it was her turn to do the same. Hope was the one thing she was not about to give up.

He nodded in agreement.

"We must find a way out of here without being noticed."

"Indeed, we must," Dare agreed. But how this feat was to be accomplished, neither of them knew.

৵৵

Eustace Ludlow stared at the overturned coach. He had arrived late to Waverley Hall the day before only to find the house in chaos, his mother frantic, and Emma St. James gone. He had questioned the staff, threatening more than just their positions if they did not tell him everything, but everyone pleaded ignorance. The missing coach, however, was a clear sign of Emma's escape.

He had left early the next morning to find the brat and drag her to an asylum, where she belonged. He could not believe that such a little country nothing had the power to destroy his whole life. It was entirely unfair. It had taken him most of the day, but he had finally found the coach, crashed in a gully on the side of the road. The scene had gathered a small crowd of rustics, who had come to gawk.

Eustace tramped through the muddy slush, cursing Emma under his breath for ruining his polished Hessian boots. They had cost him dear and now were a complete loss. He looked through the smashed window, hoping to find evidence of a bloody demise, but none could be found.

"What happened here? Where is the occupant of the coach?" he asked a man with a silver mustache who had taken charge of trying to remove the coach from the side of the road.

"They're looking for 'em," replied the man.

"Them?" A shiver of dread crept up his spine. His mother had assured him that Emma had no contact with any man who could remotely be seen as marriageable. If she were to wed, all was lost.

The man tied a sturdy rope around a broken axle. "'Tis all the talk. They say a man and woman were in this here coach and run into another coach, robbing them and killing one o' them. The body was found right in the middle o' the road, shot dead." He leaned closer. "Bad sort, you could tell, and not just 'cause he was dead. They moved the body out o' respect for the ladies."

"What?" Eustace rocked back on his heels, trying to make sense of what the man was saying. He thought very little of Emma, but she was no murderer.

"'Course, they couldn't just leave the body there in the mud. Blocking the road, it was."

Eustace checked again to make sure the coach was indeed Emma's. What had happened here? "You say there was a man and woman?"

The man tugged on the rope that connected the overturned coach and a team of black horses. "I didn't say it. The men they robbed did."

"And where are these men now?"

"Here now, I got a job to do. I've got to get this here coach off the side o' the road."

Eustace rubbed two shillings together, making a distinctive metallic noise. "Where can I find the woman from this coach?"

In one swift move, the shillings disappeared from his hand and the man doffed his cap revealing a mostly bald head. "Don't know where they are, sir, but they can't have got far, not with the weather we've been having. They'd be on foot too, 'cause we found the nags from this here coach, the harness cut with a knife."

"Where is the nearest town or hamlet?"

"Straight that way, through the hedgerows, about two miles. Follow this road here and it'll take ye 'round the fields."

"Thank you," muttered Eustace and mounted up again, squinting into the cold rain as he trotted down the road to the little hamlet. He would not be kind when he found Emma. If anyone deserved a sound beating, it was she.

When he arrived at the hamlet, he was pleased to see only one inn. If Emma had come this way, she must surely have stayed at the Green Man Inn. Fortunately, the news of the robbery and murder was all the talk, so information was not difficult to glean. He heard of strangers in town, a Mr. and Mrs. Anders who arrived the night before on the mail, which Eustace found suspect.

"I would like a room for the night," Eustace said, addressing the elderly landlord. "I would like to inform my mother I have arrived safely. Could you post a letter for me?"

"Yes, of course, sir." The landlord gave him a nod of the head and a genial smile.

"I've heard a Mrs. and Mr. Anders are staying here," commented Eustace in what he hoped was an offhand manner. "I believe they may be friends of mine. Could you describe the lady?"

"She's a pretty, young thing, she is—head full of blond curls, bright-blue eyes. Why her smile could—"

"Yes, yes, that sounds like her." Eustace did not wish to hear anyone sing the praises of his stepsister. "Could you let me know the room? I'd like to surprise them by giving my regards."

"Oh, I don't think that would be good." A cloud fell over the landlord's countenance. "Mr. Anders is quite unwell, in fact…" The landlord leaned close and lowered his voice to a whisper. "I don't want to spread rumor and cause a panic, but the magistrate thinks he's got the pox."

"How dreadful." Eustace was not sure what to make of it but decided against a knock on the door. It would not do to expose himself to illness only to find the lady in question was not the one he sought. "Could you let me know when the lady emerges? I should very much like to offer my assistance to Mrs. Anders."

"Yes, of course, sir."

Sixteen

DARE AND EMMA REMAINED ALL DAY IN THE INN, discretely querying the maid who brought up dinner as to the latest news. The overturned coach and corpse had been found, and it was the talk of all in the heretofore-sleepy little hamlet. The highwaymen had not left but roamed freely, receiving the sympathy of the hamlet, who believed them to be the victims. It was impossible that they had not heard about the arrival of a Mr. and Mrs. Anders. So far, the men had stayed away, most likely for fear of smallpox, but Emma had no hope they would not eventually come to see "Mr. and Mrs. Anders" for themselves.

Dare's progress had consisted of not developing a fever, which was Emma's primary concern. They still did not know why the men had targeted Dare, but both agreed they would be best served to retreat to a place of safety.

To do that, they had to leave. And that was proving difficult.

"You need to leave tonight," declared the Earl of

Darington. The day had almost passed and the sun hung low in the sky.

"I prefer to help you continue to recover from your injuries," replied Emma mildly. She checked his wound once more to ensure it did not appear red, hot, or swollen. If the wound were to fester or turn septic, it would not matter if they managed to evade the highwaymen, for it would be fatal on its own. The wound continued to seep, but so far everything looked as well as could be expected.

"I do thank you for your assistance," said Dare, grimly submitting to her ministrations. "but I cannot consider myself a gentleman and continue to allow you to put yourself at risk. You must leave as we agreed on the next mail coach."

"That was before I realized those men were still here."

"You will be on the next mail coach."

"I most certainly will not." Emma folded her arms across her chest.

"You will, if I have to put you on it myself." Dare's lips were a thin line, and Emma did not doubt his tenacity and determination in carrying out his threat.

She changed tack and attempted reason. "I doubt they will allow me to travel by mail if they think I have been exposed to smallpox. Besides, there must be some other way than abandoning you to your fate. I did not help to heal you just so you could get yourself into more trouble."

"I appreciate your help. I doubt I would be alive now without it. But the truth is I can fend for myself more easily without you."

"I beg your pardon?"

"You and your maid will only slow me down. I am sure I can escape more easily without you," he said without compassion.

Emma blinked at him. Was he saying this because it was true or because he was trying to protect her? She chose to believe the latter. "We are at an impasse then, for I cannot see that the way to repay the man who saved my life is to abandon him to the men who shot him."

Emma wandered to the window as she spoke, looking out over the small village on the gray, winter day. The clouds had hung low all day, casting the landscape in a dim, subdued light, as if everything was waiting for night to arrive. She feared their unwanted acquaintances might be waiting for night too.

Dare responded not in words but in a growling sigh that she had come to interpret as one of displeasure. She wanted to leave for safer lodgings as much as he did, but abandoning him could not be right.

She watched out the window for the comings and goings of the brigands. It had become something of a nervous habit for her. As she idly watched the sleepy hamlet going about its business, two people caught her eye. They were gentry by the cut of their cloth.

"Oh no!" exclaimed Emma, staring out the window. She had seen that many riding capes on only one man before. It was Eustace. He had found her. Cold dread filled her veins.

"What is it?" asked Dare, struggling to sit up.

"I fear Eustace has... Oh, wait. No, it is not him." Emma put a hand to her chest, relieved. "There is a gentleman down there who must have at least fifteen riding capes on his greatcoat. I feared it was my stepbrother, but it is not."

Dare's interest perked up. "How many?"

"Too many to count. He is with a lady in a plain black coat, such a contrast."

"The lady, what does she look like?" asked Dare with an urgency to his tone.

"She is wearing a bonnet, so I cannot rightly see— Oh! What are you doing out of bed? You should not get up." Emma gasped at Dare who stood slightly hunched over and shirtless next to her. It was one thing to see him lying down; it was another to have him tower over her, the muscled perfection of his form drawing her attention from the couple in the street.

"My word." Dare's face was twisted with surprise and pain. He held himself up on the windowsill with one hand and pressed the other onto his wounded side. "That is my sister."

❧

"No," said Darington as the unrelenting pain forced him to allow Emma to help him back to the bed. What was he thinking, getting himself shot? Damned nuisance. "No," he said again as he watched her grab Sally's plain cloak and pull it around her. "No, it's too dangerous."

"Yes, I know," said Emma with a gleam in her eye. She was an unusual girl, he had to give her that. "Those brigands are nowhere in sight," she continued in a cheery tone. "We have no time to waste."

"No," he said for a third time through gritted teeth, trying to get back out of bed. "I will go make contact with my sister."

"I fear you will do nothing of the sort," said Emma with a hand on his bare chest. At the merest touch, he complied and lay back down. "You are not even dressed. Even if you tried to stagger down the stairs and cross the street, you would more likely fall on your face and cause a scene, which would no doubt alert our enemies to our presence. No, you will have to stay here."

"It is not safe," growled Dare, angry at his own impotence. "Send Sally if you must, for she is less recognizable than you."

"I ain't going down there!" cried Sally.

"I must alert your sister to your whereabouts before she leaves," said Emma practically. She looked at him with sparkling eyes. What could she do if those men attacked her? Charm them to death? Maybe…

"It's too dangerous," Dare repeated.

"She must have come looking for you. We must tell her where you are. How else will she find you?" Emma asked, picking up her bonnet.

Dare shook his head. "I do not know, but my sister is…tenacious."

"A good thing too," said Emma, tying on her bonnet. "I'll be back in a twinkling."

"Please." Dare's strained voice did not sound like his own.

Emma paused and looked back at him.

"Please be careful."

A slow smile brightened her face. "As you wish."

And with that she was gone.

Dare waited for a minute before struggling out of bed again and staggering to the window. He could not lie helpless and do nothing while Emma and his sister might be in danger.

"Bring me my coat," he demanded of the frightened maid.

She squeaked in fear and jumped up to comply. He pulled the pistol out of his coat pocket.

He opened the window a crack, ignoring the blast of cold on his bare chest. He cocked the pistol and watched as Miss St. James walked across the street to meet his sister, who stood with a man in a much-adorned greatcoat that could only belong to Wynbrook. Dare lamented his weakness that prevented him from walking, but he would still protect those who were dear to him.

Emma strode boldly across the street toward Kate and Lord Wynbrook. If anyone could approach strangers on the street and instantly bring them to her side, it was Miss St. James. He watched carefully as Emma led Kate and Wynbrook to the inn. He scanned the road for signs of danger, but seeing none, he returned to his bed with a groan of pain.

Emma entered a few minutes later looking triumphant, followed by a hesitant, then surprised Kate and Lord Wynbrook.

"Robert!" His sister raced across the room to him and gave him an uncharacteristic embrace. It was more emotion than she had shown in years. Or ever.

"Kate, good to see you. Ow! Easy there."

"Do be careful, Lady Kate," said Emma, coming up beside them. "You might rip out the stitches."

"Stitches? Where were you shot? Are you all right? How did you get away?" Kate had nothing but questions, and demanding ones at that.

Emma quickly apprised Kate of his medical situation and introductions were made all around.

"Pleasure to meet you, Miss St. James," said Lord Wynbrook in a tone Dare could not like. The Earl of Wynbrook was a handsome, young, titled gentleman, with twinkling, green eyes. His clothes were impeccably cut and his manner pleasing. Dare had never realized until Emma looked up at him with her smiling, blue eyes how irritating Wynbrook's hold on perfection was. In truth, Emma and Wynbrook would make a lovely pair. They were both of pleasant disposition, animated, and attractive.

He had never hated Wynbrook more.

Kate distracted him from his uncharitable thoughts by demanding to know how he had escaped the brigands and made the acquaintance of Miss St. James. He knew by Kate's tone and pale face she was worried about him and had no context in which to put the discovery of him in a bedchamber with a young lady.

He spoke briefly about the events that led to their current situation but apparently did not do the adventure justice, so Emma jumped in at the part where she had come into the picture, finishing the story in grand form. Her rendition added much zest to the story and gave it the dramatic retelling of some gothic novel or romanticized tale. It did make for great theater, though, and kept basically to the facts.

Kate frowned at all the parts where they were in danger and stared at Emma in shock and surprise when

Emma confessed it was she who had performed surgery and stitched up the wound. Without waiting for an invitation, Kate pulled down the blankets and inspected his injury with a critical eye, exposing his naked chest to the room. A curious look passed over Wynbrook's face.

"You must forgive that Darington does not have a shirt at the moment," commented Emma. "The wound bled quite a bit, and I fear I ripped his linens to shreds, using them as bandages."

"Emma has been very helpful," said Dare, trying to express his appreciation for her skills as a healer and distract everyone from the fact that he was half-dressed. In an instant, he realized he had made a mistake by calling her by her first name.

The slip was certainly not lost on Kate, who raised an eyebrow at him. He deserved that. It must be the pain medication making him softheaded.

"But how do you come to be here?" asked Dare, desperate to change the subject. "How did you find me?"

"Your sister has dragged me up one frozen, ice-caked road and down the other," drawled Wynbrook. "I am certain that if we had not found you here, she would have knocked on every door and searched through the hedgerows until she did."

"After I was pushed from the coach, I ran back to the inn and found Wynbrook outside," explained Kate. "We rushed after you in Wynbrook's coach, hoping to overtake you quickly, but it was not to be. Fortunately, we got a few good leads and eventually they led us here." She said the last in an offhand manner, as if it was not unusual to chase a coach through the night.

It was Dare's turn to raise an eyebrow at his sister. So Kate had been in the presence of Wynbrook for over twenty-four hours. He noted that she did not mention where she had stayed the night. Had they traveled all night? Had they shared a room at an inn? He wanted to ask, but Kate was busy frowning at his wound and Wynbrook was suddenly busy removing a piece of lint from his greatcoat.

Guilty. Both of them. They had shared a room; Dare knew it.

"Well now, we have all had such adventures!" exclaimed Emma, breaking the awkward silence with a smile to the whole room.

What followed was a discussion of what to do next. Wynbrook was in favor of informing the magistrate, and Dare had to relate to him the dangers of that option. Emma advised that to travel at this point would put a strain on him, at a time when he needed mostly to rest, and if traveling was a necessity, they should keep it as short as possible.

"Actually, we may not be far from Greystone," said Kate.

A chill crept up Dare's back at the name. He was surprised the word even came from his sister's lips.

"Greystone?" asked Emma. "Is it a nearby town? Have you friends or relatives who can help?"

"Greystone Hall is our..." Dare paused, not sure what to call the place that haunted his memory. "Home."

Seventeen

EMMA REFUSED TO LET ANYONE SEE HER CONCERN. They had enough to be worried about without her adding to their fears. She allowed Lady Kate and Lord Wynbrook to focus on the travel plans as she quietly packed her things. Under any other circumstances, she would not have allowed the patient to move. This was the most dangerous phase of recovery, the point at which her father's wound had begun to fester and he slowly lost his life.

While she was alert for any telltale signs of fever, Wynbrook and Lady Kate took on the problem of moving their party without alerting anyone of their intended departure. Fortunately, Wynbrook's coach still held Dare's luggage, so he was able to dress with Wynbrook serving in the role of valet.

A bit of reconnaissance from Wynbrook revealed no sign of the brigands, so they decided to take a chance and hustled into Wynbrook's coach. Wynbrook continued to serve as coachman, not wanting to hire anyone who could later reveal their destination, and brought the coach around to the front of the inn. Dare walked stiffly between Emma and Kate, leaning on them as needed, and after some difficulty entering the coach, collapsed onto the velvet squabs. Sally followed behind with the luggage.

Dare and Kate took one side of the coach, and Emma sat with Sally, facing them. Wynbrook hardly gave them time to sit down before he got the coach moving, not wanting to linger.

Emma took a deep breath of relief as the coach rolled out of the hamlet and onto the dark road. "I am glad to put the Green Man Inn behind me," she confessed.

Lady Kate nodded in mute agreement, her angular face appearing even harsher in the flickering light of the swaying coach lantern. She was a tall, thin woman who had a strong resemblance to her brother, except where his eyes were dark as night, hers were an alluring silver. It was the only thing flashy about her, as her clothes and demeanor might have best been described as reserved.

Kate and Dare shared a penchant for taciturnity, for neither spoke. Kate turned toward the dark window without a word, and Dare's eyes closed. Emma knew the best thing he could do was rest.

Emma had hoped that Sally would be cheered with the prospect of escaping the inn, but her maid only scowled at her feet. Without anyone inclined toward conversation, Emma contended herself in sending a silent prayer of thanks for their escape.

After a few hours, they appeared to turn onto a drive that was less frequented. The road was rough and every bump, every shift of the coach brought a new grimace of pain from Darington. Emma was certain a man of less fortitude would have been hollering in pain, but Dare took it with the cool detachment that was his temperament.

Finally, the coach began to climb up a windy, steep road. Lady Kate's face was pinched, and she stared out the black window. Emma knew they must have been getting close to the house. Even Dare's body went rigid, as if preparing to fight an unknown foe.

"When was the last time you visited Greystone?" Emma asked politely.

She saw at once it was the wrong question, for both Kate's and Dare's faces hardened.

"It has been a long time," said Dare in a low voice.

As the carriage struggled up the steep road in the poor, slick conditions, both brother and sister were rendered as tight as bowstrings. Even Emma could not miss the sense of foreboding as they crept slowly up the hill toward Greystone. She stared out the window, trying to make out the dark shapes of the landscape in the light of the pale moon. She wrapped herself a little tighter in her cloak.

The skies were clear, but the wind was sharp and the temperature a brittle cold. They reached the top of the bluffs, which Emma guessed must have looked out over the ocean, though at night, it was all blackness. They turned a tight corner and the imposing house came into view.

Greystone Hall stretched five stories high like a monstrous black tower. Emma searched for something pleasant to remark upon but was at a loss. Everything about the striking tower was stark and bleak. From the scraggly bushes and windswept trees along the bluff, to the sharp edges of the imposing tower house, everything about the place was formidable and barren. It was almost as if the place itself did not wish its master to return.

"My, but that is a striking hall," Emma said, trying desperately to find something kind to say. "This is your home?"

"This is where we were born and spent the first few years of our life," said Lady Kate in an icy tone. "We have not been back since our father died thirteen years ago."

"Thirteen years? But then, you haven't been back since you were children. Is this not your country seat?" Emma could not understand why Kate and Dare had not set foot in their own home for so long. According to Dare, his fortune had been restored, so why stay away?

"It has been more financially advantageous for us to rent the property." Kate did not look at her as she spoke. "We've had a series of respectable families who have lived here, though it is vacant at the moment. We have kept the house fully staffed, as we expect our land agent to find a new tenant soon."

"How fortunate that your home is staffed, as if it was waiting for you to return." Emma was determined to bring some liveliness to the grim siblings before her. Dare did not speak, but his color was pale. The main thing that pleased Emma about reaching Greystone was it meant that their journey was almost at an end. Dare needed to rest. She smiled even brighter, as if she could ward off all misfortune by determined cheerfulness.

They pulled into the drive and Wynbrook jumped down, half-frozen and shivering.

"I trust I found the right place," said Wynbrook through chattering teeth.

"Oh, you must be chilled through," said Emma sympathetically. "What you need is a good bowl of wine punch."

"Make that rum punch and I think you've about got it."

Darington and Kate both glared at her. She was taken aback at their reaction but quickly realized neither of them appreciated her interaction with Wynbrook. Instead of being offended, she chose to see this as an indication of Lady Kate's regard for Wynbrook. She smiled at them, trying to convey that they need not worry.

Wynbrook was a tall, handsome man, but he was in love with Lady Kate. Emma could tell by the way his eyes rested on Kate, the way he watched her and smiled at her when she was not looking, then pretended to be attending to something else when she turned his way. Wynbrook could be charming and flirtatious, but Emma had no doubt as to where his heart lay.

What was less clear to her was Dare's reaction. Was he displeased with Emma because he feared she might steal the affection intended for his sister? Perhaps. Or maybe it was his heart, his affection, which gave him pause. Despite the frigid wind that cut through her wrap, Emma flushed warm.

They shuffled up to the main door and Emma was a little concerned about their reception. To appear in the middle of the night on the doorstep of a house, even if it was the house you owned, was not done.

She also wondered, as she and Wynbrook assisted Darington on either side, how they would explain arriving in the middle of the night, unannounced, and with the master of the house injured.

She need not have worried though, for Kate took things well in hand. The butler and housekeeper who arrived at the door were clearly surprised and had to be convinced that people they had never met before were in truth the master of the house and his sister. Emma doubted she could have convinced anyone of such a thing, but she underestimated Lady Kate. Kate was sure and confident, with a regal manner that, despite her plain wool coat and bonnet, left no doubt she was aristocratic. She spun a story of traveling together and getting set upon by highwaymen who shot Darington.

The house was roused and Kate quickly had everyone snapping to her commands. The maids were awakened, fires laid, punch served (Emma had two cups before she could even begin to feel her toes). Emma watched in amazement as Kate managed everything, directly and precisely. She was not rude or unkind, but she was exacting and clearly in command. Emma's grumpy maid was whisked off to the servants' quarters. Kate would never allow herself to be served by anyone who was not respectful and competent.

Emma admired Kate. Greatly.

Greystone was a grand house, or at least it could have been. It was a bit of a blank canvas. The furnishings were limited, and at first, Emma had difficulty determining what made the house feel so imposing. Then she realized the sparseness of the mansion exuded a barren, neglected feel. No pictures adorned

the rooms, causing the sound to bounce off the
empty walls and carry long and loud. Emma found
herself walking on tiptoe to try to avoid being heard.
Everyone's voices were hushed, as if not to disturb the
ghosts that prowled there.

They did not linger in the drawing room, nor did
they talk much. There was often one of the servants
present to prepare the room in some way, so conversation about anything important was out of the question.
Small talk seemed irrelevant after all they had gone
through, and even Emma lapsed into silence.

"I am sorry to keep you waiting," said the housekeeper, bustling into the room. "It may take a bit to get
the master's chamber prepared. We were not expecting
you, and we had not prepared the family suite. That
wing of the house was never opened, you know."

"I think it more important that we get rest than that
we sleep in any particular bedroom," said Kate severely.

"Yes, my lady." The housekeeper curtsied and
hustled away.

Emma wondered why the family wing had been
kept unused and off limits. Soon they were shown to
their rooms by the housekeeper. The main staircase
rose up to an open balcony that looked down through
stone arches to the marble floor of the entryway
below. From there, two staircases continued up, one
on either end of the open corridor.

Emma followed the woman up the stairs on the
right-hand side, while Dare, his arm around Wynbrook
for support, climbed the other. She glanced back at
Dare, watching him proceed slowly up the stairs. She
wanted to help. She needed to help.

Emma wanted to check the stitches, and she knew Dare was due for another dose of laudanum, without which he would have a difficult time sleeping due to the pain. Despite their unconventional sleeping arrangements of the night before, as an unmarried female, she was not allowed anywhere near his bedroom at night—or ever. She supposed she could give him a dose of medicine in the hallway, but she could certainly not check the wound there. Dare did not look back at her to give any indication of his needing her. Of course, it was not the sort of thing he could rightly ask of her.

Emma was shown to a bedroom with a fresh fire lit in the grate. It was spare, but pleasantly appointed in blue and sage green. She guessed the linens and drapes had been recent additions, probably added by the current staff for the series of tenants. Sally knocked a moment after Emma arrived, and she had no choice but to submit to the questionable assistance of her maid, who helped her into her nightgown.

Emma could hardly tell the young maid she did not wish to change because she wished to visit an unmarried man—no, an unmarried *earl*. Even worse, the Pirate Earl himself.

Sally finished with a sullen frown and dragged herself out of the room without a curtsy. Emma sighed. She would work on common courtesy later.

Emma took a deep breath, grabbed a candle and her medical bag, wrapped herself in a thick blanket, and cautiously stepped outside the room. She looked back at the beckoning bed. It looked comfortable, and she knew a young maid had heated it with a bed warmer.

Her tired body ached to crawl under the goose-down comforter and fall into a deep sleep.

And yet, somewhere in the house, Dare needed her. So despite all societal rules against it, she would go to him. It was as simple as that.

Eighteen

EMMA STEPPED OUT INTO THE HALLWAY, CLOSING THE door quietly behind her. She walked down the corridor in soft slippers, careful not to scuff her feet on the floor. She slunk up the stairwell she had seen Dare ascend, wondering how she would find his bedchamber.

She wandered down a corridor of doors. She guessed one of them held the Earl of Darington, but which one? With sudden inspiration, she blew out her candle and waited for her eyes to grow accustomed to the dark. Light shone from under two of the doors. She had even odds of picking the right one.

She took a breath and knocked on the first door.

"Enter," said a muffled male voice from behind the door.

She opened the door and found Lord Wynbrook in a dressing gown and nightcap, sitting in bed, reading a book. His eyebrows shot up to see Emma standing there in her nightclothes, and he hastily attempted to hide his book, but not before she noted it was the *Captain's Curse*, one of those gripping novels young women were warned against…and she had hidden in her trunk.

"I do apologize. I am looking for Lord Darington. It is time for his medicine," Emma attempted to explain. Of course she would pick the wrong door.

Wynbrook gave her a slow smile. "I see."

She was not sure what exactly Wynbrook saw, but it was not good whatever it was. Closing Wynbrook's door, she hurried to the next lit door and rapped lightly.

She was bade to enter and this time Darington was on the other side.

"Oh, good, it is you this time," said Emma, entering quickly.

"This time?" Dare was also in bed wearing a nightshirt. He wore no cap though, and instead, his dark-brown hair, which she had only seen pulled back in a queue, hung loose around his shoulders.

"Yes, I..." For some reason, seeing him with his hair untied felt strangely intimate, which was odd since she had seen much more of him than his undone hair. "I found Wynbrook's room first."

"You went to Wynbrook's room?" he asked in a dark tone.

"Not on purpose," she explained, but he did not look appeased. Heaven help her, it did nothing to dispel the strange attraction she felt toward him. He may have been wounded, but he still held an aura of danger. "I came to give you some medicine and check to make sure your stitches held."

Dare acknowledged her with a nod. "Thank you."

She knew he must have been hurting if he accepted the laudanum without a fight. She walked to the bed and poured out a dose, which he took with a grimace.

"Has the wound bled during travel?" she asked.

"Some," he admitted.

"I had best take a look at the stitches. It will be a wonder if they are not all pulled out."

Dare gave her a quick nod and pulled down the covers to his waist and sat up farther. He was dressed much more appropriately than before in a voluminous nightshirt. No doubt it kept him warm, but she missed seeing his bare chest in all its naked glory.

She blinked at the sudden turn her thoughts had gone. When had she become a wanton? She was here to help this man, not ogle him.

"Would you mind pulling up the nightshirt so I may inspect the wound?" she asked briskly.

He paused a minute, then complied. Though now his top half was covered, his careful movements made her realize that unlike when they were in the inn, he was wearing nothing from the waist down. The mere thought brought heat to her cheeks.

He moved carefully and slowly, possibly due to the pain and possibly due to the need to pull up the nightshirt while keeping the blankets in place.

"I will be looking for any redness, heat, or swelling that might be a sign of infection," she babbled, focused on his slow, deliberate movements.

Finally, the dressings came into view, stained in dark-red blood. "I am glad I brought more bandages. That is more than a little blood."

She went to work removing the old dressing and inspecting the wound. As she did so, she could not help but notice his pronounced muscles, taut and tempting. One prominent muscle formed a ridge from his lower hip going down toward his core. What might she see if the blanket slipped down a few more inches?

"Well now, let's see how those stitches are holding," said Emma as if she did this all the time. She examined the entry wound and was relieved to see that it looked as well as she could hope.

"Could you roll over so I can examine your back?"

Dare nodded and rolled onto his side, away from her. She had begun to examine the larger wound on his back when the blanket slipped a bit and she could see the top part of his derriere. She forgot to move, forgot to breathe. Surely he was the perfect form of a man.

"Did I rip out stitches?" asked the man whose backside had captured her entire interest.

"I…err…" *The stitches. Look at the stitches.* She forced herself to look at the wound and was pleased to see no sign of infection.

"Does it look good?" he asked.

Very, very good. She cleared her throat more easily than she did her mind. "There has been some slight tearing, which probably accounted for the bleeding, but it has stopped now. I think it will heal well." She was pleased she sounded reasonable despite the flight of her unruly emotions.

He rolled onto his back and met her eyes. "Emma." He said her name with such sincerity it made her heart pound. "Thank you. I am greatly sorry for embroiling you in this escapade. You deserve better."

"No, indeed, I have found our adventure excessively diverting, especially now that we are safe. I would not change one second of it." Her words were true.

She dressed the wound, her pulse increasing every

time she touched his skin. She must get herself under better control. She needed to leave the man's bedroom before she did anything untoward. She found the Earl of Darington more attractive than was good for her. "Sleep now. I shall come again in the morning."

Dare's eyelids grew heavy. "Thank you, Emma."

Emma crept back to her bedroom, knowing who would be featured prominently in her dreams.

❧

Dare listened as she crept away from his room, down the hall. Truly, he owed Emma more than he could repay. Even if she was promised to another in marriage—an engagement that seemed rather suspect to him—an offer of marriage from him was due. Though the proposal might be obligatory, his intentions were decidedly sincere. He was determined to change her mind and secure her hand in marriage. The thought of her marrying another set his teeth on edge.

He would ask her tomorrow. He just wanted to be fully dressed and on his own feet when he did so.

❧

"What do you mean they have gone?" Eustace Ludlow ground out, trying unsuccessfully to conceal the anger in his tone.

"I'm sorry, sir. They didn't tell me they was leaving. When the maid went to check on them to see if they done with the dinner tray, they were gone." The landlord stood at the door of Eustace's room wringing his hands on a dirty apron.

"I am very concerned for my friends. I thought I requested you to let me know when they emerged."

"Well now, that's the thing. I'm not sure when they left. I don't stand at the door all the time, you know, but one o' the lads said he seen them get into a coach with two others."

"And where did they go?"

"I don't rightly know."

"You don't rightly know?" Eustace repeated at a shout. He was too angry to keep a level tone. He could not have come all this way only to have her slip away in the presence of some strange man…if it was her.

"I am sorry, sir. But…but this came for you." The landlord held out a missive with a shaky hand.

Eustace snatched the letter and slammed the door in the man's face. The letter was from his mother, sent express. He ripped it open and scanned the contents.

Eustace took a breath, allowing himself to smile for the first time since he had learned of Emma's flight. His mother had intercepted a letter for Emma from the secretary for Lord Langley. Within was a revelation of all his stepsister's conniving plans.

Eustace took a flask from his coat pocket and took a generous swig, welcoming the burn as the liquor poured down his throat. He had to hand it to his stepsister; she certainly had plotted her escape quite nicely. She had accepted an arranged marriage with an American and planned to meet her chaperone in Portsmouth in three days' time.

He reclined on the bed and made himself comfortable. Mrs. Anders must not be the person he sought. He did not know where Emma was now, but that didn't matter, because he knew where she was going to be. When she arrived in Portsmouth, he would be waiting.

The only place she was going was the asylum.

Nineteen

EMMA WOKE WITH A SMILE ON HER FACE. IT WAS already midmorning, and she realized she had slept long, waking refreshed. For the first time since she'd left her home, she felt safe.

In a series of circumstances she could not possibly have predicted, she had found herself in the company of new friends—and not just friends, but members of the aristocracy. Her stepmother would grind her teeth to the bone if she knew Emma was fraternizing with two unmarried earls. Eustace would be positively livid. He had such hopes of elevating his position, and here Emma was in the company of those he could not possibly hope to gain an acquaintance.

Emma indulged in a smile of vindication but did not enjoy the gloat as much as she had imagined. It was not through any of her own doing that she found herself in such company. No, that was firmly in the hands of her maker. She readjusted her attitude, felt better, and decided it was past time to check on her patient.

She feared Dare may already be awake and in pain, so she rang for Sally and dressed as quickly as she could. She took her medical bag downstairs and was informed by an aloof butler that Lord Darington was in the drawing room.

It was hard not to feel a little cowed by the formality of it all. It was one thing to take care of an injured man in the heat of a crisis; it was another to be staying at his estate. She had believed him before, but it was not the same as seeing it for herself.

She entered the drawing room and was a little taken aback. Dare was sitting on the settee, newspaper in hand. No, not the Dare she knew. This was the Earl of Darington. His clothes, his bearing, his rigid posture—all revealed him as an aristocrat and master of the house. Gone was the injured man she had known. This was a peer of the realm in his element. She paused, not sure if she should approach. He must have sensed her presence, for he looked up.

"Miss St. James." He pushed himself up slowly, a tightness in his jaw revealing the pain required to do so. Suddenly, she felt more at ease. This was the same man she had met on that muddy road. And he still needed her help.

"Please do not rise." She rushed into the room and sat in a chair next to him to prevent him from the obligation of having to stand. "I see you are doing better."

"I am, thanks to you."

"I brought you another dose to ease the pain."

Dare nodded. "Half dose if you please."

"Half of this dose will not deaden the pain."

Dare nodded. "Need to keep my wits about me. Half dose."

"As you wish," she responded, keeping her admiration

for his choice to herself. She had seen people become so attached to laudanum that they became no earthly good and seemed to slip deeper and deeper into pain and self-destruction. She admired a man who regulated himself against such an unfortunate outcome, though it meant living with pain for a time.

She prepared the dose and he drank it down in one gulp, though she knew it was dreadfully sour. He was not one to complain, this Earl of Darington.

"Did you sleep well?" he asked.

"Yes, very well indeed. I confess I was rather exhausted from all our adventures, though I feel quite myself now," she hurried to add as a frown came over his face. "Did you sleep well?"

"I did. Thank you."

"I suppose we will need to do something about those dreadful men today."

"Already done. Wynbrook and I met with the local magistrate here and explained things. He will straighten out the other magistrate and will look for the brigands."

"You explained everything?" asked Emma, wondering how candid Darington had been.

"We kept to the same story Kate told the staff. I did not feel it necessary to involve you in the incident."

"Thank you," said Emma, appreciating his protection. She wondered what would happen next. Did he still need her? The truth was, if he was well enough to walk to the sitting room, he was well enough to take care of his own wound. "I shall give the housekeeper some bandages, so you may tend your injury. I imagine she should have laudanum in her medicine cabinet. You know the dose that is right for you."

"Yes, of course. Thank you, Miss St. James." He paused. She waited, but he paused, seeming unsure how to proceed. "I do not suppose you found my signet ring in my waistcoat when it was removed?"

Heat ran up the back of her neck at the memory of removing his clothing. "N–no, I fear not. Is it missing?"

Dare gave a quick nod. "No matter. Probably fell out in the coach." He took a breath as if he wished to say something else but paused, frowned, and looked away.

"So this is your home." Emma attempted to fill the awkward silence.

"Yes." Dare seemed relieved she had changed the subject…or started one. "I have not been back here since the day of my father's funeral."

"The memories must be very difficult."

Dare looked past her to the bare walls beyond. "My father returned from sea in poor condition. A cannon blast had backfired and nearly blinded him. We were away at school. I knew his health was not good, but I had not thought him close to death. When we received the letter, it was a shock." Though Dare's tone never changed, he closed his eyes for a moment and opened them before continuing.

"We returned to find the house…" He gestured to the sparse furnishings, which made the room feel neglected and forlorn. "I wish I knew who was responsible."

"Have you no idea? Did your father have any enemies?" Emma checked herself. "Forgive me for such a forward question."

"No, it is a relevant question." He met her eyes with his dark ones. "My father was a captain in the Royal Navy. He was in command of a flotilla when he discovered a plot to capture a ship carrying four of the royal princes. It was one of his own fellow commanders, Captain Harcourt, who had accepted a large sum in gold bars to deliver the princes into the hands of their enemy."

"That is horrible. How could an Englishman and a captain in the Royal Navy betray his country?"

Dare gave a slight shrug. "The love of money must have poisoned his soul. My father revealed the plot and Harcourt was taken into custody for treason. Unfortunately, the ship taking him to court martial was engulfed in a storm and never seen again. They found nothing but wreckage. It is assumed all hands perished."

Emma shook her head. "A horrible end to a horrible man."

"Aye. My father was rewarded with the gold bars that had been intended as the blood money for Harcourt, was promoted to admiral, and given the title of the first Earl of Darington."

"So you are the second."

"I am. Though I would give much to have my father still in possession of the title."

"Yes, of course." Emma leaned closer. "You have endured much."

"It was worse for Kate. We were both betrayed into debtor's prison. Even as the Earl of Darington I could not protect her. I regret not being able to keep her safe."

Emma knew this admission was not made lightly or easily. He was letting her into his world and she was honored. Emma put a hand on his sleeve, unable to resist the desire to comfort.

Dare stared down at her hand. Becoming self-conscious, Emma pulled away just as Dare raised his other hand and their hands collided. Somehow, in a manner that felt natural, fingers intertwined until they were holding hands.

"Lady Kate is a strong and capable lady," encouraged Emma. "I am quite impressed. And you managed to protect her from those highwaymen."

Dare shrugged. "Did what was required."

"You did more than that," she argued.

"No, you did that," he said firmly.

"Oh, I did not do much." Emma shrugged off his praise out of habit. "I am just a silly country girl, after all."

"No." Dare's eyes blazed fierce. "Do not diminish yourself. Ever."

"I…I beg your pardon." Emma was taken aback. Usually people appreciated when she lowered herself. It made everyone more comfortable when she took herself down a few pegs. But not Dare.

"You saved my life. You are a better doctor than any I have ever met." He held her hand tighter. "You are not silly. And you are not 'just' anything."

Emma stared at him in surprise. Most men felt threatened by a capable woman. It put them more at ease when she told them it was all her father's teachings. She never mentioned the countless hours she studied medical texts and how she took her work seriously. Yet Dare was not one to allow her to be denigrated in any regard, even if it was at her own hand. Only an extremely confident man could do that. And the Earl of Darington was an extremely confident man.

"Forgive me. It was wrong of me and I apologize," she said sweetly.

Dare gave her a quick nod and lowered his head in a sheepish manner as if just becoming aware of how harsh his defense of her had sounded. "Not accustomed to talking with ladies."

"Perhaps you'd best just think of me as a friend then, and forget about the female part."

"I would be honored," he said gallantly. "Though I could hardly forget the latter," he added softly.

Emma felt heat rise in her cheeks. He knew she was female. Of course he was aware she was female, yet somehow his recognition of her made her feel shiny inside. "Shall we be friends then?"

"As you wish." He met her eyes and held them. His dark eyes were piercing, the tiny gold flecks blazing.

She leaned closer, fascinated by the unique color of his eyes. He mirrored her, drawing near, pulling their joined hands closer to him. They leaned closer until they were inches apart. His lips parted and she suddenly became enchanted with his mouth.

"Emma," he whispered. "There is something I must ask you."

"Yes?"

Footsteps from outside the drawing room made them both start, and they jerked back to their original seated positions. Wynbrook's voice could be heard in the hall.

"Perhaps another time," muttered Dare.

"Yes, yes." Emma was suddenly feeling rather guilty, though she was unsure of her crime. "I should...I should give these medical supplies to the housekeeper." She grabbed her medical kit and almost flew from the room, barely acknowledging Wynbrook in the hall as she passed.

Something had just happened…or was happening. She was not sure what to name it, but she could not wait to see Darington again.

What had he wanted to ask her?

Twenty

DARE CURSED HIMSELF AS HE WATCHED EMMA LEAVE. Why had he not asked her to marry him? He had planned to. He meant to. But somehow, when he looked into those deep, blue eyes, his tongue grew heavy and the words stuck in his throat. He wanted the proposal to be perfect, but how could he find the right words when he couldn't find any words?

Dare cleared his throat and reached for the familiar comfort of a freshly ironed newspaper. The butler had provided him not only with the most recent paper, but also with the copies from the past two days, so Dare could catch up on his reading. He opened the paper and skimmed it, though his mind was focused more on his current situation than on the state of the war on the Continent.

He and Wynbrook had dealt with the magistrate as best they could. He had informed the staff of possible danger and to be on the lookout. It was his job to keep everyone safe, and he would do it to the best of his ability.

Of additional concern was the loss of his signet ring.

He never wore the thing, but kept it in the pocket of his waistcoat. With all the excitement, he had not thought to look for it. And now it was gone. He hoped the ring was truly lost and had not fallen into the hands of his abductors.

"Dare! How are you doing old man?" Wynbrook strolled into the room, looking well and back to his good cheer.

"Feeling older by the minute," Dare admitted. Wynbrook took a seat opposite him by a cozy fire, which was the only thing cheerful about the otherwise barren sitting room. Their voices echoed in the room without any pictures, throw rugs, or ornamentation to break up the drab space.

"I hear that's what getting shot can do to a man," laughed Wynbrook, who had an uphill climb in his attempt to drag Dare into good humor. "Though I do not know this from personal experience, nor do I wish to."

"I am glad my misfortunes can be used for the edification of others."

Wynbrook raised his eyebrows with a smile. "Quite right. I will learn from your mistakes, though in truth, this was no mistake but an act of unparalleled heroism in which you sacrificed yourself to save your sister."

Dare shrugged off the compliment. "You would have done the same."

"Oh, you think too highly of me. Though I might have been willing, I doubt I would have had the skill to do so. And yet, I am honored by your faith in me, so I shall pretend that I too could act the part of the hero should the need arise."

"Marrying my sister will be proof of your courage."

Wynbrook stopped short, his smile fading into something more earnest. "That is indeed what I intend to do."

Dare gave him a quick nod. Wynbrook and Kate had spent the night together. They should be wed. Besides, they liked each other; even Dare could see that. The men shared a look, for even between two men who shared a mutual affection for Lady Kate, neither was so blind as not to recognize her faults. Wynbrook might have a tough time convincing Kate, who had on numerous occasions expressed her intention never to marry, but if anyone was up to the task, it was Wynbrook.

Now if only Dare could produce a similar outcome with Emma.

Kate entered the room with her perpetual scowl and Wynbrook greeted her warmly. Though Kate did not readily reveal her emotions, Dare could see how her eyes softened when she looked at him. She was not immune to Wynbrook's charms, and he hoped after all the difficulties she had experienced, she would allow herself to find happiness.

Miss St. James also reentered the room and Dare forgot what he was thinking, reading, and possibly his own name. In the morning light, her golden ringlets glowed, framing her face, a contrast to sparkling, blue eyes and a perfect peaches-and-cream complexion. Her gown clung to her curvy shape as she walked, and her plump décolletage drove out any rational thought.

Dare forgot himself and leapt up from his chair, grimacing at the sudden shock of pain. "Miss St. James." He remembered not to address her informally before his two witnesses in the room. He motioned for her to take his own seat and sat down across from her.

"What brings you on your journey, Miss St. James?" Kate asked Emma.

Dare leaned forward so as not to miss a single word of Emma's reply.

"Oh, I have embarked on a remarkable journey," said Emma with a wide-eyed smile. "My…stepmother has arranged for me to marry a man in America. I know it seems a bit unusual to wed someone you've never met…" Emma proceeded to tell the others of her plans to accept an arranged marriage.

As she did so, both Kate and Wynbrook shot glances at him. Not even Emma's determined optimism could prevent a widespread sense of apprehension regarding her situation. There was more to the story than she was telling, that much Dare was certain. He was determined to uncover the whole situation and remedy it in his favor.

"I do not suppose I could trouble you for a look at one of your newspapers?" Emma asked, breaking the uncomfortable silence. Dare handed her the entire stack of papers, including the one he was reading.

"Thank you. I am so glad to catch up with my reading. I have not been able to get the *Times* for several days since I began my travels."

"You enjoy reading the paper? Capital," praised Wynbrook. Dare was pleased his future wife enjoyed the paper as he did but felt Wynbrook had no business commenting on it.

Emma gave a shrug. "I mainly read the gossip columns."

"I also enjoy glancing at them from time to time," said Wynbrook with a social ease that Dare did not share. "Mostly, of course, to see if I am listed." He continued to ask if Emma would see how his sister's wedding was mentioned and raised his eyes at Dare when Emma's golden head disappeared behind the paper.

Dare realized he must have been glaring at Wynbrook and attempted to school his features, though he did wish Wynbrook would cease any conversation with his Emma. How was Dare to stand a chance if Wynbrook showed her how a gentleman was truly supposed to behave?

Emma read a notice about Wynbrook's sister's wedding and went on to the next day.

"There won't be any mention of us the next day," said Wynbrook.

"But I believe there is," said Emma, her head behind the newsprint. "Oh!" She looked up over the paper, her mouth a perfect oval. She bent back down and read a passage about Wynbrook and Lady Kate. The society paper had done little to hide their identities and shockingly claimed Wynbrook and Kate had eloped.

Dare was confused for a moment, but then remembered that Wynbrook and Kate had taken off after him in Wynbrook's coach. Apparently, someone had seen them chase after the coach that held Dare and jumped to conclusions. He shook his head. Why had nobody been looking out the window of the posting house when Kate had been abducted?

"This is nonsense," said Kate in a slightly strangled voice that did not quite seem her own. "We simply need to tell people that…" She paused, looking at Dare, unsure.

"We shall tell people we planned to meet Darington on our journey," said Wynbrook. "We then traveled together to your home, where we were married."

"Married?" Kate glanced around the room, silently pleading her case to all present. "Surely there can be no cause for anything so extreme."

Dare hated to see her uncomfortable, and certainly this was not the way he had hoped Wynbrook would propose, but it was done and hopefully for the best.

"Robert?" Kate barely mouthed the word at him. Her eyes were desperate. Though he thought she should marry Wynbrook, he hated to see her so unhappy. It was now up to her whether or not to accept the proposal.

"I think I should attend to some of my correspondence," said Emma with a tight smile, rising to her feet. It was clearly time to leave Kate and Wynbrook alone.

Dare rose with Emma and gave his sister and Wynbrook a brief nod. "Good luck," he said as he walked to the door. It was directed at both of them, though for different reasons.

"I am so sorry," apologized Emma in a fervent tone as Dare shut the door to the drawing room.

Dare was confused. What had the lovely lady done to require such an ardent apology?

"I should not have read the society pages. I fear I have made things difficult."

Dare waved off her concern. "You have nothing to apologize for. Best they know."

"Still, I hate to see your sister so distressed." Emma looked up at him, her cheeks plump and rosy, her eyes compassionate. She was as beautiful as any siren and Dare was hopelessly entrapped.

There was a pause and he recalled that staring silently at her was perhaps not the best social response. He had to struggle to remember the topic of their conversation. "Wynbrook is a good man. I hope she will accept the offer. Her decision though." He had given up long ago trying to figure out why his sister did things the way she did. His job was to simply support her, and so that is what he did.

"I am sure she would not want to marry someone who was offering just because they were caught in a compromising situation." Emma stopped short as if recognizing that her description was rather similar to their own situation.

Dare also saw the clear similarity between Kate's situation and theirs. He hoped Wynbrook could help Kate to see that marriage might suit her. He further hoped he could convince the lovely lady before him to accept his proposal.

"Shall we retire to the library?" he asked. This would allow him to speak with her without any interruptions.

"Oh, yes, I would like that exceedingly well."

"I should have asked this before, but is there anyone who will be missing you that we should alert to your safety?"

"Well, I am sure that Eustace will have noted my departure, but I certainly do not wish him to be alerted."

"He cannot touch you here at Greystone." Dare would defend her against whatever unpleasantness her stepbrother might bring. In truth, he hoped to be given the honor of protecting her for life.

"Thank you. That is very kind." She smiled and her whole face came alive.

"I do hope you will stay with us here. My sister would appreciate your company."

"And I would like to see the wound heal a little more, if you are amenable."

"Yes, I think that would be essential." He would agree to anything if it meant she would stay.

"Then stay I must, at least for a few days. I am supposed to meet the lady who is to be my chaperone to America in Portsmouth in a few days. The ship is scheduled to leave in four or five days, I believe."

Dare's mouth went dry. He could not let her sail away. He gave a nod, his mind spinning. He only had a few days.

They reached the end of the hallway, and Dare pointed in the direction of the library, motioning for her to proceed down the next passage. His step grew slower as the pain in his side demanded that he pause for a moment to catch his breath. The medicine helped, but he felt much better when sitting.

Emma glanced back, concern instantly shining in her eyes. "Oh, you poor thing. Let me help." She rushed to him, but he put up a hand to stop her.

"No!"

She blinked at him and he realized that had sounded more forceful than he intended, but he did not want to be her "poor thing."

"I am fine. Just walking a bit slowly." Dare put a hand on the wall to brace himself.

The housekeeper made an appearance, probably drawn by his loud voice as it echoed down the empty hall.

"Mrs. Brooke," called Dare to the housekeeper. "Could you show Miss St. James to the library?" He turned to Emma. "I need to attend to something and will join you shortly." He stood up tall and bowed slightly, ignoring the angry complaint from his injured side.

There was nothing Emma could do but follow the housekeeper, though she threw him a glance of concern over her shoulder as she left. He doubted she was fooled by his attempt to prevent her from knowing how much he hurt. In truth, if it hadn't been for his desire to see Emma and, more importantly, her to see him as something other than an invalid, he would not have left his bed.

When they were out of sight, Dare leaned back against the wall to rest. He wanted to sit down, but he feared someone would turn the corner of the hall and see the master of the house sitting on the floor. Emma might be alerted to the situation, and that was the last thing he wanted.

As he rested, he thought about how best to conduct the proposal. What would be the best words?

Miss St. James, you are the loveliest creature ever born. You have saved my life and I am forever in your debt. Would you do me the great honor of becoming my wife?

That was good. Or maybe...

My dear Miss St. James. With your own blessed hands, you have healed me and given me back my life. I am forever in your debt, and my deepest desire is to spend the rest of my days repaying this debt as your devoted husband and slave.

Hmmm…maybe too much. How about…

Miss St. James. You are eminently practical, reliable, and levelheaded in a crisis. Your beauty is beyond compare. You stand as a shining exemplary of womanhood. Your hair is golden, your mouth like rosebuds, your eyes deep pools of timeless beauty. You are like the sirens of myth. Your breasts alone could drive a man into madness…

No. No. NO.

Dare took a few more steps and leaned against the wall once more, though this time it was his mind he needed to get into better regulation, not just his body. He wished to propose marriage, not terrify the girl. He had done this before. How could it be so difficult now? Of course, his previous attempts had been flatly refused, so perhaps it was best not to try to replicate a failed offer. Still, it didn't seem like it should be so difficult. He just needed to propose sensibly. And yet, he could not shake the fear sparked by his past rejections.

He did not want to fail.

Really, truly did not want to fail.

Young, unmarried females typically terrified him, but he felt comfortable when he was with Emma— and desperately uncomfortable, but never in a manner that made him want to run away. No, he only wanted to see her more.

She was beautiful, intelligent, kind, skilled, beautiful, sensible, practical, cheerful, beautiful…really, really beautiful. Maybe her breasts *had* driven him to madness. They quivered when she walked. Or laughed. Or breathed. *Quivered!* How was a man supposed to think when something so tempting was trembling right under his nose? It was impossible.

If he could pull himself together enough to make an offer she would accept, he would be allowed the opportunity to introduce himself more formally—or, more importantly, informally—to her breasts. He could actually touch them. Cup them. Hold them.

"You all right, my lord?"

Dare was brought forcibly back to reality and realized he was leaning on the wall, his hands outstretched, fondling the air. He dropped his arms immediately and stood upright no matter how it pained him to regard Mrs. Brooke.

"I...I was just... I'm not myself." He ended in a mutter. There was no way to explain his actions.

"It is the laudanum, I warrant," she said kindly. "When Jonathan, the footman, hurt his ankle, he took a goodly amount. Helped with the pain, but he also had an entire conversation with a set of fire irons. Later, he said he was sure they were talking back."

"Yes. Laudanum. Very bad. Not in my right mind." Dare was relieved for a plausible explanation.

"You ought to be upstairs. I warrant Lady Kate will be quite irritated by you walking about. And Miss St. James as well. They seem very attentive."

"Cannot stay in bed. Just catching my breath before going to the library."

"I'll call Jonathan to help you, then."

"No, I'm perfectly fine. Do not trouble yourself." But the housekeeper was gone, and before he had reached his destination, the footman appeared and offered to help. The assistance was helpful, but Dare's grand entrance was rather marred by being assisted into a chair by a ruddy-faced footman.

Emma sat in a narrow block of sunlight from the one open window drape. She smiled when they entered, the pale winter light illuminating her golden hair and giving her an ethereal presence.

This was the woman he would marry. If only he could get her to say yes.

Twenty-one

DARE WAVED OFF THE FOOTMAN AND ATTEMPTED TO regain his dignity by walking stiffly to a chair beside the lovely Emma St. James.

"You should be resting," chastised Emma.

"I am fine."

"Here, this should help." She darted up and grabbed a cushion from the settee across the room and shoved it behind him before he could even think of standing. Her movements were so bright, quick, and easy, he cursed himself for being slow and injured. He would have resisted her ministrations, but the pillow did help.

"Are you comfortable?" asked Emma with a cheery smile.

Comfortable? No. "Yes, thank you."

"Good, good. Shall I call for some tea?"

"I am fine. Unless you are hungry. Yes? Is it tea-time? Tea, tea would be nice," Dare stammered. This was not going well.

Emma jumped up and pulled the bell and was back at his side. "You really ought to be resting. I shall be grieved if you pull a stitch."

Before Dare could answer, Mrs. Brooke was at the door. Everyone looked expectantly at him, and he realized since he was the host, he should do the ordering. He had not been the master of his own home in so long he did not know quite what to do. "Some tea?" he finally managed.

Mrs. Brooke nodded with a curtsy and was gone.

Now was the time. He needed to say something. He looked around the vacant room for inspiration. Bookcases stretched from floor to ceiling on three walls and heavy, dark drapes covered most of the windows. It might have been a pleasant library—had there been any books. The bookcases were all empty, a towering monument to a life stripped of all the things that make it worth living. This was a tomb—silent, empty, dead.

Emma also looked around the room, following his gaze. In a flash, she jumped up and flung open all of the green drapes to allow in the natural light. Dust filled the air, dancing in the shafts of sunlight. "I like this room. 'Tis good place to read."

He stared at her. "We have no books."

"This room is like the opening beat of a song: full of promise. You can fill these shelves with anything." She gazed wistfully at the empty shelves and sat back down beside him.

He continued to stare back at her. How did she do it? How could she be so cheerful, even in the face of loss?

"Miss St. James," Dare began, trying to remember the words he had practiced.

"Yes?" Emma leaned forward, her ample décolletage on full view, and it must be acknowledged there was undeniable quivering. *Quivering!*

His mind went blank.

Don't stare at them. Do not *stare at them. Look away.*

"My lord?" she asked.

The formality struck him odd, and he dragged his focus back to her face. "Robert or Dare, please."

"If you wish. You started on a very somber note with the 'Miss St. James,' so I thought we were back to formalities in this setting."

"No, no I just… I wanted to say something of import."

"Yes?" she prompted.

His attention was now captured by two bright-blue eyes and plump, pink lips. *So delicious.* He shook his head and put a hand over his eyes. She was dangerous to look at. There was no place he could focus that didn't make his jaw go slack and his mind go blank.

"Oh dear, have you a headache? Sometimes that is an effect of the laudanum."

"No, I am quite fine," he lied. Actually, he did have something of a headache, probably from trying to focus on what he wanted to say. How was he going to do this?

"Miss St. James," he began again. At her raised eyebrow, he amended it. "Emma, I owe you a debt I can never repay, even if I follow you all your years as your faithful slave."

Emma blinked at him, unsure. This was not coming out right. He needed to flatter her.

"You are as beautiful as any siren who led sailors to their deaths."

"Errr…my thanks."

This was a disaster. "I want you to know… That is, you slept with me… I mean, we spent the night together in an inn. Feel the obligation is mine to—"

"Oh dear, let me stop you there. I can see your discomfort. You think that because Lord Wynbrook feels obligated to offer for Lady Kate, you should make an offer to me too. That is very kind of you, and it does your scruples credit to think of it, but please do not make yourself uncomfortable on my account."

"Not uncomfortable," protested Dare, desperately uncomfortable.

"Yes, of course you are. Let me assure you that there is no need to trouble yourself on my account. No one has noted us together who can besmirch our characters. Thus, we do not need to concern ourselves."

"I still feel that I should offer—"

"No," she said, louder than he was expecting. Perhaps louder than she expected for she seemed startled at the sound of her own voice.

"That is," she amended, "I do not wish you to feel obligated to me in any way."

"But I am. The honor of the marriage for you… I…I would live in obligation of an unpayable debt…" He didn't even know what he was saying anymore. Everything was coming out wrong. He could see the conversation sailing straight into the rocky shoals but could do nothing to prevent the worst string of words from emerging from his lips. "I think I might be concussed," he muttered.

"There now. Do not worry yourself over me."

"But…but you need the protection of marriage."

"I am on my way to America to be married."

Dare frowned. "Why?" It was not the most tactful of questions, but he did not care anymore.

"I beg your pardon?"

"I asked you why. You told me you were running away from home. You told Kate and Wynbrook your stepmother arranged the match. You have refused my offer because you wish to wed an American you have never met, and I would like to know why." His voice was gruffer than he intended, but he could not help the emotion his bluster betrayed.

Emma looked down and straightened her skirts. She was spared from having to form a hasty reply by the entrance of the maid, who arrived with the tea tray. Emma busied herself in setting up the tray and served out.

"Forgive me. I have no right to ask," Dare added in a softer tone when they were alone again.

Emma glanced up at him and then looked back down, a guilty expression on her face as if she had been caught. "No, I do not mind. My stepmother initially brought the option to my attention, but I am sure Eustace would never have approved. In the end, it was my choice. My decision. It was the best option I had and I took it. I am quite excited about the prospect of going to America. It should be a grand adventure." She straightened her skirts again. "So you see that you do not need to worry about me. All is well." Her eyes gave him the opposite message of her words.

If he were any gentleman at all, he would have let it be. She clearly did not wish to speak of it, but he was too angry to let it go. He was angry at her refusal, and even angrier at the unknown American who was ruining his chances to pursue an acquaintance with the lovely Emma St. James.

"You have another offer," he said quietly.

"Oh, but I could not trap you into marriage. What a horrid way to repay you for saving my life."

"You saved mine."

"So we are even and can part as friends." She looked up rather timidly and must have been flustered by his expression, for she looked down again and busied herself with the tea. "Milk or lemon?"

"Black."

She handed him the cup.

"Forgive my rudeness, but I must know. Why did you say marrying an American was the best option you had?" demanded Dare. He was well past attempting to be civil.

Emma took a sip of tea but did not look up at him. "My father left the estate to me, to be held in trust by my stepmother and stepbrother until I reached my majority. They did not feel I was competent to take over management of the estate. It all got rather unpleasant. Leaving to marry the grandson of the Earl of Langley, even if he is an American, seemed preferable."

A new target of fury blasted through Dare. "They are trying to get rid of you so they can take over your estate," he said without mercy.

Emma took another sip of tea. "Leaving was my idea." She finally looked up at him, a steely resolve in her eye.

"Did they threaten you?" he asked darkly.

"No, no, not physically." She looked down and gave an audible sigh, continuing in a voice so soft he had to strain to hear. "I did overhear Eustace considering to have me committed, for he felt my refusal to marry him and sign over the management of the estate was a sign of madness."

"The bastard!" Dare slammed down his cup. "I will take care of him. No need to go to America."

Emma looked at him squarely in the eye, her back straight. "Accepting this arranged union was my choice and done on my initiative. I am sorry if you disapprove, but I am of majority and can make decisions irrespective of what any other person thinks."

Dare belatedly realized his fury at her mistreatment might frighten her away. "Yes, of course. I just…do not want you to be forced into anything you do not want."

"I am in no way disappointed with my decision thus far. I am away from a situation that was making me greatly unhappy. And see what fun I've had so far?" She gave a determined smile.

Dare decided that Emma had a much different definition of *fun* than he did. "I see. I wish you every happiness," said Dare, his words not in concert with his emotions.

She had refused him. Three proposals, three rejections. He sighed and slumped back in his chair.

"Are you well?" she asked, true concern in her eyes.

No, he was not well. His heart hurt. This was one hurt his pain medication would not help. Dare closed his eyes. "A little tired," he confessed.

He had lost her. Not that she was ever his.

He had not thought his heart could be touched, not after all he had done and experienced. His heart should have been beyond the reach of unfamiliar emotions, such as affection or loss. But he was wrong. And now his heart was squeezed tight.

He had feelings for Emma St. James, that much was clear. He was too unfamiliar with the territory to hazard a guess as to which one it was. The one that made him grind his teeth at the thought of Emma marrying someone else.

"I think I must insist that you go lie down," said Emma kindly.

He had proposed, been rejected, and now was being sent to bed. All in all, one of his worst days, which, considering his history, was truly saying something.

"As you wish," he conceded.

He had lost this round…but he had not given up.

Emma stared at the door long after Darington had gone. She had been proposed to by the Earl of Darington, the man who made her heart skip a beat. She had never wavered in her refusal…well, maybe a little, but that was ignoble of her. She could not trap a man into marriage; the thought was too dreadful. And she would not be coerced into marriage either, not by Eustace and not even by Dare. She was done with men deciding how her life would be lived.

No, she would go on with her original plan, but… She closed her eyes and indulged in a small flight of fancy in which she could have said yes to the handsome man with the serious eyes. She could be mistress of this house; she could bring back the joy to it and to Dare.

She could make him smile.

She opened her eyes and took stock of the empty library. It was just holding its breath, waiting for a new mistress to breathe life into it. Someone would fill that role. But the new mistress would not be her.

Twenty-two

DARE WENT BACK TO HIS CHAMBER IN DEFEAT AND DID take a rest. He needed to regain his strength, and fast. Somewhere, there was a group of men who were determined to do him, and now possibly Emma, harm. He suspected they would not give up, whatever their plan had been. When he met them again, he would be ready.

It was late afternoon by the time he slowly got out of bed again, taking his time against the pain. It hurt considerably, but it was better than the day before, which was encouraging.

A knock came at the door, and he stood taller, thinking Emma had come to check on him. He struggled into his coat and called for her to enter, but it was Wynbrook who opened the door.

Dare sat down in a chair in disappointment. "How did things go with Kate?"

Wynbrook slouched into the chair on the other side of the fireplace and stretched out his long legs. "I fear my efforts to win the hand of your fair sister have not proven successful. But I shall continue the pursuit. Can you offer any advice for a hopeless case such as this?"

Dare carefully chose his words. Kate had experienced more than her fair share of troubles, but it was for her to choose what to tell Wynbrook. "Kate has lived a hard life. I fear I have failed to provide the type of upbringing a lady deserves. She has erected battlements against pain, but her heart is true. Do not attempt to breach the walls, but wait for her to open the gate."

"Any chance of that happening in my lifetime?"

Dare shrugged. "She likes you. It is possible."

"Well, that tepid hope will be all I have to cling to," laughed Wynbrook. "And how is your pursuit going, if I might be so bold as to inquire? I assume you made an offer to the lovely Miss St. James."

"Yes." Dare did not wish to elaborate.

"And may I wish you every happiness?"

"She refused me."

"Well, what a pathetic lot we are! Two peers of the realm, plump of pocket and fair of face, and we cannot get a single damsel to accept our names and titles. That is a sad state of affairs in England, I tell you!" Wynbrook jumped up at his proclamation. "There is only one thing a true Englishman, lord, and master can do at such a time."

"Drink." Dare knew his friend well.

"Drink!" proclaimed Wynbrook, and pulled the bell for the butler. Mr. Foster appeared at once. "The makings of wine punch, if you please. Only substitute rum for the wine, come to think of it."

"Very good, my lord." The butler bowed himself out the door.

Wynbrook continued to pace the floor, lamenting their misfortunes in good humor. "I tell you, I am shocked that sweet Miss St. James refused you. I saw that way she looked at you and I could have sworn her affection for you was sure."

"I cannot begin to pretend to understand her heart, but she has informed me that she is engaged to another."

"Yes, so she said. Seems rather havey-cavey, if you don't mind me saying."

"Quite dodgy. But she's determined to go through with it."

"Oh, well, there you have it. Tough luck, old man." Wynbrook slumped back down in his chair with the sigh.

"I have…I have not entirely given up hope. The marriage has been arranged, but she has never actually met the man in question."

"Well then! Seems an easy fix. Surely her papa would rather her wed a peer of the realm than be shipped off to the savage Americas."

"Her parents have passed and she has a stepmother with an elder son who have acted as her guardians. Now that Miss St. James has come to majority and will inherit the estate, they wish her to Jericho, hence the foreign groom."

Wynbrook leaned forward, his eyes bright. "Ah, my friend, your life could be the basis of one of those horrid novels that I secretly love so much. So tell me, what do you plan to do next?"

"Don't know. In truth, I have no standing in this case at all unless Miss St. James wishes me to become involved. But how does one contrive to convince a lady to accept your proposal?"

"I fear I cannot be of much assistance on that count!" laughed Wynbrook.

"If you have any advice to offer, I would appreciate it. I know I am poor company, especially with ladies, but I should like to improve myself."

It was not an easy request for Dare to make. He had spent his life avoiding company, particularly female company, and had assumed that he could find a wife who would fulfill her obligations without putting demands on his company or his time. The thought that he had found someone for whom he would be willing to step into the unknown abyss of human relations was something foreign and unnerving to him.

Wynbrook opened his mouth, his eyes laughing, and Dare was sure he would be the recipient of another glib reply. Yet Wynbrook stopped himself and gazed at Dare more thoughtfully. "Miss St. James seems a very good sort of gentlewoman, and very capable too," he observed. "Though I do not know her in particular, it has been my understanding that females like to know that they arouse a special feeling of affection in their prospective husbands. They want to know that you will care for them and treat them with a special kindness." Wynbrook had lost the irreverent playfulness that often accompanied his speech and spoke with less confidence.

"And how does one express or show this special feeling of affection to the lady in question?"

"Damned if I know," muttered Wynbrook. "Tokens

of affection? Demonstrating your care by being steadfast and kind? Stealing a kiss?"

"Is that why you and Kate…"

Wynbrook glanced up and swallowed hard. "You know?"

"That you kissed my sister? Yes."

"Is it pistols at dawn or have I your forgiveness?" Wynbrook laughed with a tremor of nervous energy.

"You have my blessing to marry her."

"Which is what I am trying to do if she were not so recalcitrant! I mean, not that your sister is not delightful. She is very… Well, that is to say… Oh, here is the punch! Thank goodness. I was drifting out to sea." Wynbrook jumped up and directed the butler into the room. "Put it here by the fire, my good man, and I will mix it for us. I do not wish to boast, but I am said to have a clever hand with punch. Are you a married man, Mr. Foster?"

"No, sir, I have not had that honor."

"Well then, by the master's leave, grab a glass and join us in a bachelor's toast!"

The butler looked to Dare, who gave a nod.

"Perfect!" announced Wynbrook, who stood and poured glasses for the three men. Dare rose for the occasion and Wynbrook held up his glass for a toast. "For the bachelors three, may we live forever in blissful harmony, until such time as we embrace matrimony!"

Esqueleto bit into the end of his cheroot in anger, half smoking, half chewing his cigar. He had boldly sailed into Portsmouth flying an American flag on board the renamed frigate, the *Kestrel*. He dared not show his face in the harbor, not with its Royal Navy shipyard and so many officers, marines, and sailors about. He was much too crafty to be caught so easily. No, he remained in his cabin, relying on his agents to carry out his orders.

He had been informed that his son, a man he now considered dead to him, had lost their fortune to the Earl of Darington. That same son had run from him, not telling him of the loss, and instead sailed to England. It had taken a month to find him, but Esqueleto had his own cruel means, and had his men drag his son to him.

"You lost everything! My gold. My jewels. My silver. You lost it! Lost it to that bastard Darington, the only man I hate more than you!" Esqueleto hit his son hard across the face. Again. Silas stumbled but did not go down. He stood before him, and it was all Esqueleto could do not to wring the life out of the man with his own hands. "And then instead of coming to me, you ran."

"I was trying to retrieve the treasure." Silas wiped the blood from his nose with the back of his hand.

"What have you retrieved?"

"Well...nothing yet."

"Nothing?" Esqueleto bit through the end of his cigar and spit it into his son's face.

"I have his signet ring," offered Silas.

Esqueleto grabbed the ring from his hand. "This will not repay me, though it may prove useful. Where is Darington?"

"I...I...am not certain to his exact location."

"You let him get away?" Esqueleto clenched his hands so tightly they began to shake. "You let him get away?" he shouted into the face of his son.

"Darington cannot have gotten far. He is shot. He may be dead by now."

Esqueleto backhanded his son, this time sending the man sprawling. "Idiot! He is close to Greystone and must have gone there. Should be easy enough to determine if the master is at home, even for one so pervasively stupid as you. I don't care what you have to do, but bring me back my money."

"There may be another way," stammered Silas as he struggled back to his feet. "I saw on the deck of his ship a piece of wood with the word *Merc* on it."

Esqueleto's interest was instantly captured. "Did he find the ship?"

"He must have found something, but not the treasure. I would have heard if he had."

"Where is the ship?"

"I don't know."

"Don't know? It will be in his damned captain's log. Go get it, you fool!"

"Aye, Father."

Esqueleto lunged forward until the tip of his lit cheroot singed the tip of his son's nose. "Kill every bloody bastard in the house if you have to, but don't come back without that damn book!"

Twenty-three

EMMA PROWLED THE HOUSE, GIVING HERSELF A TOUR. With Darington resting and Kate and Wynbrook locked away in yet another heated discussion, she found herself at her leisure. She walked down a corridor past the library, to an area of the house that appeared unused. She hoped she was not snooping, but there was hardly anything to see, so she opened one door after another to peek inside. All she found were empty rooms.

One room had a few pieces of furniture covered with white sheets. She flung back the drapes to allow light into the corner room. Though the room was clean, it had a musty, unused smell.

She lifted the edge of one of the sheets and found a pianoforte. She pulled back the cover and sat at the instrument, running a finger along the smooth ivory keys.

"Haven't opened this wing of the house." The Earl of Darington walked slowly into the room.

"Oh! I do beg your pardon. I should not have trespassed." Emma jumped from the piano bench.

"You may go anywhere you wish." Dare leaned on the pianoforte.

"Are you in pain? Have you given yourself another dose of the medication?" asked Emma, concerned for the patient.

Dare slowly shook his head. "I want to keep my wits." He said nothing more, and she knew the burden of conversation would fall on her.

"This is a pleasant room."

Dare seemed pleased or perhaps relieved at her comment. "It was the music room."

"Does anyone in your family play?"

"Kate did." A heaviness descended on him once more. "After we were forced to leave she never played again."

"I am sorry for that. What a terrible thing to happen," said Emma with sincerity.

"No one should have their inheritance stolen and be forced from their home." His dark eyes seared through her.

She turned away, not sure what to say. Waverley was being taken from her, but she did not wish to dwell on it. She hoped if she ignored the problem, it would somehow get better, or simply go away.

"Forgive me. I did not intend to make you uncomfortable. I have not the fortune of conversing easily with ladies."

"Do you not? I have not noticed." That was not entirely the truth, but Emma was not beyond saying kind things because she wished to be nice.

Dare gave her a look that said he did not believe her.

"I'm sure it cannot be quite as bad as you imagine," she reassured. "You are too harsh on yourself."

Dare raised an eyebrow. "I have no conversation. I do not dance. I lack social conventions."

"Such as inviting a lady to be seated when you wish to speak with her?" teased Emma, who was still standing beside him as he had never invited her to sit.

"Oh! A thousand pardons. Please, do be seated."

Emma only smiled at him. "Here, let us sit in the window seat over there. It seems a pleasant vantage." She led the way and he followed. His face was grim and Emma repented her tease.

"In truth," she said as she settled herself on the window box with Dare next to her, "lack of conversation in a gentleman is not as grievous as it is for ladies. And dancing, while preferable, is not everything. And can be learnt."

"But there is the rub. I do not wish to learn. I tend to avoid females of all sorts," he admitted, looking out of the window at the sweeping view of the ocean.

Emma followed his gaze to the dark-gray, white-tipped, churning seas. For a man who had spent most of his life at sea, that must be where he felt the most comfortable. "But you have many other qualities to recommend you. I am certain you have had many an admirer who had her heart broken for lack of your attention."

"I doubt I have much to recommend me."

"My dear sir, you are a well-heeled peer of the realm. Please forgive me for being so gauche, but that must make up for any reticence in social company."

"They dubbed me the Pirate Earl," he muttered.

"Oh! Those society papers, they are full of gossip, designed to ruin people's lives. I apologize for ever reading such nonsense," declared Emma. "Besides, some ladies prefer a man of action, a man they know can defend them, a man who is kind, maybe even shy with ladies, but ferocious to his enemies."

He raised an eyebrow at her. Maybe she had spoken too candidly.

"I fear my slights are more substantial than you think," he countered. "For I have pressed my case to two ladies of my acquaintance, three counting yourself, and all have turned down my suit."

"Oh." Now Emma was at a loss. The knowledge that he had asked two ladies before her to marry him did not sit well with her. Had his heart been captured by some young miss? Was that why he offered for her, because he no longer cared about a love match? "I am sorry if such refusals caused your heart pain."

"My heart? Why would an offer of marriage affect that particular organ? No, I believe it only confirmed my suspicions that I have nothing to offer a member of the fairer sex."

"Well, I'm glad to hear it hurt nothing but your pride. But I wonder why— Oh, but you are trying to trap me into asking you impertinent questions and thus showing my lamentable country manners." Emma smiled at him, only half joking at her unconventional upbringing, for she did feel quite out of her element in such illustrious company.

"Your manners are such that I like. I tell you the truth, I far prefer your company to any young lady I met in London." He spoke with a simple earnestness that gave added meaning to the compliment.

"Thank you," she murmured, feeling the weight of his praise.

"I did offer my hand to two ladies while in London. Kate was insistent that I find a wife or I would not have asserted myself. Both ladies were in circumstances in which I believed an offer of marriage would have been appreciated. They did, in truth, quickly enter into the marital state. Just not to me."

"Their loss, I am sure."

"They did not seem to agree with the sentiment."

"So you offered your hand for marriages of convenience?"

"Yes, though it was apparently not so convenient that either would accept it. And now I have once again…" He paused and she was afraid he would bring up the fact that she had refused him too, but he changed course. "So you see it is a hopeless case."

Emma smiled, for she assumed his words were in jest, but he remained somber, and she realized he was being entirely sincere with his assessment of his lack of social graces. "So you plan to die a bachelor?"

"It does seem likely."

"Well, that is the saddest thing I have ever heard. I wish there was something I could do to provide assistance."

"You could accept my offer." He did not pull his punch this time.

It was Emma's turn to look away. She gazed through the frosted pane at stormy seas, attempting to calm her flustered mind enough to form a cogent response. "I would not do you the injustice of accepting an offer made only out of obligation. You deserve more than that. You deserve to find someone you can truly cherish."

"But you do not?"

She was indeed advocating a love match for
Dare while accepting an arranged marriage with a
stranger for herself. Her words and actions were not
in concert and she felt an uncomfortable dissonance
between the two.

"Perhaps I can be of service to you in some other
way," she continued quickly, not wanting to discuss
the obvious contradiction. "I should not like to see you
become discouraged and remain forever a bachelor."

"I am resigned to my fate." Dare wiped the con-
densation from the windowpane to see more clearly to
the rolling seas below. Perhaps he was already planning
his escape.

"I fear no challenge. Even a lump of coal can
become a diamond under the right circumstances."

"But a sow's ear will never become a silk purse,"
argued Dare.

"Ah, you have thrown down the gauntlet and I
must accept the challenge! Now if I am to help you,
you must explain the approach you took in making
these previous offers, so we can discover the difficulty.
If I can be so bold."

Dare turned back to her, tilting his head slightly. "I
wish you would be. For it is considerably easier when
you take control of the conversation rather than rely
on me to devise my own topics of discussion. If you
could form your questions such that I could answer
only in yes or no, that would be appreciated."

Emma searched his expression, wondering if he was
being earnest. She detected a slight softness in his eyes
and a slight quirk to his lips. It was not quite a smile,
but it revealed he was in jest. The man had made a joke!

She laughed out loud, placing her hand on the sleeve of his jacket in her mirth. His lips twitched, and he rested his hand on top of hers for a moment before they both jerked their hands away.

"Well then." Emma cleared her throat. They had certainly entered into an interesting topic of conversation. It was not quite proper, but considering everything they had shared, the usual social boundaries on conversation seemed irrelevant.

"When you made your proposals, did you use flattery or make an argument for why the lady would be a suitable countess for you?"

Dare shrugged. "I'm sure either one would have performed the office adequately."

"Did you express any particular affection for either one?"

"I could not express an emotion I did not feel."

Emma was secretly reassured that Dare's heart remained untouched. "I see. I do believe ladies do like to feel that their groom holds for them some sort of affection. Even a little bit."

"I am not one to flatter and flirt."

"I think that is a positive thing. I would rather one word of true praise than a thousand of false flattery."

Dare's eyes warmed as he looked at her. "Very wise."

"Thank you." Emma's heart beat a bit faster at his compliment. "Did the ladies in question go on to marriages of convenience or love matches?"

"I would not be the best to judge such things, but I heard talk that there was true affection between the pairs."

"Then there you have it. In order to find a marriage

partner, you must learn to woo the lady of your interest."

Dare paled and leaned away from her. "I could not begin to conduct such an endeavor."

"All activities can be intimidating when first tried, but with practice…" Emma paused, for Dare had taken on a sickly hue. "Perhaps start small by giving banal compliments or small gifts."

"Gifts?" asked Dare, and Emma suspected he was interested in anything that did not require conversation with the female in question.

"Yes, like flowers. Of course, one must be careful, for a single man cannot give an unmarried lady a gift, but one can bring a bouquet to the mother of the girl of your fancy. She will understand the token is for her."

"Flowers," said Dare carefully. "Sounds tedious."

Emma smiled again, humor bubbling up at his morose assessment of wooing. "Perhaps it is. I suppose it is only worth it if the lady is worth the effort. I suppose that is the whole point. The object should not be the goal, but the fact that it cost the gentleman time and effort, which indicates affection."

"Affection. Is that also a requirement?" Dare stared at her with his dark eyes, full of an emotion that was hard to name. Longing perhaps. Sorrow. This time, he was not in jest.

"I should hope that all marriages should have at least a little love between them. It can be a difficult world and it helps to have a friend by your side."

"And you?" His eyes burned into hers and she once again realized her words were contrary to her intention to marry a stranger.

Emma took a deep breath and nodded. "Yes, you are right. I suppose my decision to wed a man unknown to me was primarily based on my desire to escape my situation at home. But I hope that when we meet, a connection can be found. Perhaps, even in this strange beginning, a love match can be formed."

Dare scowled at this. "And if he is not the man you deserve?"

"Then I return home. I have ensured I have enough funds." Eustace did not know, but Emma had been saving the little pin money he gave her for years. "Do not fret over me. I am actually excited to take this chance. I do wish to travel the world."

Dare pressed his lips together, unconvinced.

"No, truly. Men have advantages you cannot comprehend. You get to travel, see new places, go where you want to go, do as you wish. I would like to take to the seas, learn to navigate a ship and take sail." She paused at the incredulous rise of his eyebrows. "I'm sure that seems rather silly to you."

"Not at all. Those are all things I like too."

Emma opened her mouth to say they were quite a match, but thought better of it. She coughed to hide the awkward pause.

"Oh, Lord Darington, there you are. Please forgive the interruption." The housekeeper entered the room. "We have supper ready and are waiting on your pleasure to come to table. Lord Wynbrook and Lady Kate show no signs of exiting the drawing room."

"Actually, Mrs. Brooke, I prefer to take my meal in my room," said Darington, rising stiffly from the window seat.

"I shall as well," murmured Emma, not wanting to be the only person at the table. She had thought they had established a rapport, but now he apparently did not wish to extend his time with her.

He gave her a nod. "I hope to see you later tonight," he said after the housekeeper had gone.

He did not wish to eat with her but wanted to see her later? What was this man about?

Twenty-four

EMMA ATE HER SUPPER OFF A TRAY IN HER ROOM BY herself. She was not sure what was happening between her and Dare, if anything. Were they... flirting? No, he was not the sort. But perhaps, if she was honest, she was. But what did he mean by seeing her later tonight?

She opened the door to her room and tiptoed out into the darkened, empty hall. She felt like a guilty child sneaking out of her room to do mischief. But what mischief did she want to do with Lord Darington?

Unfortunately for her peace of mind, the question brought the image of Dare in his glorious state of undress. He had chiseled features, with the tanned face of a man who had spent much of his life out of doors. He was not handsome in the same way as Lord Wynbrook, but his strong features and utter sincerity drew her to him with a force stronger than anything she had ever experienced.

She reached the landing and wondered where she should go. Should she even be doing this? It was growing dark, and there was no chaperone. Still, she continued to tread softly toward the drawing room. Maybe she could ask to check his stitches again, just once more...

"Miss St. James."

Emma turned to find Dare walking slowly down the stairs. Her heart tripped over itself at the sight of him and she had to remind herself that he could not possibly have known what she was thinking. "I...er... Lord Darington."

"I have taken the liberty of collecting your wrap." He held out her scarlet, fur-lined pelisse.

"Are we going somewhere?" she asked, putting on her coat.

"Yes. As you requested." He pulled on his own greatcoat. "This way, please."

She followed his direction toward the front door, utterly baffled. When had she requested to leave the house? "I fear you have me at a disadvantage," she said as he opened the door. "Where are we going?"

"This way," said Dare and walked away from the house toward the edge of the cliff. It was a barren landscape, dotted with occasional scraggly trees, gnarled from the almost constant wind.

He produced a walking stick and leaned heavily on it. Though he walked relatively slowly due to his injury, his long legs kept him at a good pace. Unlike most men, he did not offer his arm or wait to see if she followed. Still, she suspected he was not being rude, just oblivious, and took pity on him, following him along a narrow dirt path.

"Where are we going?" asked Emma.

Dare turned to look back at her, his head tilted ever

so slightly as if confused by the question. "You said you wanted to learn to use the sextant."

"A sextant?"

"To navigate."

"Yes, I suppose I did say that." Emma wrapped her red pelisse tighter around her against the bitter wind.

"You need to see the horizon."

"Oh. I did not know that." Emma stepped closer and reached out a hand. He took the strong hint and offered his arm. They continued to walk toward the cliff, and Emma instinctively drew close. Most likely for warmth. Or maybe something else. Either way, Dare made no protest and they walked forward toward the sound of the crashing waves.

Dare stopped them a few feet from the edge of the cliff, and Emma marveled at the view. In the pale moonlight, the waves crashed foamy and white below. The dark, churning sea stretched out to a distant line, where it met with the sky and a bounty of twinkling, silver stars.

Dare removed a metal object from his greatcoat pocket. The instrument was made mostly of brass and had a rounded ruler on the bottom, a movable arm, two small mirrors, and a small telescope. Emma's curiosity got the best of her and she leaned closer to see how he would use it.

"You take a sight by measuring the angle between the horizon and the sun or a star." Dare held the telescope to his eye and made some adjustments.

"Which star? There must be millions."

"The North Star. There." Dare pointed, but there were so many points of light in the night sky, she could not tell one from the other.

"Where?"

Dare leaned closer until his face was next to hers. Emma's heart began to stutter. He was so close she could smell his own unique scent, something of a mix between leather, sailcloth, and freedom. She breathed deeply.

He pointed at a bright pinprick of light. "You see it?"

She nodded, paying more attention to him than whatever was happening in the night sky.

"Good, now take a sight. First, you focus on the object and turn this knob to divide the image into two. Next, move the arm of the sextant so the second image rests on the horizon." He made small adjustments, talking knowledgably about angles and arcs and the best way to fine-tune the instrument.

Emma, however, was much too distracted to pay attention to her sextant lesson. Her heart fluttered again such that she pressed her hand to her chest to try to stop it. She had never felt this way before and was not sure what to name the strange sensation. The Earl of Darington made her feel slightly ill, but there was no one she would rather be near.

"Here, now you try." Dare shifted back and handed her the instrument. It was heavier than she had expected from the easy way he held it. She hoped he would explain it again, since she had not been attending to anything he said. Something about using the contraption to navigate across vast oceans with nothing more than the stars as a guide?

"I…er…" said Emma, taking the brass instrument awkwardly. It had a lot of moving parts and looked complicated.

"Here, look through here and find the horizon,"

said Dare patiently, standing so close it made her catch her breath. "Do you have it lined up with the horizon?" he asked, his breath on her cheek.

Forcing herself to attend to her lesson, she looked through the glass and saw two images. He took her hand and moved it to the arm, helping her make the adjustment. Her heart pounded at his nearness. His hands were rough, but his touch was gentle. At his urging she adjusted the arm of the sextant until the image of the North Star rested on the horizon.

"I think I have it," she said excitedly.

"Very good," he praised, his words warm in her ear.

She turned and realized they were close, very close. She stared at his lips and felt a strange draw. He must have felt it too, for he leaned in slowly before he caught himself and cleared his throat, pulling back.

She swallowed, glad he was in control of himself, for she could not be trusted. Although…perhaps he could have been a little less than strictly honorable. All things in moderation.

He cleared his throat again and took the sextant from her hand. He focused on the object, not making eye contact. "Then you take the reading here and note the time very precisely." He pulled out his watch and began to describe some complicated calculations that she could not begin to follow. Instead, she was more interested in the way he looked in profile in the moonlight. His features were strong with high cheekbones and a long, straight nose. In the cold, silver light, she saw true nobility.

"Do you understand?" he asked, finally giving her a furtive glance.

"Not in the least," she confessed.

He looked at the sextant and watch in his hands. "Takes a bit to get accustomed to it. Sometimes takes the young gentlemen a whole cruise before they can come up to scratch."

"Young gentlemen?"

"The ship's boys. Start around twelve. Sometimes they're with us; sometimes they just put their names on the roster to count as experience so they can enter service at a higher grade."

"That does not sound fair."

Dare shrugged. "Common enough."

"Did you do that?"

Dare shook his head. "First sailed at twelve, joined right after I escaped Fleet. Not much else I could do. First tour saw action at the Nile with Nelson."

"You were with Nelson at such a young age? Why, you are quite the hero."

"I ran powder. Tried not to get shot."

"An admirable goal. I fully support it!"

Dare turned back to her with warm eyes. "Considering my recent experience, I quite agree." His dark features gleamed a roguish enchantment in the moonlight.

A shiver ran down her spine.

Dare shrugged out of his greatcoat and, ignoring her murmurs of protest, put it around her shoulders. The heavy wool coat was warm from his own heat and stoked a fire within her. His scent lingered and she breathed deeply, feeling a little giddy at being draped in his coat as if wrapped in his arms.

"You should keep your coat. It is cold and you are still recovering," Emma protested.

Dare gave her another of his shrugs and stepped close to her, reaching into the pocket of his coat that was wrapped around her. "This is for you." He held out his hand, revealing a small, white shell.

Surprised, Emma took the small shell from his hand. It had a light gray, curved outside shell and a glossy, smooth, pink surface within. She looked up at him, wondering its significance. He continued to stare at her with an expectant air, and she wished she understood the meaning of the gesture.

"Thank you."

"It is for you," he explained. "A gift. There are no flowers in January and your guardian is not present so…"

"Oh! A gift for me?" Emma realized this was his attempt at wooing her and her heart cracked open. "But how did you…? Please do not tell me you walked all the way to the beach to find me a shell." She looked down from the edge of the cliff to the beach below.

"I confess Jonathan assisted me."

"But you should not attempt such a thing. You are still recovering."

"You said the purpose of the gift was not the object but the effort involved in the giving."

"Oh, Dare!"

"Did I do it right?" The earnestness in his eyes made her heart ache.

"Yes, yes, you did it very well. Thank you. I will cherish it always."

"Good." Dare opened his mouth to say something but turned away instead, staring out over the ocean. She could not begin to guess his thoughts. Without his greatcoat, he appeared thin and lonely in the pale light, leaning on his walking stick.

Clearly, he had not given up his attempt to convince her to marry him. She would never take advantage of the situation to accept an offer made only out of obligation, but what if his heart had been truly touched? He certainly had gone to great effort. Would he act the same way out of a sense of honor? Given what Emma knew of the enigmatic man before him, he probably would.

Though she was already standing next to him, she stepped closer. "I must insist you take back your coat. I do not wish you to catch cold in your condition. And truly, you should rest."

"No, no, my condition is very well, thanks to you."

"But that does not mean you should freeze. Here, take back your coat. I am very warm, I assure you." She stepped forward and attempted to place the coat back around his shoulders.

"No, I insist you keep it," he protested, trying to keep the coat around her. Somehow, they ended up with one shoulder of the coat on him and one on her, standing so close their bodies brushed against one another.

Emma froze at the contact, looking up at the dark eyes of the Earl of Darington. His eyes burned with a fierce intensity, his lips parted. His dark look was similar to when he had defended her from the highwaymen. This was the true Darington. He kept a calm, distant facade, but raging beneath the surface was something wild and dangerous. Her heart pounded, but instead of pulling away, she pressed closer.

He slowly wrapped his arms around her, inside of the greatcoat, pulling her closer to him. Her hands flew to his chest, but she did not push him away. Without a word, he slowly lowered his head. He stopped just inches away from her lips. She waited, the air between them crackling with anticipation. Was he going to kiss her? Was he going to come so close and not kiss her? Waiting was agony.

Swiftly, he put an end to the debate and claimed her mouth with his. His lips pressed against hers and he pulled her closer, parting her lips with his tongue and deepening the kiss. Emma reached up and wrapped her hands around his neck, holding on tightly as her heart soared. She had never experienced anything like the sensation of kissing Darington. It was like flying, though her feet never left the ground.

When they finally parted, they both took deep breaths. His greatcoat slid to the ground, forgotten. She was certainly more than warm now. When his hand slid away from her waist, she noticed that it trembled.

"Forgive me," he murmured, turning to face the crashing waves once more, holding his hands rigidly behind his back.

Emma took several more breaths before attempting speech. "That was…" She had not the words to describe it.

"An imposition on your person," finished Dare without turning to her.

"No, no, that was not what I was going to say."

"It was not?" He turned slightly to her, a note of hope in his voice.

"No," she replied firmly. "That was…quite remark-able." Surely this must mean his offer was not just out of obligation. He actually had feelings for her. If his emotions were anything like what she was beginning to feel for him, then it was a powerful attraction.

"Wynbrook suggested I steal a kiss," Dare admit-ted. "Trying to get you to change your mind about your betrothed. Not sure the action recommends my person to you, but there you have it."

"Oh." So his kiss did not stem from his own desires. He was merely following the suggestion of his friend. Emma stepped farther away, embarrassed at her own assumptions. His kiss had seemed demanding and passionate, but she had never kissed anyone before, so perhaps she had read more into it than there was.

"Emma," he spoke her name like a whisper on the wind. "Only one task remains. I must share with you my…my feelings regarding you." He cleared his throat and directed his attention to the rising moon. "I can say unequivocally that I greatly admire you. I cannot speak more on matters of the heart, for I fear I am not practiced and can hardly speak to things beyond my ken."

He turned back to her, his eyes black against the night sky. "My offer remains unchanged. If you should decide to accept my suit, I am entirely at your service." He bowed, picking up the coat and his walking stick. "Please allow me to escort you back to the house."

Emma nodded mutely, unsure what to say. She took his arm and walked slowly back to the house. Her mind swirled with questions she had no idea how to ask.

It was her first kiss. Her *first kiss*! It had rocked her to her core—her legs were still like jelly—but Dare did not appear to be similarly affected. No, he seemed more aloof than ever. He had even admitted he had only done it on Wynbrook's suggestion. Did this mean his feelings were indifferent?

Yet his words of praise, though not a declaration of love, seemed genuine. She believed he truly appreciated her care for him, but that did not mean he genuinely wished her to be his bride.

If he continued to offer out of obligation, then her answer to his proposal remained unchanged, no matter how much she longed for another kiss—and another and another. She would not trap anyone into marriage. No, that was something she would never do.

But what if his emotions were touched? If that was the case, things would be different entirely. If he truly liked her, wanted to marry her for her own merits, would she accept his proposal?

She glanced up at the tall, solemn man who walked stiffly back to the house as if in a funeral procession. He certainly was not the most cheerful of men, but she could not imagine wanting to embrace anyone else. Wanting to kiss anyone else.

Of course, she had gone to great lengths to arrange a marriage for herself, and it would certainly cause a dustup with the Earl of Langley and his American grandson, whichever one it was, but it would be worth it if she could marry Dare.

The man she loved.

She took a deep breath and shivered at the recognition. But could he ever love her in return?

Without a word, Dare removed his coat and once more draped it over her shoulders as they walked back to the house.

Emma held the simple shell in her hand. It was a small thing, a little rough, with a few grains of sand still attached. It might be of no real value, but to her it was precious.

They entered the house and he bowed, a slight grimace betraying the pain it caused him to do so. "Until tomorrow, my lady."

"Good night, my lord."

She watched for a moment as he proceeded stiffly toward his bedchamber. She walked slowly back to her own as she turned the shell around in her fingers. Considering how much Dare was hurting, it must have cost him a great deal to be helped down to the beach to find the shell and struggle back up again. The gift was not the object, but the time and effort it took to give it. Would he have done so much purely out of obligation?

Perhaps his cold manner was merely his natural reserve. Wynbrook might have suggested the kiss, but it did not mean Dare was uninterested. Maybe his proposal was more genuine than she realized.

Emma flung herself on her bed, wishing she better understood the true motivations of the Earl of Darington. And yet...maybe she was thinking of this the wrong way. She had developed feelings for him, her response to his kiss proved that. Perhaps it was enough to be true to her own feelings.

She had wanted a love match, was willing to settle for a marriage of convenience to avoid an asylum, but now she was offered the chance for both. She could find a convenient marriage with a man she loved who might be beginning to feel something for her in return.

The decision was a big one. She prayed for guidance. Earlier in the day, she had felt rejecting his proposal to be the right thing to do. But now…now her heart was leaning in quite the opposite direction.

That kiss might have been only her first, but surely it demonstrated at least a spark of interest. She would have a lifetime to fan than spark into a flame. She squeezed the small shell in her hand. Tomorrow, she would accept his proposal. Tomorrow, everything in her life would change.

She fell asleep with the shell still in her hand.

Twenty-five

EMMA WOKE THE NEXT MORNING WITH A SENSE OF expectation. This would be the day her entire life would change. She was going to accept the proposal from Lord Darington. She scrunched her toes under the warm bedsheets with anticipation. She was going to say yes. She was going to be married!

She flung back the blankets, jumped out of the tall bed, and twirled around, ignoring the cold floorboards under her feet. She jumped back into bed and decided one of the first things she would do as mistress of this house was put rugs on the bedroom floors.

She paused even as her breath hitched. *Mistress of this house*. She was going to be the *mistress* of this house. She would be Lady Darington, a countess no less! Of course she was not marrying Dare for his title or his money or his house...but she could not deny that it was rather nice all the same.

What would Regina and Eustace say? Oh, they would be furious when they found out and would probably try to make things difficult, but no matter. She was of majority, she could do as wished, and once married to Darington, there was not a thing they could do about it.

Emma rang for Sally, who arrived with her usual ill humor, but Emma was too happy to care. She dressed quickly and proceeded down to the breakfast room. Dare and his sister, early risers both, were already there deep in conversation.

"Good morning," Emma said brightly.

Dare rose as she entered, and she was pleased to see him move a little faster than he had the day before. It was a good sign that he was healing well.

She was a little disappointed that Kate was present— not that she did not like his reserved sister, but she wished to speak to Dare alone. The two siblings, however, were clearly discussing something of particular import, for they both had stopped as soon as she entered, their faces even more grim and serious than their usual bleak manner.

"Kate and Wynbrook believe they have found our housekeeper," explained Dare as Emma sat beside him at the table.

"I did not know she was missing," responded Emma.

"Our old housekeeper," explained Kate.

Still Emma did not understand the importance of such a discovery.

"The one who worked here when our father died," explained Dare. "And the house was—"

"Looted," finished Kate.

"Oh!" The significance dawned on Emma. "She may have answers about what happened."

"Yes." Dare gave a curt nod. "We had been told she had died."

"Took her own life," added Kate. "But apparently she survived the suicide attempt and was sent to an asylum for many years. She has returned and is now living in the village with her daughter."

"Excellent!" cried Emma. "I hope your audience with her will prove informative."

"Awkward thing just to knock on the door," Kate muttered.

"Oh, but I think it would be perfectly normal. Why, I often visit people who live in the village near my father's estate and our tenants too. People appreciate a basket of treats and good company."

"Good company is beyond my ability to provide," said Kate with frank honesty. "But the basket sounds like a good plan. I wonder what to put in it."

"If I could be of service, I could pop down to the kitchen and see what might be on hand. Those biscuits cook served yesterday were heavenly."

"That would be appreciated," admitted Kate.

"And you must come with us too," Dare demanded, then continued in a more hesitant tone. "If it is not an imposition. I imagine Wynbrook will want to come as well."

"I would be delighted," Emma cried, truly happy he had included her. She knew he was a taciturn, private person. If he invited her to come, then he saw her as family. His family. Emma beamed broadly at the glum brother and sister and hastened to prepare a basket for a social call.

After a nice chat with the cook, Emma assembled a basket of tea and biscuits wrapped in a lovely tablecloth. She returned to the drawing room, hoping for a private audience with Darington. She was in luck, finding him reading the paper with his greatcoat lying beside him on the settee, ready to leave as soon as the party was assembled.

"I have chosen a few tempting treats," said Emma, holding up the basket before placing it on a side table.

Dare immediately rose, flung his coat to the side, and motioned for her to sit.

Emma sat beside him on the settee, her heart beating loudly in her chest. How was one to broach the topic of marriage? "I do hope you will be able to gain the information you seek today."

"Thank you. I do too."

The clock ticked loudly as the seconds dragged along. She was not typically at a loss for words, but then she was not typically accepting a marriage proposal. His demeanor was so reserved it was almost fierce, which did not provide much encouragement for what she intended to say.

"I...I was thinking about our conversation last night." She boldly initiated the topic, watching carefully for his response.

"Yes?" He remained somber but a certain softness crept into his eyes. It was the most encouragement she was going to receive. It would have to be enough.

"Yes, I would like to—"

"Robert. Miss St. James. We are ready to leave." Kate strode into the drawing room, followed by Wynbrook.

"Looks like rain," commented Wynbrook. "With any luck, I can get soaked through again."

"Not if we leave now. I believe the weather will

hold for a while at least," declared Kate, looking at them expectantly.

"I was having a conversation with Miss St. James," said Dare with a scowl.

"Perhaps you can finish it later," returned Kate with an equally ferocious frown.

"Yes, of course," said Emma, jumping to her feet. "We can certainly talk later over tea." She was not sure if she was relieved or disappointed to be saved from declaring herself. Maybe she could think of a clever way to accept his proposal as they visited the old housekeeper.

A few minutes later, Emma sat in between Lord Darington and Lady Kate in the coach as Wynbrook drove them to the village. The invalid housekeeper, by the name of Mrs. Hennings, was rumored to live there with her grown daughter.

Though the dark clouds threatened rain, they drove down the five miles to the small fishing village without incident. The village was nestled around an ocean cove. Emma surveyed the small, white houses, closely clustered together, with interest. Would the villagers be her new friends? Would they accept her the way the villagers around Waverley had?

They found the house, and Dare knocked on the door. She watched him carefully for signs of pain. Though he shifted from one foot to the other, he remained upright. He was no doubt hurting, but he was improving and Emma was happy to see it. Now if only he could find the answers he sought, maybe he could discover some peace, even joy, in his life.

A middle-aged woman in modest attire opened the

door and gaped at them, her eyes wide at having such illustrious guests. Despite her deference, she resisted the request to meet with Mrs. Hennings.

"Me mother is ill, sir. She sees no one." The housekeeper's daughter shook her head, her distress clear.

Emma could practically feel the frustration and anxiety rise in Darington and his sister. They needed to have answers and she immediately jumped in to help. "Lord Darington and Lady Katherine have brought gifts for your table. May we come in?" asked Emma sweetly, holding up the basket.

"Yes, yes, of course!" The woman opened the door wide and ushered them into the simple dwelling. Several openmouthed children stared at them from the corner of the room that would be best described as "homey."

Emma smiled at the children, made introductions, and chatted to put everyone at ease. The woman, who introduced herself as Mrs. Saunders, reluctantly granted an audience with her mother. Dare and Kate went to a back room to meet with the elderly Mrs. Hennings while Emma and Wynbrook took to keeping everyone else in the house entertained to give them time for their chat.

In this regard, Emma had a capable partner, for while she made the tea they had brought, Wynbrook regaled them with entertaining stories and kept the children amused, even wining a smile from the unsure Mrs. Saunders. When an anguished sob escaped from the room next door, Wynbrook spoke louder and Emma practically forced the biscuits on the family, both doing their best to give Dare and Kate more

time. Emma prayed they would be able to find the
information they needed to finally answer the question
of who had attempted to destroy their lives and left
them in debtor's prison.

All was quiet again for several minutes and then
the sound of mournful wailing grew so loud not
even the combined efforts of Emma and Wynbrook
could prevent Mrs. Saunders from rushing to check
on the welfare of her mother. Emma and Wynbrook
followed her to the door of the small room, where all
three stopped, transfixed by the sight before them.

A small woman with thinning, gray hair was
hunched over on a chair, while Kate knelt beside her,
trying to provide comfort. Mrs. Hennings was talking
of her time in service at Greystone. She was recalling
the time just before the first Darington died, when the
master lay ill and things were disappearing from the
house with no explanation.

"She never speaks of this," whispered Mrs. Saunders
to Emma and Wynbrook. "Never."

"More and more things went missing." Mrs.
Hennings stared straight ahead, wringing her hands.
"Finally, the steward told me that the earl was in dire
financial straits and the things must be sold to pay his
debts. Most of the staff was let go and we shut up
parts of the house. I was glad you and Master Robert
were at school, and I hoped Lord Darington would
recover and be able to set things to rights. The doctor
came more frequently and stayed with us for a while,
him and his son. By this time, practically everything
of value had been sold. I was starting to look for a
new position, you understand, not knowing how

much longer they could afford to pay me. In truth, toward the end, I had not received my pay in over four months."

"You are a good woman, Mrs. Hennings, to continue to serve my father so," reassured Kate in a kind, compassionate tone Emma had never heard from her before. Kate may have had a cool exterior, but she had a true heart.

"Then came the night his lordship passed away." The housekeeper's scratchy voice was strained. "It was late and I wished for some tea to steady my nerves, so I went down to the kitchen to prepare it. I heard voices. It was the doctor, berating the cook, saying 'You gave him too much' and 'I didn't want him to die yet.'"

"He didn't want my father to die *yet*?" asked Kate.

Emma gasped. Lord Darington's father had been murdered? She stared at Dare, her heart breaking for the man who stood perfectly still and silent as Mrs. Hennings went on to describe how the cruel doctor had threatened to kill her children if she ever spoke a word, and so to protect them, she had tried to kill herself.

"Oh, Mama!" cried her daughter, running into the room. "You were trying to protect us? Why did you never tell us?" They embraced each other tightly. Emma reached for her own handkerchief, while Wynbrook handed his to Kate. Dare said nothing, his countenance frozen.

"I do not suppose you know the name of this evil doctor?" asked Kate.

"He went by the name of Dr. Bones, but I am certain that was not his real name. He was in his midthirties perhaps, a muscular man, with black hair and gray eyes that squinted when he talked."

Wynbrook stepped up to Kate and put a hand on her shoulder. Emma longed to do so for Darington too, but his eyes were blazing with fury and she did not dare.

"I wish there were a way to know who this man was or why he did something so horrible," said Wynbrook.

"I do not know why," Mrs. Hennings looked up with tears in her eyes, "but I might know his name."

Everyone in the room held their breath.

"The doctor, he stayed at Greystone before his lordship passed and I did his laundry. In one of his coat pockets, I found an old letter."

"Did it have a name?" whispered Kate.

"Captain Harcourt."

The name meant nothing at first to Emma, though she noted Dare's hands balling into fists and his jaw growing tight. He knew that name. Where had she heard it before?

"Captain Harcourt?" asked Wynbrook when they were back outside the cottage. "The Captain Harcourt whom your father exposed as a traitor?"

"Oh my stars!" gasped Emma.

"They arrested Harcourt for treason, but the ship taking him back to England was lost at sea. He and all souls aboard were presumed dead," said Dare, his voice like gravel.

"That is why we have been so cursed. He came back to effect his revenge. Evil, hateful man!" Kate paced back and forth.

Dare said nothing more, but his look had turned

murderous. Kate and Wynbrook decided to walk back to Greystone, while Dare would drive Emma. Emma wanted to ask if he was strong enough to handle the coach, but she wisely held her tongue. He had just discovered his father had been murdered. Dare wanted vengeance not sympathy.

Dare offered to have Emma sit in the coach, but she swung herself up to the box instead to sit beside him. There was no way she was going to sit by herself in the coach while her future husband wrestled with such devastating news. Now was her time to let him know her decision and her regard for him. She would tell him he would not have to face this alone; no, she would be at his side.

He looked as if he was going to protest but sat beside her on the coach box and clicked for the horses to get moving.

"As soon as we get back to the house," he said in a tone so low it was almost a growl, "you need to leave."

Twenty-six

EMMA SAT NEXT TO DARE AS HE DROVE BACK TO Greystone Hall along the sea cliff. He said nothing, but his jaw was tight, and he held the reins so firmly that his knuckles showed white. She wanted to ask what he meant by wanting her to leave but could not find the words. Instead, she remained silent and placed a gloved hand on his shoulder for a moment before returning it to her lap. She wanted to provide some comfort yet was unable to shake the ominous cloud that had descended upon them.

"I am sorry you have received such dreadful news," began Emma, painfully aware how inadequate her words were.

Dare gave a nod of his head without looking at her, his jaw still clenched.

"I had hoped you would find answers and that would bring you peace. One could not have suspected such a revelation as this."

"I have answers but no peace."

"I am sorry," Emma murmured. "I wish I could be of service to you."

Dare met her gaze with a look of intense longing, only to have it cloud over the next moment and he returned to staring at the road ahead. "No. There is naught you can do. My father was murdered many years ago, but this crime will be avenged, I swear it."

Emma said nothing, for she feared the vehemence with which he spoke.

Dare glanced again at her and must have seen the fear in her eyes, for he forced a breath and continued, "Forgive me for speaking of this before you. I do not wish to frighten you with such talk."

"I am not fearful of you. I am afraid for you. You are going to track down this Harcourt, aren't you?"

"I am."

"Do you know how to find him?"

"No, but I warrant the bastard is near." Dare coughed. "Forgive my language."

"Oh no, think nothing of it. I was thinking something much worse."

"So was I." Dare pulled up, bringing the pair of horses slowly to a stop on the empty road. Wind whipped along the bluff and buffeted the white-capped sea. They stood on the edge of a storm.

"My father was a good man." Dare stared out over the churning waves. "Had he not discovered Harcourt's treachery, many would have lost their lives, and the princes either captured or killed. I wish I could have known him better." Dare closed his eyes and hung his head.

"He was a hero. Just like his son," said Emma softly.

"I never got to spend much time with him. He was away at sea, and when he returned the last time, he had been injured in a cannon misfire, which affected his eyes. We saw him briefly and then were away at school. I had hoped to spend time with him at holiday. Instead, my father was slowly poisoned as everything he owned was stolen from him, and then he was finally killed." Dare worked his jaw, grinding his teeth.

"Oh, Dare, I am so sorry." This time her hand lingered on his arm.

He turned to her, the frozen mask cracking open to reveal the anguish beneath. She opened her arms and he fell into her, holding her so tight it almost hurt, but she would never let him go. She pressed herself closer and tried to soothe away the hurt and pain, though she knew the depth of emotion was far beyond healing with an embrace.

"We will work through this together," murmured Emma.

Dare jerked back and looked around the barren landscape as if worried they might have been seen. "No. You need to get away from here."

Emma's stomach clenched as the growing sense of doom washed over her. "I could not think of leaving you at such a time."

"And I could not think of having you stay. You are in danger if you do."

"Danger?"

"Those men who attempted to abduct Kate and shot me—they are surely Harcourt's men. He must have heard that I had managed to crawl back from ruin and regain my fortune. He is determined to destroy me and anyone around me. No, you must go immediately. I can only hope that Harcourt will not connect you with me."

"But—"

"At least you had the good sense to refuse my offer," continued Darington, snapping the reins and getting the horses moving again.

Emma's heart dropped with a sickening sense of falling. "You no longer wish to marry me?"

"What I wish does not matter now. As long as Harcourt lives, I cannot take a wife. I would only put her in grave danger." Dare looked at her, his eyes softening. "I would not put you at risk for the world."

A lump formed in Emma's throat. What could she say in return? She suddenly had the urge to cry but stifled the impulse. She did not wish to burden him with her emotions. This was no time to focus on her own distress. Her mind spun, looking for a way to stay by his side, even as her darling dream crumbled before her.

They reached the house and pulled up to the stable. A stable lad ran out and held the heads of the horses, while Dare helped Emma down. Despite his injury, he lifted her down, his hands lingering for a moment about her waist before he turned back to the house.

They trudged against the wind, but Emma put her hand on his sleeve to stop him. She could not give up. She needed to tell him how she felt. Maybe, somehow, that would make a difference.

"Lord Darington, I cannot begin to express my sorrow for the difficult information you learned today." She paused, not quite knowing how to proceed.

He stared down at her, his eyes dark, full of longing.

"I want to let you know that, though I have not known you for long, I have come to admire you greatly. I would like to… That is, I should very much…" Emma was not sure how to accept the proposal of a man who had just rescinded it.

"Stop!" Dare yelled past her and pulled her behind him.

Emma was shoved to the ground, hitting the cold mud hard. The dark figure of an unknown man ran from the side of the house. Dare ran after him as fast as he could manage. "I command you to stop!"

The stranger sprinted behind a copse of trees and the sound of hooves could be heard a moment later. Dare did not make it far before he doubled over in pain. He pulled a pistol from his pocket and shot.

Emma scrambled up off of the cold, wet ground and ran to Dare, who was still holding his side. Several members of the house staff ran outside toward them.

"Are you all right? Did you shoot that man?" she asked, her voice drowned out by the others demanding what happened.

Dare was breathing hard, holding his side. "I did not stop him. Go catch him. Quick now!" he commanded, and the men hastened to follow his commands, though the stranger was no longer in view.

"Forgive me." Dare turned to her as the heavens opened up and began to pour down rain. "Did I hurt you?"

"No, no, I am well," she answered. She had lost her bonnet and so rain streamed down her face.

Dare took her arm and tugged her back to the house. "Probably best for you to stay here tonight and then I'll take you to Portsmouth tomorrow. Glad you are going to America. You need to get away from me. Far away."

Emma was glad for the torrential rain, for he would not be able to distinguish the rain from her tears. The dream was gone. She had lost him.

And now he would never know.

Twenty-seven

EMMA WOKE EARLY THE NEXT MORNING WITH HER two familiar companions: hope and resolution. The dream of marrying the Earl of Darington may be gone, but she was accustomed to loss. She had weathered many a storm in her life, and she would weather this one too.

Emma dressed quickly, not wanting to linger in her farewells. She had only known the Earl of Darington for a few days—surely her attachment could not be too strong. Yet, she suspected what she had experienced with Dare was not something that came along often. No, it was a rare thing. And precious. And lost.

She pulled out her small Bible and penned verses for Dare and Kate. If she must leave, at least she wished to leave them with hope. She knew Darington would never pursue any sort of connection with her as long as his father's murderer roamed free. Harcourt had gone undetected for over a decade. How long could he evade Darington? Months? Years? Would Dare ever bring him to justice?

The uncertainty of Darington's quest made one

thing clear. This would be where they would part ways. She needed to return to her original plan, which meant meeting her chaperone today in Portsmouth. So much had happened since she had left home, it was odd to think she was right on schedule.

No doubt Eustace would be looking for her, but he would have no reason to suspect she had gone to Portsmouth. Even if he had found her overturned coach, he could not possibly guess her plans.

Emma pasted on a smile and walked down to the foyer, where Kate and Wynbrook stood, holding hands.

"Am I to wish you every happiness?" she asked Kate.

Kate gave her a small nod with a rare smile.

Emma's forced smile warmed into a real one. "I wish you and Lord Wynbrook all the joy in the world." At least Kate had finally accepted Wynbrook's offer of marriage. Emma was genuinely pleased... though not without an aching longing to become part of the family.

Emma continued to exchange pleasantries with Kate and Wynbrook, but her mind was on Darington. She had assumed he would see her off as well, but he was not present in the hall. Her stomach sank as she tried to attend to what Kate was saying. Where was he? Would he not even say goodbye?

Emma paused, looking around to see if he was coming down the stairs. He was not.

Wynbrook sensed her concern and leaned toward her with a conspiratorial grin. "Hope you don't mind riding with Darington to Portsmouth. He's off to take the fight to Harcourt and we have a dearth of carriages I fear."

"Oh! I don't mind." Relief flooded through Emma followed by a rush of apprehension. She was to ride all the way to Portsmouth with him? It was to be a long and painful farewell.

She walked outside, the wind instantly tugging at her red cloak. It was not raining, but the blustery wind was having its way with anyone foolish enough to step outdoors. Darington stood by the open door of the carriage, solemn, grim, handsome. Her heart squeezed at the sight of him.

He helped her into the coach and she struggled to know what to say. Sally entered next, taking the seat across with an audible sigh. Emma had forgotten the presence of her sullen maid. Darington climbed in next, sitting beside her, but now all meaningful avenues of conversation were closed. Emma struggled to find something to say to Dare that could be expressed in the presence of her maid.

"So you travel to Portsmouth, my lord?" Emma asked, the formality sounding strange in her ears.

Dare nodded. "Harcourt is a man of the sea. The only way he could have evaded justice for so long was by leaving England. Portsmouth is the closest port that can handle a ship of any significant size."

"So you expect to find him there?"

"We shall see." His eyes were dark, but they blazed with emotion.

"I wish you well," she murmured, not knowing what more to say.

"And I you."

She was struck with the finality of the interaction. Were these the last words they would utter to each other? Dare turned to the window, staring at the gray landscape. She wished to embrace him one last time, but despite their proximity, there was no way to reach him.

Her heart splintered, close to breaking. She watched him from under the edge of her bonnet. His face was stoic, impassive. He was not one to let his emotions show, even if they had not had their unwanted witness.

The carriage bounced on the road, and her hands flung to her sides to steady herself on the seat. Her fingers brushed against his, their hands hidden by the folds of their respective outer garments. Slowly his fingers curled around hers, until his gloved hand was holding hers. It was everything they could not say. Whatever emotions she was feeling, they were shared.

She tried to draw comfort from the warmth of his hand, but instead, her chest tightened. This was her true love. And the last time she would ever see him. She squeezed his hand. He returned it. They passed the remainder of the journey to Portsmouth in silence, hand in hand.

The coach bumped with jarring rapidity as it reached the cobblestones of the Portsmouth streets. A few minutes later, it slowed to a stop before the weathered inn. They had arrived. Emma would say farewell to Dare and resume her own journey into the unknown.

"Forgive the rudeness, but it would be best if I am not seen with you," said Darington in a solemn tone. "I do not know who is in the employ of my enemy. I will not put you in danger by being seen with me."

Emma nodded.

"If anyone asks about the friends you stayed with, please do not mention my name or that of my sister. I fear it is not safe to do so."

Emma nodded again, slower this time. Her heart was breaking and she could not even share her pain with anyone.

Emma stared at Dare, but he looked straight ahead with unseeing eyes. Was this all? Was this how they were to part? They were still holding hands; Dare had not let go. If anything he held on tighter.

"Sally, please take the bags in with the coachman and tell the innkeeper I would like a room," Emma said to her maid in a brisk manner. She needed to be able to say goodbye without an audience.

Sally stepped outside and Dare reached across and pulled the coach door closed. The intensity of his gaze was fierce. She knew she was safe with him, even if he was not completely safe himself. Darington held himself rigid. She doubted the man knew how to relax. He was all angles and hard edges. Yet he still held her gloved hand.

"I… That is…" He struggled to express himself.

She wanted to help but did not know the words he could not find. She also struggled to put her feelings into cogent expression. Everything she wanted to say seemed wrong. She felt for him a powerful attraction, but should such a thing be acknowledged?

"I wish things were different," Dare whispered. "Wish I could say something, but I ought not."

"What would you say if you could?" She had to know.

"I'd say you ought not let the bastards run you off.

You shouldn't marry some American. You should marry me instead."

Emma's mouth dropped open.

"Shouldn't have said that," he muttered.

"If the offer of marriage still stands..." began Emma, but Dare shook his head.

"I do not want you to marry someone else, but I can't make you an offer. Can't let you get connected to me."

"I am not afraid."

"But I am. They killed my father and sent Kate and me to Fleet. I cannot think of what he might do to you. Best thing is to let you go." Dare took a shattered breath. "Only thing is to let you go."

"I could wait..."

Dare shook his head again. "Not fair of me to ask. Not safe until I kill him and any he had working for him. Don't know how long that will take. Could be years. Don't know if I'll be coming back at all." He bowed his head and leaned closer to her. "Sorry, but that's the truth."

Emma leaned toward him until the brim of her bonnet was almost touching his head. "If we are to be honest, then you must know I had decided to accept your proposal."

"You did?" His eyes were wide.

"Yes."

A look of hope sprung on his face only to be shattered a moment later. His shook his head. "There is no way we can be together. Damnation, but that is another reason to kill Harcourt. I am so sorry."

"You have caused me no ill."

"Then why are you are crying?"

He pulled his hand from hers, removed his gloves, and wiped a tear from her cheek with his thumb. She blinked and more tears fell. She did not mean to cry but could not help it. Her heart seized, and she could not think of how she could continue on her journey to marry another when she was so much in love with the man before her.

"Please, please forgive me," he murmured.

"For what?"

"For this." He cupped her face in both hands and kissed her hard. Heat surged through her and she felt weightless and limp yet empowered by the strange sensations building within her. She clasped her hands around him even as he drew her closer to him, wrapped in his long arms. This was their last moment together. Time suspended and everything seemed to stop. She did not dare even take a breath. The moment had to last forever. It was one perfect sliver of time when everything was as it should be.

And then it was over. He sat back and turned away from her. "Had no right." He shook his head.

"But I'm glad you did," she blurted out.

He turned to her, surprise flickering in his eyes.

"I must be turning into quite the wanton." She attempted to smile but instead another tear traced a path down her cheek. How could she experience such a kiss and say goodbye?

"I must go," he said but made no move to leave.

"Do be careful."

"You as well."

Silence grew between them, but neither attempted to move.

"Everything happens for a purpose," said Emma, trying to make sense of the growing ache in her heart.

"Do you really think so?" It was an honest question.

"I'd like to." Emma was honest. "I do believe God can use whatever hardship we face for good."

"His good or our good?"

"His good is our good."

"Do you really think so?" This time bitterness laced his tone.

"I do. I truly do." Her answer remained honest.

One side of his mouth slowly drew up, but his eyes remained sad. "Then I also will try to believe. You are like none I have ever met."

"And I have never met anyone like you."

"I...I..." Dare stumbled over his words and paused, shaking his head slightly before continuing. Emma wondered what he censored himself from saying. "I wish you a pleasant journey." He leaned forward again and kissed her on the cheek, his lips warm against her cool cheek.

Lingering in the coach was sheer agony, but she did not wish to leave. Her mind scrambled for some way that he could remain with her, but she knew it was not possible. He must go. And she must also.

"This is for you." She handed him the verse she had chosen for him and boldly returned his kiss on his cheek. He pressed his lips together, the pain clear in his dark eyes. She quickly opened the coach door and jumped out, the cold wind stinging her face.

Tears sprung to her eyes and she wiped them away with the back of her hand. She reached the entryway to the inn and turned back to wave farewell. The coach ambled away, the curtains closed. She doubted she would ever see him again.

She wiped more tears from her eyes.

Stepping into the inn, Emma took a deep breath. It was a large establishment with a brisk, businesslike feel. Voices could be heard coming from the common room, with the low rumble of conversations and the occasional peal of laughter. Emma felt at once how unequal she was to public viewing. Sally stood in the entryway before the wooden staircase, leading to the guest rooms upstairs.

"Has our room been acquired?" asked Emma.

Sally nodded.

Emma followed her upstairs to a comfortable room and dismissed Sally to get some food in the kitchen. She needed to be alone.

Emma tried to keep her emotions in check but could do so no longer. The tears fell hot and fast down her cheeks, another one appearing as soon as she wiped one away. She gave up and collapsed on the bed, letting the tears fall.

Twenty-eight

Dare instructed the coachman to continue on toward the docks and pushed aside thoughts of the lovely Emma St. James. At least he tried to do so. Thoughts of her kept rising to the surface, unbidden, unwanted, and unwilling to subside. He doubted he would ever stop thinking of her.

He unrolled the small scroll of paper she had given to him, wondering what she had written. Did he have the courage to look? He had to know. On the page was a simple verse.

> *O lord, thou hast searched me, and known me...If I ascend up into heaven, thou art there: if I make my bed in hell, behold, thou art there. If I take the wings of the morning, and dwell in the uttermost parts of the sea; even there shall thy hand lead me, and thy right hand shall hold me.*
> —*Psalm 139:1, 8–10*

It was her encouragement to him. He stared at the words. He was not sure if he believed in a compassionate God, but he did have faith in Emma. If she believed, then maybe that was good enough for him. He carefully rolled up the small paper and placed it in his breast pocket. It was a message of hope in a world devoid of it.

He had never anticipated developing feelings toward a member of the fairer sex. The thought of experiencing strong emotions at all had seemed inconceivable. No, the experience he had in his chest was something completely foreign to him. He had the sickening sensation of falling. He gulped air, but it did not help. He could not shake the feeling that he had been hollowed out from the inside and there was something missing. Something important. Something like Emma.

She was a bright light, making him realize how dark and dreary his life truly was. To be shown another way only to have it ripped away was cruel. To think of her giving herself to another man made him rage within.

Dare directed the carriage to pull to a stop at the Round Tower, an old fortification built by King Henry V to protect the harbor from invaders. The old tower stood with its base in the choppy waters and its cannon trained on the harbor opening. Nothing could get by without being raked by the thirty pounders.

Dare jumped out of the coach into the blustery winter day and directed the coachman to take his sea chest to the *Lady Kate*, while Dare walked along the battlements toward the royal dockyard. He welcomed the stinging wind blowing the sharp saltwater spray into his face. The slap in the face helped him to think.

Until Harcourt was dead, everyone around him was in danger. Kate was at risk. And Emma too. He would protect them no matter the cost. He had to find Captain Harcourt. And fast. Then return to Emma and convince her not to marry that American sod.

Dare shook his head, not wanting to give himself false hope. And yet if he could eliminate Harcourt quickly...

Dare turned his focus on finding Harcourt. He was a naval man and would no doubt captain his own ship. If Harcourt was after Dare, he would start with the *Lady Kate*. She was moored in Portsmouth, and so Dare bet Harcourt was too. He just needed to figure out which ship.

It would have to be a ship that would not raise suspicion, but also not be known, for Harcourt could not show his face in Portsmouth, where the locals knew all the captains and most of the crew. One place he could not be was on a ship of the line. The ladies of the Royal Navy often knew more about the disposition of the ships and crew than did the admiralty. So he must have been on a fishing or merchant vessel.

Dare walked along the sea wall, squinting into the wind at the ships in the harbor. All sorts and sizes of vessels were moored in Portsmouth—frigates, schooners, brigs, hulks, ships of the line, and modest fishing vessels dwarfed by their larger cousins. One of them might be holding Harcourt, but which one?

Dare studied the small shipping fleet with a critical eye. No, he reasoned, as in any tight community, the fishermen would all know one another. They would know if there was someone who did not belong. Harcourt would have to be a stranger in a situation where being a stranger would not be unusual.

Dare continued his walk along the wall, trying to discern where Harcourt might be hiding. A merchant ship, the *Kestrel*, moved slowly out of the harbor. It was a frigate with smooth lines, flying the flag of the Colonies, or rather the new United States of America. Could that be Harcourt?

Or maybe Harcourt was on the brig with a sturdy build and a floating armament. Dare didn't know. But one thing was for sure, Harcourt certainly knew him. He might be watching him even now. Was he aware that Dare knew he was alive?

Darington continued along the sea wall, passing the mud flats toward the bastion. It was low tide, and the little rivulets ran through the mud, silt, and sand, waiting for the tide to swallow them up again. The wind stung his face and Dare pulled his greatcoat tighter around him. It was January in Portsmouth, and a cold one.

The streets were unusually vacant and Dare guessed the cold was keeping everyone indoors. He ducked into the Mariner Pub and walked past weatherworn men in blue naval coats to lean against the bar.

"Cap'n Dare!" A young lad greeted him informally, earning him a cuff from a large man with beefy arms.

"You talk proper now," the landlord admonished, shoving the lad back to his work. "Greetings to you, Cap'n Lord Darington. How can we be of service to you?"

"Got something warm?"

"Ah yes, mulled wine, just the thing to put the heat back into your heart."

Dare doubted anything could do that now that

Emma was gone, but he accepted a warm cup with a nod of gratitude. "Most folks staying in with the cold," commented Dare, attempting to engage the landlord in conversation for the first time. The man had started to walk toward the other end of the bar and stopped short to turn back to him in surprise. Dare had frequented the pub when he had first weighed anchor in Portsmouth harbor months ago, generally eating in a far corner in silence. He had never been the conversational type.

"I warrant the cold has got people staying by the hearth," replied the landlord, striding back to him. "'Course, the *Victory* and twenty ships of the line sailed out yesterday. Things were all a rush before, but now it's a little thin on company."

"There are the merchant ships," said Dare, hoping to find out as much as he could about the ships in the harbor. "I warrant they are good for business if they grant shore leave."

"Some do, some don't. Some of them foreign ships don't let off their crew, same as the navy." The man shook his head sadly, for a crew unable to leave the ship was of no use to his livelihood.

"Truly? I thought all merchant ships allowed at least some shore leave."

The man shook his head. "Wish they did, and that's the truth."

"But at least you see the captains."

The man shrugged. "Some prefer to stay with the ship. Especially them foreign ones."

"I saw a Spanish galleon far out there. Strange to see it here, since I remember Trafalgar so clearly. I suppose we are at peace now." A Spanish galleon was suspicious to Dare.

"Aye, strange though it may be. The captain and crew, they nearly drank me out o' rum and paid in doubloons for it, so I'm inclined to think charitable like toward them." The man gave Dare a smile.

So maybe it wasn't the galleon. Perhaps it was a ship Dare suspected of smuggling. Maybe they were hiding more than French wine. "I saw the *Rooster* in the harbor. I'm sure they are good for business."

The landlord straightened his back, his smile fading. "Aye, they be loyal customers."

Dare took the hint. Smugglers provided the shop-keepers with valuable commodities and everyone turned a blind eye when the officers' love of French wine was at stake.

"What about those Americans?" Dare tried to change the subject. He wished Emma were here, for she could charm anyone into talking about anything. "I'm sure they are no match for our lads when it comes to a pint or two."

The landlord laughed and the easy smile returned. "No, they aren't, though they give 'em a run for it."

"Too bad for you the *Kestrel* just left."

"Nay, they stayed mostly on board. Only saw a few of the crew, and they were a sullen lot."

"Damn Americans," Dare muttered with feeling.

"Now the *Alliance*, she's an American too, but she pours out her crews and they drink up their pay like good sailors." The barkeep wiped glasses with a towel as he warmed to his topic. "The *Maiden Lilly* never let a single man off, but kept running bumboats back and

forth. I think every harlot in Portsmouth got a tour."
The man laughed heartily.

Dare nodded mechanically and drained his mug.
He would have to get information on every potential
ship, forcing him to frequent every public house in
Portsmouth to do it. The more questions he asked, the
more likely Harcourt would be to hear about it and be
able to slip away.

Dare paid for the drink with resignation and walked
to the door to continue his search with heavy feet.
Raised voices caught his attention.

"You gave him another bottle?" exclaimed the
landlord, chastising his young apprentice. "What's
wrong with you, boy? He hadn't paid for the first
dozen and run off without paying his shot."

"S-sorry," stammered the lad.

"Well, if Silas Bones wants another drink, he needs
to pay up first!"

Dare had his hand on the door latch when the
landlord's words froze him in his tracks. Silas *Bones*?
That was the same surname Harcourt had used to
masquerade as the doctor. Could it be a coincidence?

Dare stalked back into the bar. "Forgive the intrusion, but I might know the man you speak of. Silas
Bones?"

"Friend o' yours?" asked the landlord, wiping his
hands on his white apron.

"No," said Dare in a low voice, leaning closer over
the bar. "But I'd like to find him."

"He sped out o' here today, he did. Got no idea
where he might go."

"Could you describe him to me? I'd be willing to

pay his shot for your trouble." Dare pushed a crown toward the landlord across the polished wood bar.

The landlord palmed the coin with an easy swipe of his large hand. "Younger man, late twenties I'd say. Short, curly black hair, blue eyes."

If he were a younger man, then it could not be Harcourt, but didn't the old housekeeper say Dr. Bones had a son? "The man I'm looking for had some friends. Last I saw them, they each had a different color muffler, one black, one red, one blue."

"That sounds like them," said the lad, joining the conversation. "Was the man in the black muffler a big bloke with a low voice?"

"That sounds right. Which ship was Silas Bones from?" Dare clenched his fists at his sides, trying to keep the urgency from his tone.

"He never said." The bartended shook his head.

"I saw him go a few times to the *Kestrel*," the lad interjected.

The *Kestrel*! The American ship whose captain had not been seen with his officers. It must be it, but it had just left.

"Thank you." Dare strode with purpose out the door. The chilling blast did not bother him anymore. He was on the hunt once more.

Twenty-nine

EMMA BLOTTED HER EYES WITH A MUCH-ABUSED handkerchief. She had heard the talk that she was beautiful, but no one would think so now. She was not someone who could cry without her face telling the tale. Her eyes swelled up and her nose turned red and ran, making her look like a victim of influenza.

Emma pushed herself off the bed and tried to calm herself. She needed to believe things would work out for the best, but the evidence at present was not in her favor. Her father had died, leaving her alone in the world. Her stepbrother wanted to send her to an asylum. And then, just when she had been ready to accept a proposal of marriage, Darington was taken away from her too. It all seemed so futile. Why open her heart up again if it was only to be broken?

A lump formed in her throat and she wiped her eyes again with her much-abused handkerchief. She feared she might dissolve into tears once more when Sally skulked into the room. With a glance, Emma realized she was not the only one feeling out of sorts.

"Sally? Are you well?"

Sally slumped down on a chair by the window and turned to her with sad eyes brimming with tears. "I don't want to go to America. I don't want to be on a ship."

Emma was not terribly surprised by this confession. "You certainly do not have to do anything you do not wish. I understand if you do not wish to leave England." She could not fault the girl for not wishing to be banished with her. "I can travel alone with my chaperone, I'm sure."

"But what of me?" cried Sally. "I want to be a lady's maid for a fancy, rich lady and live in a nice house. I thought you was a fancy lady, but it turns out I was wrong."

This outburst was so outside the bounds of what would be considered an appropriate utterance for a lady's maid, Emma was taken aback and found herself without words to reply.

"I need a good reference so I can get a position with some fancy lady," continued Sally with a pout. "I want you to write one for me before you leave."

Emma felt strongly that the position of lady's maid was not quite in keeping with Sally's natural skills and abilities, whatever those might be. "Perhaps you should think of employment outside of service," she suggested.

Sally's eyes flashed. "You ain't going to write me a letter?"

"I do not think you are well suited to the position of a lady's maid and I do not wish to sign my name to something that is untrue. However, I will provide you with your remaining wages plus some extra, with which you can return home and look for other

positions." Emma fished a generous sum out of her
reticule. She had been saving her meager pin money
for a long time, and though it left her with less than
was entirely comfortable for her journey, she wished
to be more than fair to Sally.

Now that she had caught up with her designated
chaperone, she could survive on what little she had
left until she met her future husband. Of course it
meant she no longer had funds to return if she wished,
but she would deal with that problem if it came. She
certainly could not send Sally away empty-handed.

"Here you are." Emma handed Sally the generous
sum. "That should provide enough for you to return
to your parents and start over with whatever you
should wish to do."

Sally took the money but stared at it with a glower.
No thanks emerged from her lips. "It's cold out there.
I'll freeze trying to get back home." She spoke with
a sob.

"I did not realize you had been uncommonly cold.
Let me see what I have to make you more comfortable." Emma turned to rummage through her traveling chest. Sally already had a wool cloak and heavy
wool gloves with a cotton liner. Still, everyone was
cold traveling in January and Sally seemed more sensi-
tive than most. "Would an extra muffler do for you?"
she asked, turning back around with a scarf in hand.

"No. No, I just want to go." Sally edged to the
door. "I just want to be done with the whole mad lot
of you."

"Well then! I do wish you the best."

Sally said nothing more but dashed out the door,

slamming it behind her. Emma sighed and sank back down to the bed, feeling heavy with the tremendous events of the past few days. She had lost her home, her maid, her chance to wed her true love.

Emma took a deep breath and then another. She had to remind herself that this was exactly her plan all along. Nothing had changed.

Except her arranged fiancé was not the sea captain she wished to marry.

Emma took another breath and forced herself to her feet. She had chosen her fate, made the arrangements. It was time to face whatever her life would be. She squared her shoulders and held her head high. She would at least meet her chaperone with dignity, even if her heart was breaking.

She walked down the wooden stairs of the old Portsmouth inn, worn smooth over the years. She gave the name of her chaperone to a harried maid and was informed that the good lady was in a private dining room and was expecting her company.

Emma followed the directions through the smoke-filled common room to a door on the other side. She paused a moment, her hand on the latch, trying to steel her nerves.

"Please give my apologies to Lord Langley," came a familiar voice on the other side of the door. "But I fear Miss St. James is in no condition to marry anyone."

Emma clapped her hand over her mouth to keep from crying out. It was Eustace. He had found her.

"Lord Langley will be greatly disappointed," responded a female voice Emma could only assume was her chaperone. "I cannot fathom why anyone would attempt to arrange a marriage to the grandson of the earl to a girl who is, as you say, quite mad."

"Yes, I quite agree, it was ill-fated from the start. I only just found out about the plot and set out immediately. I felt it my duty to set things right."

"Yes, yes, of course. I do appreciate your scruples."

Emma's heart beat so loud in her chest she feared it would be overheard. She backed away quietly, fearful the door would open at any second and Eustace would find her. She turned and strode back through the common room, smoke swirling around her.

She retreated to her room and bolted the door. She put a hand to her chest, forcing herself to think logically. She needed to talk to her chaperone and somehow convince her that Eustace was the one who was mentally unstable.

The ship did not leave for another day. She had to find a way to speak to her chaperone alone and enlist her help to sail away without alerting Eustace. It would be a difficult thing to manage, but the alternative was the asylum.

Emma would not surrender easily.

❦

"The *Kestrel*—where is it heading?" asked Dare in a tone that was more a demand than a question.

"The *Kestrel*, ye say, my lord?" asked the harbormaster, removing his cap and scratching his gray head. "Sailed out not long ago. Not sure where she was heading. Can see her there bearing for the Isle of Wight. She'll be turning into the Channel soon." He pointed to the black outline of a ship.

"Thank you!" Dare kept the ship in sight as he strode down the sea wall. He could not lose Harcourt now. He passed the *Venture*, the ship Emma would be taking to America. Despite his great hurry, he slowed his step to give the ship a good look. It was a sturdy brig and would see Emma safely to the New World.

To his surprise, the sails unfurled and the ship began to move slowly from the harbor. The captain must have decided to leave early. It was a good thing he had brought Emma to her chaperone in time. Wasn't it?

Dare's gut clenched as he watched the ship slowly sail out of the harbor. He scanned the rail, looking for her. Would she stand and watch the shore drift away? Would she see him and wave? A fresh wave of agony washed over him as he watched the ship leave, taking away the light of his life. He could not even see her one last time.

He wished to chase her and beg her not to leave, but to be with him was to put her at risk. The thought of her being hurt made his blood a molten fire even as he shivered from the cold. No, Emma could not be anywhere near him.

He must let her go.

He turned his collar up against the bitter wind and continued down the sea wall, keeping the outline of the *Kestrel* in sight.

He was not sure how many of his crew would be available. He had requested they not leave town, though he had no way to ensure they did not go home. Even if he could not find them all, he would make do with what he had.

"Cap'n Dare!" said a cheery voice, a jarring dissonance from Dare's dark thoughts.

Dare turned to face his first mate. "Everett, you are well met."

"I am much surprised to see you." The young man pushed back his dark hair.

"Why should you be surprised?" Dare frowned.

"Because you gave us all extended shore leave." Everett tilted his head to the side. "Your orders were to leave the ship and see our families. 'Course, I have no family so—"

"I gave no such command," said Dare, his apprehension rising.

"But…" Everett stared at him wide-eyed. "Got your letter two days ago, commanding us all to go home to our families. Said not to return within two months or you'd never sail with us again. It had your seal."

"Damnation!" Dare swore a string of curses. He did not typically give vent to emotion, but considering the day he was having, he allowed the indulgence. After keeping himself in check around polite company for months, it was a relief to express his feelings to one who would not take offense. "My signet ring was stolen. I never sent that letter."

"I am sorry, Cap'n. I was fooled. I knew it was not your hand, but it had your seal, so I thought it was dictated."

Dare shook his head. "Not your fault. Everett, we need to sail. Today."

The man smiled as if Dare had said a joke, but the smile faded when he realized Dare was serious. "But we got no provisions, no crew."

"There must be some sailors left in Portsmouth."

Everett shook his head. "A few, maybe, but no

good ones. The Royal Navy just sailed out, and they pressed every able sailor from eight to eighty into service. It's mighty thin 'round these parts."

"Round up the bad ones then, and get ammunition over food."

"Oh, our ammunition's full and loaded. The *Lady Kate* is never caught unawares." The man gave him a sly smile.

"Good. I'll round up the men. You get the provisions. We leave as soon as may be. See that ship?" Dare pointed to the shrinking form of the *Kestrel*. "That's our quarry. Take a reading on it and mark its course."

"What?" Everett stared at him aghast.

"Everett, we are going after Captain Harcourt."

"Harcourt the traitor? But is he not dead?"

"No. But he will be."

Thirty

DARE SOON FOUND THAT EVERETT HAD NOT BEEN exaggerating when he told him that there were no sailors to be found. It was January, the time when many a ship wintered in the harbor and many a sailor rested by his hearth. Of course, there were always a hardy few who sailed, but with the departure of the navy with a full complement of impressed sailors and the interference from Captain Harcourt, Dare was thin on able seamen.

Dare had no doubt it was Harcourt who had deprived him of his crew. He wondered if Harcourt knew Dare had finally figured out who he was. Had Harcourt sent the crew away because he knew Dare was coming for him?

No, Dare reasoned, Everett said they had been dismissed a few days ago, before Dare knew Harcourt was alive. Harcourt had simply been causing trouble and ensuring that if Dare ever did suspect him, a quick chase would not be possible. If Harcourt was unaware Dare was coming for him, Dare might finally have an advantage, slim though it may be.

He glanced at the silhouette of the *Kestrel*, getting smaller every minute. He needed to hurry. After checking all the main pubs, a few gambling dens, and even asking about at a local church, Dare had had little luck finding eligible men. He was told by one lonely barmaid that the press gang had rounded up every able seaman not in jail.

So Dare headed to the jail. He was desperate. He could not come so close to apprehending the man who murdered his father only to remain in port because he did not have enough hands to make pursuit.

Dare spoke briefly to the warden at the local jail. They had about thirty men who had been arrested and convicted for one offense or another, mostly fighting, assault, or disorderly conduct. They were serving out their time, for none could afford the fine. These were not the seamen Dare would choose to man his ship, for he had seen the effects of poor seamanship and wanted nothing to do with it, but these were desperate times.

He walked into the jailhouse, the acrid smell of misery and human waste bringing back memories of being forced into Fleet prison. His boots scuffed down the stone staircase into the dank, cold darkness. The haunting memories of panic and desperation slithered through him. Walking farther into the bowels of the jail was like ripping the scab off his memory and watching the wound bleed.

The cells were mere alcoves in the stone wall, barely big enough for a cot or two and a bucket. Shaggy heads of dirty men lifted as he walked by.

"How do, gov'nor?" said one man who despite the several days' growth of beard on his face obviously had attempted to keep his personal hygiene as best as could be done. The man leaned on the iron bars of his cage and regarded Dare with desperate eyes.

Dare gave the man a nod. "Looking for sailors."

"Well then, you're in luck, yes you are. For we're sailors. I'm Davy Pricket, at yer service, sir." The man gave a rather gallant bow for his circumstances. He was a wiry man who shifted from foot to foot, unable to stay still. Behind him in the dim cell, two other men stood, a balding man with two missing front teeth and a shorter man with wide shoulders.

"What was your crime?" asked Dare.

"Ah, I was caught in the right place at the wrong time." The man swayed from side to side like a caged animal.

"He got caught by a pretty face," smirked the toothless man behind him. "And her husband took offense."

"Alas, I was not aware of the husband until too late."

"Weren't aware the cuckold was coming home, ye mean."

"Aye, for I would have chosen a more opportune time for our tryst if I'd known."

"You do say the damnedest things. But you started the biggest brawl I ever saw, I'll give you that." The old sailor spat on the floor through the hole in his teeth.

"What experience have you?" Dare asked Pricket.

"Well, I've sailed since I was a wee lad. Able seaman, I am. Been to Australia and back." The man winked and Dare wondered what crime he had committed to be banished to the penal colony of Australia.

"And you two?" Dare addressed the men behind Pricket.

"I've been a sailor all my life," said the older one. "Tom Bean is my name. And my friend is Tobias Stalk."

"And you are a sailor as well, Mr. Stalk?"

"I've been many things," said Tobias Stalk with a deep, reverberating voice. And then he stood up.

Dare suddenly realized Tobias Stalk was not a short man with wide shoulders but a tall man with shoulders to match the rest of his large frame. The man had to hunch over, for the height of the cell could not accommodate his size. He stepped forward to the iron bars, forcing Dare, who was a tall man in his own right, to look up at him. The man had to be over seven feet tall.

"Even a sailor?" Dare was doubtful. Could this man even fit belowdecks? He would forever be hitting his head. And how could he possibly fit into one hammock?

"Aye, sir. They pay me two men's wages and give me two men's portions, and I do the work of three."

"I see," said Dare, deciding to move the conversation along. "I am Captain Lord Darington. I am looking for sailing men who can fight well. The target I am pursuing is a difficult one and will test the mettle of my crew to the utmost." Dare walked up and down the jail corridor, inspecting the sad state of the men locked inside. The men were a sorry lot, but he hoped they would serve. Besides, given his current mission, it was probably best not to take his own crew. He would hate to make an honest man an accomplice in his crime, for Dare intended to engage Harcourt at sea, no matter what flag he flew.

"Captain Darington the Pirate Earl who returned rich as Midas?" asked Davy Pricket.

Darington had always bristled at the title. There was

always a thin line between a privateer and a pirate. Standing in the jailhouse of Portsmouth, Dare realized he was about to cross it. To attack a ship without a letter of marque was piracy. To take down Harcourt, he would become a pirate.

"I will pay to release all who will serve, but I will demand absolute obedience to my orders. I served in the navy and I run my ship like it. Know that before you sign. I will push you to perform better than your best. And this mission is personal. If any of you want to keep your hands clean, you best stay where you are. I'll not lie to you. I may not follow all the dictates of this great empire. In fact, I intend not to."

"What's the man mean?" asked Bean.

"It means he will treat us harsh but fair and he plans to do something illegal," said Pricket, rubbing his hands together.

"Smuggling?" asked one man, licking his lips with glee.

"Worse," replied Dare in a grim tone. "Who's with me?"

All the men, about thirty in all, volunteered.

"We leave immediately," said Dare and went to find the warden.

"Ye want these scurvy dogs, do ye?" The grizzled warden gave him a sharp look with his one good eye when Dare presented him with the news.

"I am in immediate need for hands on my ship. I cannot wait."

"Ye must be hell-bent desperate if ye want these blackhearts. I'd rather sail with the bashi-bazouk than these louts."

The warden's comparison of the men he was freeing to mercenary Turks known for their savage brutality did not bode well. Dare would not have done it, except for the dire circumstances in which he found himself.

If Dare could dispatch Harcourt quickly, he could sail to America and find Emma. With any luck, she would not have yet spoken her vows to some ill-mannered American and then he could…

"M'lord?" The warden narrowed his good eye at him. "Ye want to pay the fines on these bastards or no?"

Dare plunked down the required coin. He had his crew.

Thirty-one

DARE STEPPED ON BOARD THE *LADY KATE* AND TOOK A deep breath. The familiar aroma of tar, cordage, and sailcloth welcomed him. He might have been an earl on land, but he was a captain at sea. It was here that he was home.

He glanced about with a nervous eye, for he had harbored a fear that Harcourt had done some mischief to his *Lady Kate* while she was anchored in the harbor. A quick tour of his flagship reassured him that no sabotage was in play.

Dare strode down the single, continuous battery deck and mounted the armed quarterdeck. The bumboats had arrived with his new recruits, and he watched them with resignation.

"Those are some rum-looking cullies, they are," muttered Everett, shaking his head. "Some of them look like drunken lubbers."

"They are," admitted Dare with a sigh.

"Here we are, Cap'n!" shouted Davy Pricket. "Ready and willing to make you proud."

Dare acknowledged the man with a brief nod. The

first test of this ramshackle crew would be to attempt to make sail.

"Have we the water?" Dare asked his first mate.

"Aye, and the stores, though it be but meager fare on short notice. I did secure seven chickens, but a goat was not to be had."

"Good man. And the cannonade and powder?"

"Aye, fully stocked."

Dare stared out at the Isle of Wight where the *Kestrel* had been last seen. It was time to make sail. Dare paused for a moment, almost afraid to give the order. With the surly lot before him, he felt sure disaster was brewing. Still, one could not live a coward.

"All hands to make sail," he ordered. The call was repeated, and with some confusion over who was to do what, the men found their places, or were shoved into place by Tobias Stalk, who by sheer dint of height and girth had taken charge of the deck.

"Away loft," Dare called, and the men who knew what they were about raced up the shrouds with practiced skill. Those who were learning their craft took longer and were subjected to many a curse and jab for slowness.

Dare nodded to Everett, and he continued to give the calls. "Trice up. Lay out!" The men worked to free the gaskets, the lines that held the sails furled to the yards.

"Let fall. Sheet home. Hoist away. Watch the lines now! Look lively."

A commotion in the foretop caught their attention as Davy Pricket lost his footing on the upper topsail yard. To Dare's horror, the man fell with a shriek, only to be caught by the ankle by an errant line and swung helplessly across the deck, screaming with all his might.

"Grab him, men. No, not all of you. Look to the sheets. Hands to braces. Belay!" yelled Everett, running down to the deck to help the men rescue the howling lad who was hanging upside down, rotating slowly.

Dare stood as still as a statue, his hand clasped tightly behind his back. The sails filled gently at first, then the wind took hold and the *Lady Kate* was under way.

"We shall endeavor to improve that performance, Mr. Everett," Dare commented without emotion.

"Aye, though I doubt I shall ever be able to show my face in Portsmouth again," moaned Everett.

"You and me both," muttered Dare.

᷇

Emma cracked open the door of her guest room and watched carefully for anyone who might be walking by. She needed help and prayed that support could be found. Finally, a maid strode up the stairs, a basket of linens in hand. Emma took a chance and stepped outside to speak with her.

"Hello, I am looking for Mrs. Atwood. I wonder if she is in her room and if you could direct me to her?" Emma spoke in a hushed tone, fearful to be overheard by her stepbrother.

"I'm sorry, miss," replied the maid. She pushed a lock of hair out of her eyes as she balanced a basket of linens on her hip. "Mrs. Atwood left immediately after speaking with the gentleman downstairs."

Emma stared at the maid, unable to speak for a moment. "She...she left?"

"Yes, miss. She said the captain of the ship wanted to leave a day early and was only waiting for all the passengers. She had been waiting for someone but said she was no longer— Oh! Was that you, miss?"

"I… Yes."

"If you be Miss St. James, then there's a gentleman waiting for you in the common room."

Emma's face must have gone pale, for the maid continued in a friendly manner.

"You don't want to meet with him?"

"No, indeed. I must reach the ship without alerting him." Emma had no choice but to take the girl into her confidence. "Is there a way you can help?"

The maid looked sympathetic. "What is he? A jilted lover? A debt collector?"

"Worse. An unwanted relation."

"Ah, those are the worst. Well now, I don't know what I can do. That man's been pacing about, watching the door like a hawk."

"Would five shillings help you think of something?"

The maid gave her a wide grin, highlighting a spate of freckles across her upturned nose. A few moments later, Emma and the bright-haired maid were carrying her trunk down the side servants' stairs and out the back door into the alleyway at the back of the inn. A shivery boy held the leads to a pony cart as he waited for the owner to return.

"Here you go. Get in," commanded the maid, and Emma shoved her large trunk into the cart and jumped in after it.

"Hey! What's you doing?" cried the boy.

"You said you wanted to drive this," replied the

maid. "Now's your chance. Take her down to the docks, to the *Venture*, and come back as quick as may be."

"What about 'im?" The boy pointed to the kitchen door and presumably the owner of the cart.

"You know he likes to chat it up with Beatrice. He won't be back out here for a while. You want to freeze or have a little fun?"

The boy, who could not have been older than ten years, gave a wide grin and hopped up, giving a smart crack of the leads over the pony's back. The cart jolted forward and they careened down the narrow alley. Emma clung to the pony cart with one hand and her case with the other, praying that she would not be flung from the open bed. They rounded the corner and whisked past the front of the inn just as a man wearing a greatcoat with multiple capes was backing out of the door. Was it Wynbrook? Maybe he could help. The man turned. Their eyes met.

It was Eustace.

"Hurry!" Emma called to the lad, her heart in her throat. It was an unnecessary rejoinder to the boy who was already urging the pony into a gallop as the cart skittered across the icy cobblestones. Emma's heart pounded, though she was not sure whether from fear of being caught by Eustace or being overturned in a pony cart. By the time they reached the docks, she was just happy to be alive and able to jump down from the cart without injury.

"The *Venture* is in the harbor. Step lively. I've got to get this back or I'll get a whipping," the boy cried with a wide grin.

"Thank you!" called Emma, having just enough time to grab her trunk before the boy snapped the reins once more and was gone. She turned toward the harbor, freezing salt spray stinging her eyes. Ships of all shapes and sizes were anchored in the harbor. She wondered which one was the *Venture* and how she was to get to it.

She walked along the sea wall, struggling with her large trunk. A group of women, laughing and talking, were walking toward her at a fast pace.

"Excuse me," Emma said to a woman with heavily rouged cheeks and a bright-yellow gown. "Could you tell me which of these ships is the *Venture* and how I might get to it?"

"Don't know the names, my sweet," she replied in a drawl. "But if ye want to get to a ship, ye got to take the bumboat."

"*Bum*boat?" asked Emma.

The women all laughed at her confusion and made some remarks about the anatomy of sailors that were certainly not for maidenly ears.

"It's what the gigs are called what take folk to the ships in the harbor. You coming?" asked a young woman with short-cropped, black hair.

Emma joined them, and they led her down to a dock, where gigs were rowed back and forth. One was just leaving, and the women all called out for it to hold and scrambled into the wooden boat, crowded with sailors, women, and even a few children. Everyone seemed to be talking at once, with the patrons who were there earlier protesting the addition of the women.

"Make room! Make room!" demanded a sailor holding

the oars. "You coming?" he asked Emma, beginning
to push away from the dock.

"Emma! Come back here at once!" Eustace was
running down the dock after her.

"Yes!" She jumped into the boat, trunk and all, to
the shouts and curses of the people in the boat. She
ended up crammed in between two of the women as
they all used her trunk as a seat. The man pushed off
and Emma struggled to maintain her balance as the
small gig bounced in the waves, splashing everyone
with freezing spray.

"Stop! Come back here at once!" yelled Eustace,
panting at the end of the dock.

"No more room! Wait for the next one!" called the
sailor, and the two-man crew set to the oars, rowing
out into the harbor.

"Emma! Emma, you come back, or I swear, you
shall be sorry!" yelled Eustace.

"She don't want you no more!" shouted one of the
women.

"You ain't nothing to her no more!" shouted
another, along with a variety of insults and uproarious
laughter from the women.

Eustace sputtered and cursed and paced on the
dock. Had it not been for the freezing water, Emma
was convinced he would have jumped in after her.

"There now," reassured the woman in the bright
yellow on her right, patting her shoulder. "He can't
hurt you anymore."

Emma took a shaky breath. "Thank you. I…I
cannot fall into his control."

"No, not a prig like him. Right flash cove," said

the woman with cropped hair on her left. If Emma didn't understand everything she said, at least it sounded sympathetic.

"I am trying to reach the *Venture*," she said to the men at the oars.

"Outta luck there, missy. She sailed out an hour ago," replied the sailor at the oars.

"The ship left?" Emma once again felt she was sinking. She took a stuttered breath. She knew that she was not supposed to contact Dare, but these were desperate times. "Could you take me to the *Lady Kate* instead?"

"The *Lady Kate* just set sail herself. Made a mess of it," he added with a laugh.

Emma's heart beat loudly in her ears. What was she going to do now? She could not return to the dock. Though she could no longer hear him, she could still see the dark figure of Eustace Ludlow pacing the dock.

"Aww, now, don't be upset. Was your man on one of those ships?" asked the woman with black hair.

"He... Well, yes." Emma's heart felt heavy at the thought that Dare was gone. "I am not sure what I am to do next."

"Come with us!" declared the woman in yellow. "A face like yers could make a fortune."

"Awww, no," argued her companion. "Can't you see she ain't no light-skirt?"

"Excuse me, miss," said a man in the bow of the gig with a weatherworn face and white, straggly hair sticking out of a blue cap. "Seems you're a bit distressed."

"Yes, I have missed my friends who have sailed on the *Venture*, and now I am not sure what to do."

Emma forced herself to smile. "Forgive me for burdening you with my troubles, sir."

"I am Captain Grimes, happy to be of service to such a fine lady as yourself. Why, I warrant I could get you to the *Venture*."

"You could? But how?"

"Ah, she be a large ship. I got me a smaller frigate. No doubt I could catch up with them before the sun sets. They do it all the time. Takes them bigger ships a while to navigate out of the harbor."

"Does it?" Hope crept up. "I do greatly appreciate the offer, but...forgive me, Captain, but you are unknown to me. I fear protocol is not on our side."

"I understand, understand completely. Wouldn't want me own daughters to run off with some strange sea captain. Wouldn't be right—no, not right at all. I only offered because I thought I could be of service."

"He might be able to help," whispered the woman beside her with the cropped hair.

"Or make you his doxy," countered the woman in yellow.

"Too old," argued her friend.

"Them's the worst. They can be a randy lot, them old salts."

"Awww, he looks nice. I'd go wi' him."

"You'd go wi' anyone."

Emma considered what other options she might have, but her choices were few. She could begin a new occupation with the women beside her or remain in the boat and meet Eustace when she returned to the dock. He was so angry she feared she might not live to see the asylum. No, she could not do either of those.

"Did you say we could meet with the *Venture* before nightfall?" she called to Captain Grimes.

"Have you sitting down with your friends to supper." The man gave her a creased smile, rows of wrinkles forming around his mouth. He did seem a kindly man. It may be unorthodox, but given her current predicament, it was her best choice.

"Thank you for your assistance, Captain Grimes. I do hope we can overtake the *Venture* as quick as can be." She was certain Darington would be angry to see her in such circumstances, but she was stuck taking her chances with Captain Grimes.

Thirty-two

DARE SHRUGGED OFF THE INAUSPICIOUS START AND focused on catching his quarry. They rounded the Isle of Wight and sailed into the channel. Far on the horizon were two ships. One of them had to be the *Kestrel.*

He took a bearing and set his course. Attacking a merchant vessel flying an American flag was against maritime law. He would face charges unless he could prove his claim that the captain was the traitor Harcourt—something that would be difficult.

No matter. Dare would face Harcourt and deal with the consequences later. There was no other option. If he had to break every naval law and become the basest of pirates, he would do it.

Dare walked to the worn wood railing of the quarterdeck. At least he had the *Lady Kate.* He had never captained a ship in which he had more confidence. She was fast, sure, and surprisingly strong. She could be a bit temperamental if not treated right, but for those who knew their craft, the *Lady Kate* was the best ship a captain could want.

"Let them fly. Full sheets to the wind," Darington commanded.

"Stiff wind," commented his first mate, giving voice to his concerns.

"You doubt my powers of observation, Mr. Everett?" Dare gave him a cold look.

"Nay, Cap'n. Full sheets to the wind!" called the first mate. The cries were taken up and the top sails unfurled without further incident.

The *Lady Kate* crested and fell as she sliced through the waves. Dare held his ground as the ship creaked loudly and tilted hard to the port side. A few of the crew looked at each other as they grabbed the railing, and Dare felt more than one pair of eyes on him, silently asking if he was trying to kill them within a league of the shore.

Dare ignored them. He knew what his *Kate* could do.

He lifted a glass and swept the horizon for a glimpse of his quarry and narrowed in on a speck on the horizon. Determination soared. He was close to ending Harcourt's reign of terror. Even pushing their speed, night would fall before they caught up with the *Kestrel*. That could be beneficial, since Harcourt would not be able to identify the *Lady Kate* in the darkness and be warned that Dare was on the hunt. This time, Dare had the upper hand.

The shouts and guffaws of some of his unruly men caught his attention, and he glared at the men in question. They were staring at another ship that had emerged from the harbor into the channel. This was not the conduct he appreciated in a controlled crew. He turned back to the horizon but was distracted by shouts of, "Get her! Don't let her go! I'll take you, sweetheart."

Dare raised an eyebrow to Everett, who explained. "Apparently there is a commotion aboard the *Rooster*. A woman is being chased across decks."

Finally, out of sheer curiosity, Dare turned his glass to the *Rooster* behind them. He focused on the form of a woman, struggling in the arms of a sailor.

Dare's blood ran to ice.

It was Emma St. James.

∽

"Let's get to know each other better."

Emma perched on a chair in Captain Grimes's quarters. Warning bells rang through her mind, but since they were heading out to sea, there was precious little she could do about it now.

"Please make yourself at ease." The captain smiled at her in a manner that was decidedly unkind. Emma feared she had made a horrible mistake.

"I would like to return to my ship, if you please," said Emma firmly.

"Ah, now, a prime article like you? You'll be much happier here wi' me."

"No! I must insist that you either help me reach my ship, or return me to the shore. Let me be clear: I do not wish for your advances." Emma's heart beat in her throat.

"Ah, now, I know I got some years on me, but once you get to know me, you'll like me better." The captain moved his chair closer and put a hand on her knee, slowly sliding it up her thigh and squeezing.

Emma stared at the man's hand on her thigh, too shocked and scared to move. Silently, she prayed as the man leaned closer, the smell of whiskey on his breath. She had always believed that the Lord was with her, that he would save her. She had always tried to do the right thing. And look what it got her. She was trapped on a strange boat, with some lecherous captain, and none of it was fair.

There could only be one conclusion. Either God wasn't watching, or he just didn't care. Perhaps Dare had been right all along.

Tears sprang to her eyes. More from the thought that the Lord had abandoned her at the moment she needed divine protection most, than at the prospect of being mauled by some elderly lecher.

Emma blinked back the tears in disgust. If this is what being good got her, it was time to start being bad. A cold, calculating chill spread through her, starting with her soul. She looked at the captain and forced a smile. "Why, Captain, I thought you would never ask. Can you assure our privacy?" She motioned to the cabin door.

"No one will disturb us."

"Oh, but I do prefer a locked door."

"Well, what the lady wants, the lady gets," said Captain Grimes, wiping a line of drool from his mouth. He stood and walked to the cabin door, and she took the opportunity of his momentary distraction to grab the heavy brass lantern off the table and creep up behind him. Her heart pounded, but she silenced it with disgust. She would not be anyone's toy to use and throw away.

Emma paused for a moment, but a cold fury at everything that had befallen her suddenly flooded her, starting with the accident that claimed her father's life, the horrid way her stepfamily had treated her, the abuse hurled at her by Eustace on the dock, and ending with this man who could meet a vulnerable young woman and think only of how he could use her for his own despicable advantage.

With an unladylike grunt, she swung the heavy lantern.

"That should keep us—oh!" The man turned around just as the lantern glanced off the side of his head, bringing him down.

Emma gulped air, staring at the man at her feet. She felt an instant pull to tend the cut on his head but pushed down the treacherous thought. She was going to look out for her own interests now. The only hope she had was to somehow hail someone on the shore and get them to rescue her.

To signal for help meant going up to the deck with all the sailors. She took a steeling breath. Hiding here would not help her. She had to get off the ship. She held her back straight and wiped tears from her eyes. She would not cry before these men. This was her last shot. A long one, but it was all she had.

She unlocked and opened the door to the cabin and walked boldly out, leaving the body of the still-breathing captain on the floor, shutting the door behind her. She held her skirts out of the way and climbed up steep, narrow steps to the deck. Immediately, her presence was noted.

"Hey there!"

"What's doing, pretty lady?"

"Come to spend some time with me?"

A man who looked to be in charge grabbed her arm with a fierce scowl. "What are you doing up here? Get back below. You're distracting the crew."

Emma held up her chin. "The captain is resting and gave me leave to get some fresh air."

The man did not release her, but the glint in his eye turned mercurial. "He done wi' you, eh? You can let me have a turn."

Emma wrenched her arm from his gasp. "You best take that up with the captain. He wanted me back within the quarter hour."

The man glared but stepped back, and Emma quickly moved away. She walked along the length of the ship, all the while conscious of the heated stares of the men. She needed to escape…but how? She proceeded to the bow of the ship and squinted into the setting sun. She leaned against the railing, holding on as the ship gently rolled and pitched. Ahead of her she saw the outline of a ship. She could not identify it, but they were close enough that she could see the individual men as dark silhouettes against the sun, attending to their duties. Since she could see them, they must be able to see her. But how to hail them?

She removed her bonnet and started to wave it back and forth, trying to catch the attention of the men of the far ship, without calling attention to herself. Of course this was no use, for immediately the men on the *Rooster* started to comment on her behavior.

"What's she doing?"

"What you want, sweetheart?"

"I think she wants someone on that ship."

"I got everything you need. Just lift your skirts and I'll show you."

"I gots to have a turn too!"

"Don't worry. The captain probably let her come on deck so we all can have a turn."

Emma waved her bonnet furiously, trying to ignore the comments behind her. She took a chance and, holding tight with her white-gloved hand to some of the rigging, she pulled herself up until she was standing on the railing and waved her bonnet back and forth, the ribbons streaming in the wind. It was no use to scream, for they could not hear her. She was not even certain that they could see her.

The ship pitched in the rolling waves, and she grabbed the rigging with both hands, her bonnet falling into the sea. She watched as it fell gracefully into the ocean and was immediately overrun by the bow of the ship, disappearing from sight. Would she be next?

She was grabbed from behind and screamed as she was wrenched off the rail and thrown down on deck in a heap. She rolled back to face her attacker. It was the captain, with murder in his eyes and a stream of blood running down the side of his face.

"Look what you did to me, wench!" the captain shouted. "You gonna regret that, I swear you will."

Emma struggled to her feet and ran away from him, desperate to escape, terror coursing through her. Her feet flew down the deck to the other end of the ship, though she knew with cold dread that there was nowhere to go. There was only one way to prevent her body from being used by these men. She would run off the back of the ship.

The desperateness of the situation and her response shocked her, but she ran on. She was going to use her last seconds of freedom to make the only choice she had left to her. She was going to jump and try somehow to swim to shore. She knew she would most likely drown.

She reached the back of the ship and climbed up the railing on the stern. Her skirts got tangled, and she wrenched them free, but before she could jump, more hands grabbed her from behind and dragged her off the railing. She fought them off with desperation, tears streaming down her face, unable to see what she was doing or who she hit.

"Get her!"

"Tame that hellcat."

"I likes 'em feisty!"

Emma punched and kicked and somehow managed to wrench herself free and run along the length of the boat once more toward the bow. The men laughed and let her go, enjoying her panic. She turned to the side and blinked back her tears, looking to the other ship. Had they seen her? Did they even care? They sailed along without notice.

No one was going to help her now.

Once more, she pulled herself over the side, and once more, rough hands dragged her back, laughing when she struck at them, mocking her misery.

Suddenly, an explosive noise shocked everyone into stunned silence. They all looked over at the far ship, which was coming about and drawing near.

"What are they doing?"

"They shot at us."

"Take that doxy down and lock her in my cabin. I'll deal with the wench later," growled the captain.

Once more, hands were all over her, grabbing, pulling, squeezing, forcing her down the hatch. She was shoved into the captain's cabin and the hatch slammed behind her.

Had the other ship seen her? Were they coming to rescue her or just doing some military exercises? Repenting her earlier lapse of faith, she sank to her knees and prayed.

She could hear men's shouting above her and she wondered what was happening. The ship shuddered and bounced awkwardly in the waves. An unlatched window swung open.

Emma went to the window and looked out. Land was still in sight. Could she swim to it? She did know how to swim, thanks to her local pond and a father who thought it a harmless amusement. But could she survive the icy winter waves?

She knew her chances were slim, but her chances with the captain were slimmer. She quickly divested herself of her gown, knowing it would only drag her under. She searched the room for something that would float.

She would wait to see who entered the cabin next. If she were rescued, she would explain why she was in her chemise later. If it were Captain Grimes...she would jump.

Thirty-three

"MR. EVERETT, TELL ME, DID THE *ROOSTER* OFFLOAD her cargo when she was in port?" Dare asked evenly, making an effort to keep his voice calm.

"I do not believe so."

"Mr. Everett, think very carefully, for your answer may be the difference of your life or hanging from a yardarm. Did or did not the *Rooster* offload her cargo?"

Everett paled at the seriousness of his comment. "No, they did not. At least, not that I noticed."

"Let us hope you are right. All hands, prepare to come about."

"But...what are we...?"

Dare glared at Everett, who stifled the question. He passed on the order, and the men, though confused, obeyed. Dare feared they were more curious than faithful, but it would have to do. He took one last, fleeting glance at the *Kestrel* on the horizon. He did not wish to let go of his one chance, but given the choice, he would protect his Emma.

Hold on, Emma. Keep fighting. I'm on my way.

"All hands, come about!" shouted Dare.

Lord, please protect her. Keep her safe. And please let that hold be full! It was the first prayer he had said in a very long time. For some reason, he believed God might hear him now, for God would surely want to help Emma. Emma trusted the Lord, and Dare trusted Emma, thus Dare's sudden turn to faith.

The ship turned more sloppily than Dare would have liked, but it was done, and they began sailing toward the *Rooster*.

"All hands to quarters!"

Everett saw it done but came close to whisper, "What are we doing, Cap'n?"

"I will ensure the record shows that you have counseled me against this," said Dare, striding to his cabin to secure his sword and a brace of pistols.

"Against what?" asked Everett, strapping on his own sword and pistol, and following Dare back onto the deck.

"Mr. Bean," Dare called to the older man who had been made master gunner. "Run out your gun and prime."

"You want me to shoot on an English ship?" Even Tom Bean was shocked.

"I expect you to follow orders."

Everett's eyes widened. "Cap'n Dare—"

"Duly noted, Mr. Everett," said Dare to his first mate in an undertone. He turned and continued to shout orders to the master gunner. "Let's get the attention of the *Rooster*. Aim out to sea. Fire!"

A loud boom echoed across the water, and smoke rolled down the deck. He was committed now.

"Hail the *Rooster* and tell her to drop sail and prepare to be boarded," commanded Darington.

"Heaven's bells, we're still within sight of the shore," pleaded Everett.

"Can't be helped."

"They ain't slowing," called Pricket. "Making a run for it."

"Put one over the bow, if you please, Mr. Bean," said Dare calmly, hoping his crew were better gunners than sailors.

A loud blast rocked the ship and a cannonball sailed across the deck of the *Rooster*, splintering a railing and causing the captain and crew to hit the deck.

"I said over the bow, Mr. Bean," growled Dare.

"Sorry, Captain!"

"Well, at least we have his full attention," Dare muttered. "Put us alongside her. Prepare to board." Dare raised an eyebrow as his first mate crossed himself. "Wasn't aware you were a Papist."

"I'm not, but I'm thinking of converting. You've gone mad."

Dare was not surprised his first mate was baffled by this sudden attack on the *Rooster*. It was so out of character for himself he hardly knew what he was doing. He wanted to explain about Emma, but for her own privacy and reputation, he could not say a word.

His mercenary crew, on the other hand, nodded and smiled. Perhaps they were even a bit impressed. They had been promised evil deeds, but none had anticipated their dive into criminality would proceed quite so quickly and without even leaving sight of the shore.

The *Rooster* dropped her sails.

"I'm Captain Grimes of the *Rooster*. What the hell do you think you're doing?" demanded the captain, who stormed back and forth, a trickle of red blood down the right side of his face. Had they done that or Emma?

Dare grasped his sword with a viselike grip. If Emma was hurt, Captain Grimes would die. "I am Captain Lord Darington of the *Lady Kate*. By the right of the King, I demand you allow me to board and inspect your ship for contraband. Refusal will be taken as an act of aggression and I will respond accordingly."

"You got no right to board this ship!" yelled the captain.

It was the truth, but Dare proceeded anyway, bringing them alongside the *Rooster*. "Surrender your ship!" Dare had no idea if they would put up a fight, but he was ready for anything. The only thing worse than being a pirate was to be a bad one.

Whatever happened, he would get Emma to safety. Nothing else mattered. She had been dragged belowdecks and he had not seen her again. If any one of those dogs was inconveniencing her in any manner, he had no qualms over killing them.

"What is the meaning of this?" demanded Captain Grimes, wiping the sweat and the blood from his face. "This is an outrage!"

"Surrender your ship!" Dare demanded again.

"Have ye gone mad? Aye, I surrender. I surrender! But I swear the admiralty courts will hear of this!"

Dare turned to his crew, who lined the railing of his ship, ready for him to give the order to attack. From the glint of glee in their eyes, they were ready for a fight. "The *Rooster* has surrendered. Anyone who does not respect this surrender will be strung up from the yardarm." The last thing he needed was a fight between the crews. "We are going to board the *Rooster* and take her cargo, and we're going to do it without violence. Is that clear?"

This disappointed his crew, but they grudgingly nodded their heads.

"Prepare to board!" commanded Dare.

When it came to boarding ships, his questionable crew was well skilled. Grappling hooks flew, and they neatly pulled the ship to theirs. Dare jumped on board, followed by his boarding party. He towered over the sweating Captain Grimes.

"I am Captain Lord Darington," said Dare coolly. "I have reason to believe you are in possession of goods smuggled from our sworn enemy, France."

"I... That is a lie... You cannot board this ship!" spat Grimes.

"I have already boarded this ship. I have the right to search and seize any goods smuggled into the country and to take the captain back to face justice."

"I... But..." the captain sputtered, his face turning a shade of magenta and then slightly green. Dare might have had sympathy for the man had he not seen the man's hands on his Emma.

"Search the ship!" Dare commanded and unleashed his swarm of unsavory characters. "No crew member or passenger is to be harmed."

"You cannot do this," said Captain Grimes, but he was much less sure of himself.

"The admiralty is concerned with flagrant disregard

for the embargo. It has determined to increase patrols and bring captains who traffic in smuggling to justice."

Captain Grimes turned a shade of sickly green.

"How many souls have you on board?" Dare asked the man quickly. "Have you any passengers?"

"There be forty crew and…and one passenger."

"Where is this passenger?" Dare took a step closer, his hand on his pistol.

"What can this have to do with her?"

"She may be a witness to these proceedings. Where is she?" Dare demanded, his voice rising.

"Looks like there be crates of French wine in the hold," shouted up a man.

"French wine?" Dare turned to Grimes.

"I…I can explain."

"Save it for your trial. I shall arrest you on grounds of treason."

"Treason!" The captain went almost as white as a sheet.

"Aye, unless I can speak to your passenger. Witness statement. Very important. Might be able to find extenuating circumstances in these cases."

"I…I… But …"

Dare heard a female scream and pushed past the captain, catapulting himself down the hatch, toward the direction of the sound. He burst into the cabin to find Emma, wearing nothing but a thin chemise, fighting off one of his own men.

Dare grabbed the man, wrenching him from Emma and sending him flying out the door.

"But she's the ladybird," defended the man. "She was trying to jump from the window."

"Remove yourself from my sight before I kill you!" Dare slammed the door in the face of the man.

Dare stared at Emma with a heart beating faster than he could ever remember. She was barely clothed. "Are you all right? Did they hurt you?"

"Dare?" Emma gaped at him. "I…I am all right. How are you here?"

"Saw you on the deck and so I had to take the ship. Your clothes…"

"I was going to jump and try to swim for it, but I lost my nerve at the last second, and that man grabbed me."

"You were going to swim?" His Emma was going to drown herself?

Emma shrugged "You were right. God doesn't care."

His heart sank. He took her hands in his, needing her not to abandon her faith that had given him strength. "No, no, you are the one who was right. I prayed today that I could see you safe."

"You…prayed?"

"Yes. If you knew me better, you would know that to be a miracle itself. But now I need to keep you safe."

"That man, he is on your crew?"

"Yes." Dare realized that he could not walk her up to the decks and onto his ship. His own crew would mutiny to get their hands on her. He could hear more men outside the cabin door. No doubt the sailor had told others of Emma's presence. He needed to keep her safe.

"Do you trust me?" Dare moved fast, seeing her trunk and opening it.

"I…I suppose so."

He pulled out medical books and some other miscellaneous items to make room. This had to work. "Please do as I say and whatever you do, do not say a word."

"But what are you—"

"Get in the trunk."

"What?" She was half-dressed and confused, but he had no time to explain. He heard the voices of men outside the door.

"She's in there!"

The shouts from the men were followed by the pounding of feet down the hatch.

"Damn!" swore Dare, and then wanted to curse again at himself, for Emma's blue eyes were wide with fear. "Scream."

"What? Why?" she asked, backing away from him.

"Scream!" he hissed and closed the distance between them and picked her up.

She yelped with surprise. He put her down feet first in the trunk and pushed. She screamed, the panic sounding all too real. He was frightening her and he hated himself, but he needed to keep her safe, and this was the best he could do.

"I will protect you. Not another sound," he hissed in her ear and, with one final shove, closed the trunk. He grabbed the books he had taken from the trunk and threw them overboard with a decided plunk.

Dare rushed to the door and faced the men. "Quick! She jumped overboard. Do you see her?" he demanded.

"Jump? Why she do that?"

"Probably saw your ugly face," replied another.

The men ran to the deck with calls of "man over-board" followed by "doxy overboard."

"Get the cargo. Seize the wine!" demanded Dare. This was followed by whoops from the men, shouting and hollering.

"What did you do wi' my company?" Captain Grimes appeared in the cabin door, huffing for breath.

"She is no longer your concern," said Dare coolly. "I will be reporting your treasonous actions to the port authority. 'Tis possibly a hanging offense."

The man put his hand to his throat. "Now I ain't done anything worse than what many others have done. Why, the admiral himself likes a glass o' wine."

"Perhaps you will remind him of that fact once the rope is around your neck."

"No, now, please, sir. I am an honest smuggler I am. I've got a family what depends upon me."

"My condolences. I might be able to look the other way and not say a word if you will surrender your cargo and forget this ever happened."

"Yes, sir. Very good, sir."

"Remember, never speak of it, for if you do, I will have to make my full report."

"Aye, Captain. Fully understand." Captain Grimes mopped his face, wiping away the sweat and blood that trickled down.

"I will be taking the poor girl's things too. Must be returned to her kin. Mr. Pricket, your hand with this chest."

Dare heaved the chest and carried it with his crew-man carefully over to his ship.

"This is a heavy chest," said Pricket, his eyes gleaming with greed. "I wonder what's inside?"

Dare needed to get Emma out of the chest and hidden somewhere without being seen. If his men knew he was concealing a half-dressed young woman on board, they would mutiny without thinking twice.

Thirty-four

EMMA WAS TRAPPED. SHE WAS CRAMMED IN HER OWN large trunk, on top of her gowns and medical kit. Was Dare trying to help her? Why had he stuffed her in a crate? Nothing was making sense and she was having a difficult time catching her breath.

Should she try to break free? Pound on the lid until someone released her? Panic surged through her. She needed to get out!

The lid of the trunk suddenly lifted, and Dare's face appeared once more. "Stay hidden. I swear I will see you safe or die in the trying."

Emma took a breath and only had a second to shift her position before the lid was shut once more. The sounds became muffled as she tried to ascertain what was happening. If Dare was there to rescue her, why did she need to hide? Something was very wrong. No, everything was very wrong.

Voices drew near, commands were barked, and the chest was lifted up and swung around. She clenched her jaw tight to avoid screaming and giving herself away. One side of the trunk dropped, and she banged her head against the side. She bit her tongue to keep from crying out.

Dare cursed at someone, using a tone and language she had never heard from him before. Another man responded in an apologetic manner, and her trunk was lifted again. She had no choice but to trust Dare, and she prayed he knew what to do and would keep her safe. The trunk swayed again, and she began to pray earnestly that she would not be dropped into the ocean. Her pulse pounded so loud in her ears she feared it could be heard by the men outside. She almost wanted to scream just so she could be released from her prison. Her coffin.

The trunk was moved and jostled and tipped until she felt she could take it no longer. Dare's voice came again, near yet muffled, and she focused on the sound of it. As long as she could hear him, she had hope. He was there. It was all she had to hold on to.

At last, the trunk was set down onto solid ground. "Oh!" cried Emma when the lid of the trunk finally swung open and she was allowed a breath of fresh air. Immediately, a hand clamped down over her mouth.

Emma stared into the eyes of a man she thought she knew. Captain Lord Darington glared back at her with a ferocity she had never before seen. His hand over her mouth was rough, and he made no attempt to be gentle about it. Dare demanded silence, and even if she not been inclined to comply, the shock of seeing such a wild man would have stunned her into remaining mute.

Dare pulled her from the trunk, glancing over his shoulder. She was in a different ship's cabin and she guessed Dare had taken her on board the *Lady Kate*. They were alone in what appeared to be the captain's dayroom, the door shut and bolted. Emma was relieved to be out of the trunk and away from Captain Grimes, but her hope that she was now in safe hands was lessened greatly by the unorthodox manner of her arrival on board and the stern manner of her reception.

He drew her to himself, so close her bosom pressed up against his chest in a manner that would have made her gasp had she not feared reprisal for a sound.

"Not a word," he breathed into her ear in so low a register she could barely make out the words. It was an unnecessary rejoinder, since he had made his wishes quite known.

She gave a quick nod of understanding as a knock came to the door. Before she could react, Dare grabbed her elbow and shoved her through a narrow side door with a hatch so low they both had to duck their heads to get through. The smaller cabin appeared to be Dare's private quarters. He gave her an ominous look and shut the door in her face.

Emma took a deep breath and leaned on the nearest object for support, only to jump back when she realized she was resting on the barrel of a cannon.

"Enter!" came Dare's voice, and she could hear a man enter the captain's dayroom. She pressed her ear to the door, trying to discern what was going on around her and why her entry onto Dare's ship had taken place in such a clandestine and uncomfortable manner.

"Mr. Pricket, we must take inventory of the transferred cargo."

"Aye, Cap'n, the tally's underway," the man replied with confidence.

"I hope by honest men, if they can be found on this ship."

"As honest as we have," replied Pricket with less certainty.

"Do you know your letters, sir?" asked the captain.

"Aye, sir, for me job, I can function."

"Good. This trunk needs to be inventoried with the rest. Take note, if you please."

"Aye, sir."

"Let the log show six gowns of various types, one coat—"

"That's a pelisse, Cap'n, and a nice one. And that one there is a ball gown, while those two are day gowns," said Mr. Pricket with surprising accuracy.

Emma's face heated substantially as she listened to the men describe her belongings. The thought that her personal effects were being inventoried by Darington and a common sailor sent her heart racing into some sort of palpitation.

"Thank you, Mr. Pricket," replied Dare in quelling tones. "There are additionally two wraps and sundry unmentionables."

"Oh, now, let me see those ladybird's knickers. Oh, she was a fancy thing, weren't she?"

"Mr. Pricket!"

Emma feared she might expire on the spot while the men inspected her unmentionables.

"Oh, lacy, they are. Good quality. You think she was one of those fancy high fliers? These is nice things. She weren't no wharf wench."

"Enough, Mr. Pricket!" said Dare in a warning tone.

"Aye, Cap'n."

"Let the log show a medical kit and articles for a lady's toilet. Do we have a surgeon aboard?"

"No, ain't got no bone setters or limb launchers."

"Then I will keep these items here and use the medical kit to treat ailments as necessary and to the best of my ability."

"Very good, Cap'n."

The voices went silent, and Emma leaned against a small desk for stability. Her hands shook and her legs threatened to buckle. The captain's quarters consisted of a small, unadorned room containing a built-in bed, a small desk, a chair…and a cannon.

The door opened once more and Dare stood before her. She had thought she could not blush any more, but at the sight of him, her cheeks burned. Not only had her unmentionables been inspected by Darington, but she was also still dressed only in her thin chemise.

Dare opened his mouth and then shut it again. It was the first time she had seen him unsure since her awkward arrival. For her part, she was too mortified to speak. He leaned in close to her ear, his cheek brushing momentarily across hers. Her heart, which had been beating at a gallop, skipped a beat and she pressed her hand to her chest.

"I do apologize," he whispered in her ear. "It was against protocol to bring a trunk into my private quarters. Makes the men think I'm hiding something. Can't have them sneaking in to look at what's inside."

Emma nodded, trying to understand. She turned

her head to whisper back into his ear and brushed her lips across his jawline in the process. It was accidental, but the contact sent thrilling ripples through her. "Why put me in the trunk?"

He clenched his jaw before leaning back toward her to answer. "These are men without scruple. If they saw you so attired, they would take you for... They would not understand. They would not show restraint. Must keep your reputation intact and can't do that if they know you're here. Best to keep you hidden until I can return you to shore."

"Have you settled accounts already with Harcourt?"

Dare shook his head. "I tracked him to the *Kestrel*."

"You found him?"

"Yes, I hope so. We were following him, but lost him..."

"Because you stopped to rescue me." Realization dawned at what Dare had given up to attack a British ship and save her. "No, you must go on to find him. Heaven only knows when you could find him again and what more trouble he could make for your family if you do not stop him now."

Dare shook his head with grim determination. "I must set you safe on shore in Portsmouth. But why... why were you on the *Rooster*?" Dare gave her an anxious glare.

Shame at being found in such a compromising position pricked at her skin. With as few words as possible, not wanting to linger on the unfortunate situation, she explained how running into her step-brother had led to the unfortunate decision to put her faith in Captain Grimes.

"Oh, Emma," whispered Dare, his breath hot on her neck. "I should not have left you."

Her body shivered in response. Immediately, he grabbed a folded blanket from his bed and wrapped it around her. She breathed in his scent, knowing it was only making her body tremble even more.

"I shall have you back to port soon," he reassured, standing close so his faint whisper to her could be heard.

It was Emma's turn to shake her head firmly. "But I cannot go back to Portsmouth. Eustace is looking for me."

"My sister can—"

"Your sister is much engaged at present, and I would not think of interfering with her wedding plans. Besides, if you return now, Harcourt will get away."

"I fear that has already occurred, so it does not matter."

"No, I refuse to give up. Did you not tell me the *Lady Kate* was one of the fastest ships on the seas? Could you catch up to him?"

Dare paused. "It is too dangerous for you."

"I fear it will be dangerous for me, and all of us, if we do not. What is to keep him from coming back and effecting revenge against you again, and me as well, since he knows my attachment...my connection with you?" Emma stuttered, not sure how to phrase her relationship with the Earl of Darington.

"I cannot put you at risk. I had to take on a new crew, one that I do not trust. You are not safe if they find you."

"I trust you can keep me safe." Emma's hand brushed against his as they stood near. She trailed a finger across his hand and he took it in his.

Dare looked down, shaking his head.

Emma knew what she needed to do. She had questioned her faith in a moment of desperation, but seeing Dare restored it once more.

"God has brought you to rescue me twice, but I cannot think that it was done to prevent you from confronting Harcourt. I have faith that I will be safe with you. I fear I must insist that you apprehend the criminal Harcourt." Emma spoke in a hushed whisper, trying to keep her words soft yet convey her determination.

Dare took a deep breath. "If we go after him, you will not be safe."

"There is nowhere safer for me than with you," she replied. She had fallen into doubt today; she would not do it again.

He shook his head, but he was clearly torn. "I cannot assure your safety."

"Truly, only the Lord can do that. You prayed today, and it seems your prayers were answered. Maybe you should do it more often."

"Maybe." He bowed his head, touching his forehead to hers. "I hope going after Harcourt is the right choice. Stay hidden." He gave her hand a slight squeeze before releasing her.

Dare straightened and his face hardened into a cold mask. He brought her trunk into his quarters and, with a final grim-faced nod, locked her in without further commentary.

Emma took a long, shaky breath and collapsed onto the bed. She stared at the long, iron barrel of the cannon. She was committed now.

Thirty-five

DARE RETURNED TO DECK AND WAS IMMEDIATELY consumed with responsibilities. His crew was in high glee that he had managed to rob a smuggler while convincing the man Dare was doing him a favor. Whatever might come next, at least Dare had won their immediate approval and perhaps a bit of their loyalty. Whether that appreciation would extend to accepting a young female passenger on board was not something he wished to test.

He gave the order to turn the ship back toward the setting sun. He scanned the horizon for anything that might be a speck of the *Kestrel* but saw nothing. Once again, he gave the order to press for speed and the *Lady Kate* groaned under the strain but held steady as she flew across the waves.

Working some mental calculations, Dare attempted to estimate when he would catch up to the *Kestrel*, if he could ever find her again. He did not have long to ponder as a fight broke out over some of the men trying to sneak into the wine and his presence was immediately required.

Dare calmed the crew and established discipline and order, but he could not shake the ever-present awareness that Emma was on board. He could not stop thinking of her. Emma in her chemise. A very thin chemise.

"One of those sea dogs has taken his hand to cooking," said Everett, strolling up to him on the quarterdeck. "Supper is ready, in whatever form that might take."

Supper. Emma would want to eat. Dare considered taking Everett into his confidence. He had no qualms about her safety in his presence. Yet that would compromise her reputation and put Everett in the awkward position of having to lie to conceal Dare's secret. Everett was an honest young man, and Dare feared he might unconsciously give something away. It would be safer for everyone if Everett did not know.

"Thank you, Mr. Everett. I am fatigued from today's excitement. I believe I shall take my supper alone in my cabin tonight."

"Oh, yes, I understand." The disappointment in Everett's face was clear. "Some doings today."

Dare rested a hand briefly on the man's shoulder. "Thank you for your support. It means much to me." Everett was the one man on the ship he could trust.

"I'll sail with you, wherever you might go. You know that."

"I do and I thank you."

Dare retreated below, relaying the request for a hearty supper, claiming he had worked up an appetite, something that was not far from the truth, since he had not eaten since breakfast back at Greystone. He accepted his meal with appropriate resignation, telling the lad he would return the tray himself when he was through.

After the sailor left, he locked the main cabin door behind him and stared at the smaller, side door to his captain's quarters where Emma was hidden. He had known of officers and crew who attempted to sneak a girl on board, keeping her hidden until, invariably, she was discovered by someone unwilling to turn a blind eye. Now he was the one with a girl in his cabin—no, a true lady. What was he going to do next?

Dare rested his hand on the latch. She was in there. Miss Emma St. James. He was not sure if this was the worst or the best thing that had ever happened to him. He had wanted her back from the second he'd let her go…but had not imagined anything like this.

He unlocked the door and slowly opened it, pausing at the picture presented to him. Emma had donned a white frock and straightened herself into order. Her hair was smoothed back, but still, little curls managed to escape and frame her face. She sat primly on the chair by his desk, her hands folded neatly in her lap. Had it not been for the cannon with which he shared his cabin, she could have been in any drawing room anywhere in Mayfair.

He bowed low with a grimace, for his wound still pained him, and she gave him a slight incline of her head. He held out his hand and she took it, allowing him to lead her to the main cabin. His day cabin stretched the length of the ship and boasted a long oak table, polished smooth. Paned windows graced the length of the cabin, revealing a stretch of stars in the cloudless sky.

He silently pulled a chair for her and she sat before the table with the supper laid out for one. Supper consisted of some sort of stew, which he hoped she would find palatable. He sat beside her, motioning her to begin to eat.

It was a relief that the clandestine nature of her presence on board required their silence. It was so much easier for him without the expectation of conversation. Emma, however, was proving recalcitrant when it came to supper and refused to eat, motioning for him to go first.

Seeing that speech was required, Dare leaned forward and whispered in her ear, breathing in her scent and almost forgetting what he intended to say.

"I've already eaten. Please eat," he lied.

She raised an eyebrow, questioning his veracity, and his stomach chose that moment to betray him with a loud growl. She frowned and shoved the spoon at him.

He relented, seeing that he was not going to win, and took a hearty spoonful of the stew, pleased that it was reasonably edible. He handed her the spoon, since of course only one had been provided, and she took a bite of the stew, smiling her appreciation.

He buttered some bread and handed it to her, pleased that she accepted it with a bite. They took turns eating from the soup bowl and sharing the bread. There was one glass of wine, most likely from his recent smuggling acquisition, which they shared.

The intimacy of eating in silence, sharing a meal from the same bowl and glass struck him powerfully. He was not accustomed to happiness, but breaking

bread with Emma filled him with an easy content-
ment. When at last they had eaten their full, he was
still hungry for more—more Emma.

He was treading on dangerous ground, for he knew
she was trusting him to keep her safe. Still, when he
looked into her large, blue eyes or glanced down at
her generous décolletage, he could not keep his body
from desiring more.

They had been alone in a room before, even over-
night if one could count the time when he had been
shot and she performed surgery. But this was different.
He was recovered enough to act on his desires. There
was no chaperone. He needed to speak to her but realized, to do so, he needed to be close. And to be close
to her was dangerous. For him. For her.

He leaned toward her, her unique scent of lavender
soap filled him with longing. "Miss St. James," he
whispered, and then realized he had nothing more
to say. What could he say? He paused and the silence
stretched on awkwardly. He pulled back only to be
arrested by her wide eyes, staring at him intently. He
floundered, unsure.

She leaned forward and whispered in his ear, her
breath warm on his skin. "Thank you, Lord Darington,
for saving my life." She paused, then added, "Again.
I cannot think of what would have befallen me if you
had not interceded."

Dare nodded and leaned in, breathing faster than he
was accustomed to. "It was my pleasure." He paused
at the word, surprised it had emerged from his mouth.
It was truer than perhaps he should admit.

"It has put you in an awkward position." When she

leaned forward to whisper to him, her bosom brushed across the back of his hand as it rested on the table, driving out all logical thought. "This crew…it is new to you?"

He blinked at her, struggling to focus on her words, not the gentle pressure of her breast on his hand. He murmured an explanation of the loss of his crew and the unorthodox way he found a new one, though all his focus was on her bosom.

"Oh, that is terrible!" Emma leaned back, which Dare did not appreciate in the least. She leaned forward again and it was all he could do not to turn his hand over, so he could cup her breast. "I am sure you can inspire those men to reformed behavior."

Dare wished he could agree with her, but he was better acquainted with the sort of men who were now his crew.

"I am sure you will find Harcourt." Emma smiled with confidence.

The ocean was a big place, and all he could do was continue the course Harcourt had laid and hope for the best. His chances of success were slim, but if Miss Emma St. James would accompany him on his search, he would spend the rest of his life a happy man.

❧

Emma stared into the dark eyes of Captain Lord Darington knowing two things. First, she should not be with this stoic man alone in his cabin. And second, there was no place she would rather be.

It was getting late, the time when people considered going to bed. The ship had grown quiet, and it was clear the majority of the crew had retired for the night. There was only one bed in the side room. It was one thing to spend the night with an injured man who needed immediate medical attention. It was another to spend the night in a small cabin with a man who was fully functional…with only one bed.

"It is getting late." His breath was soft on her cheek. "You must need sleep."

Her pulse rose, and she glanced into his cabin, where the bed was clearly visible. Where were they going to sleep?

"I will sleep here in the ready room. You will take my cabin." He stood from the table, straight and tall. He offered his hand and she took it, allowing him to help her rise.

"No, I insist you must get your rest. You are still recovering." She stood on tiptoe to whisper back. It was impossible to be close enough to speak in a hushed tone without brushing up against him.

"It would be most improper." He looked down at her, and she realized her chest was brushing against his arm. There was no way to avoid it, and if she was honest, she hardly even tried.

"I do believe we left propriety behind a while ago, probably at the point you shoved me into a chest. Or possibly when we checked into the hotel under an assumed name as a married couple."

Dare sighed. "Definitely when I fired on an English ship within sight of the shore."

"Oh goodness! Shall you get in trouble for that?" Emma said, gasping and causing Dare to put a finger to his lips to remind her to keep her tone low.

He leaned down to her again. "Only if it is reported. They cannot report what I took without admitting they were smuggling, so I hope we are in the clear."

"You did it for me."

"Of course."

"But why?" Emma asked. She was pushing, but after all she had been through, she gave herself license.

Dare frowned at her. "You must think very little of me if you think I would see you in peril and not act to correct the situation."

"Yes, of course. You would do the same for any lady." Emma looked down. Of course he would protect any lady in distress. She knew that full well.

"I would," agreed Dare. "But…"

Emma looked up. "But?"

"But none would cause me such pain to see in a similar situation." Dare's demeanor had not changed, but the admission, Emma knew, was not a common one.

"Thank you."

"Emma," he whispered to her, his cheek brushing against hers.

She stepped closer and placed a hand on his chest. His arm naturally wrapped around her. She leaned into his embrace, resting her head on his chest. This was where she belonged. She belonged to Lord Darington.

She looked up, and he brushed his lips against hers. Tremors of excitement coursed through her. She was not satisfied with just a taste. She ran her hands up his dark-blue naval coat, twining them behind his neck. She pressed closer and their lips met, slowly at first, then with growing pressure and need.

Suddenly, Dare broke off the kiss and stepped back,

breathing hard. He shook his head and stepped to her side to speak. "Forgive me. I should not…will not take advantage."

"You did not."

"I did. Forgive me, I… You are too tempting… Must not." He shook his head and took her by the elbow, walking her into his cabin. He grabbed a blanket, then backed away from her into his ready room as though she might explode. "Stay there," he mouthed. "Sleep."

He closed the cabin door and locked it, then slid the key under the door. She picked up the key with a smile. No matter what happened, at least she was with the man she loved.

Her smile faded as she remembered she was hidden on a ship with treacherous men going after an even worse man. She stared at the locked door. She hoped she and Dare would make it through alive.

Thirty-six

Tap. Tap. Tap.

Emma woke to the sound of tapping. She was confused for a minute, trying to get her bearings. It was still dark, and she was sleeping in a small bunk in a room that was gently swaying.

Tap. Tap. Tap.

Emma sat up, her memory flooding back. She was on the *Lady Kate*, sleeping in Dare's bed.

Tap. Tap. Tap. Tap.

Emma grabbed the blanket and flung herself out of bed, having to catch herself, as she was not accustomed to the roll of the ship. She fumbled for the small key in the darkness and struggled to unlock the door.

Finally, she was able to open the door to find Dare in his shirtsleeves, illuminated by the orange light of a lantern. Of course she had seen him in states of much less dress, but still her breath caught.

"What is wrong?" she whispered.

"Nothing. Past four. Morning watch already up." He stood tall and solemn.

Emma rubbed her eyes. "You start the day at four in the morning?"

"Aye." Dare ducked his head as he entered. "Forgive me. Need fresh linen. Go back to sleep." He walked past her and opened his sea locker, pulling out some items.

Emma wrapped the blanket tighter around herself and stepped onto its edges to protect her bare feet from the cold. Watching him gather his clothes to dress for the morning was rather domestic. She liked it.

He leaned down to her, and she thought he was going to give her a kiss on the cheek, as if they were an old married couple. "Lock the door and stay hidden" was what he whispered instead.

"When will you return?" she whispered in return, feeling now she was becoming a little too domestic.

"Noon."

That meant she would have the next eight hours to sit by herself, locked in his small sleeping cabin. "Forgive me but where are my books?" asked Emma, hoping she was not pushing too much.

Dare frowned. "Books?"

"My medical books. And my novels. I would like to read to pass the time if you do not mind."

Dare's frown turned into a painful expression. "The books went overboard, so I could make room for you in the trunk."

Emma was silent for a moment. "I see. Well, it was done in my service, so I will thank you. Of course, now I will never know how the *Captain's Curse* ends." She meant it as a joke, but Dare took it to heart.

"If we survive, I shall buy you—"

"No, no, do not trouble yourself. I am indebted to you in ways I can never repay. I was only thinking of how to pass the time."

Dare frowned again and returned to his sea chest, retrieving a burgundy-leather-bound book. "This is my logbook. Only book I have. Very dull perhaps, but it records the actions I have taken."

"Oh, yes, that sounds interesting. What better than to read about a real naval adventure." Emma grabbed the book eagerly, relishing the opportunity to know her enigmatic sea captain better. She tried to take the book, but Dare held it fast, frowning at the leather volume.

"Did you not wish me to read it?" she asked, wondering why he had not let go.

"Yes. If you wish." He slowly peeled his fingers off the leather book and she took it. He continued to regard her and the book, so she opened it up, curious what he had written the day before.

"You did not write in your log yesterday," she observed.

"Much of yesterday will never go in the log," he muttered and with a last, longing glance at his log, he left the room.

Much to Emma's dismay, he took the lantern with him, so she had to wait until dawn to begin reading his log. She dressed in her warmest frock and wrapped her cloak around her against the damp sea air. There was no window in the room, but a hatch, which could be opened, so the cannon could be rolled out to fire. Cracking open the cannon hatch for light, she eagerly began to read of Darington's life.

Emma pored over the pages of the log, each page drawing her deeper into the life of the Earl of Darington. The log was a study in understatement. He was careful to note details, longitude and latitude, actions taken, accountings of prizes secured, all written in a simple, straightforward, detached prose.

He wrote about the most harrowing and exciting of times, but all without emotion. He was not a man to let his sentiments show. In fact, if she had only read the log, she would think he had no emotional reactions to anything in his life.

Reading the impassive prose, she realized he had been positively gushing with emotion when he had been with her. Far from being reserved because he was indifferent, he only appeared indifferent because he was so reserved. If she had any lingering doubts regarding his affection for her, they faded as she read his log.

He must love her. The truth was in his kiss.

Despite the uncertainty of their situation, there were a few things of which she was sure. She admired him. She loved him. And she had every reason to hope he loved her in return. Perhaps they should kiss some more, so she could better ascertain his true feelings.

Emma lay back on the bunk, hugging the logbook to her. Yes, she must explore this further.

❧

As soon as the light would allow, Dare scanned the horizon for any sign of the ship. He even climbed up to the crow's nest himself to scan the horizon for any sight of the *Kestrel*. He saw none. He had continued in a straight line from the last sighting of the *Kestrel*, hoping for luck to be on his side, but apparently it was not.

How long would he continue to look for Harcourt with Emma hidden in his cabin? How long could he hide her from view?

The morning seemed to drag on. He saw no sign of the *Kestrel* and all he could think about was Emma in his cabin, reading about his life. He had never before allowed anyone to read his private log. Not even Kate had ever cracked it open.

He wondered what Emma thought of him. Was she repulsed by the life he had led? His log certainly chronicled life at sea without flinching. It described the actions, the ships he had taken, the men he had lost. He had been in Emma's presence with hardly a stitch on, but felt more naked, more exposed now, knowing she was reading his log. What must she think of him?

Dare had never been so eager for the midday meal. He waited in his ready room for the tray to be brought, then locked the outer door and tapped on the door to his private quarters to release his female contraband.

She opened the door, holding her precious log. Her face was bright but inscrutable. He motioned for her to enter the ready room to eat, and they both sat down at the table. He wanted desperately to know what she thought of him now, but could not find the words to ask.

"Are you finished?" he whispered gruffly, pointing at the log.

Emma leaned close, her breath in his ear. "Yes, it is a fascinating read. Thank you for lending it to me."

She leaned back to eat, though he wished she would say more.

"Hope it was not dull," he whispered, desperately fishing for answers.

"Not at all. I have admired you from the first day we met, and I admire you even more now." Her breath in his ear sent shivers down his spine. She gazed at him with warm eyes. It was everything he needed to know.

"Was there a reason you removed some of the pages?" she asked quietly.

Dare frowned. "Removed pages?"

"I was reading along in your log and was just getting to an exciting part when I came to a section where a page was missing. I thought perhaps they contained scenes too bloody to have me read," she whispered with a smile, putting her hand on his arm.

Dare took his logbook and flipped through the pages. "No, I have not removed anything. Though…" He paused, belatedly realizing that some of his adventures were not of the sort a lady ought to read. "Perhaps you should not have been reading the log."

"Oh pish! I love a good adventure. And I have enjoyed getting to know more of your life."

Dare flipped through his log, trying to find what pages she thought were missing. Much to his surprise, he found a page had been cut from his log. Only one was missing, and it was done carefully, so unless you were reading through the log, it would be difficult to notice. Who had cut the page? And why?

"What did the page contain?" she whispered, her eyes wide with curiosity.

"Nothing of consequence." He flipped back and forth to remember. "We had been asked to deliver some messages for the Crown to the governor at Madeira."

"Madeira?"

"Small island off Morocco. Has an English governor. We anchored off the shore and rowed in but got lost in heavy fog. When we got closer, I realized we had rowed into Ilhas Desertas, a rocky island next to Madeira. Took us a while, but eventually we made the delivery."

"Was there anything important about the messages?"

"It was wartime correspondence, but most likely routine."

A little crease appeared between Emma's eyebrows. She was adorable when she was thinking hard. Of course, to his mind, she was always adorable.

"Did anything of import happen around that time?"

"Soon after I took a French privateer. Large prize." He flipped through the log. "Strange, but the only page taken was the day before we took the *Jade*."

Emma chewed on the corner of her plump lower lip and Dare had to struggle to attend to anything other than his desire to kiss her. "Did anything interesting or unusual happen when you got lost?"

Dare shrugged. "Found a submerged gig. It was washed into a sea cave cut into the cliff. It was low tide, and a bit of the bow was visible, so one of the men was able to remove the name. It was the *Merc*. At least that was all that was left."

"The *Merc*? What an odd name. Unless it had lost a *y* and was originally the *Mercy*."

"We were in Spanish waters so that would be…" Dare stood up with a sudden epiphany. "*Mercedes*!"

This time, it was Emma who reminded him to remain quiet. "*Mercedes*?" she mouthed.

"*Mercedes* was one of the ships carrying a large payment to France before war broke out between us and Spain," he explained in a hurried hush.

"Oh, I remember it in the papers. It was one of the treasure ships that Commodore Moore fired on, which led to the destruction of one ship and the capture of the three others."

Dare was impressed at her knowledge of the war campaign. "Yes. You are familiar with it?" he whispered as he sat back down beside her.

Emma shrugged. "I do read more than the society columns. But that was seven years ago. Were you there?"

"No, I was at university at the time. The declaration of war on Spain brought me back to the navy and I served in the battle of Trafalgar."

Emma beamed at him and he sat a little taller.

"You think the boat you found could be from the *Mercedes*?" she whispered.

"Perhaps. The magazine of the *Mercedes* exploded, destroying the ship. I imagine the gig could have been blown free and drifted a ways to be found where we located it."

"Why would anyone want to know the location of the *Mercedes* gig?"

Dare shrugged. "Shortly after we found the gig, we took the *Jade* and everyone forgot about it."

"Do you still have the piece of wood you found?" asked Emma. "Maybe we should inspect it."

Dare gave a nod, appreciating her determination to solve the mystery. He paused for a moment to remember where it had gone. "Last I saw, it was on deck after we captured the *Jade*. Brought the French captain and his officers aboard as we unloaded the ship. He was none too pleased. He picked up the piece of wood and dropped it again."

"So if there was something important about it, that French captain would have known it. Who was this captain?"

"He gave the name Capitaine Desos."

"*Des os*? Like French for 'the bones'?"

Dare stared at Emma and said nothing, the light dawning suddenly and brilliantly. "Damn, I've been a fool. It must be him!"

"Him? Who?" Emma blinked at his sudden proclamation.

"Silas Bones!"

"Oh!" said Emma a little too loudly and clapped a hand over her mouth. "So you think you actually captured Harcourt on the *Jade*?"

"No, the captain I met was too young to be Harcourt, but remember Mrs. Hennings said Harcourt had a son. In Portsmouth, I heard of a Silas Bones seen in the company of men who fit the description of those who attacked us. I wager Silas Bones and Captain Desos are one and the same."

Emma's eyes shone with excitement. "So you captured treasure from Harcourt's son. Little wonder he came after you again."

"They must have wanted their money back. Probably why they tried to kidnap Kate."

"So you think Harcourt was sailing with his son?"

"Not on board the same ship, but perhaps close. I was searching for Esqueleto at the time I found Harcourt's son."

"Esqueleto?"

"A notorious pirate."

"Does that not mean 'skeleton' in Spanish?" Emma tilted her head a bit to the side. "That is almost like 'bones.'"

Dare slammed his hand down on the table, startling Emma into hushing him. "Esqueleto must be Harcourt!" He jumped back to his feet.

"You found him!" Emma rose next to him and held her arms open in excitement. He took the invitation and pulled her to him, her body melting into his.

"So why would Harcourt want to steal your log pages?" she asked, her cheek resting on his chest.

Dare stepped back slightly, instantly missing the sensation of her in his arms. "Harcourt's son must have told him of seeing the plank and knew the location of the gig would be noted in my log."

"But what could he want with the gig from the *Mercedes*?"

"I do not know, but at least now I know where he's going!"

Thirty-seven

DARE STRODE FROM HIS CABIN AND SET A NEW COURSE, sailing toward the deserted island of Ilhas Desertas. Whether the gig was from the *Mercedes* or not, if Harcourt was after it, then at least Dare knew where to find the man.

For the first time since his search for Harcourt began, he felt he might have the upper hand. He had Emma to thank for that. Without her, he never would have realized pages were missing from his log.

It was all starting to make sense. Harcourt had not disappeared; he had reemerged as a notorious pirate. This was not going to be an easy fight.

"Mr. Everett, we will be at quarters," said Dare.

"Captain?" Everett glanced around, looking for the unseen foe.

"It is time to work on our aim."

"Oh! Aye, sir."

If they were going to be able to capitalize on the element of surprise, they had to be able to shoot straight. The day was fine and the wind steady. It was a good day for target practice.

"We won't be able to run all the guns," commented Everett.

"I'd rather have six guns blazing with accuracy than fifty without."

Everett was skeptical, but the men were brought to quarters and six cannons selected for practicing their skill. If there was any good side to being short of crew, it was that the cannon in his cabin would go unused. If he had been sailing with a full complement, the dividing walls would be removed, and the cannon rolled out for use. Fortunately, they had not the men for it, so Emma remained in relative peace.

Mr. Bean organized them into teams, with Tobias Stalk demanding absolute obedience should anyone stray or look as if he was not paying attention. Mr. Stalk certainly lived up to his promise and worked tirelessly to get the rowdy crew to stand at attention.

Dare had directed a few crates be bound, and a pole attached with some streamers, so it could be seen readily. Dare tossed it overboard, then worked with Everett to bring the ship around to take a shot at their target.

"Run out your gun. Prime. Aim. Fire!" commanded Dare. He watched with some disappointment as only half the guns rang out, while the other teams dissolved into heated arguments over who was at fault for not firing. Of those who did fire, none hit the target.

With considerable effort to overcome the chaos and disarray, the teams were formed once again, and the order given to shoot the target. All of the guns sounded, which would have been more satisfying if even one team had been able to hit the target.

Dare shook his head and went down to the gun deck to assist the teams directly. They had to do better if they had any chance of defeating Harcourt.

"Congratulations on making your gun sing," began Dare to his men. "But the only safe place to be is sitting atop our target. Now let's review how to aim."

The men began to take instruction, learning how to aim with precision. Next, Dare worked on speed. Accuracy and speed were vital. It was what he was known for. And while he could not turn them into his experienced crew in an afternoon, he could make them a good deal better.

One team was struggling with the reload and Dare strode down the battery deck, acrid smoke swirling in his wake. Dare began to give instruction to one team when a shout from Mr. Stalk grabbed his attention.

The crew behind him fired out of sequence, leaving Dare directly in the path of its recoil. Dare dove out of the way, knowing he could not get clear of the cannon before it smashed into him. He rolled and came up surprisingly unhurt. But how was that possible?

The large form of Tobias Stalk lay at the base of the gun.

"My word, Cap'n," gasped Mr. Bean. "He done stopped that gun from hitting you with his own bare hands."

"Quickly now, free him!" commanded Dare.

The men jumped up and quickly rolled the gun away. Tobias Stalk had a bad knock on the head and one of his hands had been crushed by a cannon wheel.

"Is he dead?" asked Everett, removing his cap out of respect.

"No," replied Dare. "He breathes still but is grievous hurt."

"I wish we had a surgeon on board." Everett shook
his head. "I suppose we should take him down to the
infirmary, though I doubt he'll fit on the table."

"No, he certainly won't."

"Only table long enough on board this ship is the
one in your ready room," observed Everett.

No. He could not bring a man into his ready
room, so close to Emma. Of course, if anyone on
board knew what to do, it would be her. Maybe she
could give him advice. He had been busy with battery
practice all afternoon and had not seen her.

A sudden realization gripped him. He had not
thought to tell her he was conducting drills with the
men. What must she have thought when she heard the
cannon blast?

Oh. No.

"Captain?" asked Everett, confused by Dare's sudden
silence.

"You're right. Best to lay him out on my long table
in my ready room. The man may have saved my life.
Least I can do. Wrap the wound and be careful with
him. I'll prepare the room."

Dare ran to his quarters, knowing he must face Emma.
He rapped quietly and she opened the door immediately,
her face white, her eyes wide. He stepped inside quickly
and shut the door behind him, lest she be seen.

"What happened?" she asked in a hoarse whisper.

"The men are bringing an injured man into the
ready room," he whispered in a rush. "Stay hidden.
All is well. Target practice."

"Target practice?" she mouthed back to him. Recognition dawned and her eyes narrowed. She put her hands on her hips and glared up at him. "Target practice?" she mouthed again.

"Should have told you." He could not come up with a plausible excuse. He was simply not accustomed to thinking about anyone besides himself. He had never before seen Emma St. James angry, but her plump lips thinned into a straight line and her jaw set. He would not be kissing those lips anytime soon.

"I thought we were under attack!" she hissed. "I have spent the afternoon praying for your safety!"

Dare cringed, knowing he had wronged her. "Sorry?"

Emma crossed her arms over her chest, which only pushed her décolletage higher, as if mocking him with what he could never have. The voices of the men bringing Tobias into the ready room grew louder and he knew he must go.

"I…I must attend….injured man. He saved my life."

Emma's glare was withering. Dare wished Tobias Stalk would jump in between and rescue him once more. He had a feeling, though, that Tobias might take her side.

"I will dine with the men tonight. Again, I apologize. Must go."

She put a hand on his sleeve to stop him and reached in her bag to pull out the laudanum and a dosing cup. "Give the man this much."

"Thank you."

He exited the room just in time to help the men lay out the injured Tobias Stalk. He did not know how he was going to save the big man any more than

he knew how to repair the rift he had caused with
Emma.

❧

Emma had spent the afternoon on her knees praying
for their safety as their ship was under attack. Cannon
fire blasted through the day, shaking the ship. She half
expected someone to barge in to use the cannon that
lay dormant in the cabin, but nobody did. She did
expect that Dare would come and tell her what was
happening. But he never did that either.

When Dare informed her it was all just practice, a
hot rush of anger flushed through her. She wanted to
scream at him for putting her through such agony and
then embrace him, for her prayers prayers for his safety
had been answered.

She paced in his small chamber, trying to think
of what to say when next he came to the door. She
would let him know exactly how he had wronged her.
It would cause him pain no doubt, but he deserved it.

When he finally returned, he only slipped in briefly
to give her some food he had managed to hide under
his coat. Voices came near, and he whispered quickly
that he would be on watch that night, and left without
giving her a chance to respond.

Emma glared at the door, hoping he would return, so
they could continue the conversation, but clearly he was
a man who knew how to avoid a fight he could not win,
for he did not return. Finally, the ship quieted down,
and Emma's anger began to subside. She supposed Dare
was unaccustomed to having to answer to a lady hidden
in his cabin. He was under considerable strain.

She tried to sleep, but the occasional groan of the injured man kept her awake. She remembered Dare had said the man had saved his life. She knew Dare had demanded she stay hidden, but how could she let a man suffer? No, Dare must act within his nature, and so must she.

Emma slowly opened the door a crack. A large man lay covered with a sheet on the long table. They had left a lantern, but otherwise, the man was alone. He groaned again in his sleep, and Emma slipped out into the ready room and locked the door, so she would have privacy.

The dose of laudanum she had suggested should have been enough to put down a man for a good, long time. She was not sure what she could do to help the man, but she did know for a certainty that she could not leave the poor man groaning in pain without doing something to render assistance.

Emma stepped closer and lifted her lantern to assess the patient. At first she was not sure what she was seeing, for the shape was unusually large and she thought perhaps a bundle of clothes or other items had been left on the table with the man. But no. As she crept closer, she realized this was one large man—about seven feet tall.

"My, but you are a tall one," she whispered.

"Always have been." The giant opened his eyes.

Thirty-eight

EMMA FROZE. SHE HAD BEEN SEEN. HOW WAS THIS possible? The man should have been unconscious. But of course—the dose she had given was for a regular man, not a giant.

"You that ladybird. The doxy from the *Rooster*. Cap'n Dare is the very devil, he is." He tried to lift his head but winced and put it back down.

"You have hit your head and have been given laudanum. I am naught but a vision," Emma whispered.

"Are you sure? You look real enough."

"I am sure. I am the hallucination. I would be the one to know."

He could not argue that logic so he gently shrugged. "Pretty vision. Never saw anyone so pretty."

"Thank you. I will be your guardian angel if you will cooperate."

"Yes, Miss Angel." He gave a look of innocence itself.

"Let me see your head first," said Emma, removing the bandage from his forehead. "A pretty good whack, but a few stitches and you'll be all right. Now let me see your hand."

Emma turned her attention to the bandaged hand, soaked red with blood, but he held it away from her. "Now, do not be skittish. I just want to look at it." She tried to grab hold, but he was faster, and clearly she would not be able to examine it if he was not willing to let her. "What is the matter?"

"They said they was going to chop it off."

"Well, sometimes that is the only option. You do not want to get gangrene, do you?"

"Rather that than lose my hand."

"You must not talk so," she scolded.

"But without my hand, I can't work. Need two hands to work. Can't become a beggar. Look at me! I'd starve to death."

"But surely you could find other gainful employment. Did not Lord Nelson sail with only one arm?"

"Aye, he did." The giant was thoughtful for a moment. "But he was an admiral. Didn't need to make sail."

"I see your point. Let me look at it and I will see if I can save it. You must let me examine it and hold very still."

The big man stared at her and slowly raised himself from his prone position, so he was propped up on his elbow. Emma took a step back. She had taken the risk that the large man was injured and medicated and could do her no harm. She had been wrong.

He gave her an appraising look. "Can you help me?"

"I can try. I have set bones before."

"Like Mrs. Mapp the bonesetter?"

"Yes, like her."

"All right then." He lay back down and rested his

arm on the table, making no further complaint. She carefully unwrapped the bloodied bandages and inspected the mangled hand. She had seen grievous wounds before, but even she had to take a breath to settle her stomach. Still, she had a job to do. She cleaned it as best she could with water and a clean cloth. The man grit his teeth and broke out into a sweat from the pain.

"If I am to save this hand, I will need to set each finger, which will be painful. To tell the truth, amputation may be the more merciful."

"Not for me," the man growled.

"Then let me give you another dose of laudanum. I cannot give you too much more, for there is a thin line between sleep and death, and we shan't wish to cross it."

The man nodded and she poured another dose, which he swallowed down with a grimace. She went to work, and he was good to his word, never moving his hand, gritting his teeth against the pain. She had hoped the medicine would put him under, but it did not, and she did not dare give him a larger dose, for she had already given a dose that could have been fatal to an average-sized man.

She carefully straightened and set each bone of his fingers, though one was so badly mangled she was forced to cut off the ring finger. He persevered manfully through the ordeal until each of his remaining fingers were wrapped and set carefully, his wounds stitched and fresh bandages applied.

"There, now. I cannot do more for you," whispered Emma when she was through.

"Thank you," he said in a shaky voice. "Will I keep my hand?"

"Only time will tell. I will pray for your healing."

He turned to give her an appraising look. "Never had no one pray for me before."

"Well, you do now."

"Thank you." He voice was low and sleepy.

"You are very welcome." Emma began to pack her kit to remove all evidence of her presence in the ready room.

"Miss?"

"Yes?"

"I know you ain't no vision. You be the best lady that ever lived. You need anything, you just come to old Tobias Stalk."

"Thank you, Mr. Stalk. I will do so."

❧

Tapping came early in the predawn hours of the morning, but this time Emma was ready for it. She opened the door to Dare, and he quickly entered the cabin and shut the door behind him. He glared at her with a ferocity she felt she was beginning to understand.

"You treated that man," he hissed.

"Yes," she answered simply, unperturbed by Dare's anger, for she had expected him to react in that manner. "Of course I did."

"Was he conscious?"

"Yes."

The glare intensified into something of desperation. He stood as close as he could without actually touching her. "He will tell the ship. You will not be safe."

"I doubt it. I think he is a good man." Her heart beat faster as she sparred with Darington. She wished to keep distance between them, but the need for secrecy kept them close, whispering in each other's ears.

"I bailed him out of *jail*."

"Perhaps not a perfect man," she amended.

"I thought I made it clear you were to remain hidden in this cabin."

"Perhaps you should work on your powers of communication. For instance, you could try telling me when you plan to conduct target practice from the gun deck." She folded her arms across her chest and refused to back down.

He opened his mouth to respond but paused, his lips apart. Slowly, he leaned toward her, until the stubble of his jaw brushed against her cheek. "You are right. I should have told you. I was a complete arse."

His self-deprecating assessment defused her anger, or possibly it was the touch of his cheek on hers that caused her to lose all rational thought.

"I suppose you are not accustomed to having a guest on board," she acknowledged.

"No. Never. I am not accustomed to having people...ladies in my life. Ever."

All traces of her irritation with Dare melted away and compassion returned. She brought a hand up to gently touch his cheek. "You have done much for me and I find no fault in you."

"My faults are legion."

"I must disagree in the strongest of terms."

"Thank you, Emma. You are very good."

The intimacy of him calling her by her first name flooded her with comfortable warmth.

Dare leaned closer, his lips dangerously close to hers,

and she feared—or rather hoped—that he was going to kiss her again. He pulled back at the last moment and cleared his throat.

"Need fresh linens," he whispered.

Emma stood aside as Dare rummaged through his sea chest. "Have you been on watch all night? You must be exhausted."

"My watch ended a few hours ago. Did not wish to wake you, so I slept a few hours in the purser's room, which is currently vacant." He stood tall and looked down at her, his dark eyes black in the dim room. "I shall be back for supper."

A tremor of excitement rippled through her. "I shall be here waiting."

❧

Dare changed his linens and prepared to face the day. He walked over to the prostrate form of Tobias Stalk to inspect the patient. Though he had chastised Emma for revealing herself, he was secretly pleased that she had, for he owed Tobias a life debt.

The large man was sleeping and had fresh bandages on his head and hand.

"Heal well, Mr. Stalk," he said in a low voice.

The man's eyes flew open. "Thank you, Cap'n."

Dare gave him a nod. "Thank you, Mr. Stalk."

"Cap'n? Who is she?"

"My future wife," responded Dare without hesitation. He was on his way to confront Harcourt, but before he did, he wanted to settle things with Emma. It was time to begin wooing once more. And he was going to start tonight.

Thirty-nine

EMMA WOULD HAVE BEEN LYING IF SHE DID NOT ADMIT to taking a little extra time with her appearance. She did not have a maid to help her, so it took longer to ensure that she was appropriately attired. She chose a more formal gown of sage-green silk, with a slightly lower neckline than she typically wore during the day.

The buttons in the back gave her trouble, and despite all her maneuverings, she could not wrap her arms to her back to button a few of the little rascals. So she put on a cream-colored, cropped spencer to hide whatever mistakes she made in the back. The spencer was clasped together with a stout gold broach beneath the bustline. If anything, she feared it might make her look even bustier, but there was little she could do about it.

She did not have to wait long before she heard the rapping at the door. Dare was dressed in his blue coat as usual, looking every bit the sea captain. He held a tray of food in one hand, and in the other, a leather logbook. His eyes lowered and his jaw dropped ever so slightly, before he trained his gaze back on her face.

He stepped in quickly and closed the door behind

him with his heel, putting the tray of food on the small desk. "We must remain in here," he explained as he took her key and locked them inside his small cabin.

A tremor of excitement coursed through her. They were locked inside. Together.

"This is for you." He handed her the logbook with a hint of anxiety. "Forgive me, for I left you today without diversion. I found one of my old logs for you to read."

"Thank you. That is very kind," whispered Emma, pleased at his conscientiousness. "I am fortunate that your many years at sea provide me with multiple logs to read. I did find my Book of Prayers though, so I passed the time quite well."

"Good. Very good." He appeared relieved. He clasped his hands before him, then clasped them behind his back, as if unsure what to do with his arms.

Beyond the walls of the cabin, the ship seemed to have come alive, with loud voices and hints of something that might have been music.

"Your crew appears to be in a fine mood tonight," she commented.

"Should be. Gave them a crate of smuggled wine to reward them for a job well done."

"That is kind of you."

Dare shrugged his shoulders with a guilty expression. "I wished to have time alone with you undisturbed. You are...beautiful."

Emma looked away as heat crept up the back of her neck. "How is Mr. Stalk today?" She had to change the subject or die of embarrassment—or possibly sheer desire.

"Improved, thanks to you. He has returned to his regular quarters."

"I do hope he will be able to keep his hand." She did not know what else to say.

Dare nodded. "Would you care for supper?"

"Oh, yes, please. I am hungry."

"I apologize," he murmured and motioned for her to sit at the desk, while he sat on the bed next to her. He waited for her to begin to eat and so she did, listening to the sounds of the men carousing on deck, wondering what would come next.

Emma motioned for Dare to eat as well, and they shared their meal as they had the first night.

"Dare?" she asked, leaning close to him and keeping her voice low.

"Yes?"

"I know this will betray my lack of manners, but since we seem to have thrown propriety overboard, perhaps I could ask you a bold, rather impertinent question?"

Dare's lips curved up ever so slightly. He was almost smiling, something she had never seen before. "I sincerely wish you would ask me a most bold, impertinent question."

"Oh, now I fear I shall not amaze you."

"You always amaze me." His voice was a low rumble, his breath hot in her ear. Maybe this was answer enough.

"Do you feel for me any...special regard?" Emma whispered, not daring to look at him.

"Yes" came the simple answer, hot on her neck. "Ask me another question."

"You prefer me asking questions? It is quite gauche."

"Easier for me. Now, ask me another bold, impertinent question, only this time, answer it also for yourself."

"So I am to both ask and answer my own questions?"

"Yes."

"That does sound like a rather one-sided conversation."

Dare's lips twitched up again. "Perfect."

Emma gave him a rueful smile. "I do believe you have found a way to engage in conversation without actually having to extend yourself in any way."

Dare moved closer, so his cheek brushed against hers. "Want to court you but do not know how."

Emma's heart skipped a beat. "You are doing a fine job at raising my heart rate."

"Good. Now ask me your bold questions."

"Did you ask me to marry you because we stayed together at the inn or because you wanted to?"

"I asked because I had to."

Emma drew back at this, but he caught her arm and drew her close to him once more. "Had to because we were together in the inn. Had to because I never before met anyone I wanted to spend my life with."

The tension Emma had carried within her ever since meeting Darington melted and she rested her cheek against his once more. "I see."

"May I ask an impertinent question?" he queried.

"Only seems fair."

"Why did you refuse me?"

"Because I could not trap anyone into marriage. I could never do that to anyone. Especially not to you."

"I see."

But Emma could tell he did not see it all. "In truth,

had I thought your heart was touched, I would have said yes."

"And your heart?" His voice trailed off into such a faint whisper she could hardly hear him.

"Touched." In a bold move, Emma placed her hand on his. "Very much touched."

His eyes softened and his lips twitched, and then, gradually, the Earl of Darington smiled.

Emma's jaw dropped. It was the first real smile she had seen from him. He was the most handsome man she had ever seen. Tension crackled between them.

"Emma." Dare whispered her name with a breathless tone. "I am...forgive me but I am much distracted by your presence." His eyes dipped toward her bust and then back to her eyes again.

"Are you?" She smiled in return. She usually was self-conscious of her curves, but with Dare, she only wanted him to notice her more.

"Yes. Quite. All I can think about is...is..."

"Is?"

"Kissing you."

A warm tingle flushed though her, hot and tremulous. "I see," she responded, for she could think of nothing else to say. "I think about it too," she blurted out. And there it was, the truth. She had been lusting after the Earl of Darington.

He stood slowly, reaching out a hand. She took it and allowed him to help her rise. Slowly, carefully, allowing her time to voice complaint if she wanted, he drew her closer, wrapping his arms around her. They swayed slightly, moving gently with the rise and fall of the ship. She put her hands around his neck and hugged him close, feeling safe for the first time since leaving Greystone.

Suddenly, his lips were on hers, urgent and demanding. He pulled her closer and she wrapped her arms around him, holding him tight. She forgot to keep her footing in the rocking of the ship and lost her balance. Dare prevented her from falling, though they both tipped over onto the bed, her practically in his lap.

She knew she should resist, but the sensations he was drawing from her with his kiss made her press herself closer and return his kiss with such ardor that he pulled back for a moment, stunned at her response.

She froze, surprised by her own desire and shocked that she could do that with her tongue—or maybe it was his tongue. Either way, she had never even dreamed a kiss could be so intimate, passionate. Did he think her a complete harlot?

"Saints above," he murmured and pulled her close once more. This time, he slowed the pace, taking his time, initiating an intimate dance between them. She followed his lead…until he did not move fast enough, and she pressed closer to him, lifting herself full onto his lap.

He moved his hand up her side until he caressed her breast. She pressed into his hand until he ran a finger underneath the material of her bodice, sending shock waves through her body.

"Oh!" She pulled back out of surprise.

"Forgive me. I forget myself." He removed his hand at once and tried to stand, but she was still sitting on him and had no inclination to let him go.

She wrapped her arms around him once more and rested her head against his shoulder. "Perhaps I should ask your forgiveness, for the only thing I wish you to do is continue."

"Truly?"

"Truly."

It was more than enough encouragement. He leaned back, taking her with him until they were both lying on the bunk. It was a narrow bed, made for one person. She ended up on her back with Dare on his side beside her, his leg over her.

"I tried to leave you behind," he breathed.

"Clearly that was not to be."

"I shall never do it again."

Emma drew him closer. This man was to be her husband. She knew that with a certainty. They had tried to part, but clearly their fate was to be together…though with the danger of Harcourt looming over them, she did not know how long their forever would be.

He leaned closer and kissed her again, his hand caressing her breast. The sensations he built within her were like nothing she had ever experienced. She felt like she might explode.

He unpinned the broach holding her spencer closed, revealing more of her ample bosom. He kissed down her neck until he pressed a kiss between her breasts in a manner that made her gasp. She wanted him to do more, much more.

"Buttons in back," she gulped. Without further comment, he released her, so she could roll to her side and he could undo the buttons. When she rolled back he slowly pulled down her bodice, revealing her with a sharp intake of breath. She felt momentarily self-conscious, for she had never been so exposed, but the look of pure adoration in his eyes reassured her that she was safe and her natural endowments had never been more adored.

He kissed down one breast until he took her in his mouth and drew from her a gasp. This time, he did not stop but increased in pressure, which made something tighten in her core. He moved his attentions to her other breast, and she felt like she was in heaven. She had never experienced anything like it and never wanted it to end.

"Forgive me," he panted as he came up for air.

"Only if you don't stop," she gasped in return.

"As you wish." And he kissed her again.

She felt it was desperately unfair for her to be exposed while he was still wearing his coat, so she began to help divest him of it. He was wearing much too much clothing, for she knew the muscular chest hidden beneath his tailored coat.

He cooperated with her wishes, throwing off the coat and making short work of the waistcoat. His simply tied cravat was next and his shirt was quickly pulled up and over his head. He embraced her, rolling onto his back with her lying on top of him, skin to skin. She reveled in the warmth of his skin on hers. His long arms encircled her, and she snuggled on top of him. She had never felt so shockingly intimate as lightning coursed through her veins at his touch.

He slowly ran a hand up her leg, over her stocking, past her garters, sliding up her thigh until it rested in the crest of her bottom. Her breath came in short gasps.

This was where she belonged. This was where she needed to be. She could not stop him. She could not stop herself. She loved him. And more than that, she needed him. Needed him in a carnal manner she had never experienced before.

"Captain!" Someone banged loudly on the door.

Dare jumped and Emma scrambled off him.

"Yes?" he answered, scrambling for his shirt.

"Captain, lights ahead. Might be the *Kestrel*."

Forty

DARE SCRAMBLED TO FIND HIS CLOTHES. HOW HAD things gotten so out of control with Emma? He had planned to attempt to woo her. He had intended to ask her to marry him. Instead, he ended up ravishing her. Not an all-bad outcome, but not the action of a gentleman with a lady under his protection.

He would have been more ashamed of himself if she hadn't been quite so beautiful and quite so delicious. She was remarkable. Amazing. He wanted nothing more than to smother himself in her bosom. He took a breath at the thought and his mind wandered astray.

He forced himself to focus back on the situation. "Douse the ship's lights. Don't let him see our approach," he called. "Be on deck in a minute."

"Aye, Cap'n," said Everett.

"I must go," he whispered to Emma. "I do apologize for losing my control. I...I cannot explain my reaction to you."

"I cannot explain mine to you either." She gave him a bashful smile with heightened color. "Most unlike me."

"I should hope so."

She was so beautiful, and the image of her glorious body was etched so indelibly in his mind, it was all he could do to continue to get dressed.

She smiled at him and he paused a moment, actually debating whether or not he wanted to go after Harcourt. But they would never be safe if the demon was allowed to get away. This opportunity may never come again.

"I must go," he whispered.

"I know. I will be praying for you."

"I should pray for forgiveness," he muttered.

"Fortunately, we have a merciful and gracious God."

"Emma, if God brought you to me, which I concede might be the case, then you are correct: God is more gracious than I can ever deserve."

She gave him a brilliant smile. The ship tilted, and he had to brace himself to keep his balance.

"Weather's coming up," he noted. "Stay here. Stay safe."

"Will you return tonight?"

Dare shook his head. "The chase is on."

"You need to rest."

He placed a hand on her shoulder. "Here with you, I would not sleep."

Her color heightened again. "I suppose you are right."

"That is one thing of which I am certain." He kissed her cheek. He paused, trying to find the words to tell her what she meant to him. She gazed at him expectantly. What did he need to say? His mind went blank.

"I… Lock the door after I leave." He turned to go.

It wasn't until he was on the quarterdeck, scanning the dark horizon for a pinprick of light that might be Harcourt's ship, that he remembered what he meant to say.

He had forgotten to tell her he loved her.

✖

Emma stared at the cabin door long after he had left.

Despite the fact that things had become more heated than she had anticipated, she could not regret any of what had transpired. She only hoped they would both live to find a life together.

She had no illusions about the danger they faced. If they were right and Harcourt was also the feared Esqueleto, he was more than dangerous; he was deadly. The odds of going after him and surviving were not high.

The ship groaned and pitched as rain began to pelt the roof of her cabin in a constant drumbeat. Going after Harcourt was dangerous enough, let alone doing it in a storm.

She should have been terrified. She should have been miserable. And yet…all she could think about was how Dare kissed her. And every time she thought about his kisses, she smiled. His emotions had not been declared, but his kiss said everything he could not say.

He liked her. A lot. And that was good enough for her.

Despite being in the midst of a desperate situation, she hummed to herself in a slightly giddy manner. She was glad no one could see her, for she was heading into danger grinning like a madwoman.

Death might come, but she would face it with a smile on her face.

❧

Dare searched the dark night for any sign of light. He found it and leaned against the railing, trying to identify the ship. Suddenly, lightning flashed and he saw it—the dark outline of a frigate matching the lines of the *Kestrel*.

"We will be at quarters," called Dare.

The ship's bell chimed to rouse the crew as Everett came to his side.

"Is it the *Kestrel*?"

"I believe so. More than that, I fear Harcourt may also be our pirate Esqueleto."

"Esqueleto?" Everett's eyes widened.

"Aye, and with the lightning, if we saw him…"

"Then he saw us." Everett shook his head. "That's not good."

Orange lights flashed in the distance.

"Get down," cried Dare as cannon fire ripped through the night. They were at a considerable distance and nothing struck the ship. Perhaps it was a warning shot. Dare hoped Harcourt did not know who it was coming up behind him.

Dare listened carefully to the cannon fire and the repeat, counting as they fired. He hoped Harcourt had also sailed with a light crew; otherwise, they were horribly outgunned. Dare cursed under his breath as he counted volleys. Harcourt had a full crew and could blast at him repeatedly.

"Hold back," commanded Dare, letting the *Kestrel* pull away. "We are no match for her firepower."

Cannon fire rang again through the storm, matching the thunder and lightning for flash and roar.

"I don't think they are going to let us go," shouted Everett, pointing at the *Kestrel*, which was coming about.

"Hard to larboard," called Dare. "We'll lose them in the storm."

"We'll have to go back to Portsmouth and get a proper crew." Everett held on to the railing as a freezing wave crashed over the side, drenching them.

"No, we'll lose Harcourt forever. We must take him now."

"But how?"

"We know where he's going. We can use that."

Everett frowned as rain pelted him in the face. "Terrible risk."

"It is all I have."

They sailed through the night, losing the *Kestrel* in the storm. Dare plotted a course around the east side of Ilhas Desertas, which was within sight of Madeira. He reasoned that Harcourt would avoid announcing his presence to the British-controlled Madeira, so he would want to approach from the west side of the island. This would allow Dare the opportunity to sneak up from the opposite direction, as Harcourt searched for the sunken gig. Hopefully, they would be able to surprise Harcourt and take the ship before he had time to respond.

At least, that was the plan.

Forty-one

"FIRE!" COMMANDED DARINGTON.

So far, his plan was working. He had sailed along the coastline of Ilhas Desertas in the early dawn. With break of day, the clouds parted and the sun began to shine. He hoped it was a good omen.

His guns were primed, his men ready. Emma was well and hidden. They sailed around one of the rocky cliffs that formed the desolate island and found the *Kestrel,* just as he had suspected. Now he just needed to blast the traitor from the earth.

Cannon blasted through the peaceful morning, sending huge flocks of birds into the air, basking seals jumping for the ocean, and the men on the *Kestrel* scrambling. The attack shot through their rigging, made a mess of the quarterdeck, and blasted holes through their sails, but did not cripple their ship.

"Over again! Fire!" Dare commanded.

This time, only three of his cannons responded amid the shouts and curses of the men below. The *Kestrel* was not long caught unawares, and a volley blasted from the enemy ship, ripping into their hull and across their deck.

"Fire again!" shouted Dare, running to the gun deck. Men and guns and power were in chaos. The *Kestrel* had aimed true, blasting into their gun deck and causing havoc. The men struggled to move the debris and reset the guns. Even Tobias Stalk pushed a cannon back into place with his one good hand.

Another volley blasted from the *Kestrel* and Dare ran back to the main deck. With a sickening sound, the main mast was struck, violently shooting splinters across the deck.

Dare watched in horror as the main mast of his beloved *Lady Kate* splintered, cracked, and collapsed, taking the sheets with it as it crashed over the side, into the ocean. Dare's stomach sank with it. They were dead. They were all dead. He had failed. He had cost Emma her life.

They had drifted just beyond the range of the *Kestrel* and he watched helplessly as the wind filled the sails of the enemy ship and she slowly began to approach. There was nothing he could do. He was dead in the water. He had been in many battles, but never had he felt such a clawing desperation. Never had he had more to live for or more to lose.

The initial yelling and shouting of the crew had given way to silence, and everyone watched as the *Kestrel* charged toward them, slicing through the breakers like death's own scythe. All eyes were on him now. What would he do? He was the undefeatable Captain Darington. Yet he had been defeated. Would he call the men to the guns for another pointless volley?

"Strike the colors. Raise the white flag." Dare did

not raise his voice; he did not have to. Everyone heard him in the silence. There was an awful pause, a moment for the awful truth to become reality as his crew registered the meaning of his words.

With a heavy sigh, Everett struck the flag. "Do we even have a white flag?" he grumbled. Dare had never used one. In truth, he had never thought to use it. He would fight until he won or he was dead. It was simple. But now, he had Emma to protect. Nothing else mattered.

Lord, please, help me keep her safe. He needed help and he trusted her faith to save them both.

The *Kestrel* leveled her guns and slid closer. They would soon be in range for a broadside, the enemy ship ready to strike the final blow.

"Captain Harcourt, a word with you if I may," called Dare with an air of false calm. "Or perhaps I should call you Esqueleto."

"So you finally know my name." A weathered man in an ornate coat called back to him. "Took you long enough to figure it out."

"You are responsible for my father's death." Dare's voice rang out across the water.

The *Kestrel* sailed so close he could see the smirk on Harcourt's face. "I was. And now I will be responsible for yours."

"You killed him with poison," observed Dare. "A woman's weapon." Crew on both ships gasped and Captain Harcourt's smirk vanished. "For the murder of my father, I challenge you to a duel." Dare was generally calm in battle, but this time, his heart was pounding.

"You have no right to challenge me to a duel. I've

got you dead to rights. I can give the command and blow you into the surf!" shouted Harcourt.

"I should have known you would not have the courage to face me in combat," Dare yelled in return. "That is why you snuck into my home and killed my injured father with poison—because you feared him as you fear me. Go ahead and give the command. But everyone will know the truth of what you are: a sniveling coward who is afraid to face me man to man."

Dare's crew shouted in agreement. Harcourt's crew stared at their captain. If he did not meet Dare in combat, he would lose face. Dare only hoped he had baited him enough to accept the challenge, but not enough to blast him on the spot.

Harcourt's face flushed red, his eyes narrowed into angry slits. "Cast the hooks! Bring her in!"

Dare held a hand to still his crew as the *Kestrel* slacked their sails and threw their grappling hooks, lashing onto the *Lady Kate* and bringing her in with a crunch. Dare tried to ignore the splintering sound of his ship as the two collided.

He stared at the man who had killed his father, robbed his inheritance, caused his sister no end of misery, and now threatened to kill him…and Emma.

Captain Harcourt leapt over the railings and was suddenly before him, seething with fury, breathing through his teeth. Dare was sobered by the muscular build of the man before him. The man was broad shouldered and thick necked. His presence oozed power, strength, and cold malice. "You will die today."

"A duel to the death." Dare knew this was how it must be. "Let us set terms."

"Let us fight!"

"Since I have challenged you, you have the right to choose the weapon." By convention, seconds would take up the negotiations of terms and attempt to dissuade the fight. No such civility would occur here.

"Swords, as we are gentlemen." Harcourt smiled something malicious. Esqueleto's skill with the sword was infamous.

"You, sir, are a traitor and no gentleman."

Harcourt's smile faded into a glare. "Duel to the death. Winner takes the ship, the cargo, and the crew."

"And whatever it was that you wanted from the gig of the *Mercedes*."

Harcourt's nostrils flared and his eyebrows rose before he schooled his expression once more. "As you wish."

Dare's guess was right. The gig was from the *Mercedes* and Harcourt wanted it badly.

Dare had learned to size up any enemy and determine his best course for victory. He had hoped to find Harcourt past his prime, but this was not the case. The man was tall, strong, and vigorous, a worthy opponent. If Dare should fall to him, what would become of Emma hiding in his cabin?

"I have one request before we begin, if you would consent to indulge me," said Dare in a calm, neutral tone.

"I have little care for your desires. What do you want?"

"I would ask that you preside over my wedding."

Harcourt's eyebrows soared up, his wide eyes a contrast to his usual squint. Harcourt stared at him. The crew on both ships gaped at him.

"Your wedding?"

Forty-two

"MR. STALK, PLEASE ASK MISS ST. JAMES TO JOIN US ON deck." Dare hoped he was not committing the biggest mistake of his life.

Complete silence fell over the two crews, broken only by the occasional creaking of the ships as, lashed together, they rode the waves. Everyone stared at the open hatch, wondering what might emerge. Slowly, a bonnet appeared, and with no apparent distress or hurry, the figure of a woman became visible.

Emma kept the brim of her bonnet low, looking down to ensure her steps on the steep, narrow hatch stairs. She was dressed all in white, as if emerging for her coming-out ball, beautiful and unsullied by the ugliness of life around her. She paused a moment once she was standing on deck before lifting her chin, revealing her face to all assembled.

An audible gasp came from the crews of both ships. Dare had seen her every day for the past week and still his breath caught at her beauty. Her rosy cheeks, pure-blue eyes, and primrose mouth were a vision to behold. Blond curls escaped the bonnet and framed her face to charming effect.

She surveyed the assembled men and gave the company a gracious nod of her head. "Good morning, gentlemen."

"But that's the chit from the—" Whatever the sailor was going to say was instantly silenced by Tobias, who slammed his good fist into the man's head, knocking him to the deck. Tobias bowed low to Emma and stood behind her with a menacing glare at all who faced her, her self-proclaimed protector.

The indomitable Miss St. James gave the crowd a warm smile and more than one sailor stood up straighter and tipped his cap. She looked as if she had walked into the hallowed halls of Almack's itself. The men knew how to act at war. The men generally knew how to act in the presence of a lady. Put the two together and everyone was off balance.

"If you think trotting your trollop out on deck will make me spare your life, you are sadly mistaken." Harcourt had overcome his initial surprise and narrowed his eyes once more into a penetrating leer.

"I do not require your leniency, for I will grant you none of my own. My request is simple—to witness my wedding. Then, we may proceed." It occurred to Dare, belatedly, that perhaps he should have asked Emma to marry him before announcing this to all the ship. If she should refuse him now, it would make him look the fool and put her in grave danger. The first was of no consequence, but the latter was untenable.

He sought her eyes and held them. *Please, please understand*, he tried to send her the silent message. He

was going into mortal combat with Harcourt, a dangerous man and formidable opponent. If Dare should fall,
Harcourt would take the ship and find Emma. Harcourt
would think her a common doxy, even Dare's own
crew would think the same, and she would be subjected
to the worst treatment imaginable and either dumped
at some port as a common whore or simply thrown
overboard when the crew was done with her.

"Considering my current situation," said Dare, too
far into it to back down now, "I will write in the presence of these witnesses, my last will and testament."
He nodded at Everett, who scrambled below, returning with paper and quill.

"I hope you know what you're doing," muttered
Everett, turning around so Dare could use his back to
write on.

"I hope so too," murmured Dare in an undertone.
"If I should fail…"

"Don't fail," said Everett in an urgent hiss.

Dare scratched out several lines, containing the
most important aspects of his will. He hoped to live,
but if he did not, he had to protect Emma even in
death. Harcourt glared but made no attempt to stop
him, waiting to see if the terms he had written were
to his liking.

"There. I have completed my will, in which I leave
all my worldly possessions to my future wife, Miss Emma
St. James," said Dare in a loud voice. "Mr. Everett, if
you would sign as a witness." Dare turned and Everett
put the paper to Dare's back to sign his name.

Emma's only chance, should Dare fail, would be to
have some value in the eyes of Captain Harcourt. As

the widowed Countess of Darington, Emma would inherit everything. Harcourt would certainly not let the opportunity slip by to take advantage of the situation. It was still bad for Emma, but at least it brought her back to London in order for Harcourt to use her to get at Dare's fortune currently held within the Bank of London. If nothing else, it kept her alive and gave her time to escape.

Dare took the will from Everett and slowly waved it in the air, drying the ink. He hoped Emma would understand. But would she accept such a backhanded, unconventional marriage proposal?

Dare walked up to her, giving a nod to Tobias, who narrowed his eyes even at him. "Miss St. James. Please...please make me happy by becoming my wife." *And forgive me for these unfortunate circumstances.*

Emma's smile lit his heart and radiated sunshine even amid the growing danger.

"It would give me great pleasure, my lord, to do so."

Dare closed his eyes a moment and breathed deep in relief. *She said yes. She said yes!* If he had not had ample reason to defeat Harcourt before that time, he did now.

"Fine, then. Let's proceed with the wedding," said Harcourt with a greedy grin. With control over the beneficiary of Dare's will, if Harcourt killed Dare, he could gain more than just Dare's ship—he could gain all of Dare's fortune.

Dare stood before the man he was about to kill with Emma St. James at his side. It was the happiest, worst moment of his life. Emma was presenting an admirably serene exterior, but at closer inspection, the vein in her neck pulsed rapidly, and fabric stretched over her bosom with every quick breath.

Still, she presented such a pool of calm he wished nothing more than to remain by her side for the rest of his life. How many other society ladies could remain steadfast in such circumstances? He had admired her for some time, but now he had fresh cause to appreciate her. She was unique. And she was his. And he loved her more than he had thought possible.

Love? Was he truly in love?

He had heard the phrase "falling in love" but had thought it a far-fetched notion of romantic tales and opera plots. He had been certain it would never happen to him.

He had been wrong.

He stood next to the lady who made his cold heart skip a beat, the lady who made him lose his precious self-control, the lady who was about to become his wife. The lady he loved.

As a child, Emma had dreamed of her wedding. What little girl did not? Marriage was the object of her life—or at least, that was what most of the women of her acquaintance had taught her. Somehow the concept of marriage had become warped in her life. Initially, she was pressed to accept a match with her own stepbrother. Then she sought a marriage of convenience to some faraway American to protect herself. Clearly, her romanticized dream of weddings and marriage had gone by the wayside.

And that was a good thing. For now the prospect

of marrying the Earl of Darington on a disabled ship, moments before he was to engage in mortal combat, attended by the most disreputable wedding guests imaginable was still better than marrying Eustace.

She was not sure why Darington wished to marry her at this moment, but she did know he would not bring her on deck without a very good purpose. If he wanted to marry her now, it could only be for her benefit.

Did she trust him enough to marry him on a ship full of thieves and murderers?

Yes, yes she did.

She smiled, and much to her surprise, he slowly returned it. And she knew. She knew without the fleeting whisper of a doubt that he loved her. Even though he stood on the deck of his ruined ship before the man who had destroyed his life, he smiled. He *smiled* at her. Whatever happened next, it was worth it for this moment. She had not been sure she could claim Dare's heart or even that he had one to claim. But he had. And it was hers.

"Fine, now let's get on with it. Who will perform the ceremony?" growled Harcourt.

"As captain of your ship, I would ask that you observe the rights of captains to serve as the officiant," declared Dare.

The snarl on Harcourt's lips twitched up. "You want me to preside over your wedding? Oh, by all means."

"Let us adjourn to your ship, where you hold domain," said Dare.

"Oh no, it is not necessary to inconvenience the lady. You have struck your colors and I claim this ship as mine."

Dare's jaw tightened, but he gave a quick nod of assent. There was a moment of confusion as people searched for a Book of Common Prayer. Harcourt did not sail with one, but then, neither did Dare.

"Here, please use mine," said Emma, handing over her small copy from her reticule.

Harcourt squinted at the words on the page and, after some deep growls, produced a monocle from his waistcoat pocket with which to read the tiny script. "We are gathered here today in the sight of God to join this man and this woman in the bonds of holy matrimony."

Harcourt clearly took no pleasure in the proceedings, other than a few mercurial glances at her. Emma was not sure why he would look at her so, but she had never before wished more ill to another human being. Her circumstances were so unusual it was surreal. If she suddenly woke, she would not have been surprised to learn it was all a dream.

But no, only the real, live Earl of Darington could make her heart beat so or her breath catch in her throat. This was no dream; this was very real. And despite it all, despite the officiant being the worst traitor in all of Britain, despite standing on a crippled ship surrounded by men who at any moment might attack her, and despite the fact that Dare was about to fight this man to the death—yes, despite even that—her heart thrilled with a sudden burst of heedless joy.

She was marrying Robert Ashton, the Earl of Darington, the captain of her heart. She was marrying the man she loved. She prayed she would not soon be made a widow, but for this moment, she was being united with the man she adored, and somehow, when she looked into his dark eyes and stoic face, she was happy.

"I, Robert Ashton, take thee, Emma St. James, to be my wedded wife." Dare spoke the words solemnly, but with a tremor of emotion that was real and true. "To have and to hold from this day forward, for better for worse, for richer for poorer, in sickness and in health, to love and to cherish, till death us do part, according to God's holy ordinance, and thereto I plight thee my troth."

She tried to restrain her smile. Truly, it was not appropriate, like a bird singing in the mouth of a fox, but somehow she could not squelch it. She spoke her vows to him with such a cheery smile she might have been in a London chapel, and even then, it would have been gauche, for marriage ceremonies were supposed to be solemn affairs. Dare, however, did not seem to care, for he gazed at her with a sort of awe-like wonder, as if surprised she would actually marry him.

When it came time for rings to be exchanged, Dare frowned. "I would wish to give you a ring, but I have none to give."

"I have no need for a ring," assured Emma.

"Oh, but you do. Indeed, you must have a ring." Harcourt gave her a malicious smile and produced from his waistcoat pocket a silver ring.

Dare's jaw tightened at the sight. "My signet ring."

"But of course. How else could I grant your crew the leave they were due?" He handed the ring to Dare with mock civility.

Dare took the ring and held out his hand to her. Emma placed her hand in his.

"Now you say—" began Harcourt.

"I know the words," growled Dare. He took a breath and focused on Emma. His features softened when he looked at her, and she felt herself melting into the dark pools of his eyes.

"With this ring, I thee wed. With my body, I thee worship." He paused and heat ran up her spine with the memory of their time in his cabin. "With all my worldly goods, I thee endow. In the Name of the Father, and of the Son, and of the Holy Ghost. Amen." He spoke the words slowly, deliberately, and she knew they were his true vow.

The ring was too big for her finger, but she curled her fingers to ensure it did not fall off. He was supposed to drop her hand but continued to hold it as Harcourt read the service.

"Those whom God hath joined together let no man put asunder." Harcourt paused and looked at them over the prayer book. "Actually I intend to do just that when we are finished here."

"You are welcome to try," countered Dare. "Proceed."

"Forasmuch as Robert Ashton, Earl of Darington, and Emma St. James have consented together in holy wedlock, and have witnessed the same before God and this company, and thereto have given and pledged their troth either to other, and have declared the same by giving and receiving of a ring, and by joining of hands; I pronounce that they be Man and Wife together. In the Name of the Father, and of the Son, and of the Holy Ghost. Amen." Harcourt scanned the page and snapped the book closed in disgust. "There proceeds a series of lengthy prayers and sermonizing, which I assume we can all skip, having done the essentials."

Dare lightly squeezed her hand and she squeezed it back. It was all they could not say.

Harcourt handed Emma back her prayer book. "Keep the ring safe for me for a few minutes. I shall come to collect it from you directly."

"Forgive me for being disobliging, but I fear I shall be attending your funeral in short order," said Emma boldly. "But do not fear. I have the page here for the order of the burial of the dead."

"Don't bother to mark the page," sneered Harcourt. "But stay and watch your new husband's death. I will take great joy in seeing that pretty smile turn to tears."

"Enough!" Dare stepped between her and Harcourt. "You are naught but a dog, unworthy to lick her boots. You will not speak to her."

"Good, good. Now we do what needs to be done. Allow me to offer my ship as the location for our brief encounter. Yours seems to have something blocking the deck." He gestured to the crippled mast.

"As you wish," replied Dare grimly.

Harcourt sprang up lightly onto the rail and jumped nimbly to the deck of his ship.

Dare turned to Emma. It might be their last moment together. He drew her close and pressed a kiss to her lips. This brought a cheer from his men, a sound that faded away as she became wholly captivated by the feel of his body pressed to hers, as if he could protect her from what was to come. For one shining moment, everything was right in her world.

Dare broke the kiss and everything was wrong. "If he wins…" he whispered in her ear.

"He will not."

"But if he does, things will become very difficult for you, but he will not kill you for he will need you to try to get my fortune. I hope somehow you can escape."

"Oh!" Emma suddenly understood why he had wished to marry her. He was protecting her just in case. "You have done so much for me."

"And you for me."

"I have not even given you a token. You are my knight and I must give you a token of my love." Emma remembered the stories of the ladies and knights of old. If ever there was a chivalrous knight, it was Darington. She searched through her reticule. "Goodness, I was so surprised by your summons I have not even a handkerchief. Here, take this instead. God's word is a much better token anyway."

Emma handed Dare her small Book of Prayer and he placed it in the breast pocket of his coat. "Thank you."

She clasped her hands on either side of his face, looking up to him. "I have no wish to be a widow," she said earnestly.

"I have no wish to be dead."

And with those parting words, he was gone.

Forty-three

DARE FACED THE TRAITOR TO THE CROWN. THE MAN who killed his father. The man who would do worse to Emma if he let him live.

Cold desperation snaked down his spine. Harcourt was renowned with the sword. Dare too was experienced with the weapon, but he had never gone up against a pirate legend. Unfortunately for Dare, his analytical, calculating mind knew the odds were not in his favor.

Harcourt drew his sword with a flourish and held it in salute, with a mocking grin. Dare drew his, the ringing of steel echoing across the deck. The crews of both ships were silent, watching. Even if Dare managed to triumph over his foe, Harcourt's crew outnumbered Dare's by about a hundred. No matter what happened, it would be a miracle if Dare and Emma survived the day.

Dare stood taller. Emma must survive. So Dare must win. There was no other option.

"Say goodbye to your bride," Harcourt said, mocking him.

"For your crimes against the Crown and against my family, I demand justice."

"The only thing you'll get from me is my steel through your heart!" Harcourt struck fast, forcing Dare to jump back and block the strike.

Harcourt lunged again and Dare blocked and parried in quick succession, keeping close to prevent Harcourt from striking true. Harcourt was fast and nimble, and Dare worked furiously to defend the onslaught. Frustrated by Dare's defense, Harcourt pressed hard. Dare ducked to avoid the deadly attack, and Harcourt's blade sliced his cheek.

"First blood to me," Harcourt gloated.

Harcourt lunged again, but this time Dare was more prepared for the speed and ferocity of the attack. The rumors of his skill as a swordsman were in no way embellished. The man was a master. Sick. Cruel. But a master with a blade.

Dare pressed on, trying to find a weakness. Harcourt lunged and Dare backed up the stairs of the quarterdeck to gain the advantage of higher ground, the clash of the swords ringing in the early morning light.

The men began to cheer, urging on their man as if Dare's fight for his life was nothing more than common entertainment. He was a gladiator of old, fighting in the arena for the amusement of the masses.

"I fear your intent with the gig from the *Mercedes* will come to nothing. I have already been here." Dare tried to distract Harcourt to gain the advantage.

Harcourt snarled. "Your log states differently."

"I do not put everything in the log."

Doubt flickered across Harcourt's face and Dare

used his momentary distraction to attack. Harcourt parried, blocking the attack with a grimace.

"You hypocrite! You come after me, but you also have been stealing treasure from the Crown. So you didn't want to go through the admiralty courts after you found the treasure from the *Mercedes* and kept it for yourself."

The gig from the *Mercedes* had treasure in it? This was news to Dare. If he survived the duel, he would certainly inspect this for himself. Harcourt slashed at him with malice. Dare had gotten to him, and he hoped that would mean the man would make a mistake.

"It was quite a prize," Dare drawled.

Harcourt attacked again, his eyes blazing. "How did you know? I killed the man who told me the captain hid treasure in the gig."

"Because everything you ever had or ever wanted is now mine," Dare taunted.

Harcourt roared in fury, a guttural, primal yell. If Dare wanted to aggravate Harcourt, he certainly had gotten his wish. Harcourt surged in attack, his movements quick and sure. Instead of getting sloppy, Harcourt got even better when angered.

Dare had made a terrible mistake.

"You are outclassed, boy," sneered Harcourt and Dare knew it to be true. "So sad your lovely bride will have to watch you die."

Dare wanted to glance at Emma once more but feared if he took his eyes off Harcourt for a second, it would be the last thing he ever did. "You will not speak of her." He lunged, and Harcourt quickly parried, slicing the coat of his forearm and stinging his flesh.

Dare cried out and struck again, but Harcourt was too quick.

"Oh, I'll do more than speak to her. She is a young widow, ripe and ready for the plucking. She will need company on the long voyage home."

"Do not speak of her!" Dare's pulse pounded in his ears. He attacked, but Harcourt blocked it and nearly struck home before Dare parried the thrust.

"I shall do more than speak," panted Harcourt. "You may have married her, but I'll be the one enjoying the wedding night."

Even in his rage, Dare knew he could not beat him. Dare stepped back, and in the second he had before Harcourt attacked again, he knew what he had to do. He would do it. His only regret was that Emma would watch him fall.

Dare lunged with determination, leaving himself open. Harcourt seized the opportunity and struck true at his heart. Dare did not pull back but crashed into him, Harcourt's rapier burning as it plunged into him. Dare grabbed the hilt of Harcourt's sword with one hand, preventing the man from withdrawing it, and plunged his own sword into Harcourt's chest.

Harcourt screamed in surprise and fury. His eyes bulged, staring at Dare with shock and loathing. Locked together, both swords pierced through, they both fell to the deck.

Dare collapsed to his side and struggled against the sword stuck deep in his chest. He gasped for breath.

"Dare!" Emma skidded down to her knees before him. "Oh, no. Oh, no, no."

"Harcourt?" asked Dare.

"Dead. Very dead. Now let me look at you. Stay still!"

Dare complied, willing to do anything she asked. Her eyes were brimming with tears. She blinked and her expression turned to confusion. "Does it hurt to breathe?"

Dare took a deep breath. "No."

"Well then." Emma stood, placed a foot on his chest, and pulled the sword out with a grunt.

Dare clenched his teeth to prevent from crying out in pain as the sword burned its way out of his flesh. It would not do to act the coward in his last moments on earth. The men of both crews, who had been creeping forward, gasped at her bold move in callously removing the blade.

Emma kneeled beside him once more. "Can you sit up?"

To his surprise, Dare found that he could. Emma opened his jacket and inspected the wound, which was spreading a bright-red stain on his waistcoat and linens, yet the puncture was far more to the side than he had thought.

"As I thought, he caught you through the skin under your right arm." Emma's countenance brightened into a smile. "I don't think it struck anything vital."

"He missed?" How was that possible?

Emma felt in the breast pocket of his coat and removed her prayer book, which had a deep gash across the leather cover. "He struck true, but the book diverted his blade."

Dare and Emma looked at each other in wonder. Slowly, Dare regained his feet, Emma rising with him.

Dare pulled her into an embrace, ignoring the pain. "Lord, thank you. Emma, I am so glad you forgot your handkerchief."

Emma burst out laughing, tears streaming down her face. "Please do stop getting yourself shot and stabbed."

"With Harcourt dead, I hope I can oblige. Of course, I know where to find a good doctor."

"Is that so?" Emma smiled at him, and he wanted nothing more than to continue where they had left off when he suddenly remembered the danger was not over.

The men of the *Kestrel* were creeping forward, malice in their eyes. Dare needed to do something. And fast.

Forty-four

"MEN OF THE *KESTREL*," CALLED DARE, HIS MIND racing. He might have killed Harcourt, but he was still outnumbered. "With the death of Harcourt, I have the right to claim this ship and his crew, but my fight was with him alone. I have no quarrel with you and I am willing to let you all go with the *Kestrel*." Dare hoped to avoid yet another fight.

"Harcourt's dead, so I'm captain now," said a large man with a bushy, black beard and a gravelly voice. "The way I figure it, we got a hundred and fifty men on this ship, and you ain't going nowhere."

The voice was familiar. Dare exchanged a glance with Emma. She recognized it too. It was the broad-shouldered man with the black muffler who had shot Dare and accosted Emma on the road.

"With the black beard, he almost looks the same," murmured Emma. Dare had to agree.

"What's to keep us from killing you and taking your ship and your cargo?" continued the new captain.

"Because with Harcourt dead, I am the only one

who knows where the gig of the *Mercedes* lies and the treasure she carried with her."

"But you said you took the treasure." The man with the black beard glared at them.

"I lied."

All were silent as the men considered this new information.

"If you make an accord with me, I will show you where the treasure is and we can all share the prize," offered Dare.

"We have an accord," said the captain with an ominous tone. Dare knew the accord would last only until he showed the pirates where the treasure was hidden. Hopefully, whatever Harcourt was looking for would still be there.

Dare collected his sword and, with Emma at his side, climbed stiffly back to the *Lady Kate*.

"You need to be tended," whispered Emma.

"It will have to wait," muttered Dare in return. His men surrounded him with anxious glances at the pirate crew.

"I will have to show them where the gig is," said Dare in an undertone to his crew. "While we are gone, cut us free from the *Kestrel* and the ruined mast, and prepare to make sail with the fore and the mizzenmast. Do it without drawing attention to yourselves. Reset the guns and prepare to fire but do not be seen. We'll have to shoot first."

"You think they will fight?" asked Everett in a hushed tone.

"I know it," Dare responded. "As soon as they have the treasure on board, they will attack. Everett, stay

with the ship. If there is any trouble, I want you to sail
and leave me behind."

"I won't let him do that," said Emma quickly. "So
you do what you must, but return to this ship. Return
to me."

"Best do what she says," advised Everett.

"My new wife is a determined soul." Dare smiled
at Emma. The expression was becoming more natural.

"And she's still holding Esqueleto's sword,"
observed Tobias.

Dare's crew regarded Emma with a certain wariness.

"I am going to need some men who can swim,"
continued Dare in a low tone, sharing the rest of his
plan with the crew. His chance of success was slim, but
he knew Emma well enough to know she would not
leave without him.

So he would just have to come back to her.

Emma watched the small boat as it rowed toward rocky
caves eroded into the cliff walls of the inhospitable
Ilhas Desertas. By mutual agreement, the gig contained
Dare and the new captain of the *Kestrel*, each bringing
a few of their men. Fortunately, while the *Kestrel's* men
outnumbered Dare's, in the small gig, they were evenly
matched and everyone was armed, which hopefully
would keep peace until the treasure could be retrieved.

They needed to make the preparations Dare dis-
cussed, but both crews were topside, keeping a wary
eye on each other. Other than the lapping of the
waves against the hull and the creaking of the ships as
they gently rose and fell, all was silent.

Emma stood beside Everett, whispering her question. "Can the men work without drawing attention to what they are doing?"

"Not like this," said Everett in an undertone, never taking his eyes off the gig as it rowed farther toward the cliff-lined shore. "Too quiet."

"I recall one night there was some music," said Emma with sudden inspiration. "Could those men play again?"

Everett turned to her with a cautious smile. "They could indeed, my lady."

Emma took a breath and called out in a loud voice. "Men of the *Lady Kate*. Men of the *Kestrel*. Why are you so glum? This is a time for celebrating! Our captains will return with treasure beyond your dreams. You all shall be rich men!"

Everett began the cheer on the side of the *Lady Kate* and Emma noted a few smiles from the crew of the *Kestrel*.

"You shall never have to work again!" shouted Emma, which brought huzzahs from the crew of the *Lady Kate*.

"You shall live like kings!" More cheers erupted, this time from both crews.

"Come, let us celebrate our good fortune. Let us have music. I should dearly love to dance."

A few musicians assembled on deck, and their band, consisting of a fiddle, a flute, a mouth harp, and a drum, took up a jaunty tune.

"May I have this dance?" asked Everett with a bow.

"I would be delighted," said Emma, glancing over at the enemy ship and noting with satisfaction that all

eyes were now on her. They began a country dance
with a few of the sailors, one with a mop on his head
as a humorous female costume who took up dancing
to the jeers and hollers of the men.

Everett passed her off to another partner and quietly
slipped aside to direct the work of the men in preparing for their hasty retreat. Emma gasped for breath at
the energetic dancing, doing her best to be as distracting as possible.

The men on the *Kestrel* began to clap their hands to
the music and shouted out comments about her person
that made her cheeks burn. Still, if they were focused
on her, they would not notice the men cutting the
ship free from the main mast and repositioning the
cannon belowdecks.

"Hey, what are you doing?" demanded a man on
the *Kestrel* whose voice Emma recognized as one of
the brigands who had attacked her on the road. He
pointed at Everett, who, axe in hand, was cutting the
ships free from each other.

"Cutting us free," replied Everett, as if it was nothing unusual. "Your ship is scraping our paint."

"I know what you're doing," accused the man who
still walked with a limp. "You're trying to steal our
grappling hooks!"

"Not at all, not at all," reassured Everett. "Come
assist me and you can personally take possession of
each and every hook."

Emma took another deep breath as she was twirled
around by a strong hand. She looked up, way up, into
the face of Mr. Stalk. "It is good to see you on your
feet, though you should rest."

"And you should not put yourself in the line of fire, but I see what you are doing. Good work, my lady," responded Tobias. He stepped aside for her to be granted another partner, but she demurred for a moment, quite winded.

The gig had disappeared into one of the sea caves, giving the *Kestrel* crew nothing to focus on except the activity of the *Lady Kate* crew. Emma needed to hold their attention.

"My, but I am so hot in this climate. I can scarce believe it is January." She removed her bonnet, along with a few of her hairpins, allowing her hair to fall down her back. She flipped her hair back, gaining the stares of many from the *Kestrel*.

Below her, the telltale sounds of grinding metal indicated the canon were on the move. She needed to distract them further. She moved to the railing, noting that they were now cut free from the *Kestrel* and were slowly drifting apart.

She leaned over the railing, gaining the full attention of the crew who gawked at her natural assets. "How will you spend your fortune?" she called over to the *Kestrel* crew, beginning a lively discussion on the benefits of wealth.

Emma motioned for the musicians to play a lively country reel and began to dance once more, with more than just her hair bouncing in time with the music. She knew she was making a spectacle of herself, but Everett gave her a small nod, indicating her efforts were appreciated and working.

The musicians continued to play and occasionally dance themselves and Emma personally danced with every soul on board the *Lady Kate*. She hoped Dare would return before she collapsed from exhaustion.

"Emma!" Dare's voice cut across the water, decidedly displeased.

Emma ran to the side of the ship and waved at her returning husband in the gig. The men strained at the oars, rowing back to the ship as fast as they could. Along with the men, the gig now carried three wooden chests.

"Did you find the treasure?" she asked.

"Aye. We opened one of the chests. Gold coins. And lots of them," responded Dare.

This brought cheers from the crews on both ships.

"Now get below," ordered Dare, looking only at Emma.

"Look out!" called Emma, seeing the captain from the *Kestrel* raise a knife to strike Dare from behind.

Quickly, without even taking time to look back, Dare and his men in the gig dove into the water. Shots rang out from the *Kestrel*, as sharpshooters suddenly appeared, shooting at Dare and his men in the water, then aiming at the crew of the *Lady Kate*.

With a sudden jolt, Emma found herself under the large form of Tobias Stalk as he pinned her to the deck, protecting her with his considerable bulk.

"Fire!" shouted Everett and the cannon from the *Lady Kate* sang out, blasting the *Kestrel* a fatal shot at the waterline. Men from the *Kestrel* shouted and swore as their ship began to sink.

"Cast off the mast. All hands make sail!" commanded Everett. The crippled mast had been cut free and was tossed overboard. The sails were raised on the two masts they had remaining, and they began to move away from the *Kestrel*.

"Wait! Dare!" shouted Emma from underneath her large protector.

"Get off my wife, if you please, Mr. Stalk," replied a cold voice.

Tobias moved at once, and Emma tried to sit up, but a sopping wet Dare only took Stalk's place until they were out of range from the *Kestrel*.

"You came back," Emma cried, welcoming him with an embrace so firm he winced. "Terribly sorry. Are you all right?"

"I am alive and married to you. I am more than all right." Dare looked back. When they were a safe distance from the sinking *Kestrel*, he stood and pulled her up beside him.

"Good work, everyone." Dare nodded his approval in his understated manner.

"Too bad we had to leave three chests of treasure behind," sighed Everett.

"Mr. Bean, were you successful?" asked Dare.

"Aye, Captain," responded a wet Bean, who, along with several members of the crew, was holding on to a rope dangling over the edge. "A little help?" Crewmen assisted and up came one of the chests, which Bean had tied to the end of the rope before he had jumped.

The men gathered around with eager eyes as Dare smashed off the lock with an axe and opened the chest, revealing the glittering contents to the amazement of all. "You all will have a fair share. Mr. Everett, please proceed to count the prize and make note of the portion for each man."

The men cheered this order.

"Make sail for Madeira. There, we can make repairs and alert the authorities of pirates off their coast," commanded Dare even as he pulled Emma next to him, his arm remaining around her waist. "I am certain they will be interested in pressing the attack once we inform them of the presence of treasure."

Emma looked up at him in admiration. Much to her surprise he pulled her closer, pressing his wet body to her and kissed her with abandon, as his men rang out a huzzah.

"I keep forgetting to tell you something," Dare said with a small smile.

"What is it?" Her eyes were only for him.

"I love you."

A warm tremor of joy rushed through her. "Truly?"

"Truly."

"Well then, I should tell you that I love you too!"

Forty-five

DARE AND EMMA STOOD HAND IN HAND ON THE
quarterdeck, watching Ilhas Desertas shrink as they
sailed around the rocky island to Madeira. "Perhaps
I could persuade you to return to my cabin, and we
could begin where we left off," whispered Dare.

Emma smiled. "We could, but you have once
again been injured. My first object will be to treat
your wounds, and of course, you must change into
dry clothes."

"Perhaps I could beg your assistance," returned
Dare slyly. "Nothing can restore me to health faster
than being close to you."

"Then as your physician, I shall prescribe heavy
doses of my company."

Dare's mouth twitched into a smile, and then to her
great surprise, and the shock of the men around them,
Dare broke into a laugh.

Everyone stared.

"You've made him plumb lose his mind," stammered Everett, wide-eyed.

"Mr. Everett?" asked Dare, returning to his senses.

"We are almost in sight of Madeira. Go tend to your lovely bride."

Dare led her down the narrow stairs to his ready room. He locked the door behind them, then guided her into his private quarters and locked that too.

"I see I will not be getting away," Emma observed with a smile.

"Never. I've spent too long trying to catch you as it is."

"Now that you have me, what shall you do?"

Dare motioned for her to sit on the bed and he sat beside her. He leaned close and whispered in her ear. "I might have a few ideas."

She brushed her cheek against his and spoke softly into his ear. "Why are we whispering?"

"Because I like it." His breath was warm on her neck. He followed the statement with a line of kisses down her neck, to the hollow of her throat.

"Oh. Yes. I like it too."

"Emma?"

"Yes?" She looked into his eyes, wide with an earnest emotion she had rarely seen on his face. She had rarely seen any emotion on his face.

"Could I be so bold as to request the removal of your gown?"

Emma smiled. "Since we are husband and wife, I think it is customary."

"Good."

"But you must join me in a state of undress. I should really look at your wounds."

"They are fine," he said, having to tug a bit to remove his wet jacket.

"You've bled through your linens, again," she accused, looking at where he was stabbed through the skin under his arm.

"Don't care." He divested himself of his waistcoat and cravat. "May I help with the buttons?"

Emma turned to accept his assistance, and soon she found herself wearing nothing more than her chemise.

"You are beautiful."

"And you are bleeding!" Emma shook her head. "I really must ask you to stop this." She helped him to remove his shirt and admired his muscular chest as she wrapped a bandage around him to dress the wound.

"Perhaps this is my way of getting your attention." He smiled at her again, soft and quick, one that might easily be missed, but it was a smile all the same.

"Choose another way," she directed.

He pulled her into his embrace and ran his fingers through her loose curls. "Why is your hair down?"

"I was distracting the enemy crew so your men could prepare to attack and flee."

"I cannot approve of you revealing anything to anyone," he growled. "Except me," he added. He drew her to him, kissing her decidedly on the mouth.

"There is one thing about my time with you that has been a great disappointment to me," whispered Dare into her ear.

"A disappointment?" Her heart sank.

"Yes. The night we first met, you undressed me. And I was not awake for it," he accused, a glimmer of humor in his eye. "Quite unfair."

Emma tried unsuccessfully to suppress a grin. "Yes,

I see your point. Is there anything I can do to remedy the situation?"

This time, Dare smiled wide. "Do it again."

"What?" A blush so hot she wished to fan herself spread across her cheeks.

He did not respond but lay down on his bunk with a look of hopeful expectation. With the rippling muscles of his chest, how could she possibly resist?

"Well, first I removed your boots."

"Allow me." He quickly dispensed with the boots and stockings, and lay back down, wearing nothing but his buckskins.

"Well, then I… Your clothes were wet… I needed to remove them…" Heat singed her cheeks as she remembered how she had undressed a perfect stranger.

"Saved my life. Let's do it again."

Emma laughed out loud. "Well, first I… Well, I unbuttoned…"

"Yes?"

Emma unbuttoned the fall of his trousers, her hands hovering over him in an intimate manner that made her cheeks burn. She hoped blushing was not a fatal condition or she was doomed. She paused, not knowing how to proceed.

Dare took pity on her and sat back up to kiss her again. This time they both lay down together, covering themselves with a blanket and they both, in between kisses, helped the other remove the remaining layers between them.

Emma sighed contentedly as her skin warmed to his. Despite being a reserved man, his skin was warm, and she snuggled close. He also seemed to be enjoying the closeness, exploring her body with his hands and mouth. Soon, she wanted more. A throbbing need she had never before experienced took control, and she wanted him in a manner quite carnal.

"Emma," he gasped, emerging from his devoted attention to her breasts. "You must tell me what you like and do not like. I wish…I wish to please you as much as you are pleasing me."

"Do not stop, for everything that pleases you seems to please me too."

"I do love you." He rolled on top of her, propping himself up on his elbows, his chest skimming across hers in a manner that brought stars to her eyes. "I never thought I would ever say that to anyone, ever. But I love you, Miss…" He smiled and closed his eyes, correcting himself. "Lady Darington."

She was a countess? She could not quite believe she was actually married to the Earl of Darington, the man that she loved. She could not stop smiling. "I love you too." She pulled him closer, wanting him, needing him.

"With my body, I thee worship," he said, quoting their marriage vow, and joined with her in a consummation of their love and marriage. There was pain and there was desire as he moved slowly, building up within her a tightening pressure until finally she was tipped over a precipice and waves of pleasure rolled through her as he gasped and shuddered. He collapsed beside her and drew her close.

"My Emma," he sighed as he fell asleep beside her. His smile never faded.

Forty-six

EMMA KNOCKED ON HER OWN FRONT DOOR WITH A feeling of dread she could not quite shake. This was the monster she had run from. It was time to face her stepmother and the man she once thought of as a brother, Eustace Ludlow. This time, she was not alone. Next to her stood her husband, the Earl of Darington.

Emma glanced back at the carriage, where Mr. Stalk stood at the ready. Despite her efforts to repair his hand, it was clear his sailing days were over. So Dare had hired him as a "footman" and instructed Stalk to act as her own personal bodyguard. Stalk gave her a small nod of encouragement and she waved in return.

The butler opened the door and his white eyebrows shot up. "Miss Emma. It is good to see you."

"Actually, I have acquired a new name," she said sweetly.

"Lord and Lady Darington to see Mrs. St. James and Mr. Ludlow," said Dare gravely, handing the butler his card.

Dare's expression had taken on the firm, dispassionate

disregard that had been his general countenance before his marriage. After spending the past several months with her new husband, first repairing his ship, then sailing back to London, where they reconnected with Wynbrook and Kate, now happily married, Emma knew Dare was quite capable of smiling, and even laughing on occasion.

"My Lord." The butler bowed, took their hats and coats, and led them into the drawing room—their best drawing room, Emma noted. "Mrs. St. James and Mr. Ludlow will attend you directly," he said with another bow.

They were alone in the house that had been her home. Was still her home. Emma took a breath, allowing memories both good and painful to wash over her. Dare raised an eyebrow at her and she nodded. She was well. She could do this.

It did not take long for Regina and Eustace to appear at the door. Both held grim looks. Regina was still regal but pale, with a dangerous glint to her eye. Eustace looked positively murderous, his hands balled into fists at his side.

"Good afternoon, Regina," Emma greeted. "May I present my husband, Lord Darington. Dear, this is my stepmother, Mrs. St. James, and her son, Mr. Eustace Ludlow."

Bows were exchanged, but other than fierce glares, neither man said anything. It was as tense as standing on the deck of the crippled *Lady Kate* next to the murderer Harcourt.

"I cannot believe that you ran away from home. That you would treat us with such disregard," said

Regina with an attempt at a sob. "I have always been to you a mother."

"No," said Emma. She would no longer be manipulated. "You have always been a mother to your son. When I was inconvenient to him, I was dispensable to you. But that is not why I am here. I had hoped you would wish me happy and we could forget any unpleasantness of the past."

"Not likely," spat Eustace. "I have heard of your marriage. Highly irregular. Officiant was a captain of disrepute. Occurred on board a ship. No proper bans read. Won't stand up in court."

"Eustace! Do you intend to challenge the marriage?"

"I do. Invalidate any brats you have breeding too."

Dare stepped toward Eustace, murder in his eyes. Emma placed a hand on his sleeve to stay him. She had requested to deal with her family in her own way. Dare had faced his demons; this was her dragon to slay.

Dare had agreed not to say a word but she had forgotten to make him promise not to silently strangle her brother-in-law, which Dare seemed to be currently contemplating. If Eustace had any sense, he would keep his mouth shut.

Emma took a breath. "Eustace, I do appreciate you speaking plainly. I confess, I feared you might be unpleasant, so Lord Darington and I took the liberty of being married again, this time with a special license in London."

"Doesn't matter," said Eustace with a sneer. "I have gone to court to have you declared insane. Therefore, you are not competent and your marriage to Lord Darington is invalid. I am your guardian and I forbid the union. You can persist in this marriage if you will, but you will forfeit your inheritance and I will continue to manage the estate."

Emma took a sharp inhale of breath. She had not expected that he would go to the courts to have her declared incompetent. "You can certainly contest my marriage and my inheritance, which would no doubt result in a lengthy court battle. However, I would advise against it. I have interceded with Lord Darington on your behalf and he is willing to offer you and Regina a monthly stipend, provided you agree to our terms and cause us no further distress. If you pursue this ill-advised litigation, after we prevail you will be cut out of everything and will receive nothing from us whatsoever. Your name will be denied in all polite society. You will be a pariah."

"You cannot do that," declared Eustace, haughty to the last. "Nobody in society even knows you, and hardly Lord Darington either. The Pirate Earl indeed! You are nothing. The courts have ruled in my favor, and if you try to take back this house, I will see you locked in Bedlam for a madwoman—aaarrrgh!"

Dare's fist connected with Eustace's nose and he went flying across the polished floor.

"Dare!" chastised Emma, running to Eustace's side.

"Sorry," said Dare without a hint of apology. "Promised not to talk. Never promised not to defend your honor."

"Well, thank you," said Emma, folding Eustace's handkerchief and shoving it up his right nostril to stanch the bleeding.

"Get away from me," grunted Eustace, clawing at

the furniture to pull himself up. He faced Emma with disdain, though his attempt at superiority was hindered by the handkerchief sticking out of his nose. "I will contact the magistrate. You will be arrested for assault."

"Speaking of my good friends, are we?" Lord Wynbrook walked in before the harried butler, who quickly announced Lord and Lady Wynbrook. The couple swept into the room, Kate looking quite dashing in a gown of scarlet. She carried a parcel of papers under her arm and gave Eustace and Regina a hawkish look.

Eustace and Regina made their bows, Regina's expression turning positively ill.

"I see you found our dear Darington is not quite civilized," said Wynbrook with the good humor that characterized him. "Well, Mr. Ludlow, quite the trick you tried to pull on our dear Emma. Unfortunately for you, she is not quite as friendless as you supposed. Allow me to make your situation clear. I will ensure that you are never admitted within polite society and your attempts to steal the inheritance from a poor maiden, now countess, will be seen for the despicable crime that it is. I can ensure that London becomes quite an inhospitable place for you." Despite his pleasing looks, his threat was well placed, and Emma knew from the shades of white in her stepmother's face that his arrow had hit home.

"You cannot… I won't let you…" sputtered Eustace.

"Enough, Eustace," quelled Regina. She gave the room a calculating look and shook her head in an expression of surrender. "Lord Darington, Lord Wynbrook, please forgive any unpleasantness. Emma, of course we rejoice in your marriage, my dear. I have always admired you, my dear daughter, and I am so pleased that you have made such an advantageous match. I wish every blessing upon you."

Regina's sudden reversal was so sudden it left Emma a bit dizzy. She knew Regina was a cold, shrewd woman, and her words were spoken with no genuine warmth, but Emma was so happy with her new life that she was incapable of responding as harshly as the situation deserved.

"Thank you, Regina," said Emma with a smile.

"I thank you, my dear daughter, for not forgetting the only mother you have ever known, the one who raised you and nurtured you to become the fine lady that you are."

Kate snorted. It was all a bit much for her. "Well, if you have had enough of the false pleasantries, let us get down to the contract." She pulled out the documents Emma had asked her to prepare and placed them on a side table. "I have documents laid out for Mr. Ludlow and Mrs. St. James, which allow for a monthly stipend, providing you agree not to contest the marriage or the inheritance. It also includes specific clauses against defamation of character I recommend you read closely, for any slander will result in the termination of the stipend. Robert, I also have something for you to sign."

This caught both Emma and Dare by surprise.

"For me?" Dare asked.

"Yes. Mr. Ludlow was correct in one thing: the marriage was an unconventional one and Emma did not have the advantage of marriage settlements. No lady should ever marry without them. I have prepared them, if you are willing, which allows for her care should you die and settles her inheritance on any children you produce."

Dare shrugged. "I am willing. Though I have one more condition for Mrs. St. James and this man she claims as her son. You both must leave this house within the hour and never, ever return."

"Within the hour? Is that necessary?" asked Emma.

"Only if Mr. Ludlow would like to live until tomorrow. I can only hold my temper so long." Dare glared at Eustace. "You will be out in the hour. I will pay for lodging at any suitable inn. But you both must go. Any personal effects will be shipped to the location of your choice."

Regina and Eustace, with straight backs and tight lips, signed the papers and left the room to prepare for their sudden departure.

"Well." Emma took a shaky breath. "I cannot believe it is over. I have been greatly blessed."

"No," disagreed Dare, "it is I who have received the greater blessing."

"I believe this calls for a celebration," declared Wynbrook.

The butler anticipated their desire by entering with a bottle of champagne.

"To Emma," pronounced Dare, raising a glass.

"To Emma," said the company.

"To you three, my dear friends," responded Emma. "I do love you, my dear." She gazed up at her husband.

"And I you." Dare pulled her close for a champagne kiss.

Author's Note

One of my favorite classic movies is *The African Queen*, featuring Humphrey Bogart and Katharine Hepburn, based on the book by C. S. Forester. Set during WWI, my favorite scene is when Bogart and Hepburn, who have overcome impossible odds only to be captured by the Germans, ask the German ship captain to marry them before they are to be executed. Can anything be more romantic? I won't give away the ending in case you have not seen the movie, but rest assured Bogart and Hepburn are not hung as spies. Loving this scene as I do, I always wanted to have a similar type of scene, where the enemy captain marries the hero and heroine, and in *Earl Interrupted* I finally had my chance.

Unfortunately, as I was researching the well-known fact that sea captains can marry couples on board ships, I found that this was not quite the case. In fact, there is no evidence that sea captains were ever officially given this authority. So was I back to the drawing board? Well, maybe not quite so fast. Although sea captains were never officially given this power, it seems they would occasionally exercise the privilege, officially sanctioned or not. Certainly popular opinion going back hundreds of years believes that ship captains do have this power, so might there be some truth in it?

For evidence of this, I turned to the nineteenth-century court case of *Fisher v. Fisher*, in which a couple was married in international waters by the ship's captain. If nothing else, this case clearly shows that ship captains did occasionally marry people at sea. The marriage was contested but upheld, with the winning argument stating that a consensual marriage conducted by a ship's captain was to be considered valid. So I decided to go forward with Captain Harcourt marrying Dare and Emma and then had them follow the wedding with a more official ceremony in London off screen.

I wish you all the best in your romantic adventures and I hope you have enjoyed *Earl Interrupted*!

Acknowledgments

This story has been percolating in my mind since I first thought of writing a book. It was a winding path to finally get it to paper, and I greatly appreciate those who have helped make it possible. Thank you to my agent, Barbara Poelle, and my editor, Deb Werksman, who encourage me to be my best. Thanks to my beta reader, Laurie Maus, who reminds me to describe my hero. I could not do this without the support and encouragement of my husband and kids, who give me the time to do what I love. The next one's for you.

About the Author

Amanda Forester holds a PhD in psychology and worked many years in academia before discovering that writing historical romance was way more fun. Whether in the rugged Highlands of medieval Scotland or the decadent ballrooms of Regency England, her novels offer fast-paced adventures filled with wit, intrigue, and romance. You can visit her at amandaforester.com.

READY FOR A LITTLE HIGHLAND TROUBLE?

Enjoy these sexy, adventurous Scottish Highland historical romances

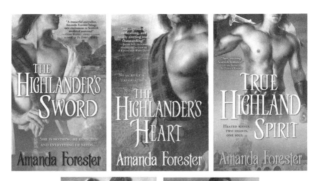

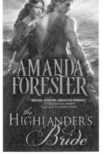

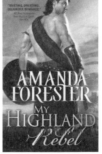

PIRATE EARL SEEKS WIFE.
SQUEAMISH LADIES NEED NOT APPLY.
ABILITY TO TREAT GUNSHOT WOUNDS A PLUS.

AFTER RESTORING HIS FORTUNE AS A NOTORIOUS privateer, Captain Robert Ashton, Earl of Darington, goes to London in search of a bride. Instead, he finds unexpected dangers and unknown assailants. He is shot and left for dead. Life on the high seas was far calmer.

Enter Miss Emma St. James. She may appear sweet and demure, but she quickly proves herself to be equal to any challenge, including saving Darington's life. Just when Darington is sure he has found his perfect bride, she reveals she's betrothed to another.

Now things REALLY start to get complicated…

"Adventures, mysteries, secrets, fun, and romance.
I can't wait to read the next one in the series."
—*Fresh Fiction* for *If the Earl Only Knew*

EBOOK EDITION ALSO AVAILABLE
SOURCEBOOKSCASABLANCA.COM
SOURCEBOOKS CASABLANCA

Romance $7.99 U.S.
ISBN-13: 978-1-4926-0552-2

S
50799